Praise for M. R. Hall

'Breathlessly enjoyable'                                      *The Times*

'Hall shows with aplomb that a coroner is just as able to become a detective as the forensic pathologists of Patricia Cornwell and Kathy Reichs'                              *Sunday Times*

'Intelligent and intricate, and grips from the beginning to end'
                                                    *Woman & Home*

'A hypnotic piece of work'
                        Barry Forshaw, *Independent*, Best
                                           Books for Christmas

'Accomplished and challenging . . . High-mindedness can be too heavy a burden for some thrillers to carry. They become all intellectual argument and no action. Equally, literary ambitions – Hall has a particular knack for conjuring up landscapes, including the Wye Valley, Cooper's base and his own home – can get in the way of the necessary narrative thrust. But *The Disappeared* avoids both potential traps triumphantly'                                          *Independent*

'A substantial and satisfying novel which adroitly combines the personal and the political into an engrossing narrative that is ultimately about international paranoia'        *Daily Express*

'It's a tribute to the author's skill that I read this book supposing it to be autobiographical . . . He really gets under the skin of his heroine . . . outstandingly interesting'   *Literary Review*

# THE REDEEMED

M. R. Hall is a screenwriter, producer and former criminal barrister. *The Redeemed* is his third novel in the Jenny Cooper series. Educated at Hereford Cathedral School and Worcester College, Oxford, he lives in Monmouthshire with his wife and two sons. Aside from writing, his main passion is the preservation and planting of woodland. In his spare moments, he is mostly to be found amongst trees.

# THE REDEEMED

M. R. HALL

PAN BOOKS

First published in the UK 2011 by Mantle

This edition published 2011 by Pan Books
an imprint of Pan Macmillan, a division of Macmillan Publishers Limited
Pan Macmillan, 20 New Wharf Road, London N1 9RR
Basingstoke and Oxford
Associated companies throughout the world
www.panmacmillan.com

ISBN 978-0-330-45838-2

Copyright © M. R. Hall 2011

1 3 5 7 9 8 6 4 2

A CIP catalogue record for this book is available from
the British Library.

Typeset by SetSystems Ltd, Saffron Walden, Essex
Printed and bound by CPI Group (UK) Ltd, Croydon CR0 4YY

Visit www.panmacmillan.com to read more about all our books
and to buy them. You will also find features, author interviews and
news of any author events, and you can sign up for e-newsletters
so that you're always first to hear about our new releases.

For my old friend, Stephen Goodfellow

For the Lord himself will come down from heaven, with a loud command, with the voice of the archangel and with the trumpet call of God, and the dead in Christ will rise first. After that, we who are still alive and are left will be caught up together with them in the clouds to meet the Lord in the air. And so we will be with the Lord forever.

1 Thessalonians 4:16–17

*I long for scenes where man has never trod –*
*For scenes where woman never smiled or wept –*
*There to abide with my Creator, God,*
*And sleep as I in childhood sweetly slept,*
*Full of high thoughts, unborn. So let me lie –*
*The grass below; above, the vaulted sky.*

John Clare
Written in Northampton County Asylum

# ONE

JENNY WAS DRINKING CORDIAL BY the stream at the end of her overgrown garden, watching a school of tiny brown trout flick this way and that, quick as lightning. It was late June and the sweet-smelling breeze was warm against her bare legs. Before the telephone intruded she had managed to lose herself – how long for, she couldn't say – hypnotized by the gently swaying ash trees and the buzz of grasshoppers in the nettles.

A moment of peace. Too good to last.

She walked back across the ankle-high lawn, hoping that whoever was disturbing her on a Sunday morning would give up and leave her to her daydreams. They didn't. She had counted eight rings by the time she stepped through the back door of the cottage onto the cool flags of the tiny kitchen, ten by the time she had lifted the iron latch to the living room, which smelled of old oak and soot from the inglenook. It was much colder inside than out. The flesh on her arms tightened into goosebumps as she lifted the receiver.

'Oh, you're there, Mrs Cooper.' It was Alison, her officer, with a note of reproach in her voice.

'I was outside.'

'CID just called me. There's a body they think you might want to see while it's still in situ. Looks like a suicide.'

She was a coroner again.

'Is there any particular reason why I should? I can't go every time.'

'You asked them for closer cooperation: this is it.'

'I thought they might do something useful like email a photograph.'

'It's progress, Mrs Cooper. Between you and me, I get the impression that they're a little bit frightened of you.'

Jenny couldn't imagine frightening anyone. 'I suppose I'd better show willing. Where is it?'

'St Peter's Church, Frampton Cotterell.'

'I don't think I know it.'

'You'll like it. It's a lovely spot.'

The Severn Bridge was all but empty of traffic as Jenny crossed the mile-wide river into England. Beneath her the tide was chasing out to sea at a gallop, the best time to jump if you didn't want to be found: you'd be halfway to Ireland before low water. That's how Alec McAvoy must have judged it, over three months ago now. She thought of him each time she crossed, picturing his hair blowing over those moss-green eyes, too young for his face, as he said his final prayers.

A forensics van, a single squad car and an unmarked pool vehicle were parked in the quiet road outside the elaborate Gothic church. A skeleton Sunday crew. A handful of teenagers were loitering on the other side of the road, a skinny blonde girl talking excitedly into her phone, thrilled with the drama of it all. It wasn't even a policeman who had been posted at the churchyard gate, but an overweight community support officer who made a meal of checking Jenny's credentials before letting her through as if he were doing her a big favour. She didn't react, the Xanax she had taken with her breakfast keeping her calm.

The activity was in a far corner beyond the gravestones,

an untended triangle that had been left to grow wild. A plain-
clothes detective glanced up and saw her coming but made
no effort to step forward to greet her, his focus switching
immediately back to the body. He watched intently while
two men in white overalls, one with a camera, the other with
a measuring tape, recorded every detail of the scene.

She made an effort to sound friendly. 'Good morning.
Jenny Cooper. Severn Vale District Coroner.'

'Tony Wallace. DI.'

Somewhere in his late forties, slim and fit, he spoke with
the clipped abruptness of a man who still entertained
ambition. He was wearing what might have been a hand-
tailored suit, far smarter than most of the policemen she had
met.

She followed his gaze to the body lying amongst the rye
grass and buttercups. It was that of a naked, well-built man
in his thirties. His head, which was facing towards them,
was shaved to a tight crew cut to disguise his balding temples. He was lying on his back, arms at forty-five degrees
to his torso. Carved into his chest and abdomen, stretching
all the way down to his groin, was the sign of the cross. By
the outstretched fingers of his right hand Jenny caught the
glint of a kitchen knife, the blade no more than four inches
long. His skin was waxy yellow and his stomach and face
had begun to bloat; bluebottles were gathering on the eyes,
lips and genitals.

'Looks like he's been here a few hours,' Jenny said, familiar
enough with corpses after a year as coroner not to recoil.

'Yesterday evening at the latest, I'd say,' DI Wallace
replied.

The men in white overalls nodded their agreement, the
larger of the two saying, 'Definitely twelve hours plus –
you've only got to look at the colour of his skin.'

'Any idea of the cause of death?'

'Not yet,' Wallace said. 'Apart from the cross, there's no sign of any injury.'

'Who found him?'

'Couple of kids looking for somewhere to drink their cider. We found his clothes in the bin over there.' He nodded towards the corner of the church.

'Do we know who he is?'

'Not for certain, but a woman who lives a couple of miles down the road reported her husband missing this morning. Sounds like him – Alan Jacobs, thirty-five, senior psychiatric nurse at the Conway Unit.'

Jenny felt a cold tightness grip her chest. The Conway Unit was a secure psychiatric facility for the newly sectioned and acutely ill. At the height of her 'episode' she had once spent a single night there. Dr Travis had persuaded her it was for the best, but it was the closest thing to hell on earth she had ever known.

She looked again at the dead man. She didn't recall seeing him at the unit, though she could imagine him as a nurse. He was big, like so many of them were, but with gentle hands and a soft face.

'What do you make of the cross?' Wallace said, his tone softening a little now he could sense she wasn't vying for control.

Jenny shrugged. 'I'd say God was on his mind, or what was left of it.'

Wallace nodded, making no comment, then said, 'I've got a busy few days coming up – I persuaded the pathologist to come in and do him straight away. Is that all right with you?'

'Fine,' Jenny said, surprised he was troubling to ask. 'What's this, be nice to the coroner week?'

'You've earned yourself a reputation, Mrs Cooper,' DI Wallace said. 'And I'm trying to make Super'.'

'Right – hence the suit.'

He looked at her, puzzled, and pulled out his phone.

'Whatever . . .' She nodded at the body. 'I'll catch up with him later at the morgue.'

Leaving Wallace to his phone call, she made her way back across the churchyard.

She had a hectic week in store, too. There'd been a messy construction accident the previous Tuesday which had prompted five separate firms of lawyers to bombard her office with demands for all manner of forensic investigations to which her puny budget wouldn't stretch. The inquest, when it came, would last the best part of a month. Two workmen and a site supervisor had been crushed to death in a crane collapse, six others injured. Compared with that mess, dealing with a simple suicide would be a holiday.

She drove into the city for a light lunch at a new Italian cafe on the waterfront, sipped her mineral water like a good girl – she'd managed to stay dry since her little slip-up with Alec McAvoy – and headed out to the mortuary at Severn Vale District Hospital in time to catch the end of the autopsy.

Dr Andy Kerr was stooping across the steel counter when Jenny entered, picking over a portion of viscera. The radio was playing the same kind of tuneless R & B her teenage son inflicted on her every time they shared a car. Andy – he had somehow persuaded her not to call him Dr Kerr – was reluctantly creeping into his thirties and trying to turn the clock back. He'd recently added a gold stud to his left ear.

She tried not to look too closely at the corpse, which lay open from neck to navel on the autopsy table. 'Find anything?'

'Hold on . . .' Andy said, concentrating on his delicate task. With a pair of tweezers he lifted something tiny out from what she could now see was the dead man's stomach and placed it in a kidney dish. 'Looks like we might have a cause of death shaping up. He had a belly full of pills.'

'That makes sense. The police think he was a psychiatric nurse.'

Andy extracted another object, an undigested white tablet, and held it up to the light. 'PB 60. Phenobarbital, probably. Used to treat seizures. Depresses respiration and leads to a fairly painless death. And there's liver inflammation, which would be a side-effect of the overdose.'

'An unequivocal suicide.'

'More or less.'

'There's something else?' She sneaked a glance and wished she hadn't: the empty ribcage was a sight from a butcher's window.

'Minor lesions on both forearms.' He looked at her over his mask. 'As if someone had dug their nails in, perhaps.'

'Violently?'

'Hard to say.' Finished with the stomach, he picked it up in both hands and placed it alongside the other major organs he had examined and cut into sections. 'You don't know if the police turned him over? Blood had pooled towards the front of his body but the photos they took at the locus show him on his back.'

'Unlikely. The DI said some kids stumbled across him – maybe it was them?'

'Kids? You think they'd touch a stranger's corpse?'

She considered the prospect. 'No, I don't.'

Andy picked up a scalpel and returned to the body. 'Well, someone did.' He began cutting around the hairline in preparation for peeling the scalp forwards over the face. It was Jenny's cue to leave.

\*

She telephoned DI Wallace as she stepped out into the welcome fresh air, the smell of death clinging stubbornly to her clothes. Wallace listened to Andy's findings and said it sounded as if it would have to remain a police matter, at least until he'd ruled out the possibility of foul play. He informed Jenny that Mrs Jacobs had identified her husband's body from a photograph but had been too emotional to talk. In the meantime he'd been over to the Conway Unit in Clifton and met Alan Jacobs's line manager, a Mrs Deborah Bishop. Jacobs had been Senior Staff Nurse in the young persons' ward, dealing with twelve- to eighteen-year-olds. As far as Bishop had been aware he'd been in good spirits; she had appeared badly shaken at the news.

'Have you got Mrs Jacobs's address?' Jenny asked.

'39 Fielding Road, Coalpit Heath,' DI Wallace said after a brief hesitation, the tightness in his voice suggesting that he'd rather she stayed away from the bereaved until it was her turn.

Jenny's gut told her there was more to his reluctance than protecting his turf. She wondered if Bishop had told him something he hadn't let on. A death, however loosely related to vulnerable teenagers, would have set alarm bells ringing all the way to Whitehall. Senior civil servants in the Department of Health would already be asking questions of their own.

Jenny thanked him for the information and let him know he wouldn't be having it all on his own terms: 'I'll have my officer take Mrs Jacobs through the procedure. Oh, and by the way – did your people alter the position of the body before I arrived?'

'Not to my knowledge. Seen as found.'

'Let me know if you hear different. Dr Kerr thinks it had been rolled over.'

The detective gave a dismissive grunt and rang off.

*

Jenny waited until early evening before calling on the widow. Technically there was no need for the coroner to disturb the next of kin while the police were still investigating, but she liked to make contact while emotions were still raw and before questions had to be thought about before being answered. And there was something about Wallace that had troubled her. From the moment she arrived in the churchyard he had seemed distracted and defensive, a man wrestling with an unspoken problem.

Coalpit Heath was an outlying suburb in the north-east of the city. She had resolved not to wake the household if she found it in darkness, but as she drew up opposite number 39 she noticed a crack of light behind the drawn curtains in the downstairs front room.

A woman in her sixties answered the door on the security chain, her face set in a hostile frown. 'What is it now?' The sound of a child's cry carried from somewhere inside the house.

Jenny passed a business card through the crack. 'Jenny Cooper, Severn Vale District Coroner. I'd like to speak to Mrs Jacobs?'

The woman held the card at arm's length, trying to make out the print. 'I'm her mother.'

'Would it be all right to have a brief word?'

Sighing, she unhooked the chain and opened the door. 'The police have been here all evening. I thought we'd have some peace.'

'I'll be as quick as I can.'

The woman led Jenny through a short hallway and into a living room that ran straight through into a modern kitchen. Her daughter, the widow, was lying on a tan leather sofa wearing pyjamas and a towelling dressing gown. A waste basket next to a coffee table was overflowing with used Kleenex.

'Ceri? It's the coroner,' the older woman said quietly. 'Don't worry about Josie. I'll see to her.'

Mrs Jacobs lowered her feet to the floor. She was thirty-five or thereabouts, pale with mousy blonde hair cut in a sensible bob. She attempted a smile with her 'hello', and Jenny saw in her face that she was suffering from shame as much as grief.

'Sorry to disturb you, Mrs Jacobs. I know it's a difficult time.'

'It's all right.' She spoke with a soft Welsh accent.

Jenny sat on a chair that matched the sofa and glanced around a room that seemed to have been disturbed. The books and DVDs on the shelves by the television were in a jumble. Toys spilled over the edges of a plastic crate.

Embarrassed by the mess, Ceri Jacobs said, 'The police were here most of the evening. They went through everything. I haven't been able . . .' She swallowed, holding back tears. 'How can I help you?'

'They might have explained that if they don't suspect foul play it's my job to determine your husband's cause of death.'

Mrs Jacobs nodded and reached for a Kleenex.

'Were they looking for anything in particular?'

'They said it was routine. I can't remember all the things they took.'

'Computer? Address book?'

'Yes, and some of his clothes.' She pressed the tissue to her eyes. 'Ones that hadn't been washed. I don't know what for.'

'Computers are always taken as a matter of course. They'll check the clothes for third-party DNA,' Jenny said. 'Just in case.'

'No one wanted to kill Alan . . . Why would they?' Ceri Jacobs shook her head with an expression of bewildered incomprehension.

'The pathologist found pills in his stomach, Mrs Jacobs. Phenobarbital. It's a barbiturate, something he might have got hold of at the unit.'

Her gaze turned inwards as she seemed to disengage, not yet ready to absorb this information.

'Was he depressed?'

'No, not that he admitted to me. Work has always been difficult, but he loved it. It was his vocation.'

'Was he being treated for any psychiatric condition, or had he ever been?'

She shook her head.

'When did you last see him?'

'Yesterday afternoon. He said he'd had a call from the unit saying they had several staff sick. They asked if he could cover for the night.'

'Was that unusual?'

'It happens.'

'What time did he leave?'

'About four o'clock. I thought he'd be back by midnight. Josie woke me about six and I saw he hadn't been home. I tried to call him but his phone was off . . . I don't know why, but I called the office at the unit. They said he hadn't been in, they had all the staff they needed.' Her eyes filled with tears. 'That's when I called the police.' The widow pressed her hands to her face. 'Why? . . . What was he thinking of?'

Jenny had tried to train herself not to form judgements on first impressions, yet she couldn't help thinking that Mrs Jacobs's knowledge of her husband might have been incomplete, to say the least. The house was a showcase exclusively for their child: framed baby photographs on every surface, nursery school paintings plastering a noticeboard that took up most of the kitchen wall, even Ceri's stretchy pyjamas were decorated with purple hippos. Alan Jacobs left here each day to work with the city's most mentally disturbed teenagers, a job he could only have succeeded in by winning their respect and connecting on their level. Yet it was as if his wife had organized her home as a shield against all that; there was nothing of him or his life outside the family home on display. It looked as if Ceri had decreed that their child was all that mattered to them.

Jenny realized that she'd missed something: God featured here, too. The simple oil painting on the wall behind the sofa was an icon – a modern rendering of the Virgin and Child – and Ceri wore a silver crucifix around her neck.

'Did the police tell you anything about your husband's body, Mrs Jacobs?'

'I know he was –' she could barely bring herself to say it – 'naked.'

'And the cross on his torso?'

She shot Jenny a look she wasn't expecting, a flash of steel as sharp as a razor. 'What about it?'

'Why might he have done that – assuming it was him.'

'I've no idea.'

'I assume you're a Catholic, was—?'

'No, he wasn't,' she interrupted. 'For most of his life Alan wasn't religious at all, his family had poisoned him against it. But he had begun to change. He was an enquirer at St Joseph's. He'd been every Tuesday night for the last five months.'

'An "enquirer"?'

'The church runs courses for those who want to learn about the faith.'

'Did he talk to you about it?'

'We talked about everything, Mrs Cooper. We were man and wife.' She stood up from the sofa. 'I'm sorry, my daughter's still crying. I'd like to go to her please.'

'Of course.'

'If you wouldn't mind seeing yourself out.'

As Jenny made her way to the front door she felt the coldness of the widow's disapproval follow her to the threshold and beyond. Driving away from the house, she was left with an image of Ceri's face, the look she had given her: like an accusation of heresy. She imagined the dead man mute in the face of his wife's silent judgement, enduring his suffering alone.

She was reluctant to trust her too-often flawed intuition, but the visit had left her in no doubt: Alan Jacobs had departed this world with many dark secrets.

# TWO

IT HAD BEEN A MONTH since Jenny last sat opposite Dr Allen in the consulting room at the Chepstow clinic. During the one session they had had since her visit to her father in his nursing home, she had neglected to tell her psychiatrist what he had said to her. In fact, she hadn't told a living soul. He had advanced Alzheimer's, for God's sake. She'd be madder than him to take any notice of his lunatic outbursts.

Dr Allen sported new glasses and a salon haircut. Finally having arrived at an age that matched his serious nature, he was beginning to find a look that he felt comfortable with: stylish academic. She had never asked him if he was married but she assumed not, and guessed that the subtle makeover was part of his strategy to remedy the situation.

He looked up from the bound notebook in which he made his precise longhand notes. 'Has it really been four weeks?' He smiled. 'Any progress on the research you were promising to do?'

She felt a rush of electricity travel up her spine and she almost said it; almost confessed that her father had told her that Katy was a first cousin, his brother's little girl. It had shocked her; her uncle and aunt had lived round the corner yet she had no memory of a little girl, let alone one her age. 'What happened to Cousin Katy?' she had asked him. Sitting

13

there in his armchair, chuckling at the seagull on the windowsill, he had said: 'You remember, Smiler. You killed her.' A minute later he was out cold, the heavy sedatives he was fed giving him the death-rattle snore she would hear all the way to the lift at the end of the corridor.

Jenny said, 'No luck, I'm afraid.'

Trying to hide his disappointment, Dr Allen said, 'Never mind. I'm sure we'll continue to make progress through regression.'

Jenny doubted that very much.

'How have you been feeling? Is the medication working?'

'On the whole.' She smoothed a wrinkle from the lap of her black suit skirt. 'It seems to hold the anxiety at bay – no panic attacks at least.'

'You've managed to avoid alcohol?'

'No problem.'

'And how does that make you feel?'

She resisted the temptation to tell him how much that phrase irritated her; she had counted him using it eight times in their last session.

'Honestly? . . . It makes me feel miserable, like there's something wrong with me.'

'Do you think there isn't?' He floated the question neutrally, as if whatever answer she gave was fine by him.

Jenny crossed her legs, trying not to let the lurch she felt in her stomach show on her face. She would tell him about her father, just not now. How could she be expected to probe an open wound first thing in the morning? And what would Dr Allen do with her answer anyway? It was her responsibility. She would deal with it when she had the time and space, which wasn't now.

'Well?' he prompted her, his eyes searching her face.

'The more often I come here,' she said in what she hoped was a calm and measured tone, 'the more I'm inclined to

believe that acute anxiety doesn't necessarily have one excit-
ing cause. As you've said, sometimes time is the best healer.'

He kept his eyes trained on the centre of her face. He was
making her nervous.

'How is your relationship with your son? Is he still living
with his father?'

'For the time being. It makes sense him being close to
college with all his commitments.' She sounded like a fraud
and could tell that he saw straight through her.

'And with your boyfriend – Steve, isn't it?'

'We've both been rather busy. He works in the day and
has to study at night. I barely get an evening to myself . . .'

'So neither of you feels the need to make the effort? Last
time we met I recall you said he'd declared himself.'

*Declared himself.* Where did he get these phrases from?

Jenny shrugged. 'I suppose I have to take most of the
blame.'

Dr Allen nodded, as if she had confirmed his theory. 'I
sense that you're feeling somewhat disconnected from your
emotions. Helpful as the new medication is, perhaps it has
allowed you to retreat a little too far from the issues.'

'I thought I was doing pretty well. No incidents, no
breakdowns.'

'On that level I'm very pleased.'

'But you'd be happier if I was suffering a little more – is
that what you're saying?'

'I'm sorry; I think we're in danger of a misunderstanding—'

She didn't let him finish. 'I know how much you want to
experience a big eureka moment, find some hidden memory
that's going to put everything right again, but to be honest,
Dr Allen, I think I've moved beyond that now. Imperfect
as things may be, I'm coping, and that's a hell of an
improvement.'

'That's all to the good.' He hesitated, glancing down at his notebook. 'I just have to check.'

She recognized that tic. He always looked down when he was hiding something. 'Check what exactly?'

His cheeks flushed with embarrassment. There. She had nailed him.

'Well, since you feel strong enough to have this conversation I'll be honest with you. I . . . I'm a little concerned that just as we were making strides you've retreated into avoidance, and you've found a way of burying your feelings that allows you to function on one level, but on another might be making things worse.'

'I thought this treatment was about helping me to cope.'

'It is, but it's also about cure, and about not making things worse. I feel we're at a tipping point, Jenny.' His left hand reached for the knot of his tie. 'Look, I think it's best for both of us if I'm completely honest. I respect the fact that you're an intelligent, professional woman, but in some ways it makes my job harder – you feel able, quite rightly, to question my approach. But I remain certain of my diagnosis: you have a buried trauma which lies at the root of your generalized anxiety syndrome. I would like to persist with a fortnightly course of regression therapy for at least six sessions. If you don't want that, I suggest I refer you elsewhere.' He sat back in his chair and fixed her with a look. 'We have twenty minutes. Shall we try?'

Jenny said, 'What, in your opinion, might happen to me if I passed on the offer?'

'Experience has taught me that there is invariably a day of reckoning. Painful as it may be, I really do recommend you give this a chance.'

She thought of the files stacked up on her desk, the emails and telephone messages that would be waiting for her in the office, the calls she would have to make, the endless petty but important battles each day brought. She wanted to say to him, *All right, but just not now.*

Jenny said, 'Can I call you?'

Dr Allen closed his notebook. 'By all means, but you'll understand that it may not be me who sees you next time.'

Jenny spent the remainder of her commute to work on the phone, the recently acquired hands-free turning the once private space of her car into an office. Government fraud officers had broken into a disused industrial unit and discovered the crudely embalmed bodies of five elderly Asians whose various pensions and allowances were still being claimed by their relatives. The last thing the police wanted was to get involved in what they called an 'all Indian', and they were trying to offload the legwork onto the coroner's office. Jenny was dealing with the crane collapse – six phone calls from victims' lawyers before nine a.m. – and told the Detective Superintendent in charge to forget it. She had barely hung up when Alison called with the news that a nine-year-old girl had been declared dead on arrival at the Vale from suspected alcohol poisoning. Jenny sent her to witness the autopsy and take statements from the ambulance crew and A & E team. The thought of a pre-pubescent body stretched out in the morgue filled her with overwhelming and irrational dread. Child deaths were one thing she had yet to learn to cope with. She tried not to think why that might be.

She approached her office at 14 Jamaica Street to find a man standing on the pavement outside. He was snake-hipped with short dark hair and olive skin, dressed in a dark suit that emphasized the narrowness of his limbs. He turned sharply at the sound of her footsteps as if startled, and she saw that he was a priest: he wore a black clerical shirt of the Roman style, a thin collar tight to his neck showing only a narrow band of white beneath his Adam's apple. She noticed his eyes were jet black, his slender features as smooth as polished walnut.

'Can I help you?' Jenny said. 'I'm Mrs Cooper. The coroner.'

A look of relief came over the priest's face. 'Ah, Mrs Cooper. I am so sorry to trouble you. Father Lucas Starr. I was hoping to make an appointment to discuss a case.' He spoke with an accent she couldn't place. She would have said Spanish but couldn't be sure.

'Have you tried phoning? We are in the book.' She stepped past him and unlocked the door.

'It's a matter of some urgency,' he said calmly, but in a way which held her attention. 'Of life and death, you might say.'

Jenny glanced at her watch: it was nearly ten and she had a hundred things that would demand her attention the moment she walked through the door.

'Look, I'm really very busy this morning. How about at the end of the day?'

The priest formed his right hand into a fist and enclosed it with his left palm, the subconscious gesture somewhere between a threat and a prayer. 'If you could only spare me ten minutes, Mrs Cooper. Your response might make all the difference to the man with whose welfare I am concerned.'

'Ten? You're sure?'

'You have my word.'

She took him through the dimly lit, windowless hallway that led to her ground-floor offices. There was a vague smell of damp; the cheap wallpaper the landlord had recently pasted up was already starting to peel at the corners. Ignoring the heap of mail waiting for her on Alison's desk, Jenny ushered the priest through the heavy oak door to her room. He waited for her to be seated behind her desk before he sat in the chair opposite, his back straight as a board, hands crossed precisely on his lap.

Jenny said, 'I'm listening, Father . . . What should I call you?'

'Father Starr is fine.'

Jenny nodded. 'You're a Catholic priest, I presume?'

'Yes,' he said, with a trace of hesitation. 'Not a parish priest, a Jesuit in formation to be precise. I'm nearing the end of a five-year ministry as a prison chaplain. One final year of tertianship and I become a brother, God willing.'

'I had no idea it took that long.'

'Start to finish, seventeen years, sometimes more.' He smiled softly. 'They don't let just anybody in.'

She placed him at about forty, but somehow his age didn't seem to define him. She was curious about his accent, though: she detected traces of American; no, Latin American – that was it. 'You said you were concerned for someone's welfare.'

'Yes, please let me explain. This relates to the death of a young woman named Eva Donaldson. I understand you are about to make the formal certification of the cause of death?'

Jenny glanced at the file bound with white ribbon sitting on top of one of three disorderly heaps on her desk.

'Eva Donaldson, the actress?'

Jenny had skimmed the Eva Donaldson file and picked up bits and pieces from news reports over the couple of months since the young woman's death, but hadn't stopped to consider the full story of her transformation from art student to adult movie star, to religious convert and full-time campaigner for Decency, a pressure group advocating a ban on internet pornography.

'The same. The man to whom I am ministering is named Paul Craven. He confessed to killing her.'

'I remember. He pleaded guilty to her murder.'

'You are correct, but he was not in his right mind. Paul Craven did not kill Eva Donaldson and he should not be spending the rest of his life in prison. I fear that unless the truth is told his life may not be very long.' A look of pain briefly passed across the priest's face. 'He is a sensitive and a troubled man, and a deeply religious man also. He had been out of prison for only a few days, having spent twenty-one years, all of his adult life, in jail.'

'Before we go any further,' Jenny said, 'you have got to understand – I'm a coroner. I determine cause of death. If you've evidence that could overturn the finding of a criminal court, the correct course is to instruct a lawyer to mount an appeal.'

Father Starr gave a patient nod. 'If we had a year or two, maybe, but Mr Craven doesn't have that long. There is a struggle within him that I sense he is losing.'

The phone rang. Jenny looked at it and pressed the divert button. 'All right, fifteen minutes. Then I really have to get on.'

Father Starr reminded Jenny of the highlights of Eva's career, telling her that she had been something of an inspirational figure to him and the prisoners he ministered to in Telhurst, a long-term prison in south Gloucestershire. At twenty she dropped out of art school and started acting in pornographic films. At twenty-five she was at the peak of her career when a road accident left her with permanent scars that disfigured one side of her face. The production company she was contracted to spat her out and sued her for loss of revenue, arguing that the drugs she had taken caused her to lose control of the car. They won. The pills she took to rev her up for a shoot cost her three hundred thousand in cash, her country house and her career.

Eva entered a downward spiral of drink, drugs and self-loathing. Later, she would tell audiences how she was on the verge of taking her own life – actually walking to the pharmacy to collect the painkillers she planned to wash down with the vodka she had ready in her bag – when she overheard a young woman telling a friend how the church she had joined had given her a permanent high. Eva caught the name of it as she pushed on the pharmacy door: the Mission Church of God.

Back then, nearly three years ago, the worshippers met in a disused bingo hall. The pastor was an inspirational young American named Bobby DeMont, who from nothing had built the mother church in Washington DC to be one of the biggest single congregations in the USA, over thirty-five thousand strong. That night Eva claimed she saw the light of God shine. It was in Bobby DeMont's eyes as he spoke, and in the faces of the young men and women around her as they heard the unadulterated truth for the first time in their lives.

Not only did the church give her back her will to live, through it she was introduced to its chief benefactor, Michael, now Lord Turnbull. At forty-one years of age Turnbull had sold his software company for two hundred million dollars, but his conscience was troubled. As a young idealist, he had pioneered video-streaming software in the hope of putting the lie-peddling media multinationals out of business. What, in fact, he inadvertently provided was the means for the pornography business to reach into every home with a computer, making a lot of disgusting people exceedingly rich. A year later Turnbull had been struggling to hold down a consultancy to a lobbying company in Washington while suffering from increasingly crippling depression. Dependent on alcohol and pills, he had started to fantasize about jumping from his penthouse balcony when he chanced on an item on the local news about a spate of miraculous healings that had taken place at the Mission Church of God. Desperate, and with nothing to lose, the multi-millionaire sobered up and took himself to an evening service. When Bobby DeMont called on all those who hadn't yet pledged their lives to the Lord Jesus Christ to do so right now, Michael Turnbull obeyed. He would later describe to television viewers around the world the feeling when Bobby first laid his hands on him as like being giddy with wine and madly in love, only many times stronger.

Born again, Michael donated generously to the church and hatched the idea of starting a sister church in his home city of Bristol. Fired up with the idea of taking the gospel back to a country that had brought so many evangelists to the US, Bobby DeMont himself came to England for the first few months to sow the seeds. Within a year the congregation had grown to a thousand members and Michael Turnbull had established a lobby group, Decency, to try to undo some of the damage he had inflicted on the world. When he heard Eva Donaldson had become a member of the church, he immediately recruited her to the cause. For the remaining year of her life she became the public face of the campaign: her scarred beauty a symbol of the ugliness of pornography; her first-hand testimony of being abused for profit a stain on the conscience of every man who heard her.

The world's media and politicians were stunned by the level of public enthusiasm for Decency's cause. Liberals poured scorn on what they dismissed as an old-fashioned moral backlash, but facing down her critics in what would become her most famous network television interview, Eva Donaldson said, 'Do you think it's right that images of me having sex with men and women I barely knew, committing acts I sometimes had to drug myself to perform, are available to your child at the click of a mouse?' She left her opponents floundering.

Jenny reminded her visitor of the time. His fifteen minutes were up.

'I'm giving you the history, Mrs Cooper,' Father Starr said, 'to emphasize how many people there were with a motive to silence her.'

'But hasn't she been made a martyr? I've read there's a good chance the Decency Bill they've been agitating for might actually become law.'

The priest leaned forward in his chair. 'Look at the circumstances of her murder. There were no signs of forced entry, indicating she opened her door to a caller. She was stabbed once, in the kitchen, with a weapon which has never been recovered. There was no evidence of sexual violation. At the time of her death Mr Craven was residing in a bed-sit in Redland, over seven miles from her home. Read the transcript of his police interview – he couldn't state her address or even describe the route he would have taken to it.'

'I've not read the whole file,' Jenny said, 'but I do recall that Craven gave himself up at a police station, confessed freely, and that his DNA was found in the grounds of Miss Donaldson's house.'

'The DNA is unreliable. They say he urinated on the doorstep. I have spoken to experts who say there are very few cells excreted in urine.'

'Then it sounds as if you've grounds for appeal. An uncorroborated confession by a man in a fragile state of mind isn't usually sufficient for a conviction.'

'The psychiatrists say there's nothing wrong with him. I know otherwise, but what notice would the courts take of a priest?'

'Surely Craven's had good lawyers representing him. What do they think?'

'He told them he was guilty. Now he insists he isn't, they

are professionally embarrassed and he has to instruct new ones. But without some evidence, some lead, he won't get legal aid. I understand that leaves him at the mercy of the Criminal Appeal Cases Review Commission. Who knows when they might get to his case – months, years?'

'Look,' Jenny said, 'where there's been a conviction a coroner is entitled to investigate the circumstances of the death, but the law states that I mustn't return a verdict which undermines a finding of the criminal court, and that includes a guilty plea.'

'I've informed myself on the point,' Father Starr said. 'But as I understand it, you would be acting perfectly lawfully in investigating the circumstances of Miss Donaldson's death. And if you were to discover evidence exonerating Mr Craven, it would be grounds for an appeal.'

Jenny smiled. 'I can't fault your optimism, Father. But is that all you've got? Tell me what makes you so sure Craven didn't kill her.'

The priest studied her, carefully weighing his words. 'When he was a vulnerable and disturbed teenager Paul Craven killed a young woman. I have now known him for five years. I know him more intimately than any other human being: I am his confessor. I have seen him turn to God and I have seen God change and redeem him. I ask you to believe me when I say I can divine whether he's lying about such a profound matter as whether he committed murder.'

'Then why did he confess?'

'I think it's best that you ask him that. It's not possible to judge a man until you have met, don't you think?'

'I can certainly send my officer to take a statement—'

'Please,' Father Starr interjected, gesturing with his hands, 'I ask this one thing of you, that you interview him in person. Then, I guarantee, you will understand.'

He was a hard man to resist, and someone Jenny already

24

felt she would like to know more about. 'And if I say I can't?'

'I shan't beg you, Mrs Cooper.' He got up from his chair. 'Thank you for your time. You have been most generous.' He produced a card from his jacket pocket and placed it in front of her. 'I'll leave you to decide what's right.'

She should have started working through her phone messages or reading her mail, but the priest's plea lingered like a watchful presence. It demanded that she make a decision on whether to rubber-stamp the Crown Court's verdict in line with usual procedure, or to risk the ire of her overseers in the Ministry of Justice and conduct an inquest of her own.

She reached for the court file and began skimming through its pages.

There was a statement from Eva Donaldson's domestic help, who had arrived in the morning to find her employer's body on the kitchen floor of her modest home in Winterbourne Down, a village just outside the northern margins of the city; statements from the several detectives who were called to the scene; a list of items that were removed from the house; a forensics report on the DNA sample recovered from the doormat; and a report by the Home Office pathologist. A bundle of photographs showed the body at the scene. Eva was curled into a foetal position surrounded by a huge pool of congealed blood. Two shots of the body on the slab showed a single stab wound to her chest midway between her breasts and her shoulder-length blonde hair. The final photograph was a close-up of her heart sitting in a kidney dish. A flagged pin marked the stab wound, which had penetrated her upper right ventricle, making death a rapid certainty.

Jenny stuffed the pictures into the back of the file and flicked through the transcript of Craven's police interview.

He wasn't much of a talker. The DI conducting the interrogation, Goodison, had had to tease him along. When eventually he found his tongue, Craven said he kept seeing Eva on the television news talking about her past in blue movies and how she had found God. He had found God, too, which was what gave him the idea of going to talk to her on his release. When the detective asked how he'd found her address, he said he had got it from contact-a-celebrity.com while he was still in prison. Jenny arrived at a section of the interview that had been highlighted:

*DI G: You say you walked all the way to her house.*
*[suspect nods]*
*DI G: What did you do when you got there, Paul?*
*PC: Hung around for a while, then rang the bell.*
*DI G: What did you do while you hung around?*
*[suspect shrugs]*
*DI G: Come on, Paul, you can remember that. What did you do? Look through the window, check out the house, go to the toilet, what?*
*[long pause]*
*PC: I think I went to the toilet, had a leak.*
*DI G: Where?*
*PC: Don't remember. No. Don't remember.*
*DI G: By the house?*
*PC: Yeah, that's it, by the house.*
*DI G: Then what?*
*PC: Like I said, I rang the doorbell.*
*DI G: What happened next?*
*PC: She came to the door. She said, 'Who are you?' I said, 'I'm Paul, like the apostle, and I think God told me to come and talk to you about all the good work you're doing, because I want to give my life to good works too.' And she said, 'Oh, well you'd better come in and tell me*

*more.' [long pause] I followed her into the house, into the kitchen, then she turned to me with this strange look on her face, and she put her hand on me [suspect indicates his chest] and she said, 'You don't have to say anything, Paul, I know what you want and I want it too.' And she moved her hand downwards, you know, down there [suspect indicates his groin area] and I said, 'No, that's not right, please don't do that to me,' but she took no notice. I said, 'Eva, that's a sin.' She said [pause] I can't say what she said.*

*DI G: It's not a problem, Paul. Just tell me what she said.*

*[suspect covers face with hands]*

*DI G: Come on, Paul. Let's hear it.*

*[pause]*

*PC: She said, [sobbing] she said, 'Fuck me for the devil.' And that's when I picked up a knife from the counter and stuck it in her, right there, in the chest.*

*DI G: How many times?*

*[suspect shakes his head]*

*DI G: What did you do then?*

*PC: I ran out of that house. I ran away from there.*

*DI G: What did you do with the knife?*

*PC: Threw it away.*

*DI G: Where? Where did you throw it?*

*[suspect shakes his head, breaking down into tears]*

The last document in the file was a report from the court-appointed psychiatrist, Dr Helen Graham, who said she had examined Craven on three separate occasions during his remand. In her opinion he was suffering from a mild personality disorder which gave him 'a sometimes tenuous grasp on reality and a tendency to fixate on abstract, often religious ideas', but there had been no evidence of violence in his character during his long prison term. He had attended classes conducted by female teachers and been in contact with a female parole officer without any suggestion of inappropriate behaviour. He wasn't clinically insane, and in her view there was no evidence to support any suggestion that he was suffering from diminished responsibility or a temporary psychological illness. During their three sessions Craven had refused to discuss the circumstances of the alleged offence, but on one occasion did express remorse for what he had done. Dr Graham concluded that there was no reason to question the validity of Craven's confession and expressed the opinion that the stress of release had caused him to commit a crime very similar to that for which he had originally been imprisoned.

Stapled inside the back cover of the file was a copy of Craven's criminal record and a handwritten statement of the facts of his first murder. At eighteen, he had met a twenty-three-year-old nurse named Grace Akingbade at a Bristol nightclub. Late in the evening they were seen leaving together. Grace's body was found in her room in a hospital accommodation block the following afternoon. She had been beaten and strangled but there was no evidence of sexual molestation. Craven was arrested the same day and made a full confession. His explanation for the killing was that the young woman had mocked him when he had failed to perform sexually.

Jenny finished reading and made up her mind that there was nothing to investigate. If Craven wanted to protest his innocence he would have to do what everyone else did and find a criminal lawyer to fight his battles for him. There were far more deserving cases on her desk.

She looked up with a start as Alison thumped through the door and dumped a fresh heap of papers in front of her.

'Are you all right, Mrs Cooper?'

'You shocked me.'

'Fun as it was watching an autopsy on a nine-year-old, I thought I'd better tear myself away.'

Jenny noticed that she was wearing shiny red lipstick and had brushed her dyed blonde hair forward over her cheeks. 'It suits you,' she said, her heart still pulsing hard against her ribs.

'Thank you,' Alison said with self-conscious abruptness and swiftly changed the subject. 'The pathologist confirmed death by alcohol poisoning so social services have asked the police to look at criminal negligence. I doubt it'll end with charges, but at least it's off our plate for the time being. We've had an anonymous email from a man who claims he was one of the gang which erected the crane and says they were using sub-standard bolts, and Dr Kerr just emailed an interim report on Alan Jacobs – it's not looking too pretty. Oh, and there's been a fatal RTA on the Portway I should probably go and have a look at.'

She turned abruptly to the door.

Jenny sensed there was more to Alison's agitation than her caseload. 'Is everything all right?'

'I've had more relaxing mornings.'

'Is it Terry again?'

'Terry?' Alison said, as if her husband was the furthest thing from her mind. 'He's no trouble to me now he's in Spain.'

'*Another* holiday?'

'I don't know what you call it,' Alison said, 'but I suppose you might as well know before you hear gossip. He's been seeing some woman he met out there last time.'

'I'm sorry. I'd no idea—'

'Neither did I till last Thursday. But I told him if there was something he wanted to get out of his system I'd rather he did it out of my sight.'

Jenny knew there had been arguments, mostly over her husband Terry's desire to sell up and retire to a Spanish condo while he was still young enough to get round the golf course, but she had no idea relations had turned this sour. 'So, where does that leave the two of you?'

'I haven't a clue, but I'm damned if he's going to have all the fun.' The phone rang in the outer office. 'That'll be traffic wanting to know if I'm coming to see the body.'

'Couldn't we make do with their photographs?'

'I'd rather get out if you don't mind, Mrs Cooper. I'm afraid I can't tolerate my own company at the moment.'

She left, thumping the door shut behind her. It seemed only a few weeks ago that she'd been wrestling with feelings for DI Pironi and had spent three days in self-pitying silence having stood him up on a dinner date. Veering between church-going piety and guilt-ridden desire, Alison spent weeks on end as moody as a teenager.

Jenny picked up Dr Kerr's single-page interim report and prepared herself for the worst. It didn't disappoint:

*Rectal examination showed fresh and semi-healed abrasions consistent with intercourse on more than one occasion; swabs show presence of semen deposited in the hours immediately preceding death. Minor lesions on both forearms appear to have been made by human fingernails. Tissue samples from affected sites have been submitted for analysis.*

*While the immediate cause of death is an overdose of phenobarbital, it is not possible to say with certainty whether consumption was voluntary.*

Jenny thought of Mrs Jacobs and tried to imagine her reaction as DI Wallace broke the news of her husband's final hours. She pictured her face set in a stony mask of denial.

How would she cope? Would she even understand? No. If Jenny had gained one insight into human nature through being a coroner, it was that two people could inhabit the same space for years and in all meaningful respects remain distant strangers.

She placed the report on the arbitrary pile at the right side of her desk which she had started with Paul Craven's court file, and was struck by the thought that only weeks and a handful of miles apart sex, drugs and God – a trinity of life's most potent forces – had colluded in the untimely deaths of both Alan Jacobs and Eva Donaldson. The thought seemed to open a door to an untravelled corner of her subconscious. She found herself in a dark and downward-sloping tunnel. And in the gloom behind her the door slammed shut.

# THREE

IT WAS IN THE EARLY evenings that the effect of her slow-release medication tapered off and the ghosts it held at bay returned to haunt her. They had no faces, these forms hovering at the margins of her consciousness, but they wanted her to know that they were only a breath away; that she had only one foot in the world of the living. Lately their presence had become sharper. It was as if the eruption of spring into summer, with all the valley humming with the urgency of life, had spurred them to greater efforts.

There was no relief from them tonight. Throughout her drive home their presence had grown. They were waiting for her in the shadows at Melin Bach, behind the trees at the end of the cottage's garden, amongst the clutter of ancient tools and implements in the dilapidated mill shed. She couldn't settle to read her papers at the scrub-top table on the lawn without feeling watched by unseen eyes, feeling the touch of their hands in the breeze on her neck. The psychiatrists would call it mild paranoia, but that didn't begin to explain the dark and complex landscape of her other world.

The scent of the newly mown meadow was overpowered by the smell of the churchyard where Alan Jacobs's body had lain. His features hovered behind her eyes, and the shame and anguish of his final moments tugged at her, as if she were somehow wrapped up in the cause of his despair.

Such irrational thoughts were nothing new. They had dogged Jenny throughout her short career as a coroner, taunting her with the notion that she was doomed to consort with the dead, denying her the chance to live unselfconsciously among the living. She had tried to pull free, to confine her imagination within normal limits, but then Alec McAvoy had arrived and flung the door to the abyss wide open. *My Dark Rosaleen*, he had called her. He had seemed to know her secrets without her saying a word and he had left without saying how. But left her to what?

Listless, and for the first time in weeks fighting the desire to drive into town to buy a bottle of wine, Jenny retreated to her little study at the front of the cottage and tried to lose herself in the most urgent files she had brought home. Top of the pile was Eva Donaldson's. There'd been an email late in the afternoon from Eva's next of kin, her father, asking when her body might be released for burial and her death formally registered. It was Jenny's custom not to allow homicide victims to be released until the conclusion of a trial; there was now no good reason not to hand her remains back to her family, especially as Craven's claim to innocence, such as it was, was based purely on the soundness of his confession.

She reached out for a Form 21, *Coroner's Order for Burial*, and began to complete it, but as she did so she heard the steady voice of Father Starr: 'Believe me when I say I can divine whether he's lying about such a profound matter as whether he committed murder.' It was illogical, precisely the sort of superstition she had strained so hard in recent months to avoid, yet completing the form suddenly felt like a betrayal. What was it McAvoy had said that morning in the car when he'd been scratchy and hung-over? 'Try going to confession once a fortnight and spilling your sins out to a celibate priest. There's something to put you in your place.' She remembered the smell of his cigarette smoke, the odour of cramped courtrooms, dirty cells and seedy nightclubs that clung to his damp woollen coat, a world she came to understand he was both called to and despised.

She flipped open the lid of her laptop and ran a search on Father Lucas Starr. He was listed as Roman Catholic chaplain of Telhurst Prison. A short biography recorded that he was thirty-nine years old, the son of American and Mexican missionaries, and had spent his early life in Bolivia and New Mexico. While still a teenager, he had entered the Seminary of the Immaculate Conception in Huntington, New York, and was now in the sixteenth year of his formation as a Jesuit. He had spent time with missions in Nigeria, Angola, the Philippines, Bangladesh and Colombia, where he served in the chaplaincy of La Modelo prison, Bogotá. She began a fresh enquiry with 'La Modelo' and learned that it was considered the toughest, filthiest, most violent and dangerous jail in South America.

What would McAvoy have said? His answer sounded clearly: give the man a chance; you don't devote body and soul to God for twenty years without becoming wiser than most. They'll scare the hell out of you, these Catholic priests, with their iron wills and cold certainty of what's to come, but they'll go to places you wouldn't dare and draw on strength you'll never possess.

Jenny typed 'Eva Donaldson' and was met with a barrage of the sacred and profane, a galaxy of hardcore pornographic websites vying with reports on the Decency campaign. She clicked 'images' and wished she hadn't. A single dignified portrait of Eva's post-accident face sat amongst a carousel of lurid shots of her in every form of sexual congress. In one scene she was a delicate virgin, in others a whore, an unwilling victim, a cheating wife. Of all the roles it was innocence she performed best. She was such a successful commodity, Jenny realized, because despite the squalor of her poses she retained an aspect of purity. She encouraged in her voyeurs the fantasy that through knowing her they would somehow lift themselves out of their own wretchedness.

Jenny quickly navigated away and scrubbed her images from the machine's memory. Be rational, she told herself, get a grip, behave like Her Majesty's Coroner and follow the protocol, but she knew the battle was already lost. Attempting to reason away her emotional decision, she tried to convince herself that it was merely a question of showing respect for Father Starr. Surely it would be a proper and humane gesture to visit Craven in prison before letting Eva's body be returned to the earth. Her thoughts were interrupted by the creak of the front gate and the sound of a man's footsteps on the flagstone path. She craned forward to see Steve approaching. He was carrying flowers.

She brought the lupins out to the garden table in a tall clear vase that had belonged to her mother and saw him crouching at the edge of the stream. He pressed his fingers to his lips as she went over to join him. She knelt beside him and followed his gaze to what she called the swimming pool, a hollow in the stream bed deep enough to wallow in. A flash of silver broke the surface and leaped among the lazily circling flies. He turned to her and smiled, a day's growth on his hollow cheeks. His face was tired, but his eyes were bright as he shielded them from the sloping sunlight with a cupped hand.

'There's scores of them. Must be the pure water,' he said.

'I suppose I should feel blessed.'

'Too right.' He held her gaze with a playful, questioning look. 'May I?'

He leaned forward and kissed her mouth without waiting for an answer, his skin rough against her cheeks as he stroked her hair.

'You don't mind?'

'Why would I?'

He drew back, letting his hand drop to her shoulder then slide down her back to her waist. 'I don't know.' He shrugged. 'It's been a while.'

Jenny stared down into the stream, watching the school of fish dart through a shaft of milky light. 'I'm sorry. I've been useless.'

'I was worried about you.'

'I'm OK,' she lied.

'Ross decided to stay with his dad?'

'Yes . . . it makes more sense for him to be in town.'

'And you've been hiding away here getting lonely.'

'I've had a lot of work.'

He gave her a look which said she could do better.

'I know I've not been much of a girlfriend.'

Steve grinned. '*Girlfriend?* I've never heard you call yourself that before. Wow.'

She contrived to look hurt, but a laugh forced itself out. One of relief, of having a distraction from herself. And he looked handsome tonight, somehow more confident in his new life as a nearly-qualified architect. He still remained partly the romantic backwoodsman who had brought the countryside alive for her, telling her the names of every plant and tree, showing her where the deer stood at night and where the fox slunk through the hedges, but he seemed to inspire more trust now that his world had expanded beyond the boundaries of his out-of-the-way farm.

'I know it threw you when I said those things . . .' He sounded almost apologetic, referring to when he had told her he was in love with her, but too embarrassed to repeat it. 'It must be tough coming out of a marriage, all the baggage . . .'

She nodded, no more ready to have this discussion now than she had been three months ago.

He paused, trying to fathom her expression. 'That day you went to see you father – what happened?'

'Nothing.'

He gave her the searching look, the one more intimate than the sex that had first disarmed her. 'The shutters came down that day, Jenny, I felt it. Was it just because of what I said? I was only being honest.'

'Partly . . . I don't know.'

'I didn't want to spoil it between us.'

'I know what you wanted.'

'If you don't want things complicated, why don't you just say so? Put me out of my agony.'

He touched her lightly on the shoulder, longing for an answer she couldn't give. As he lifted his hand she caught it and brought it to her lips. 'Can we talk about this afterwards?'

They didn't make it to the bedroom or even indoors. They made love on the grass as urgently as they had the first time last summer. She was young again, feeling his every touch, his every minute caress with an electric thrill, until at last they both exploded in the scattering colours of grass and sky and spiralled slowly back to earth, a pair of gently fading butterflies.

She brought tea outside to the table as the sun dipped beneath the crest of the hill. They sat side by side, she leaning into him as he told her about his plans for when he was qualified. The firm he was attached to had lost out on a lot of business recently: clients' budgets weren't stretching to the extra cost of the ecological buildings in which they specialized. The chances of a full-time position were slim and he'd no choice but to start looking elsewhere. So far the only interest had been from a British firm in Provence. The money was appealing, but it would mean taking beautiful old farmhouses and turning them into vulgar, air-conditioned villas for ex-pat retirees. He hadn't spent seven years of study only to ditch his principles at the first sight of a cheque.

'At least you'd see the sun,' Jenny said.

'You sound as if you're trying to sell it to me.'

'There are worse places to be than the south of France.' He looked a little hurt. 'Would you visit?'

'If you'd forgive me for using the plane.'

'We might even see each other more often.'

'Ouch.'

'I'm serious, Jenny. I'm going to get an answer out of you one way or the other.' Despite the light-hearted tone she could tell he meant it. After her months of evasion he was pressing her for commitment.

'By when?'

'I qualify in six weeks.'

'Then what? You'll give up on me?'

'No.' He hesitated. 'But after that I'll leave it up to you to make the moves.'

It occurred to her to tell him the truth then, to confess that it had taken all her strength to try to cope with her demented father accusing her of being a child killer. It would be a relief to share it with him, to have someone to reason it through with. But what if he recoiled and turned his back on her in horror or disgust? She couldn't face his rejection, not now, not on top of everything else.

Jenny felt tears in her eyes. She hurriedly moved to wipe them away.

'What's the matter?'

'Nothing. It's just . . . There are some things I need to get straightened out. It's healthy. You're giving me a spur.'

'Anything you can share with me?'

'No.'

'I'd better head back.' He got up from the table.

Jenny reached out and touched his fingers. 'I'm glad you're being honest, really. And I'm trying to be. Just give me a little more time.'

He smiled again, decent enough to give her the benefit of the doubt. Better than she deserved. He stooped down to kiss her goodbye. As he walked away towards the old cart track that led around the side of the house, he stopped suddenly. 'Oh, by the way – there was a man with a little girl who seemed to be waiting for you around the front last night.'

'A man?'

'Yes. I drove past at about six. They were still there when I came back up around seven.'

'What did they look like?'

'He was in his thirties, the girl can't have been more than five or six.'

Jenny shrugged. It didn't sound like anyone she knew.

Steve said, 'Maybe they'd got the wrong place. You'll call?'

'I promise.'

Jenny spent what was left of the evening working, the only light in the house coming from her ancient desk lamp. It was nearly midnight and her eyes were smarting from staring at the computer screen when the return email from Father Starr arrived. He had arranged for her to visit Craven the following afternoon and Craven's solicitors were forwarding their files to her office. Her diary was already full, but Starr's tone brooked no argument. She dithered, then replied that she would meet him at the reception desk. Frustrated with herself for being such a pushover, she slammed her laptop closed and switched off the lamp. Feeling her way into the tar-black hall, she fumbled for the light switch. The single bulb stuttered into life like a guttering candle. Starting up the foot-worn treads of the narrow staircase, she heard the sound of gentle rapping at the front door: the cautious knock of a small hand. She turned, startled, telling herself it was only the wind. It came again: four patient, evenly spaced taps.

She told herself it was nothing, a plant knocking against the porch, a restless bird nesting in the eaves. She listened to the reassuring silence for a long moment and resumed her climb. As she reached the landing, feet shuffled on the path outside the front door accompanied by whispered voices: a child's whimper, a man, patient and reassuring. Jenny stood frozen, her heart pounding in her ears, waiting for the next tap, willing it to be real people outside, but they faded away. She waited for the squeak of the gate, for the turn of an engine, but nothing came.

She tiptoed softly across the creaking boards and fetched her sleeping pills from the bathroom cabinet. She shook one out, then made it three.

Telhurst Prison was set anonymously outside a small hamlet on the southern plain of the Severn estuary. Surrounded by wheat fields, there was nothing to indicate its presence except a discreet sign directing visiting traffic from the main road down the narrow lane leading to its front entrance. Shielded from the surrounding countryside by a screen of poplars, it occupied a site the size of several football pitches.

The main building was of modern construction, red brick with tiny windows like the arrow slits in the walls of a medieval castle. The perimeter was contained by two twenty-foot-high fences studded with cameras and patrolled by officers with dogs.

Alison had objected on principle to the coroner being summoned to interview a convicted murderer, and having voiced her objections sat in stubborn silence for the entire journey. Still suffering the effects of the previous night's sleeping pills, Jenny was too tired and preoccupied to attempt talking her round. She was thinking about ghosts, whether they were real or imaginary, and if it made any difference either way.

Alison broke her silence as they walked across the rain-spattered tarmac to the prison's main entrance. 'They've got no sense of perspective, priests. Just because they're governed by conscience they think everyone else should be, too.'

'I thought you were a believer,' Jenny said.

'I *was*, but things change. And so do people.'

'How is DI Pironi – are you two still friends?'

'He calls now and again.'

'I see.'

'What's that supposed to mean?'

'Nothing – but I can't help remembering that the two of you used to go to church together.'

'There was never anything between us, Mrs Cooper. Certainly not in that way.' Alison tugged indignantly at the strap of her handbag. 'Anyway, I was still with Terry.'

Father Starr was waiting for them inside the door. After a polite greeting, he led them to the front of a queue of impatient lawyers waiting to collect their security tags and signed them in. The officer behind the glass screen treated him with unquestioning respect, as did each of the guards they encountered on their journey through an unending series of corridors interrupted by heavy steel gates. Even Alison started to thaw, calling him 'Father' as if she were a devoted member of his flock.

He explained that Craven was being held in the close supervision circuit inside the segregation unit while his mental health continued to be assessed. The stress of being locked in a cell around the clock was destabilizing him further, but he was caught in a catch-22: the prison psychiatrist's idea of help was to persuade him to accept responsibility for a crime he hadn't committed. Protestations of innocence were treated as delusional.

Jenny said, 'This prison must seem quite tame after La Modelo.'

Starr smiled, as if she had mildly embarrassed him. 'I see you've been doing your research, Mrs Cooper.'

'I'm intrigued to know what brought you here.'

'We're an international organization. We go wherever we are needed.' He attempted a joke: 'And you've been short of Catholic priests ever since your King Henry decided we lived better than he did.'

He stopped outside a room at the end of a windowless corridor and knocked on the toughened glass pane. The door was opened from the inside by a heavy-set prison officer with the flattened nose of an ex-boxer. Father Starr asked him if he would mind waiting outside during their interview. The officer glanced dubiously at Jenny and Alison.

'It's perfectly safe,' Starr said. 'You know I trust him like a son.'

'You're a better man than me, Father,' the guard said, and stepped into the corridor. He turned to Jenny. 'I'll be right here if you need me.'

They entered an interview room not much bigger than a cell. The man sitting at the small table in handcuffs rose to his feet. 'Good morning, Father.'

'Paul, this is Mrs Cooper, the coroner, and Mrs Trent, the coroner's officer.'

Craven glanced at them shyly and nodded in a cautious greeting. He waited for them both to be seated before following suit. Jenny had read on the file that he was in his upper thirties but his face looked much younger. A prison-issue navy tracksuit hung shapelessly from his skinny frame. There were tiny hints of his age in the creases on his forehead, but it was as if the teenage boy had been held in suspended animation.

Father Starr said, 'As I explained to you, Mrs Cooper has to determine Eva Donaldson's cause of death. She does this free of the police and criminal courts and has a reputation for dogged independence.' Jenny shot him a glance. He ignored her and continued. 'She needs to take a statement from you. You have to tell her precisely what happened.'

'I'll be taking the statement,' Alison interjected, and pushed a form across the desk. 'This states that what you have to say is the truth and that you're liable for prosecution if anything you include in it is false. Do you understand?'

'Yes.' Craven spoke quietly, looking to Starr for reassurance.

Jenny said, 'You mustn't think of this as being like a police interview. We're here to listen to what you have to say, not to judge.' She felt Alison bristle, the detective in her refusing to entertain the idea that their visit was anything other than a sop to a troublesome and bloody-minded priest. 'We'll start at the beginning, shall we? Eva Donaldson was killed on the night of Sunday, 9 May. I believe you were released from prison on Thursday, the 6th.'

'That's right.'

Alison coughed pointedly. Jenny sat back in her chair and let her officer take over.

'Where did you go when you left prison, Mr Craven?'

He stalled before answering, requiring a nod from Father Starr to prompt him. 'The probation service fixed me up with a bedsit.'

'Address?'

'19b Clayton Road, Redland.'

Alison wrote it down in laborious longhand, determined not to put him at his ease.

'And what did you do once you were installed at this address?'

Craven shrugged. 'I stayed inside mostly, went to the shops once or twice, saw my parole officer on the Friday – she'd sorted my paperwork and that, told me where to go to collect my benefits.'

'And on the Saturday?'

'I don't remember . . . I think I stayed indoors. And the next day.'

'Did you communicate with anyone?'

Craven shook his head. 'No.'

Father Starr said, 'Paul lost contact with his family when he was ten years old. He was taken into care.'

'Where were you on the Sunday evening?' Alison asked.

'Inside. I didn't go anywhere.'

'Were there any neighbours, or anyone else, who might be able to verify your movements?'

'I never saw them to speak to.'

Alison frowned. 'And when did you make your confession to the police?'

Craven looked down and shook his head.

'It was on the following Wednesday at about midday,'

Father Starr said. 'I received a phone call here at my office from Detective Inspector Goodison. He handed me over to Paul, who asked me to find him a lawyer. I arranged that for him.'

'Why did you turn yourself in to the police, Mr Craven?' Alison asked.

Jenny watched him twist the fingers of his cuffed hands together as he struggled to explain.

'I wanted it to go away . . . I couldn't take hearing about it any more.'

'What did you want to go away?' Alison said.

'The pictures on the television. They didn't stop. She was everywhere . . . looking at me.'

Alison carefully wrote down his answer. 'You're saying you went to confess to Eva Donaldson's murder because you couldn't bear seeing her picture on television?'

Craven didn't answer, his gaze fixed on the table between them.

'Did you explain this to the police?'

'I can't remember.'

'What happened when you went into the station? What did you say?'

He shook his head.

'*Do* you remember?'

'Kind of.'

'Had you been drinking, taking drugs?'

'No.'

Jenny leaned forward, lightly touching Alison's arm as she interrupted her. 'We've read your police interview, Mr Craven – was what you told them true or false?'

He lifted his face and met hers with his child's china-blue eyes. 'It wasn't true. I didn't kill her, I didn't. I didn't. That's God's honest truth.'

'Then why tell the police you did?'

Craven's eyes flitted to Father Starr, then back to Jenny. 'Because I was weak. Because I let my faith weaken.'

There were many leading questions Jenny would like to have asked but they all fell into the category of cross-examination, which wasn't appropriate unless or until she held an inquest. A statement had to be an unprompted narrative by the maker, and they had already strayed too close to putting words into his mouth. But there was one direct question she could properly ask him: 'You told the police in interview that you urinated outside Eva Donaldson's house. They later claimed to have found traces of your DNA on the mat outside her front door. Can you explain that?'

Craven slowly shook his head.

Father Starr said, 'Samples get confused or contaminated at laboratories, it happens all the time. Even experts can be mistaken.'

Alison said, 'Do you have anything to say about the DNA evidence, Mr Craven?'

'It's wrong. I never went to her house. The only times I saw it was on the TV. That's the truth.' Agitated, he turned to Starr. 'That's right, isn't it, Father? Tell them. That's God's honest truth.'

Starr reached out and put a comforting hand on Craven's. 'That's what Mrs Cooper is going to do, Paul. She's going to find out the truth.'

Losing patience, Alison kicked Jenny's ankle under the table.

Ignoring her, Jenny said, 'Do you have anything else to add, Mr Craven? This is your one chance to speak to me directly. We won't be meeting like this again.'

The prisoner closed his eyes for a moment, as if summoning the strength to force the words out of his mouth. When they came, it was in a lucid stream that seemed to bubble up from deep inside him. 'You're right to think I'm lying to you. I did once murder an innocent young woman and I know God will judge me for that, but I didn't kill Eva . . . I'm a different person now. I couldn't do that. I'd kill myself before I'd hurt another human being.'

And as he held her in his innocent gaze, Jenny was tempted to believe him.

Jenny waited for Alison to stop off in the ladies' room at reception before turning to Father Starr, who had hardly spoken during the walk back through the prison. 'There was a question I should have asked him – why wasn't he at church on the Sunday?'

'My fault, Mrs Cooper. I should have made arrangements. I was on a study retreat during the week he was released.'

'If I was a more cynical person I'd say you were finding it hard to accept that a man you'd worked so hard with could have left here and killed three days later.'

'There is more than likely to be an element of pride. I am only human.'

'I don't doubt your good intentions, Father, but I'm afraid that the scales didn't fall from my eyes. I saw a man who needs a psychiatrist, a priest and a good criminal lawyer, probably in that order.'

'You were touched by him, weren't you?'

'I beg your pardon?'

Father Starr smiled. 'Lack of prejudice is a wonderful gift. I have had to work hard to try to acquire it. I sense you possess it naturally.'

'Listen, let's be straight about this now. If I decide to hold an inquest it'll be because there are issues around the cause of death that require further investigation, not out of any desire to assist Craven.'

'Of course. I understand.'

'I may even turn up more evidence against him.'

Father Starr turned his gaze out of the rain-flecked window and up towards a moody sky. 'Do you believe in good and evil, Mrs Cooper, and that the former attracts the latter?'

'I try not to get too philosophical during business hours.'

'Really? That's not what a mutual friend of ours once told me.'

Alison emerged from the ladies in a fresh cloud of perfume and glanced between Jenny and Starr, sensing an atmosphere between them. 'Is everything all right?'

'Yes, thank you,' Starr said. 'One other thing I should have mentioned, Mrs Cooper – as far as I know the police neglected to interview Miss Donaldson's former boyfriend. His name's Joseph Cassidy. He's an actor of sorts. I understand she and he resumed their acquaintance in the weeks before her death.'

'How do you know that?' Jenny said, feeling her cheeks flush with emotions she couldn't yet articulate.

'Craven's lawyer tried to speak to him, but he was reluctant to cooperate. I contacted his local priest.'

'You're quite the detective, Father,' Jenny said, feeling an unchristian stab of hostility.

'I try to live by a very simple philosophy: there is that which is right and just, and that which is not. As convenient a belief as it may be, there is no middle ground.' He opened his hands in a gesture of gratitude. 'Thank you both for coming here today. And now I must excuse myself; I have to conduct Mass.'

With a nod he turned and retreated into the depths of the prison.

'Didn't I tell you, Mrs Cooper?' Alison said.

Jenny scarcely heard her. She was thinking of their mutual friend, and dared to wonder with thundering heart if Alec McAvoy might still be alive.

# FOUR

IGNORING ALISON'S WARNINGS that anything other than an endorsement of the criminal court's verdict would threaten her already shaky tenure as coroner, Jenny wrote to Eva Donaldson's father informing him that she was ordering a final post-mortem examination of his daughter's body before releasing it for burial. Her next pressing task was to track down Eva's ex-boyfriend, Joseph Cassidy. He wasn't hard to find. An internet search revealed that he had starred alongside Eva in a number of films, all with names as obscene as the images that advertised them, and since leaving that business he had reinvented himself as the managing director of Wild West Productions, a television production company with offices in Bristol and Soho, central London. Not surprisingly, his company website contained no mention of his past in adult movies.

Jenny called him at his office number. Cassidy answered the phone himself, no assistant to protect him from the pestering hordes. When she announced herself and requested a meeting, Cassidy said, 'I've really nothing to say. Eva and I hadn't been seeing each other for more than two years.' He spoke with a Dublin accent that made him sound endearing even when he was being evasive.

'But I understand you had recently got back in touch?'

There was a brief silence.

'Where'd you get that from?' Cassidy asked.

'You're not under suspicion, Mr Cassidy. I'm just trying to find out if there's anything more about Eva's death that ought to be known.'

'It's all been said.'

'You're sure?'

'Honestly, I wish I could help you.'

She sensed him wavering and pounced. 'Why don't I buy you a drink and you can tell me what you do know?'

They met in a waterside bar at the harbour and sat at an outside table overlooking the boats, a warm breeze playing off the water. Joseph, or Joe, as he preferred to be called, resembled an ageing surfer. Suntanned, with tousled blonde hair, he wore an open-necked pink shirt under a black summerweight suit. He ordered neat vodka with ice and a dash of lemon juice. Jenny settled on neat tonic, her nerves still held in check by the Xanax she had taken before visiting the prison.

Keeping to small talk while they waited for their order to arrive, she asked him about the television business. The small screen was taking care of itself, Cassidy said, but he already had ambitions for feature films; he had just discovered a screenwriter who was going to be hotter than Tarantino. There were plenty doing the rounds who claimed to have mixed with gangsters, but this young man was the real thing – gold dust – a former drug dealer who had served time for shooting a rival through the kneecap.

Jenny listened patiently, but was glad when the waiter arrived with their drinks. Joe waited for Jenny to sip hers before he took a mouthful of the neat vodka, pretending he could take it or leave it.

Jenny said, 'Tell me about your relationship with Eva.'

More confident now he had a glass in his hand, Joe said, 'I'd like to know what you've heard about me first.'

'Just what I told you on the phone – that you and Eva had communicated recently.'

'Yeah, but *who* told you?'

'Paul Craven's solicitors knew about it,' Jenny lied, instinctively wanting to keep Father Starr's name out of the conversation for now.

'Hmm.' Joe took a big gulp of his vodka. 'I guess they must have talked to her lawyers. Trust those bastards to break their word.'

Jenny waited for him to enlarge.

'Does what I say here go any further?'

'That depends on what it is.'

'And if I don't talk?'

'I'd probably have to summon you to my inquest and make you answer under oath.'

'And this way I don't have to do that?'

'Possibly.'

'The thing is, Jenny—'

'Would you mind if we kept it to Mrs Cooper?'

Cassidy smiled. 'Whatever you like, *Mrs Cooper*. I did have a couple of meetings with Eva at the beginning of the year, but the matters we discussed were in strictest confidence.'

'Is that still relevant now she's dead?'

'It could be.'

'I don't follow.'

Cassidy pushed his hands through his hair. She noticed it was thinning at the temples. 'Look, I get that you probably know my history, how Eva and I met, but we both felt pretty much the same way about the adult entertainment business. I didn't even make money – girls get five times as much as guys, did you realize that?'

'No, I didn't.' She took a patient sip of her tonic.

'And if there's one good thing that comes out of all this, it's that Eva actually achieved something.'

'You mean Decency?'

'Yes. She wanted the law changed and so do I. In less than two weeks from now the bill gets debated in Parliament. That's what she'd been working for ever since we split up.'

'You're saying that whatever you discussed could jeopardize that in some way?'

'It's certainly possible.'

Jenny put her hands on the table. 'Mr Cassidy, we're talking about a young woman who was murdered. Unfortunately, it seems the police didn't go as far in their inquiry as they might have done – you're one of the people they should have spoken to, but didn't. One way or another you will eventually have to reveal what you know.'

Cassidy emptied his glass and crunched on an ice cube. Jenny tried to banish the image of him she'd seen on her computer: a still from *Locker Room Orgy*. 'Look,' he said, 'it wasn't that Eva wasn't totally committed to Decency, but she needed to make money. She'd got used to a certain standard of living, and who can blame her? She'd heard I'd gone into straight film-making and she came to me in the hope of lining up some work for later. We talked about using her reputation to pitch a TV series. It was going to be about these women she used to work with who were trying to shake free of their pasts and lead ordinary lives. She had a title: *Fallen Angels*. But nothing was going to happen until after the campaign was over, OK? Decency came first.'

'Did she tell anyone else about these plans?'

'Not as far as I know.

Jenny studied his face and decided he seemed more or less genuine. He didn't come across as sharp enough to be a good liar. If he were female, you would have called him a bimbo.

'Tell me, what was Eva's state of mind when you met her?'

'To be honest, I thought she was feeling the strain of being on show the whole time. She reminded me a little of how she was after the accident, when she was depressed. She was showing the same signs.'

'Such as?'

'She was jumpy, smoking a lot, and her hand would shake – you know, like an old person's.'

'Did she have any enemies that you knew of?'

Cassidy glanced up and down the boardwalk, then leaned in across the table, lowering his voice to a whisper. 'If you're asking do I think someone other than Paul Craven killed her, I'd say anything's possible. But what I do know is the porno business, and that the people that run it are far too rich and clever to get their own hands dirty – you know what I'm saying? I've thought about it every which way, and if Craven didn't do it, he must have arrived to find her already dead, right? So it could have been a professional hit – why not? You should hear the stories this scriptwriter tells me.'

Jenny said, 'Would you like another drink?'

Cassidy said, 'Only if you're having one.'

The second dose of vodka loosened Cassidy's tongue to the point at which Jenny sensed he was trying to please her. He told her that he'd met Eva when she'd already been in the industry for some time and they were cast in the same movie. They'd bonded over their love of sixties music – a time when pop was a rebellion, not just a business. From the moment he met her, Cassidy said, he knew she was different from the other girls he worked with; there was something behind her eyes, an intelligence, depth. It was what made her so special: her audience wanted to get to know her for more than just her body. And even though she was making big money, she was always planning for the future. Way before she found God, he remembered her saying, 'There's no reason we only have to be one person throughout our lives, we can be as many as we like.'

Thinking Eva would have been an interesting woman to have met, Jenny said, 'How did that happen, her conversion?'

'Just like the story goes. "He caught me just as my fingers were slipping from the edge," is how she described it to me.'

'And you're convinced it was genuine?'

Cassidy grinned, showing off expensive teeth. 'Put it this way, I hadn't been inside a church since my First Communion. When we met that second time, in February, Eva said she'd had a word of knowledge – I think that's what she called it – telling her to tell me to go to Mass. Can you believe it? Me! But just for her I went four times in a row, confessed my many sins, and – guess what? – the first channel I talked to about *Fallen Angels* virtually bit my hand off. The only problem was they wanted someone else to play Eva's part.'

'How did she react to that?'

'Like you'd imagine – she was disappointed, but I kept telling her she'd have a share of the show and a creator credit. That would have made her a proper player, part of the business. Pretty actresses are ten a penny.'

'But it wasn't going to solve her money problems.'

'I told her she should work in PR, cash in on all the skills she'd learned with Decency.' He stared into his empty glass and shook his head. 'Let me tell you the funny thing about Eva. She could walk naked onto a set and have sex with six guys in front of a full crew, but ask her to make a simple phone call, it'd take her half the day to pluck up the courage.'

Jenny said, 'We all suffer from our contradictions.'

'Yeah,' Cassidy said, 'we certainly do.'

Unless the whispers Starr had received from Cassidy's priest contained something darkly sinister, Jenny couldn't see that Eva having entertained ambitions to be a straight actress gave her any reason to conduct a full inquest. Of course it was logically possible that Craven hadn't killed Eva; he could have gone to her house and, acting on some strange animal impulse, urinated on her door mat without actually coming into contact with her, but that wasn't what he claimed. He denied having been there at all. Her lawyerly instincts, ingrained over fifteen years of practice, told her it was unethical to explore possibilities that a criminal defendant hadn't suggested in his own defence, but as a coroner she had to force herself to think differently. She wasn't bound by any one version of events; she could investigate and test whatever theory she wished. Her overriding duty was to uncover the truth. She could feel her conscience drawing her towards holding an inquest, but at the same time another voice was warning her to beware.

Wrestling with these conflicting thoughts as she walked back to her car, she passed a fly-poster among the many plastered on the outside wall of the multi-storey. An attractive young black man pointed out of the picture above the caption, *I'm on a mission. Are you?* Beneath the caption, it said: *Come to where the love is. Mission Church of God, 5 Fleetway.*

She told herself it was purely idle curiosity that made her drive across town at the end of the day to see for herself. At the south-east edge of the city off a busy road through

Bedminster, she turned into the vast and busy car park for what she had remembered as a multiplex cinema, bowling alley and pizza restaurant. Ross had had his thirteenth birthday party here. She and her ex-husband, David, had celebrated the occasion by yelling at each other in front of all the kids, ensuring Ross never invited any of them home again. The cinema and alley had now been knocked into one vast barn of a building, in front of which stood an illuminated white cross which reached higher than the peak of the roof. The former pizza restaurant, which occupied a separate chalet-style building opposite, had been re-branded 'McG's'. All the parking spaces near the building were already taken and the rest were filling quickly. Slipping into a zone reserved for employees and official visitors, she pulled up next to a sleek maroon-coloured sports car that made her ten-year-old VW look like a wreck.

She joined the horde of casually dressed families and groups of teenagers heading for the main entrance of the Mission Church, unable to stop herself becoming infected by the excitement in the air. Black and white kids, parents and infants, all mingled together, eager to join the same party. Loudspeakers set high up on poles relayed the sound from inside: a big congregation clapping and cheering as a choir and full band belted out a catchy gospel number. Jenny found herself alongside a group of lively teenage girls who swung their bodies in time with the chorus. Straight ahead was the entrance to the main auditorium. Grinning teenage boys wearing MCG T-shirts shook hands with the faithful as they went in, saying, 'God bless you, brother,' and 'Welcome to God's house.' To the left was an open-plan retail area that resembled an airport mini-mall. Jenny's eye was caught by a sign hanging over one of the aisles that said 'Decency'.

Stepping out of the flow of worshippers, she entered the

shop. One entire centre shelf was filled with Eva Donaldson's scarred face staring calmly from the cover of *Fallen Angel: How God Saved a Porn Star*. Jenny picked up a copy and was leafing through the pages of simply written prose when she became aware of a TV screen further along the aisle on which an interview between Eva and a young pastor was playing. Dressed demurely in a dark suit and silk blouse buttoned up to the neck, Eva wore her hair back from her broken face, proud of the scars that gouged vertically through the left side of her face leaving her eye partially closed.

The pastor asked her how it felt to know that her films were still being watched by millions of people on the internet. Eva said, 'Since coming to Christ and being born again in the spirit, I know that the person they are watching isn't me. But aside from that, people should know that a lot of what I did was forced on me by contracts I was too frightened to break. Even in my state of sin, much of the time I wasn't consenting, I was letting myself be abused, and anyone who watches those films is a party to that.' Pausing to wipe away a tear, she collected herself and straightened her shoulders. 'But my real message is that the dividing line is clear – if you're watching pornography you're not with God, and if you're not with God, well, I don't have to tell you whose company you're keeping.'

'Can I help you, madam?'

A slender, red-headed boy of no more than sixteen hovered nearby. His bright yellow T-shirt read: *TEAM MCG: on mission for God*.

'No thank you,' Jenny said. 'I'm just looking.'

'I can recommend Eva's book. Lots of people say it's changed their lives. She certainly changed mine.'

Jenny placed *Fallen Angel* back on the shelf. 'Maybe I'll call by on my way out.'

She turned to go.

'Is this your first visit?' the boy asked.

'Yes,' Jenny answered, more abruptly than she had intended.

Unfazed, the boy said, 'My name's Freddy. Pleased to meet you.'

He held out a pale, freckled hand.

'Jenny Cooper.'

Freddy gave her a warm smile. 'Welcome to MCG, Jenny. We're a church, but not as you know it. You'll find everything here's very relaxed. There are no particular rules about how to behave, but if you've got any questions just ask anyone wearing a team shirt. Is there anything you'd like to know?'

Jenny asked, 'Did you say you knew Eva Donaldson?'

'She was one of the first people I met here. She was leader of my study group.' A hint of sadness entered Freddy's bright expression. 'She was a beautiful person. We all miss her very much.'

Freddy's sincerity ignited a feeling of maternal warmth inside her, and Jenny found herself wishing her son could be a little more like him. 'Why don't I take the book now?' she said. 'I don't suppose you'll be able to move in here later.'

'You know how many people we're hoping for tonight? Five thousand.'

'You're kidding. Is it that many every week?'

Lighting up, Freddy said, 'It's usually closer to three but Pastor Bobby's here – he's on a world tour. He's opening new churches in Amsterdam, Hamburg, Moscow and Sydney.'

A roar of applause issued from the auditorium as the choir reached the end of their number. The bookshelves shook with the vibration of stamping feet.

'We'd better hurry,' the boy said. 'You don't want to miss the start.'

The body of the church was the size of a small aircraft hangar and set out like an amphitheatre. Five thousand seats were arranged on a gently sloping floor facing a raised, semi-circular stage, on which stood a choir dressed in shiny purple robes alongside a twelve-piece band. Two big screens suspended on cables from the ceiling announced, 'Bobby DeMont – World Tour'. Jenny found an end-of-row seat as the man himself jogged out of the wings, his startling image filling the big screens. In his late forties, slim, tanned and with thick walnut-coloured hair, Bobby DeMont wore a suit and tie and silver-tipped cowboy boots which glinted under the lights. The preacher soaked up the applause like a movie star, bowing to each section of the auditorium in turn before holding up his outspread hands and closing his eyes.

'Dear Lord, I am truly humbled to be here today.'

'A-men,' the audience thundered in reply.

'Now, as you all know,' Bobby began, strutting to and fro across the stage, his homely southern accent picked up by an invisible microphone and relayed with perfect clarity through a network of speakers, 'it's been a little over fifteen years since a young country pastor from the back hills of West Virginia answered God's call to set up shop in the big city. Bobby, the Lord said to me that evening in my itty-bitty tin-shack church in Oakville, much as you love these good people you grew up with, I'm gonna to take you on a journey. I'm gonna take you on a journey to a city you've never been to before, the seat of your government no less, to fish for souls.' He grinned into the cameras. 'So with nothing more than four hundred dollars and a suitcase full of hick clothes I learned the meaning of what it is to be a fool for Christ. When I stepped off that bus in Washington

DC I literally did not know which way to turn. Everywhere I looked there was traffic and host'le faces, and I thought: man, you've lost your mind, this is crazy; this isn't an act of faith, it's an act of stupidity.' Bobby stopped abruptly and stared out at the sea of admirers. The air crackled with expectation. He continued in hushed, dramatic tones: 'And after I'd walked the streets for an hour or so I wandered into a poor black neighbourhood. There were kids on the corners dealing drugs, prostitutes giving me the eye, guys in bandannas who looked as if they'd shoot you down for a nickel. And I'll be honest, folks, I was afraid – I'd never been to no big city before. I tried to retrace my steps but I just got more and more lost and desperate. I was scurrying along a sidewalk that was all covered with trash and broken needles and I turned a corner and ran slap-bam into a group of bums outside a liquor store smoking what I took to be marijuana. There was four of them, all gang tattoos and gold teeth – you know the kind. Well, they took their time looking me up and down in my western boots and my cowboy hat, and then the biggest of 'em stepped toward me. I was so frightened I couldn't even run; tell the truth, I could hardly breathe. Then this fella says, "Sir, you look like a man who's lost his way. May I be of any assistance?" And in this squeaky little voice I said, "Sure. Can you point me the way to downtown?" And this fella smiled like I'll never forget: a cross between a great white shark and Charles Manson. Then guess what, folks?' Bobby smiled. 'He pulled a gun, robbed my money and took my best hat.'

The crowd roared and, watching Bobby's smiling face on the big screen, Jenny couldn't help sharing their elation.

'You see the moral of the story is, not even Almighty God can protect us from our foolishness.'

Amens and more laughter rang around the auditorium till Bobby raised his hands to call for silence.

'Four years in college and a solid upbringing, I shoulda known better,' he trumpeted, stamping the heel of his boot on the stage. 'I shoulda known that God gives us the tools and it's down to us to use 'em the very best we can. Well, fortunately, he gave me a second chance. When I'd done calling my mama and getting an ear full of I-told-you-sos, I volunteered myself at Mount Zion Church. Three weeks later I was promoted to a salaried position as an outreach worker and street pastor. My job was to pick street drunks and junkies out of the gutter and feed soup to the homeless. I worked hard and lived simple, but I'll be honest with you, my friends, it was tough, thankless toil and my faith was sorely tested. Two unbroken years of service in the Lord later, I was sent out to take over a run-down old church in a neighbourhood so wild even the rats were scared to go out at night. How I longed for green fields the day I set eyes on that place. I swear, if I could've raised the fare I'd have jumped right on the Greyhound back to Oakville. But I didn't have a penny. There *was* nowhere to run. Well, that beat-up heap of rubble was so filthy and depressing I decided the only thing I could do was to name it in such a way as to give me hope, because to be honest, people, right then I had none in my heart.' Bobby turned his gaze to the floor and lowered his voice to a whisper. 'I named it the Mission Church of God.'

A profound silence descended over the congregation, broken only by a single 'Praise be' from a lone female voice deep in their midst.

'That was exactly twelve years ago next Tuesday. Friends, I'll make a confession. Even a pastor forgets to read his scripture sometimes. There I was in a crime-ridden slum pining for the forests and creeks of my carefree youth when I should've been reading Luke 13:19. The kingdom of God is like a small—'

'Mustard seed!' the audience chanted in unison.

'That's right. And O hallelujah praise God Almighty how that mustard seed has grown. That first Sunday I preached to eight people, and three of them was asleep! Twelve years down the line there's not a stadium been built could hold all the members of this Mission Church of God. Right now, ladies and gentleman, kids, this mighty tree that's spreading across the whole wide world has more than two hundred thousand birds nesting in its branches. If that isn't proof that God holds good to his promises no matter how incredible they seem, then you tell me what is.'

The crowd jumped to their feet, hands raised, hallelujahs ringing out.

'Don't thank me, thank the Lord,' Bobby cried out and turned to the band, who struck up right on cue. The words to the worship song scrolled up the big screens:

> *Shine Jesus shine,*
> *Fill this land*
> *With the father's glory,*
> *Blaze spirit blaze, set our hearts on fire . . .*

The song was hypnotic, rousing, and as it drew to a close Jenny felt the pent-up energy in the auditorium replaced with a strange and powerful sense of collective peace, as if five thousand people were united in love and goodwill.

Suspending judgement, she allowed herself to be carried along with the tide, laughing and applauding with her neighbours as Bobby stepped up again to preach on the subject of a Christian's duty to live in the spirit, no matter where it might lead him. With a string of humorous anecdotes about his dealings with sceptical and corrupt politicians around the globe, Bobby showed his audience that speaking the truth, no matter how challenging, was the only way to walk with God. And the alternative to God, he said, was the devil.

'Any of you going to walk with the devil?' he challenged.

'No!' the audience boomed in reply.

'Well, ain't you lucky people – you've each got four thousand, nine hundred and ninety brothers and sisters here to hold you to your promise. Now I want you to turn to your neighbours, shake them by the hand and wish them *strength in Jesus.*'

Jenny found herself overwhelmed with outstretched hands, perfect strangers wishing her strength and offering ardent blessings.

'And now,' Bobby said, 'I'm going to introduce you to two men who've been towers of strength to me and have helped build this wonderful church here in Bristol, England – Mike Turnbull and Lennox Strong.'

The two men joined him on stage to a thunder of applause. Michael Turnbull was a similar age to Bobby, casually dressed and with the same glowing countenance that radiated wholesomeness and prosperity. Lennox Strong was an athletic black man in his late twenties. A tight T-shirt hugged his muscled torso.

Bobby invited each of them to give their testimonies for the benefit of all those who still doubted the truth of God's presence. Michael stepped forward first and told his story of being a wealthy, burnt-out ex-businessman who felt as wretched about his life's work and his contribution to the explosion in pornography as that great evangelist John Newton had once done about his role in the slave trade. It was hearing Pastor Bobby DeMont, over three years ago, that had finally opened the doors of his heart and changed him for ever. It was Bobby who had led him to realize that, through the Lord's infinite grace, even the most evil sinner can be made clean. He'd thrown open the doors and God rushed in as fast as daylight flooding a darkened room. But he hadn't let him rest easy. No, he had presented him with the biggest challenge of his life. Not only did he charge him with raising a church in the parched sands of a spiritual desert, he asked him to make war on pornography. It was far more than one human being could achieve alone, but God had filled him with joy and a sense of purpose which carried him from victory to victory. And now the end was in sight – an earthly law to enact the law of God was only days away from coming into existence.

A huge cheer went up like the roar of a football crowd. Michael Turnbull seemed to radiate benevolence as he graciously acknowledged it and stood aside for Lennox Strong.

The young pastor received a welcome that made even that given to Bobby DeMont seem modest. The shrill cries of young women sounded out above the crowd, prompting Bobby DeMont to whisper playfully in his ear. Lennox Strong showed no hint of embarrassment at the rapturous greeting. He clasped his hands in front of his chest and waited for quiet.

He spoke with a pronounced Bristol accent, but with the ease and confidence of a true professional. The son of a single teenage mother, he was a drug abuser, a car thief and a member of a violent gang all by the time he was thirteen. At fourteen, he was sentenced to five months in juvenile detention for robbing a defenceless old woman at knife-point. Far from reforming him, his spell inside introduced him to seasoned criminals he tried hard to impress and emulate. During the next several years he was in and out of custody as he went on a spree of burglary, car-theft and drug dealing. On his nineteenth birthday the police caught him carrying a gun.

'And every day I thank God that I was arrested before I fired that weapon in anger,' Lennox said. 'Another week and I would have to have proved to my so-called brothers that I wasn't just a boy with a gun, but a man who'd used one. I'll confess it openly, I had only darkness in my soul.'

The Lord found Lennox four months after his release from prison. He was just twenty-two, 'an angry ball of testosterone and muscle spoiling for a fight'. It was late into a wild night when he took some cocaine on top of alcohol and amphetamines. 'I thought I could take anything, but I went down like a felled tree.' Lennox was rushed to hospital suffering a series of cardiac arrests. He was resuscitated five times in the ambulance. He couldn't recall much of the journey, but he did remember suffering the final excruciating arrest which was to stop his heart for a full three minutes.

'My friends, I'd never had a spiritual thought in my life. I believed that when you died the lights went out and that was it. The lights went out all right, but it wasn't an end. I felt myself leaving my physical body and going down . . . and down, into a blackness I can't even describe. The further I sank, the hotter and more stifling it became. I could feel my lungs burning.' He paused to take a breath. 'Was I terrified? . . . There are no words to express the fear I felt as I realized I was falling into hell. I may have known nothing about the Bible, but I knew what I was looking at, and it was more real than you are now. And then this scream came from somewhere within me, "Jesus, save me!" There was no answer, and this is God's truth, my friends, I felt my flesh beginning to boil. I cried out again, "Jesus, please . . . save me!" And suddenly there was a rush of wind, and for a moment it was as if two strong men were pulling me in opposite directions, then bam!' He clapped his hands. 'I felt as if I'd split in two, but suddenly I shot upwards like a cork out of a bottle and I found myself standing at the side of the bed where the doctors were shocking my heart, and, very calmly, I lay down . . . The next thing I knew I was waking up in the ward with my mother and little sister looking down at me. And I'm telling you now, I'd never felt so much love in my whole life . . .' Lennox's voice clogged with emotion.

Bobby put an avuncular hand on his shoulder. 'Don't stop short of the punchline, Lennox,' he joked. 'Tell the people what happened next.'

A ripple of nervous laughter travelled through the crowd.

'I said to my mum, "You aren't going to believe this, but I think Jesus just saved me." And she said, "Well, you'd better make sure to pay him back." And as soon as I spoke those words I knew that my life had changed for ever. She called the hospital chaplain and, for the first time since I was a tiny child, I prayed. I prayed that I would give my life to the service of God. And that prayer wasn't answered in months, or weeks or even days – you know how they say the new wine is the strongest? – that prayer was answered the very next day when the chaplain told me about a new church in my neighbourhood that was looking for volunteers.'

'I was there the first night Lennox came in,' Michael Turnbull cut in. 'He had these dreadlocks and jeans with the seat hanging down to his knees. I thought, here comes trouble.' Bobby laughed and patted Lennox on the back. 'But in his two and a half years working for us,' Turnbull continued, 'this man has taken and kept more poor and deprived young people out of trouble than any government initiative ever could.'

The congregation rose to their feet again as Lennox bowed his head and Bobby laid hands on him, saying, 'Lord, we thank you for your servant Lennox and pray that your spirit will continue to guide and strengthen this precious child. In Jesus' name we thank you for his service and pray that this man you have named Strong will continue to bring

succour to the weak. A-men.' Bobby turned to face the
crowd, and raised his fists in a triumphant salute. 'Now
I feel strong, strong in the *spirit*! I feel invincible, folks,
because God is the greatest power there is. And I want all
of you who haven't yet given yourselves to Christ to come
forward and let him into your life. A few short words and
an eternity of salvation. Come on now, this is the moment,
this is *your* moment. If the Lord could reach down into hell
to save a sinner like Lennox, how easy it will be for him to
reach you.'

Jenny watched as a team of assistants in matching yellow
MCG T-shirts received the steady stream of worshippers
who started to come forward. The band struck up an upbeat
but restrained rendition of 'Amazing Grace'; the choir
hummed in gentle harmony.

Some stood, others knelt as Bobby, Michael, Lennox and
the team laid hands on them and prayed. The big screen
showed close-ups of the newly converted with their tearful
expressions of joy and gratitude. In a sea of whispers she
overheard snippets of prayer for relief from illness, addiction, jealousy, freedom from debt. Men and women who
had arrived as strangers wept in each other's arms.

Bobby's unexpected roar echoed like a thunderclap around
the auditorium: 'Ladies and gentleman, the Holy Spirit is
truly at work here tonight! We are being visited with the
blessing of the Rapture! A-men. A-men.'

A buzz of excitement shot through the crowd as pictures
appeared on the big screens of a middle-aged woman and
two young men who lay convulsing on the floor at the foot
of the stage.

'Praise be. Praise be for your gifts of the spirit. Praise be
to Jesus Christ, our Lord and Saviour. Welcome him into
your hearts,' Bobby cried out as the slow-moving wave

spread upwards through the rows towards Jenny's. A vast ox of a man sitting immediately in front of her sank to his knees, then fell prostrate in the aisle. A teenage girl tumbled out of her seat and collapsed next to him. Jenny heard herself dismissing the spectacle as collective hysteria even as she felt the wave breaking over her; a warm sensation spread downwards from the crown of her head through her shoulders and chest; her hands trembled and the strength bled from her legs.

On the brink of collapse and fighting the heaviness in her limbs, Jenny forced one leg in front of the other and headed towards the exit. Stepping between the fallen, she noticed Freddy among them. Lying perfectly still, his eyes shone like a child's, and for a moment she thought him the closest thing she had ever seen to an angel.

Jenny sat out the rest of the service in MCG's, drinking lukewarm coffee and watching a live feed from inside the auditorium on one of the several screens arranged around the deserted restaurant. Bobby brought worshippers who had just experienced the Rapture up onto the stage and urged them to testify. One after another they all described the same feeling: like swimming in a river of love; an overwhelming sense of happiness followed by peace beyond all description as they felt themselves floating upwards.

A waitress who had been wiping tables said, 'It started in America. First it was only a few people, now it's hundreds and thousands. It's just awesome.'

'What do you think's going on?' Jenny said.

'A new wave of the spirit. What else could it be?'

'People scream and faint at rock concerts.'

'Yes, but do they go out afterwards and change the world?'

Jenny handed the waitress her empty cup. There was no answer to that.

The church offices were situated behind a locked door at the far side of the shop. Jenny pressed the intercom and was answered by a male voice. 'Hello, how can I help you?'

Jenny looked into the lens of the built-in security camera. 'Jenny Cooper. Severn Vale District Coroner. I'd like to talk to the church administrator.'

'That would be me,' the voice replied. 'Come on in.'

She pushed open the door at the sound of the buzzer, and was met in a spacious reception area by a wholesome-looking young man in a neatly pressed shirt and tie.

He shook her hand. 'Good evening. Joel Nelson. What can I do for you?'

'I'm conducting an inquiry into the death of Eva Donaldson,' Jenny said, almost without realizing that she had just made her decision. 'I'll need statements from anyone here who had dealings with her. I thought you'd be the best person to ask who they might be.'

'Right,' Nelson said, his face devoid of any trace of alarm. 'The first thing you should know is that Miss Donaldson didn't actually work for the church. She was retained by the Decency campaign, which is an entirely separate body.'

'But she spent a lot of time here.'

'That's true, but she wasn't part of the management, so to speak.'

'A boy in the shop told me she was the leader of his study group.'

'That's a purely voluntary role.'

'I see.' Jenny cast her eyes around the comfortably decorated room. There were pastel-coloured sofas, two top-of-the-range plasma screens, and several modern private offices separated from the reception area by plate-glass walls screened with sleek Venetian blinds. The largest office was signed 'Boardroom'. 'I'd be grateful if you could at least give me a list of your employed staff so I can contact them.'

'Certainly,' Nelson said, and moved over to a computer sitting on the receptionist's desk.

'Were you friendly with Miss Donaldson?' Jenny asked.

'In as much as we all try to be friends here,' Nelson said. 'I wouldn't say we were close.' He tapped on the keyboard and strolled over to a printer, which was already whirring into life.

Jenny ran her eyes over the polished solid-wood shelving that lined the wall behind him and noticed a section of box files marked 'Decency'.

'Does Decency have separate offices,' Jenny asked, 'or does it operate from here?'

Nelson glanced back at her, then at the shelves, working out how she'd made the connection. 'They have a small part-time staff here,' he said, 'but the main office is in London.'

Jenny was about to ask if he could provide a list of their employees too when Bobby DeMont, Michael Turnbull and Lennox Strong came through the door, buzzing with excitement. Wiping his perspiring neck with a towel, Bobby was saying, 'You think we couldn't be any more blessed, then we have a night like tonight.'

'You were great,' Lennox said. 'The energy, man.'

It was Turnbull who noticed Jenny first, catching Nelson's glance before turning to greet her with a warm hello.

'This is Mrs Jenny Cooper,' Nelson said. 'She's the coroner looking into Eva Donaldson's death.'

'Ah, yes. I'd forgotten about that part of the procedure.' Turnbull reached out a hand. 'Michael Turnbull.'

Bobby stepped forward unprompted. 'Bobby DeMont. Pleased to meet you, ma'am.' He enclosed her palm with a hot, strong handshake. 'What a terrible tragedy. Each time I met that woman I came away in awe. One of life's fighters. A real inspiration.'

'Mrs Cooper would like to take statements from people who knew her,' Nelson said.

'Didn't we already do that with the police?' Turnbull asked.

Jenny said, 'Don't worry, there's no fanfare or publicity. I just have to make sure that cause of death is ascertained correctly.'

'I don't understand,' Lennox said. 'We've just had the court case. There's more?'

'An inquest may only be a formality,' Jenny said, 'but there's always the chance there were areas the police didn't look at too closely.'

'Oh. Such as?' Lennox asked.

Bobby pressed a hand to Lennox's back. 'You're guaranteed our full cooperation, ma'am. The church will help in whatever way it can.'

'Of course,' Turnbull said. 'When can we expect this to happen?'

Jenny said, 'I appreciate the timing isn't great for you—'

'Can't it at least wait until the Decency Bill has had its first reading?'

Reacting to Turnbull's anxiety, Bobby interjected, 'Hey, you don't have to worry about that, Mike. A man's been convicted. This is just a technicality.'

With a forced smile, Turnbull said, 'I do hope so.'

'There's really nothing to worry about,' Jenny replied. 'This is perfectly standard procedure.'

'You'll forgive my concern when a bill threatening a multi-billion-pound industry is about to be debated.'

'Calm down, buddy,' Bobby said, throwing Jenny a tense smile. 'It'll be fine.'

'Who knows, if everybody's helpful we might get it done before then,' she replied.

Nelson took two sheets from the printer and handed them to her. Jenny said a polite goodbye and promised to be in touch. As the reception door closed shut behind her, she could have sworn she heard Bobby DeMont mutter, 'Sonofabitch!'

# FIVE

Jenny carried her coffee out to the table on the lawn to catch the first rays of sun. The house martins were already darting out from their nests under the eaves and swooping for the insects rising up from the unkempt meadow on the far side of the garden wall. The air was filled with the hum of bees and the raucous chorus of songbirds: she envied the creatures their simple, unquestioning sense of purpose. She was loath to admit it, but her visit to the Mission Church of God had left her shaken. It wasn't the frenzy of the crowd or the sight of otherwise sane and ordinary people reduced to convulsions which had played over and over in her listless dreams, but Lennox Strong's testimony. It was only a modern retelling of the hellfire sermons of the past, she told herself, a cynical manipulation of all those members of the congregation with uneasy consciences, but it had touched her nonetheless. As Lennox described his descent into darkness she had heard her father's voice, 'You remember, Smiler. You killed her.'

It was ridiculous. Her father was senile and Lennox Strong's story, even if it were true, was merely the waking nightmare of a young man terrified of death. She had no reason to be frightened; she had progressed beyond irrational emotions. Her divorce was fading into history and she had the attention of a handsome, thoughtful man whenever she desired it. By all objective measures life was good; her only challenge was to start believing it. Once she had achieved that simple step, everything else would follow. She would be well again and her son could learn to trust her.

But simply forcing herself to look on the bright side failed to lift her mood. A persistent knot of troubling and unwanted thoughts lodged stubbornly while she washed the breakfast dishes and ran through her tasks for the day. When the phone rang it was a welcome distraction. She hurried to answer it, hoping to hear Steve.

'I haven't woken you, have I, Mrs Cooper?' It was Alison.

'I was just leaving.'

Her officer continued in a put-upon tone: 'Only I've had Mrs Jacobs calling trying to get hold of you. Apparently the police say they're not treating her husband's death as suspicious.'

'That was quick. I suppose she wants to know if we can move as swiftly.'

'Not quite.'

'Oh?'

'CID returned his computer wiped blank. They claim it's a mistake; she thinks they're hiding something from her. I tried suggesting that, if they were, it might be for the best, but she's got it into her head there was something going on at the Conway Unit they're hushing up.'

'I presume they told her about the swabs?'

'She doesn't believe it. She insists she'd have known.'

Jenny saw a long day stretching ahead. 'All right. I'll stop by and talk to her on my way in.'

'Eva Donaldson's father has been melting the answerphone. He's furious about the post-mortem and is demanding to bury his daughter.'

'Tell him to come to the office. I'll try to explain.'

'Good luck.'

Alison rang off.

Replacing the receiver, Jenny felt a cold and unexpected draught on the back of her neck coupled with the sensation of being watched. She turned slightly and from the corner of her eye saw a flicker of movement beyond the window: the outline of an adult, a man. She spun round. There was no one there. She told herself it had been a trick of the light, but as she took a step she felt her legs shaking. Heart thumping, she forced herself forwards to the window and looked left and right, half-expecting to see the postman or the old man from the village who, when the spirit moved him, cut the grass. The garden was empty.

She took a breath and closed her eyes. 'Calm down, Jenny. Calm down.'

She turned the radio on as loud as it would go as she ran around the house getting ready to leave, but the spectre refused to leave her. She saw him in every corner and shadow; he lurked on the other side of each door. Hurrying to her car, she caught a musty trace of tobacco smoke and sawdust mingled with the jasmine and rosemary. It propelled her back through decades to a garden with a swing. Sitting apart from the family circle in the long grass at the far end, Jenny watched the man pushing it. He wore braces, his shirt clinging with perspiration to his muscular back. He was her father's brother, Jim.

Her reckless days were behind her. Jenny had checked whether it was safe to increase her dosage at times of stress and had satisfied herself it was. She pulled over into a lay-by to swallow the extra Xanax tablet to allow time for it to get to work before she arrived at the Jacobs' house. It was a blip. She'd had jumpy periods before and they had passed.

The key to not letting it take hold was not to panic, to remind her subconscious mind who was in control.

The double dose did the trick. She arrived on Ceri Jacobs's doorstep feeling a little woozy but not so much that it showed. Ceri came to the door dressed in black trousers and top, a small silver cross around her neck. She ushered Jenny into the house filled with flowers.

'It took people a day or two to know how to react,' Ceri said. 'They wonder if sending flowers is the right thing to do.'

Jenny gave her the kindly but neutral smile she had cultivated during her many months of visiting the bereaved. They sat at the dining table in the kitchen area, Jenny declining the offer of a drink for fear that her hand might tremble. Ceri sat upright, composed and dignified, the bewilderment of sudden grief replaced with an air of quiet determination to soldier on.

'How's your daughter?' Jenny asked.

'I took her back to nursery this morning. There's no point disrupting her routine.'

'No,' Jenny said. Small talk eluding her, she fetched a notebook from her briefcase. 'My officer said the police have called off their investigation.'

'So they tell me. I don't appear to have any say in the matter.'

'It's a question of resources. If everything points to someone having taken their own life they tend to hand over to the coroner fairly swiftly.'

'Do they usually wipe people's computers when they examine them?' Ceri nodded to a laptop sitting on the kitchen counter.

'I understand you were told it was an accident?'

'A technician accidentally formatted the hard drive, they

said. Apparently they take the drive out and put it in another machine.'

'I'm not familiar with the technicalities, but I can make enquiries.'

Ceri shook her head. 'I don't know why I'm surprised. Why would I expect the police to be honest?'

'What were you expecting them to find?' Jenny said.

Ceri glanced down at her hands, making a conscious effort to keep her emotion at bay. 'Not even his good friends really knew Alan, not like I did. He was a big, good-natured man, just the sort you'd want looking after you – we've got a drawer full of letters upstairs from ex-patients. But what you saw on the outside wasn't the whole story.' She paused and collected herself. 'He was sensitive. He cared deeply about the kids in the unit, but he didn't always agree with the methods used to treat them.'

'In what way?'

'The constant drugs for one thing. The fact they'd be so short-staffed they'd have to knock the difficult ones out just so they could cope. Sometimes he'd come home in tears, saying that instead of helping them get better he was turning them into zombies.'

'How does this connect with what you think may have been on his computer?' Jenny asked.

'I know he used it for work. And sometimes he'd look things up, try to work out if a patient was being given the right treatment. Like last month . . . there was a girl diagnosed as paranoid schizophrenic, but Alan thought it was a reaction to her anti-psychotics. The doctor wouldn't listen—' Ceri paused, in two minds whether to continue.

'I'd like to hear,' Jenny said.

'Al took it upon himself to change this girl's pills. She was getting better, she really was. Dr Pearce found out and changed the prescription back again. He was threatening to have Alan suspended, but the girl hanged herself in the night.' Struggling with the painful memory, Ceri said, 'He was involved with each one of them, he couldn't help it.'

'You think that incident might have something to do with his death?'

Ceri's eyes clouded as she relived the memory. 'All I know is that he went through three very black days when he thought his career might be in danger. I'd never seen him like that.'

'Did you tell any of this to the police?'

Ceri nodded. 'They said they'd spoken to his superior and she insisted there had been no complaints lodged against him.'

'Is it possible something else was happening which might have led to a complaint?' Jenny asked. 'Another case perhaps?'

'I've no idea. But why this business with his computer? It's more likely he'd found out about other mistakes. He was the kind of man who had to tell the truth. It just wasn't in him to lie or cover anything up.'

'So your theory is that he had uncovered some incident or malpractice . . . then what, exactly?'

Ceri shook her head, the possibilities in her mind too dreadful to articulate.

Jenny gently changed tack to a line of questioning she felt was probably more relevant to the manner of Alan Jacobs's end. 'Would you say that your husband was a secretive man?'

'No. Not at all. We told each other everything.'

'When did he tell you about the girl and her misdiagnosis, for example?'

'He couldn't tell me about it at the time,' Ceri said defensively. 'It was difficult enough ethically without asking me to compromise my morality too.'

'In what sense?'

'You could say he was acting unprofessionally. He knows I would never have approved of him being dishonest.'

'So he was giving her one type of medication but entering another into her records.'

'Yes.'

'When did he tell you?'

'It all came out after she died. There was an inquest. No action was taken against him.'

Jenny made a note, putting off asking her next question. The silence crackled. They both knew what was coming.

Jenny approached the subject obliquely. 'I've seen enough suicides now to be able to tell you that even husbands and wives sometimes have no clue as to the depth of their partner's depression, or what's caused it.'

She waited, hoping the widow would search her memory and start to put together telltale pieces.

Ceri's expression hardened. 'I know what you're trying to say, Mrs Cooper. You think Alan was gay, and probably involved in some sordid scandal with a patient.'

'We certainly have to deal with the forensic evidence.' Jenny braced herself. 'Your husband did have sex with a man in the hours before his death, Mrs Jacobs.'

'I don't believe it.'

'It may be difficult, but there is no other rational explanation.'

'He could have been murdered,' Ceri said coldly. 'Drugged and molested. It's happened to others. There were marks on his arms, the police showed me the report. He must have been attacked.'

'Those lesions weren't very deep. They weren't necessarily caused in a struggle.'

'If he was drugged he would hardly have been able to put up a fight. The knife they found next to him wasn't even one of ours.'

'I'm not sure that's proof of very much.'

Ceri's conviction wouldn't be shaken. 'Alan went to church every week to learn about the Catholic faith. He wanted us to be able to share that part of our lives. We were happily married, Mrs Cooper.'

'I can see that,' Jenny said, deciding there was nothing to be gained from pursuing the subject. 'Just one more thing while I remember. Did he have any connection with the church where he was found?'

'We've never even been there. Our church is St Xavier's, in town.'

Jenny wrote the name down. She'd instruct Alison to talk to the priest.

'I refuse to believe he killed himself, Mrs Cooper. He loved his family too much. We were everything to him.'

Jenny gave an understanding smile. The ones left behind always said that.


Kenneth Donaldson had been waiting in reception for over an hour and was in no mood to be fobbed off. Somewhere in Eva's file Jenny had seen him named as her only family. His occupation was listed as company director, and he gave every impression of being a man used to getting his own way and at a time of his choosing. He brushed Alison's attempted introduction aside and collared Jenny the moment she walked through the door of the reception area.

'Kenneth Donaldson, Eva's father. Would you please explain why you haven't released my daughter's body? It's bad enough that you made us wait until the killer pleaded guilty.'

'Pleased to meet you, Mr Donaldson. Would you like to come this way?'

'I'd like an answer. Now, preferably.'

'That's what I'm offering you.' Jenny stepped past him and into her office.

Donaldson sighed sharply and followed.

'Please, take a seat,' Jenny said.

'Now listen,' Donaldson said, refusing the offer, 'I've already taken the advice of several very senior lawyers, who assure me that this is completely irregular.'

'It's unusual, certainly,' Jenny said calmly, 'but from what I've seen so far I'm not satisfied the police have investigated the circumstances of your daughter's death to an extent that I consider satisfactory.'

'The man confessed. What the hell are you expecting to find?'

'Please, do sit down.'

'Do you have any idea what it's like waiting nearly two months to bury your child?'

'No. I'm sorry.'

'Well try, Mrs Cooper. You might begin to understand why if you don't release her immediately I'll be lodging a formal complaint.'

Jenny managed to remain impassive in the face of his anger. 'I'm requesting one further post-mortem examination – it could happen as early as this afternoon. If nothing significant arises I will release your daughter's body at once.'

'The cause of death was established beyond all doubt. There was no dispute about it whatsoever.'

'From a forensic perspective all we know for certain is that she was killed by a single stab wound. I'd like to know a little more – whether there is any trace of third-party DNA, whether there are physical signs of a struggle, whether there is any possibility that the wound was self-inflicted.'

'That's absurd. Her killer is behind bars. I'm told that it's virtually unheard of for a coroner to continue fishing for evidence at this stage.'

'With respect, Mr Donaldson, many coroners do as little as they can get away with. I prefer to cover every possibility.'

'No matter how futile or traumatic to the family?'

'Wouldn't you like to think no stone had been left unturned?'

Donaldson placed his fingers to his temples, a look of pain contorting his face. He sank into the chair, fury giving way to exasperation.

'I went through all this with the police. Of course you'd think there are potentially thousands of men who might have preyed on her, but there was simply no evidence for it. Since she'd become synonymous with the Decency campaign all that sort of unwanted attention had petered out.'

'But before that she was harassed?'

'I couldn't say how bad it was. Eva didn't communicate very much once she'd embarked on her . . .' He faltered. 'Since she left home. The detectives just assumed that would be the case.'

'Do you mind if I ask you a couple of questions?'

He shook his head.

'Do you have any idea what Eva was planning to do with her life after the Decency campaign? Did she have any long-term plans?'

He thought for a moment. 'I really couldn't say. I assume she may have harboured a maternal instinct somewhere.'

'Do you have any insight into her mental state in the months before she died? I know she had money problems—'

'I'm afraid we didn't often talk.' He glanced away guiltily. 'She lost her mother when she was fourteen. I'm afraid I never succeeded in filling the gap my late wife left.'

'That must have been a source of sadness to you.'

His expression turned to one of mistrust. 'If you're angling for some profound psychological insight, I'm afraid I can't give you one. She had a perfectly happy childhood. She went to excellent schools and even seemed to weather

her mother's death far better than I could have hoped for, but the moment she went to college she became completely wild. What more can I say?'

Quietly, Jenny said, 'I think you know what I'm asking.'

'She didn't kill herself, Mrs Cooper,' Donaldson said sharply. 'God knows, nothing would have surprised me, but if she had the knife would have still been at the scene.'

'There are other scenarios. Craven could have entered the house and found her already dead.'

Donaldson's gaze travelled around her untidy office as he seemed to be weighing her motives. 'I don't suppose a woman in your position has many opportunities to step into the limelight. I presume it's a case of grabbing it when you can.'

'Believe me, Mr Donaldson, this isn't for my benefit.'

He fixed Jenny with a look that was more knowing than accusing. 'I'm afraid I don't believe you. You could make a formal finding of unlawful killing today. But you won't because you want a piece of the action. She's too hot a property for you simply to let her go. And you know what that makes you? No better than those parasites who made their filthy fortunes from her. Why can't you let her rest in peace, for God's sake? Leave her with some tiny shred of dignity intact.'

Jenny wavered. For a brief moment she believed he was right.

'I'll tell you what I'll do. I'll ask the pathologist to complete his examination today. That way you can have Eva's body tomorrow, and I give you my word I'll deal with this matter as swiftly and discreetly as I can.'

'Before the Decency Bill has its first reading?'

'If at all possible.'

She guessed he had been speaking to Turnbull; they were men who would understand each other.

Donaldson held her in a steady, evaluating gaze. 'You understand my cynicism, Mrs Cooper. This industry my daughter was working to shut down isn't a sideshow, it's a powerful force. Its interests are secretively owned by many hugely successful legitimate businesses. These are people who would stop at nothing, baulk at corrupting no one, to protect their revenue.'

'If anyone offers me a brown envelope you'll be the first to know. Meanwhile, can I assume you'll allow me a day before making a complaint?'

'No. You're a bloody fool and deserve whatever's coming to you.' Donaldson rose from his chair. 'If I were you, Mrs Cooper, I'd be wary of far more than brown envelopes.'

'I don't know why you're bothering,' Alison said after Donaldson had stormed out. 'Haven't we got enough to deal with?'

Jenny looked at her accumulating mountain of files. Heaped up on the floor was a newly delivered stack of document boxes marked *R v. Paul Craven*. They contained all the papers from Craven's trial and would take at least a day to digest. She was tempted to give Donaldson what he wanted: quick and easy closure and a smooth path for Turnbull to deliver Eva's legacy. A few strokes of the pen and the case would be disposed of. What was stopping her? Images of Father Starr and Paul Craven jostled with a picture, now scored on her memory, of Lennox Strong's haunted expression as he described his brush with death; and behind them all the smiling face of Alec McAvoy as he turned to her with a wise, mischievous smile on the day they first met: 'I could kneel all night in prayer, to heal your many ills, My Dark Rosaleen.'

Jenny said, 'Call Dr Kerr and tell him I want her body autopsied this afternoon.'

Alison protested, 'But Mrs Cooper—'

'Then start making arrangements for the Jacobs inquest. I want it out of the way by the end of the week.'

It took another pill to propel Jenny through the door of the mortuary. The evening was hot and the Vale's creaking air-conditioning battled to keep the temperature to anything less than mildly suffocating. The still air was heavy with the smell of disinfectant and human decay. An outbreak of summer flu had claimed the lives of tens of elderly patients in the space of two days, overwhelming the refrigerators. Gurneys loaded with bodies awaiting collection by over-stretched undertakers were parked two abreast in the corridor. Sidestepping around them, Jenny wondered why she found the sight of twenty corpses less alarming than being intimately confronted with one. Perhaps being in the presence of so many bodies at once could make one feel a grim sense of biological triumph at having so far escaped the winnowing.

She grabbed a mask, gloves and surgical gown from the station outside the slap doors to the autopsy room, braced herself, then stepped inside to find Andy Kerr stooped over an array of internal organs at the steel counter to the side of the table. She barely recognized the body as the one she had seen in the photographs. The flesh was a waxy yellow and seemed to have dehydrated and shrunk. The cheek and jaw bones jutted through tightly drawn skin, the hands were clawed and shrivelled. Avoiding looking directly at the face, Jenny came alongside Andy as he peered at a section of tissue through a magnifying glass.

'Do I get a gold star?' he asked. 'I had my first date in weeks lined up for tonight.'

'I'm sorry. I had to promise her father I'd release the body tomorrow.'

'Life as a porn star doesn't do much for young arteries, that's for sure. I've seen sixty-year-olds in better nick.'

'Alcohol?'

'And cigarettes. She may have found God but he didn't curb her bad habits. I'd say she got through forty a day. There was even a small clot forming on the left lung – could have caused her a lot of problems.'

'I didn't see that in the first p-m report.'

'The Home Office pathologist was looking for the immediate cause of death, that's what he found.' Andy put down the section of what Jenny recognized as heart muscle. 'Having said that, there's one thing about the stab wound I've noticed that he didn't comment on – it comes in almost horizontally.'

'Meaning what?'

He picked up a scalpel to demonstrate. 'If you're going to stab someone, the most natural way is either to come downwards with the blade coming out of the bottom of your fist, or upwards. To get it in horizontally requires a less natural motion.' He tried several variations, each requiring the wrist to be awkwardly bent.

Unconvinced, Jenny said, 'I can imagine holding it that way.'

'My tutor at King's wrote the textbook on stab wounds – it's not the norm, believe me.'

Jenny glanced back at the body. 'Are there any marks, signs of a struggle?'

'Nothing obvious. There may have been some minor contusions I might not be able to pick up this long after.'

'Any chance the first p-m might have missed any third-party DNA?'

Andy shook his head. 'All the nails were scraped; the lab tests came back negative. I don't think there was a struggle. She didn't even have any blood on her hands.'

Jenny tried to picture Craven arriving at Eva's front door. From what she'd read about the layout of the house it was more than twenty-five feet from the doorstep to where Eva's body was found.

'Could she have walked backwards into the kitchen after she'd been stabbed?'

Andy picked up another section of heart. 'Look.' He pointed a gloved finger. 'There's an inch-and-a-half gash in the aorta. Blood would have been shooting out of there at full pressure the moment the knife was pulled out.'

'So if she was stabbed by the front door, you'd expect to see blood there, right?'

'Almost definitely.'

Perhaps if Craven hadn't produced the knife immediately, Eva might have backed away from the door and into the kitchen, tried to talk to him, calm him down. But surely there would have been more signs of struggle? She recalled the police photographs: a heavy glass measuring jug on the counter right next to Eva's body. Why didn't she pick it up and smash it in his face?

'We're sure there was no sexual assault?'

'I'm guided by the findings of the original examination. She was menstruating. Tampon and ST were still in place.'

*So what?* Jenny thought. If a man was sufficiently psychotic to seek out a porn star and execute her, surely he wasn't going to leave without an attempt to get what he came for. Craven's first murder had been a frenzied attack; Eva's killer struck once and ran.

Jenny said, 'Can you think of any reason I shouldn't release the body? I don't want to be told in a week's time there are other tests we should have run.'

'I've got all the tissues samples I need. Do you want any more photographs?'

'If you like. I don't suppose they'll add much.'

'There is one thing that didn't show up on the ones that were taken the first time.' He turned to the autopsy table. 'What do you make of this?' He pointed to a small tattoo on the left-hand side of her bikini-waxed crotch, just below where her pubic hairline would have been. Written in copper-plate script, Jenny couldn't make it out without looking closer than she wanted to.

'What does it say?'

Andy smiled at her over his mask. 'Uh, uh. This is one you've got to see for yourself.'

Jenny steeled herself and leaned in for a closer look. The tattoo said: DADDY'S GIRL.

'That's something for the old man to be proud of,' Andy said. 'Maybe the decent thing would be to let it go un-mentioned.'

Jenny looked at it again.

'It's real,' Andy said. 'I checked. She's got another one at the base of her spine, a little butterfly.'

The two words were small enough for you to miss them at a fleeting glance, but once you'd noticed they were all you could see. The pictures Jenny had seen of Eva on the internet flashed before her eyes, most of them featuring her in close-up gynaecological detail. Surely she would have noticed the tattoo?

Jenny said, 'How recent would you say it was?'

'Hmm. I don't know if there's any way of telling. It takes a number of years for the ink to start spreading.' He reached for a magnifying glass and studied it for a long moment. 'Actually, you know what, there's been some recent scab-bing, I can see where the skin's been abraded. I think there's a chance she had it done not long before she died.'

'Months, weeks?'

'If that was scabbing from the tattoo, I'd say within her last month. Interesting choice for a devout Christian, don't you think?'

Jenny looked away, feeling suddenly queasy. 'Do me a favour – don't mention this in your report. Some things are better left for court.'

# SIX

MANY PHONE CALLS AND MUCH cajoling later, Alison had succeeded in calling in a long-overdue favour from the administrator of Short Street Courts and secured the use of their smallest, stuffiest courtroom for Friday morning. Jenny didn't mind that it was windowless and painted the same dull institutional green as prison corridors, she just wanted the Alan Jacobs case dealt with and another burden lifted from her shoulders. The previous day had been spent cooped up in her office attacking her backlog of paperwork. She had made progress, but only by ignoring everything and everyone else. Repeated messages from Father Starr and several concerned text messages from Steve had gone unanswered. She had even managed to miss her Wednesday night call with Ross. It was now officially undeniable: being professionally competent meant being a bad mother.

As well as sending Alison out to round up witnesses and gather statements for the Jacobs inquest, Jenny asked her to make enquiries about Eva Donaldson's tattoo. Since seeing it she'd scoured the internet for images of Eva and couldn't find a single one in which it appeared. She'd tracked down her last known contribution to the adult genre: *Devils Bi Night*. The butterfly on her back was much in evidence, but there was no DADDY'S GIRL. A trawl through her bank statements and credit-card transactions failed to cast any light, leaving Alison to work through every tattoo parlour in the Bristol Yellow Pages. She drew a blank. The artists who answered their phones either couldn't recall or wouldn't discuss their clients on principle. Resigned to a longer search than she had anticipated, Jenny wrote to Kenneth Donaldson telling him that she would have to break her promise to release the body, only saying obliquely that further tests might prove necessary.

The call made, Jenny pushed Eva temporarily from her mind and turned to Alan Jacobs.

She was determined that the inquest would be a discreet, low-key affair. A finding of suicide was a virtual inevitability; she didn't want it to be any more painful for Mrs Jacobs than absolutely necessary. As the death couldn't be said to have occurred in circumstances with implications for the health or safety of the public at large, it would be conducted without a jury. Jenny would consider the evidence and reach her verdict alone.

She entered from the cramped, windowless office behind the courtroom and took her place on the judicial seat. On the rare occasions on which she held an inquest in a dedicated court rather than one of the draughty, far-flung village halls to which she was normally consigned, she had mixed feelings about her elevated status. A coroner wasn't like a judge arbitrating from on high, she was a judicial officer with the role, unique in the British justice system, of asking whatever questions were required to determine the true facts of an unnatural death. Drawing the truth out of a witness was best achieved through striking up a rapport, which was far harder in a space designed to inspire fear and awe.

There were two lawyers present: Daniel Randall, a genial, silver-haired solicitor, represented Mrs Jacobs, and Suzanne Hayter, an austere young barrister with scraped-back hair and small, rimless glasses, appeared for the Severn Vale

Health Trust. Immediately behind her sat an in-house solicitor named Harry Gordon, whom Jenny recognized as the
Trust's chief litigator. In his two years in post he had earned
an awesome reputation for fighting every negligence claim
and slashing their damages bill by two-thirds. The rows
behind the lawyers were filled almost to capacity with
witnesses and members of the Jacobs family. Ceri Jacobs sat
at their fore alongside her mother, both women in identical black two-piece suits. Determinedly in control of her
emotions, the widow fixed her cool, expectant gaze on Jenny
and seemed to demand an answer that would fly in the face
of the facts she was about to hear.

Jenny began by explaining to the family that the purpose
of the hearing was simply to call evidence that would assist
in determining the cause of death. There was a range of
possible verdicts including accident, suicide, unlawful killing, misadventure (meaning that the deceased took a risk
which resulted in unintended fatal consequences) or, where
there was no conclusive evidence as to the immediate cause
of death, an open verdict. Addressing the waiting witnesses,
Jenny reminded them that they would be giving evidence
on oath, and that failure to answer truthfully was a criminal offence punishable by imprisonment. Family members
exchanged glances, an elderly priest sitting at the back of
the room frowned gravely, Ceri Jacobs stiffened. Jenny felt
for them all, but unlike some coroners, she was not inclined
to massage the truth to save people's feelings. Her inquests
were conducted strictly in the public interest.

Mrs Jacobs was the first witness to be called forward.
Composed, dignified, and displaying no outward sign of
nervousness, she placed her hand on the Bible and swore to
tell the truth. Repeating what she had told Jenny during her
visit to her home, she said that she had enjoyed six happy
years of marriage to Alan, during which time he had showed

himself to be a loving husband and father and a deeply committed psychiatric nurse. Unprompted, she produced a number of letters from former patients and requested permission to read sections aloud. Jenny granted it. In a letter dated the previous February, Chris, an eighteen-year-old drug addict with a history of suicide attempts, wrote to thank her late husband: 'for showing me that life is the most precious thing there is, no matter how hard it gets. You've taught me there's always something better to hope for and I'll always, always remember that. Thank you, Big Al. You're the reason I'm still here.'

'It was the successes that gave him the strength to deal with the failures,' Ceri Jacobs said. 'You couldn't find a nurse more devoted to his patients.'

'Did this dedication take a personal toll?' Jenny asked. 'Did your husband show any signs of depression?'

'He was low sometimes, it was inevitable. But he was never moody or bad-tempered.' She was adamant. 'I've seen depressed people. I would have known.'

Jenny said, 'Do you accept that he wasn't telling you the truth when he said he had been called in to work on the afternoon before he died?'

'Yes.'

'Did he make a habit of lying to you?'

'He did not.'

'You say he left home around four o'clock on the Saturday afternoon. According to the pathologist, he died approximately five hours later. His body was found in a graveyard a little over two miles from your home. His clothes were in a nearby bin along with the packaging for a quantity of phenobarbital. This is an anti-convulsant drug, fatal levels of which were found in his bloodstream.' Jenny paused to take a mouthful of water and seize the momentary opportunity to avoid Ceri Jacobs's gaze. 'Do you have any idea what led him to that graveyard, Mrs Jacobs?'

'None at all,' she retorted, as if Jenny's question was nothing short of indecent.

'A sign of the cross was cut into his torso with a small kitchen knife that was found close to where he lay. It seems likely he did it himself. Do you know why?'

'I don't believe it's at all likely,' Ceri Jacobs said. 'I don't believe my husband took his life. I think he was molested and left to die.' She lifted her gaze to the old priest. 'If he did make that cross, it was as a sign to me, and to God, that he was leaving this world in faith.'

'The forensic evidence shows that your husband had intercourse with an unidentified male in the hours immediately preceding his death. Are you able to shed any light on this, Mrs Jacobs?'

The widow took a moment to compose herself, then answered with a level of certainty that took Jenny and the entire courtroom by surprise. 'If it happened, it was not consensual. My husband worked with the ill and disturbed, with people who are dangerous to themselves and often to others. He wasn't just a nurse to them, he was a friend. The only explanation that makes sense to me is that he went in good faith to meet someone who attacked him. I also believe that there was some hint of this meeting on his computer, and that for whatever reason that evidence was destroyed by the police, who have chosen not to pursue this line of inquiry.'

Her accusation was met with silence from her family, a look of suppressed pain from her priest and one of resignation from DI Wallace. Alison caught Jenny's eye, her expression suggesting there was little point in prolonging her ordeal; she would only embarrass herself further.

Jenny said, 'I note your theory, Mrs Jacobs, and I can assure you your solicitor will be able to explore it fully with the other witnesses.' She addressed the lawyers: 'Any questions?'

'No, ma'am,' Randall said, with a reassuring smile to his client.

Suzanne Hayter stood abruptly, extracting a document from amongst her orderly notes. 'Mrs Jacobs, at the police's request the pharmacist at the Conway Unit carried out an audit of the stocks of phenobarbital and found that two packets, each containing a sheet of twelve tablets, were unaccounted for. Here is the report.' She held up the document. 'Your husband had access to the pharmacy and regularly signed drugs out. The pharmacy is outside the locked unit. Patients have no access to it.'

'I wouldn't know,' Ceri Jacobs answered defensively.

'But you do know that your husband had a recent history of impropriety in matters concerning drugs and their prescription.'

'It wasn't Alan at fault,' Mrs Jacobs snapped back. 'It was the psychiatrist. You know that.'

Sitting in the row behind, Harry Gordon, the Trust's lawyer, wore the smug expression of a man who felt that things were about to turn in his favour.

'The patient who killed herself following his unauthorized intervention in her drugs regime was called Emma Derwent,' Suzanne Hayter said.

'Alan saved her life. It was Dr Pearce who made her suicidal.'

Suzanne Hayter belonged to the tungsten-shelled breed of advocates Jenny had once envied with a passion. Mrs Jacobs's emotion seemed only to harden her further. 'Did you notice any change in your husband's mood following Miss Derwent's death?'

'He was always upset when a patient died.'

'I'm sorry to have to be so blunt, but what I am asking is whether his remorse at having interfered with her treatment and her subsequent suicide could have driven him to take his own life.'

Ceri Jacobs erupted. 'How dare you accuse my husband of harming that girl. It's Dr Pearce who should be feeling sorry, and all the people who have covered up for him.'

Unmoved, Suzanne Hayter turned to Jenny. 'No further questions, ma'am.'

Jenny thanked Mrs Jacobs for her patience and told her she could return to her seat. Refusing to step down, she said, 'I am not going to let them tell lies about my husband. You can see what they're doing, they're just trying to protect themselves.'

'I appreciate how you feel, Mrs Jacobs, but all parties are entitled to ask questions.'

Randall intervened before Ceri Jacobs retaliated. 'Thank you, ma'am. I'll make sure my client fully understands the position.' With a gentle smile he coaxed her from the witness box, whispering comforting words as he guided her to her seat. Her relatives traded uncomfortable glances that told Jenny they suspected Suzanne Hayter had hit a raw nerve, and quite probably the truth.

DI Wallace was showing increasing signs of impatience, but Jenny made him wait his turn and called for Deborah Bishop, director of the Conway Unit. With her untinted hair, and clothes that failed to flatter her spreading figure, she looked older than her forty-four years; a woman, Jenny speculated, struggling to manage a high-pressure job as well as care for her family.

Deborah Bishop read the oath with a nervous briskness. Jenny noticed her cast Harry Gordon a mistrustful glance. He would have briefed her exhaustively, instructing her on pain of death to stick to the corporate line and never to admit to mistakes, even honest ones. It occurred to Jenny that the future of Deborah Bishop's career might hang on her performance in the next few minutes.

Bishop told the court that she had been director of the Conway Unit for a little over two years and had been Alan Jacobs's line manager for the entire period. He was the senior psychiatric nurse in the young persons' ward and had performed his duties admirably, helping the unit gain a three-star government rating. They had held regular weekly meetings and as far as she was concerned he was as happy as could be expected, given the extraordinary pressures of his job. In fact, he coped better than most: his personnel file showed he hadn't taken a day off sick for over fifteen months. Her last meeting with him had been on the Friday morning, thirty-six hours before he died. Their discussion had been perfectly routine, and was mostly concerned with how he should deal with a black female nurse suffering racist taunts from a deeply disturbed young woman on the ward. The nurse claimed a right not to be abused, and Jacobs had argued for the patient's right not to be medicated to insensibility.

'Did you resolve the issue?' Jenny asked.

'Alan suggested the nurse be transferred to other duties. I pointed out that was a luxury we couldn't afford. We agreed to think on it over the weekend and discuss it again the following Monday.'

'Was it something that might have weighed heavily on his mind?'

'It may have done, but similar issues present themselves all the time.'

Jenny glanced at Harry Gordon, his eyes fixed on Mrs Bishop, willing her to stick to the script.

'Reading between the lines,' Jenny continued, 'do I detect

a suggestion that he suspected the patient was more likely to be chemically silenced than the nurse transferred from the ward?'

'He wasn't unrealistic. A touch idealistic sometimes, but that's what made him such a good nurse.' She attempted a smile. Ceri Jacobs glared at her. With a glance at Harry Gordon, Deborah Bishop continued unprompted: 'I had only known him make one serious lapse of judgement, which was why I felt able to excuse it.'

Jenny said, 'You're referring to the Emma Derwent incident, when he felt a doctor had misdiagnosed her as paranoid schizophrenic.'

'Yes. And unfortunately he altered the patient's medication. As I said, I took no formal action against him on that occasion.'

'Tell me, Mrs Bishop, when it was discovered that Mr Jacobs had taken the patient off her anti-psychotic medication, did he express regret?'

Mrs Bishop's eyes flitted to Harry Gordon and Suzanne Hayter. Jenny got the impression it was a question for which she hadn't been primed.

'Mrs Bishop?'

'He made a formal apology to Dr Pearce, of course.'

'But he remained adamant about the misdiagnosis. And shortly after the patient resumed the medication he thought had contributed to her symptoms she took her own life.'

'This was a suicidal patient. She was being correctly treated by a consultant psychiatrist. As far as I am concerned, the only clinical error was committed by Alan Jacobs.'

Ceri Jacobs's mother laid a hand on her daughter's arm, urging her to remain calm.

'Maybe I'm jumping to conclusions, Mrs Bishop, but I'm assuming Mr Jacobs remained convinced this patient was misdiagnosed, which leads me to wonder if the only reason he didn't seek a clinical review of her case before she died was that you could have dismissed him on the spot.'

'I couldn't possibly comment on his state of mind.'

'Try to see if you can comment on this: if Emma Derwent's death was on his conscience, would it have been because of what he did or because he wasn't prepared to lose his job for what he thought to be right?'

Mrs Bishop shot back with an answer which Jenny had no doubt had been scripted by Harry Gordon: 'When a respected professional has a serious lapse of judgement it can be a very traumatic event. He hid it well, but my personal belief, for what it's worth, is that it caused Alan Jacobs to suffer a shipwreck of self-esteem.'

'One last thing,' Jenny said. 'Did you have any email correspondence with him concerning Emma Derwent either before or after her death?'

'No, I did not.'

Suzanne Hayter offered no cross-examination. Randall, who was not a gifted advocate, attempted to extract the names of any dangerous former patients at the unit who might have lured Alan Jacobs to his death, but Mrs Bishop refused to be drawn. She had made all the patient records available to the police and detectives had spoken to each of the nursing staff. As far as she was aware, Jacobs had had no personal contact with ex-patients; it would have been highly unprofessional, and she was sure he would not have succumbed to any further lapses of judgement.

Harry Gordon smiled as Mrs Bishop stepped down from the witness box. His woman had survived her brief ordeal and kept the reputation of the Conway Unit intact. Jenny had begun to suspect there were deeper layers to the Emma Derwent story, but none of the nursing staff Alison had taken statements from would admit any knowledge of the matter. Either they were hiding something, or, just as likely, Jacobs had dealt with her alone and very much in secret.

DI Tony Wallace was the last witness of the morning session. Brusque and businesslike, he described the condition in which Jacobs's body had been found and summarized his investigations into Jacobs's recent history. He produced a lab report which confirmed that the phenobarbital in Jacobs's stomach had come from the packets which were found along with his clothing, and delivery notes that proved that the drugs matched those in a consignment delivered to the Conway Unit's pharmacy. In the absence of any forensic evidence suggesting a violent struggle, DI Wallace was in no doubt that Jacobs had taken his own life.

Jenny said, 'There is a suggestion in the pathologist's report that the body may have been turned over some hours after death occurred. Do you have any idea how or why that happened?'

'I don't believe it was the two kids who dialled 999. They claimed they were too frightened to go very close and I have to say I believe them.'

'So it's possible someone else disturbed the body beforehand?'

'Yes. Most likely they rolled him over, realized he was dead and took fright. It might even have been whoever he had sex with.'

Avoiding Mrs Jacobs's gaze, Jenny said, 'Do you have any idea who that person might have been?'

'None at all, I'm afraid. Internal swabs were taken, but the DNA profile didn't match any currently held on the national database.'

'Were you able to establish Mr Jacobs's movements after he left home?'

'We just got a piece of information through this morning

– he bought petrol at Easton Road at four-thirty in the afternoon. He used his MasterCard. We asked the filling station for any CCTV footage but it gets overwritten every day.'

'That means he was heading south from his home towards the city centre. Where was his car found?'

'Around the corner from the church. The tank was nearly full so I assume he didn't drive far.'

'Do we know when he obtained the phenobarbital?'

'According to the pharmacist, it could have been any time in the last two weeks, but definitely not Saturday. The unit has an electronic entry system; the computer log had no record of him having returned after he left work on Friday afternoon.'

Jenny made a note that Jacobs had obtained the drugs at some point during the two weeks before his death. It was looking increasingly as if he had been secretly fighting a devastating wave of depression. In common with most suicides, he could have been managing a low-level condition for some time and his part in Emma Derwent's death had probably pushed him beyond the limits of his ability to cope.

Jenny said, 'You took Mr Jacobs's laptop computer from his home but returned it wiped blank. Can you explain how that happened?'

'I have apologized to Mrs Jacobs,' DI Wallace said. 'It's nothing sinister, but I admit it doesn't cover us in glory. We employ a private contractor to carry out our data retrieval. He removed the hard drive from the laptop, uploaded the contents to his machine, and then accidentally confused Mr Jacobs's drive with others containing illegal images which he had been asked to reformat.'

'That seems a rather basic error.'

'It happens, unfortunately. I've arranged for the copied

contents to be handed back to Mrs Jacobs if she'd like them. The data, such as it was, contained nothing of relevance. Mr Jacobs seemed to use his laptop chiefly as a diary and for browsing the internet.'

'Did he visit any sites in particular?'

'Sports ones mostly. I think I'm right in saying he was a football fan.'

Mrs Jacobs smiled for the first time that day.

Jenny found it hard to believe that a man wrestling with his sexuality wouldn't have explored it online. He would be in a saintly minority if he hadn't. Perhaps DI Wallace was acting out of compassion for the widow, but it seemed unlikely. She would have expected that from a comfortable detective sergeant with no eye on promotion, but Wallace gave every impression of still being on the way up, and of going about his business strictly by the rules. Nor could she see him covering up the fact that a dangerous psychopath had been negligently released from the Conway Unit, or that Jacobs was suspected of having an affair with a former patient.

No, DI Wallace simply didn't seem the type to save others' feelings.

It was left to the quietly spoken Daniel Randall to suggest, in faintly embarrassed tones, that the police had conspired with Deborah Bishop and others to disguise the fact that the dead man was drugged and sexually assaulted, most probably by a former patient, who should have remained under lock and key.

DI Wallace said, 'He swallowed twenty-four pills, possibly without water. There were no other drugs in his system. He was six feet two inches tall and weighed fourteen and a half stone. Tell me how it could have happened and I give you my word we'll look into it.'

'At gunpoint?' Randall suggested.

'No one was pointing a gun at him when he lied to his wife and left home to drive into town.' Then, as if to mitigate the harshness of his statement, he added, 'I'm prepared to make this offer. If the family wish it, I will send officers into the gay community to try to find the person with whom he spent his final hours.'

He was met with silence.

Jenny said, 'Would you like that to happen, Mrs Jacobs?'

The widow crossed her arms tightly across her chest with a look of revulsion. Her mother answered with a firm, 'No thank you.'

Jenny declined the standing invitation to lunch in the judicial dining room, and made do with a tired sandwich from the public canteen. There were more pressing issues than lunch. Both lawyers had agreed before the break that Dr Andy Kerr's post-mortem report could be admitted in evidence without the need for him to appear in person, leaving Jenny with no more witnesses to call and a verdict to reach. The law required her to be satisfied 'beyond reasonable doubt' of her decision. She had no real doubt that Alan Jacobs had deliberately taken his own life, but such was the stigma of suicide that case law required all other possible explanations to be totally ruled out. Filling out the form of inquisition and sealing it with the official stamp should have been a formality, but a nagging voice told her that there was still more left to be discovered, and that any verdict would be open to question until Alan Jacobs's lover (if that was what he had been) was found. Despite his widow's refusal, it was within Jenny's power to order the police to go out and search for the man. With the proliferation of traffic cameras and CCTV, she had no doubt he could be found, but at what cost to Mrs Jacobs? Never having known him, not having a face forever etched in her memory, would allow her to invent her own fiction. Her daughter could grow up without being haunted by a spectre forever associated with her father's grisly death. Jenny vacillated. An open verdict wouldn't carry the stain of suicide and the bitter sense of cowardly desertion that went with it, but nor would it bring closure.

It had to be suicide. She picked up her pen to record the finding when there was a knock on the door. Alison entered.

'It seems we may have another witness, Mrs Cooper – a woman who went to the same church group as Alan Jacobs.'

'She's here?'

'Yes.'

'What does she want to say?'

'I've no idea. I just saw her in the corridor being collared by the priest who was sitting at the back.' With a faint air of disapproval, Alison added, 'I think they're discussing ethics.'

'Get her name,' Jenny said. 'I'll call her anyway.'


The elderly priest wore an expression of disappointment as Mary Richards entered the witness box and whispered the oath. She was a fragile, bookish young woman who stated her occupation as mature student. She was studying for a doctorate in tropical medicine. Jenny could picture her working for a charity in a disease-stricken part of Africa, driven by a sense of controlled compassion.

Ceri Jacobs reached for her mother's hand and squeezed it hard, disturbed and frightened by the appearance of this unexpected interloper.

Jenny said, 'How did you know Alan Jacobs, Miss Richards?'

'He and I attended the same enquirers' course at St

Xavier's. We had been going most Wednesday evenings for just over four months.' She glanced at the priest. 'Father Dermody ran it.'

'Would you mind explaining what that is?'

'It's for people who want to learn about Catholicism – its teachings, doctrine, tradition.'

'And you got to know each other?'

'A little, though not so that we'd socialize – it wasn't that sort of group. But we did participate in various exercises together. Praying for one another in pairs, for example.'

'And you prayed with Alan Jacobs?'

Mary Richards hesitated. The priest wore a look of grim warning.

'Miss Richards, you have sworn an oath to tell the whole truth,' Jenny prompted.

'I know—'

'And anyone who attempts to stop you doing that is acting quite improperly, not to say illegally.'

Father Dermody's face turned to granite. The witness gave an anxious nod, then closed her eyes, as if offering a prayer for forgiveness.

'Of course, our prayers were offered in strict confidence, but given what's happened I feel justified in repeating what little he told me.' She turned to Mrs Jacobs. 'I only prayed with Alan once. He prayed for his wife and his daughter and for several people I believe he was caring for in his work. It was all sincerely meant, not unusual in any way, but I remember he fell silent for a moment. I sensed there was something else he wanted to say and I tried to prompt him, then suddenly his face started running with tears. It surprised me. I'd always seen him as very in control, strong, but calm. I asked him what the matter was. He said, "I've become involved with some people I shouldn't have. I thought they were helping me but now I don't know. I don't know what's going on. I feel as if I don't know who I am any more." I remember the look of despair on his face. I tried to get him to say some more but he wouldn't. So I prayed for him. It must have been at least three weeks before he died, but he more or less avoided me in the sessions after that.'

'Might he have spoken to anyone else in the group before his death?'

'I somehow doubt it. He kept his distance from all of us. I think he felt he had embarrassed or compromised himself. I was in a difficult position—'

Jenny said, 'I understand.'

Neither of the lawyers had any questions for Mary Richards. The images her sketchy evidence had conjured were vivid enough without causing further distress to the widow. Jenny hastily summarized the evidence, eager to bring proceedings to an end. The faces of Ceri Jacobs, her family and priest, as they waited for the word they all dreaded, were pictures of desolation. As she started to read aloud from the form of inquisition, a lump as hard and dry as pumice stone formed in her throat. But at the last moment, as if succumbing in a struggle with a supernatural force, she struck a line through the word 'suicide' and recorded an open verdict.

# SEVEN

THE RELIEF OF SEEING THE Jacobs family greet her inconclusive finding with smiles and grateful embraces was short-lived. As if to punish her for her weakness, Alison pursued Jenny into the corridor behind the courtroom and handed her a list of urgent calls that had to be made before close of business. Jenny promised to deal with them later and locked herself in the tiny office for a few moments' peace.

She made the return journey to Jamaica Street on foot. It was only a mile across the city centre and the afternoon was warm enough for road-menders to be working shirtless and teenagers to be paddling in the public fountain while perspiring policemen stood by smiling. A few rays of sunshine and the city was transformed. All was peace and goodwill. She fetched out her phone and tried Ross's number.

To her surprise he sounded almost pleased to hear her. 'Mum. How are you?'

'Feeling guilty. Sorry I missed our call. Things got a bit frantic.'

'No problem.'

'I don't suppose you're free tonight.'

'Could be—'

'I thought we could go for dinner. It's been ages.'

'Why not?' Ross said, trying hard not to sound over-enthusiastic.

'Pick you up around seven?'

'I could come into town.'

'No need. I ought to say hello to your father.'

The heat must have gone to her head. Having friendly feelings towards David had to be a sign that she wasn't in her right mind.

Alison shoved a note into her hand the moment she stepped through the door. 'Simon Moreton called, twice. You're to phone him back immediately.'

'What does he want?'

'Didn't say. But I'd guess it was your blood.'

'What have I done now?'

Alison shrugged and went back to her emails. Jenny noticed that she had swapped her dark trouser suit for a slim-fitting skirt and matching jacket that was stretched a little too tightly across her shoulders.

'Are you going somewhere?' Jenny said.

'Just meeting a friend.'

'Oh?'

'Yes.' Alison thrust a second piece of paper in Jenny's direction, her cheeks colouring. 'You might want to look at this.'

Jenny cast her eyes over the email from someone calling himself Doc Scratch.

He claimed to be the tattoo artist who had drawn Eva Donaldson's design. He said his diary showed she'd come on the morning of Friday, 23 April, a little over two weeks before she died. She had called herself Louise Pearson and paid in cash, but everyone in the studio had recognized her from the television. You couldn't mistake the scar.

Alison said, 'I sent emails to all the studios I could find. There seems to be one on every street corner these days.'

'Have you spoken to him?'

'Only briefly. He said she was very quiet. She came in knowing what she wanted, lay back and let him get on with it.'

'Is that all?'

'He said she seemed subdued, not down, but as if she were preoccupied with something.'

The phone rang. Alison checked the caller display. 'It's Moreton again.'

Jenny hurried through to her office.

'I'll see you on Monday, Mrs Cooper,' Alison called after her. 'I'm off now.'

'Have fun.'

Jenny snatched up the receiver with a sense of dread. 'Hello, Simon. I've been wondering where you'd been.'

'It's Amanda Cramer,' a humourless voice replied. 'You may have seen the circular; I was recently appointed assistant director for coroners. Simon's concentrating more on strategy. From now on operations and personnel will be chiefly my responsibility.'

'Oh, I see,' Jenny said, taking an instant dislike to Amanda Cramer. 'I don't think we've met.'

'Briefly, at the Christmas drinks.'

Jenny cast her mind back to the tedious evening in Gray's Inn Hall spent sipping orange juice amidst a sea of anonymous, suited officials getting drunk on cheap wine. Oh God. Now she remembered. Moreton, who for all his conformism was good fun at parties, and Jenny had been laughing at one of his suggestive jokes, when a joyless young woman with bad skin and flat shoes stepped between them. 'Dear God,' Moreton said when Amanda Cramer had finally taken the hint and moved on. 'I've never said it about any woman I've worked with, but I just couldn't, not even with Viagra.'

'Of course, I remember,' Jenny said. 'How can I help you?'

'Two things. Firstly, we've received a complaint about your handling of the death of Eva Donaldson. We understand there's no reason cause of death couldn't have been formally recorded after the verdict in the criminal trial, but for some reason you've neglected to do so.'

'That would be because I'm conducting an inquest.'

'Why would you do that? The superior tribunal has reached its decision. There's no possible justification for more public money to be spent on a needless formality.'

'With respect, Ms Cramer, that is a matter in my discretion. And the Crown Court is not a superior tribunal. It has an entirely separate function.'

'But you have no power to contradict its verdict.'

'I'm well aware of my powers.'

'Then I would advise you to exercise them appropriately. You could start by releasing the body. This should have been done immediately after the Home Office post-mortem.'

'The release form is on my desk ready to sign at the appropriate moment. Is that all?'

'No. We'd like your assurance that Mr Donaldson and his family won't be caused any more distress.'

Jenny felt her fragile patience ready to snap. Civil servants had a flimsy grasp on the concept of judicial independence at the best of times. Simon Moreton would at least have tacitly acknowledged that he was merely playing the part expected of him; Cramer was a straightforward bully, unafraid to do the Minister's dirty work. The morning newspapers had reported that the Decency Bill was on the brink of winning government support. That meant Michael Turnbull and his new political allies would be desperate to avoid any hint of negative press surrounding the final surge of their campaign.

Jenny couldn't resist a retaliatory blow. 'You're surely not attempting to influence the judicial process, Ms Cramer?'

'Not at all, Mrs Cooper, but if you won't abide by your wider responsibilities, we can't be expected to abide by ours.'

'And what does that mean?'

'Let me put it this way: you'll be sailing into this particular storm without a lifeboat.'

'I can't say I haven't been warned,' Jenny said sarcastically. 'You said there was a second matter.'

'Yes: your erroneous verdict in the Alan Jacobs case. Bristol CID is furious. Your local paper is running a story saying they failed to investigate the possibility of murder.'

'I said nothing of the sort.'

'Then I suggest you issue a press release and clarify the situation. Coroners can hardly be effective without the support of the police. Goodbye, Mrs Cooper.'

Jenny collapsed into her chair. She felt shaken without knowing precisely why. There had been several run-ins with the Ministry over the past year, and each time she had been vindicated. Perhaps that was the problem: she had proved rather too good at unearthing the truth.

'Hello?'

She jumped at the sound of the voice in reception. Forcing a breath past her racing heart, she stepped out to see Father Starr standing in the middle of the room as if he had appeared out of thin air. In the shadowy light she could see the sharp outline of his skull beneath his face.

'I'm sorry if I alarmed you. One of your upstairs neighbours was leaving as I arrived.'

'You could at least have knocked,' Jenny said. 'What can I do for you?'

'You might answer my calls. Pay the slightest attention.'

Jenny bristled. 'I have been conducting an inquest.'

'So I understand,' Starr said. 'I hear you behaved very compassionately.'

She felt the tightness again, a spasm beneath her ribs.

'What is this, a Catholic conspiracy?' Jenny said, only half-jokingly.

'As we sow, so shall we reap. It may be coincidence, but experience tells me they don't happen often.'

'You've lost me,' Jenny said. The disturbing sensations gripping her body were hardening into panic. She hated being spoken to cryptically almost as much as being caught by surprise. 'What do you want, Father?'

'For you to have courage, Mrs Cooper.'

He held her gaze with a self-assurance that was not quite human. Without fear or self-consciousness he seemed to reach inside her.

'When you came to the prison I mentioned a mutual friend—'

'You mean Alec McAvoy.'

'Yes. I met him a number of times through my work there. He spoke of you once.'

'Is he alive?'

'Honestly, I couldn't say.'

'When did he mention me?'

'I took his confession while he was assisting in your investigation last year into the missing young men. It's not betraying a confidence to say that he thought very highly of you.'

'What did he say?'

'That you were one of the *few*. I took him to mean one

of the few people in his orbit worthy of complete trust. I have formed a similar opinion.'

'Even though I don't answer your calls?'

Starr smiled. It was a warm, spontaneous gesture that showed him to be human after all. Jenny felt a wave of relief pass over her.

'I'll confess,' Starr said, 'I observed your reaction when I mentioned him. It was probably a little unfair of me, and it's been weighing on my conscience. He is, or was, a very charismatic man.' He glanced towards the partially open door to her office. 'It is safe to discuss such matters?'

'There's no one here but us.'

'It's only right that I tell you –' Father Starr paused and gestured with his hands, as if rehearsing what he had to say – 'he described you as a beautiful and a troubled woman whom he felt fated to meet. I don't think I would have felt prompted to mention it were it not for that word – *fated*. It stayed with me for some reason. Finally meeting you in person seemed to suggest an answer, or at least the route to one.'

She felt herself blush. There were butterflies in her stomach. Why torment her with this when McAvoy was already dead?

'You would tell me if you knew anything, even if only a rumour—'

'You have my word. Well, there you are. My conscience is clear –' he hesitated – 'well, almost. Forgive me, I'm a priest, and sometimes far too conscientious for my own good, but I feel I ought to ask – are you troubled, Mrs Cooper?'

'I think the lines have become blurred enough already, don't you?'

Starr looked at her, as if about to say something which he then decided against. 'I apologize. It wasn't my intention to make you feel uncomfortable. You are going to conduct this inquest, yes?'

'If I were to say no?'

Father Starr looked into her eyes, then dipped his head and slipped from the room as quietly as he had arrived.

Jenny pulled up on her ex-husband's spotless driveway and parked her scruffy Golf next to a brand-new Mercedes Coupé. It was the house she had lived in for the best part of fifteen years, but crossing the immaculate paving she felt like a ragged trespasser. David demanded the same spotlessness in his garden as he did in his operating theatre. Since Jenny had left, she had noticed this tendency becoming even more acute. No imperfection was permitted. A weed between the manicured shrubs was as unthinkable as a casual slip of the scalpel: a matter of life and death.

It was his young girlfriend, Debbie, who answered the door. Not yet thirty, she was pretty, pink-cheeked and blonde, and now happily pregnant.

'Oh hi, Jenny,' Debbie said sweetly. 'Come in.' She called up the stairs: 'Ross, it's your mum.'

Jenny followed her into the large, open-plan kitchen, which shone in a way it had never done when it had belonged to her.

'Can I get you anything?'

'No thanks,' Jenny said. Drinks were too risky when she was this nervous. She'd fumble it and make a mess on Debbie's gleaming floor. 'Is David around?'

'He's late back. It was a long list today. He's getting things clear for the weekend.'

'Are you doing something special?'

'It's my birthday. He's booked a couple of nights away. Don't ask me where, it's a surprise.'

'Great,' Jenny said, remembering several such trips, David

booking the big suite and expecting non-stop sex while her idea had been to catch up on some sleep. She glanced at Debbie's pert little pregnancy bump. 'How are you feeling? It can't be long now.'

'You know, I hardly notice it, except when it kicks.' She patted her stomach. 'According to the scan it's going to be big, though. David says Ross was a big baby.'

'Yes,' Jenny said. 'But a word of advice – it's better to have the cut before it comes out than risk what happened to me.'

Debbie winced.

'Two hours stitching up. Probably why I didn't do it again.'

Ross's footsteps sounded on the stairs.

Jenny said, 'Good luck. I'm sure you'll be fine.'

The sinful pleasure of seeing Debbie's smile replaced by a look of horror stayed with her all the way to the restaurant. Hopefully it would put a damper on her weekend too.

Ross chose the little French bistro in Clifton they used to visit when David still indulged Jenny in her occasional attempts to reconnect with her brief bohemian youth. She was glad it had good associations for Ross and hadn't been tainted by his father's scathing remarks about the streaky cutlery and bad wine. She guessed he almost felt part of the university crowd that gathered here. She had to remind herself constantly that he was very nearly eighteen, a young adult, old enough to fight in a war. He had changed again in the month since they'd spent an evening together. The mid-teen gawkiness was almost gone, along with the semi-permanent sneer and ever-ready put-downs. She recognized aspects of his father in him: hints of fastidiousness in the careful way he held his cutlery, a sense that his intellect was asserting control over his emotions. And as the evening wore on, he started to ask her questions, which was another new departure. He enquired after her recent cases, whether she had plans for a holiday, and whether she seeing much of Steve. Jenny was touched.

'So you're not actually together, then?' Ross said.

'We're good friends—'

It could have been David looking sceptically back at her.

'What?' she asked.

'I thought you liked him. He likes you.'

'When did he say that?'

'He didn't have to. It's obvious.'

Jenny sensed she wasn't getting the whole truth. 'Have you been speaking to him?'

Ross shrugged. 'He's called me a couple of times, that's all, to see how you are.'

'What's wrong with calling me?'

'He says he's been trying to . . . He worries about you, you know.'

'Oh, does he?'

'In a good way. Why wouldn't he? We all do.'

'*All?*'

'I didn't mean . . . sorry. That came out wrong.'

'Who exactly sits on this committee of the concerned?'

'It's only Dad. He thinks you're working too hard, that's all.'

'Really? When exactly has he been making these pronouncements – around the dinner table with Debbie there?'

Ross squirmed in his seat. 'Look, I didn't mean to start something.'

'No, I want to know,' Jenny insisted. 'I'm your mother. If you're worried about me, ask me. I might be able to reassure you.'

Ross looked at her guiltily. She hated herself for hurting him, but she couldn't bear not to know what David was saying about her.

'He thinks you seem a bit—'

'What?'

'Shaky. He thinks you could do with a rest.'

'From a man who works fourteen-hour days, that's a bit rich.'

There was a spark of anger in Ross's eyes. 'Just because you're divorced doesn't mean he's stopped caring about you. He's worried you're going to push yourself too hard and go under again.'

'If being appointed coroner is his idea of going under, I can't imagine what he thinks success would be. You know, Ross, perhaps your father is just a little bit jealous of me. I won't deny he's a great surgeon, well respected and all that, but it's uncanny how he always seems to notice when I've had my name in the paper.' She poured more mineral water into her glass, wishing it were wine. 'Shall we change the subject?'

'Is it something that happened to you?'

'What?'

'Dad says it sounds like post-traumatic stress disorder. Apparently sometimes it can be some tiny thing that sets up a reaction in the brain, like being frightened by a dog. Something can trigger it years later.'

'He's a psychiatrist as well as a heart surgeon now, is he?'

'Was there something?'

'Ross, please. We've talked about this before. I've been through a tough time and now I'm getting better.' She forced a smile.

'Mum, you've started not looking at people when you're talking to them. Your hands shake. You don't get better by taking more pills. Someone's got to be honest enough to tell you that.'

Neither of them spoke as she drove him home. It was meant to have been a relaxing evening but instead it had ended with Jenny feeling betrayed. David had primed Ross to confront her and suggested the bistro as the place most likely to take the sting out of her own son telling her she was a basket case. She pulled up on the road outside her sterile former home, fighting a losing battle against anger she could no longer contain.

'How dare your father do this to me?'

Ross sat silently in the passenger seat.

'You know what his problem is? He feels guilty. He wants me off his conscience so he can pretend everything's wonderful in his bourgeois bloody life. Well, it isn't. He's making a fool of himself with that girl. She's young enough to be his daughter, for Christ's sake.'

'Mum, that's not fair.'

'I know. I should be a bloody saint who never gets angry, never criticizes anyone, never shows any emotion.'

'There's no danger of that.'

Ross slammed out of the car and ran towards the house. Jenny wound down the window and called after him, but her apology came too late. He was already through the door. Lost to her.

She shed angry tears as she gunned home along empty roads, throwing the Golf around the steep corners on the valley road, grinding through the gears and stamping on the brakes. Her anger with David spilled over into fury at the world at large. Everyone wanted something from her, she was surrounded by people passing judgement. It was as if, resenting her authority, they had to do all in their power to diminish her. Even her father had managed to lash out from his senility to land a sickening blow.

No more. She was Jenny Cooper, Severn Vale District Coroner, a woman who had every right to demand respect.

She pulled onto the old cart track at the side of the house as the last of the late evening light bled away. She couldn't care less if her insecure ex-husband disapproved of the way she lived or had convinced himself she was a breakdown waiting to happen. That was his problem. When Debbie was cooing over a baby he'd be desperate for an intelligent woman to talk to. There'd be no more dirty weekends for a long time, just a lot of dirty nappies. There was some justice in the world.

The creak of the gate's rusty hinge echoed off the front of the cottage. The air was dead still and humid, not a hint of breeze to stir the leaves. She stopped halfway up the path and groped in her handbag for her keys. Where the hell were they? She delved beneath the jumble of make-up, pills, purses and assorted hair brushes. She checked the zip compartments. Nothing. She shook the bag to hear the rattle that would tell her they were in there, but somehow she lost her grip and dropped it, scattering the contents over the ground.

Damn! Damn! Stooping down to snatch them up something caught her eye: flashes of colour on the flagstones. In the dim light she made out a pattern of pink and yellow chalk lines: hopscotch squares and numbers drawn in a childish hand.

Her head spun and her heart exploded. She grabbed her car keys and ran.

# EIGHT

JENNY SPED ALONG THE THREE miles of winding lanes, careered down the narrow dirt track through the woods and juddered to a halt in Steve's yard. The stone farmhouse, still rented out to the weekenders from London, stood in darkness. Steve's ancient Land Rover was parked outside the barn in which he'd improvised a flat in the upper storey, but there was no light at the window. She groped for the torch she kept in the glove box. It glowed dully for a second, then died. Jenny flung it over her shoulder. Too frightened to leave the safety of her car to stumble across the yard and pick her way through the blackness of the barn, she leaned on the horn.

No response.

She pressed it again, its ugly sound splitting the night.

Wake up! Wake up!

Maybe he had someone else up there with him? One of the admiring girls from the office he occasionally mentioned. The bastard. She fired up the engine, rammed into reverse and sped round in a backwards semi-circle. Shoving the stick into first, she shot forward, kicking up dirt and gravel, tore through the gate and slewed around the tight left bend. Two bright green eyes stared into the headlights from the centre of the track. It was Alfie, Steve's sheepdog, with Steve right behind him. She stamped on the brakes. Steve and

Alfie dived into the neck-high cow parsley on the verge as she slid past and skidded to a stop.

Untroubled by his brush with death, Alfie rested his head on her lap as she sat on the corner of the dusty old sofa, gazing at her with needy eyes. The boarded-out barn loft was more of a den than a flat. There was a bed, a draughtsman's drawing board, a few items of ancient furniture and a makeshift kitchen. A solar panel rigged up on the roof provided an occasional trickle of tepid water to the sink. It smelled of straw, dog and tobacco smoke.

Steve brought her some camomile tea and sat next to her. At least his cups were clean.

'How are you feeling?' he said.

'I don't know,' Jenny whispered.

'Are you going to tell me what's going on?'

Alfie nuzzled her, demanding a stroke. She put a hand on his soft head and scratched gently behind his ears. He closed his eyes in bliss.

'I'm not sure I can explain. You'll think I'm stupid.'

'Try me.'

Jenny struggled against a feeling of unreality. She felt foolish, humiliated.

Steve put a hand on her knee. 'What's frightened you, Jenny? It's not work this time, is it?'

She shook her head. 'How can you tell?'

He shrugged. 'I guess I must know you.'

'Those people you saw waiting outside my house the other day, what did they look like?'

'The guy was a bit older than me, the girl was very little. Blonde hair, two little pigtails at the back.'

'I know this is going to sound strange —'

'Go on.'

'The man . . .' Jenny faltered, scarcely believing she was

asking the question. 'Did he look to you like he belonged in the past?'

'What do you mean? I only saw him for a moment.'

'What about the girl? What was she wearing?'

'Something pale blue, as far as I remember. A sort of knitted cardigan thing. Why? Who are they? Hey, careful—'

He grabbed the cup from Jenny's shaking hand, slopping tea onto the floor.

'Come on,' Steve said. 'Let's have it.'

'You won't think I'm crazy? I need to trust you.'

'You know you can. I keep telling you.'

She nodded, and edged a little closer to the precipice. Once over she knew there was no going back. She stepped out.

'You know my psychiatrist is convinced I've got some buried memory, some trauma—'

'Uh huh.' He took her hand and stroked it, gently urging her on.

'I'd been having dreams about this little girl. In one of our sessions a name came up, Katy. Just the name. No memory, but it was connected to my childhood. I was about five or six. He kept pestering me to research my past, family records, anything that might stir up memories. I don't have much of that sort of stuff. I couldn't find anything except a few old pictures. My mother's dead, I've no brothers or sisters. The only person left is my father. Physically he's OK, mentally he's completely shot.'

'I remember. You went to see him.'

Jenny drew in a long breath. It was too late to stop now.

'I was showing him some old pictures. I had no idea whether he recognized them or not, and I slipped in the name, Katy, and asked him if he remembered who she was . . .'

Jenny's fingers tightened around Steve's hand.

'What did he say?'

She screwed up her eyes. 'What does it matter? He's got Alzheimer's.'

'Tell me what he said,' Steve demanded, a sudden and unexpected hardness in his voice that shocked her. 'Please, Jenny,' he said, more softly.

'He said she was my Uncle Jim and Aunty Penny's little girl. Jim was his older brother. I said, they didn't have a daughter. He said, "You remember, Smiler –", that's what he used to call me.' Jenny swallowed. ' "You remember, Smiler. You killed her." That was it. That's all he said. Then he was gone again.'

Jenny looked at Steve for his reaction and saw that he was trying hard not to appear shocked.

'I don't expect you to say anything. I don't even know what to think myself.'

'Do you remember this girl?'

'No, only their son, Chris. He must be ten years younger than me. We lived in the same part of town but didn't see much of each other.'

'There's an easy way to find out. I can look it up on the internet right now.'

'You think he might be telling the truth?'

'No. I just thought—'

'Go on. Do it.'

'Really, I didn't mean to—'

'Do it.'

Steve stood up from the sofa and fetched a laptop from a battered canvas briefcase.

'Don't you want to know what happened tonight – before you get all wrapped up in your computer?' Jenny asked.

'Of course.' He set the laptop aside as it booted up.

'I know you and Ross and my ex-husband and God

knows who else think I'm mad, but I don't hallucinate. I don't see things. Imagine them, yes, but not actually *see* them.'

'What was it?'

'On the front path. There were chalk marks. Pink and yellow chalk. Hopscotch squares like we used to mark out as kids. Someone had drawn them today. And you know when you see something and it takes you back? I was standing in the street outside my house when I was a child. I could see the little buckled shoes on my feet, the white socks, everything.'

Steve looked puzzled. 'You think someone's trying to tell you something?'

'The girl you saw outside my house . . . what if it was *her*? The man could have been my uncle . . .'

'Right. You're telling me I've been seeing ghosts?'

'My grandmother used to. She'd hear a knock at the window when anyone in the family was about to die. We used to joke about it, but she was never wrong.'

'She sounds quite a character.'

He picked up the laptop and brought up a selection of websites that would trace your family history for a fee. Five pounds bought him access to the government register of births, deaths and marriages. Jenny gave him the details of her aunt and uncle. He typed in their names and hit the key that would bring up details of their offspring.

'What is it?' Jenny said.

He was staring intently at the screen. 'It looks as if they did have two children.'

He angled the laptop so she could read with him. The first entry read: *Katherine Anne Chilcott. Date of birth: 16 June 1967.* The second recorded Christopher's birth in 1976.

For the second time that evening the world spun around her.

'Do you want me to click on her name?' Steve said.

Jenny nodded and looked away.

'Died 19 October 1972.'

Jenny lay curled up in bed in one of Steve's T-shirts with Alfie lying on the floor next to her while Steve drove back to her house to fetch her handbag, some clothes and sleeping pills. It was no longer anxiety she felt, but the leadenness that closely follows the shock of bereavement; and the dread of having to face a dark and buried past she had almost convinced herself was a fiction. Exhaustion dragged her from consciousness and she sank into a dreamless sleep.

She woke, disorientated, to the touch of Steve's hand on her shoulder. Blinking against the sharp sunlight beating through the undraped skylight, she tried to remember where she was.

'It's all right. It's still early. You can go back to sleep,' Steve said.

The previous night's events came back at her in a rush. She groaned and pulled the sheet over her head.

'Hey. You're OK. I got your bag. And there was nothing on the path. I walked up and down it ten times with a torch. Not a mark. You imagined it.'

'I didn't imagine a birth certificate.'

'No. I paid to download a copy, and one of the death certificate too.'

Jenny threw back the sheet and swung out of bed. 'Show me.'

He retrieved a piece of paper from the floor. It was a printout of a scanned copy of a death certificate issued by the North Somerset District Registry. Beneath the section containing her uncle and aunt's names, the informant was cited as C. R. Benedict, North Somerset District Coroner. In the box titled 'cause of death' was the single typewritten word, 'accident'.

'Her death was accidental,' Steve said. 'You can forget what your father said.'

'That could mean anything. I just returned an open verdict in a case where the man clearly killed himself.'

Steve said, 'We know the coroner dealt with it. There must be files there somewhere.'

'I can hardly ask for them, can I?'

'I could.'

'No. Someone will find out.'

'There must have been something in the local papers. I'll look them up. There's no danger in that.'

Jenny snatched her handbag from the sofa and tipped it upside down. 'Where are my pills? What have you done with them?'

'In the car. I'll fetch them in a minute, but first we're going to make a deal.'

'What are you, my mother?'

'Jenny, stop it.'

She turned, ready to bite his head off. Steve got in first.

'You came to me when you were in trouble. You know how I feel about you, now how about some trust?'


'Does your father have lucid moments?'

'Rarely.'

'And the rest of the time?'

'He's like a child. He has tantrums, strange outbursts, throws things at the TV.'

'And are there periods when he is wholly unresponsive?'

'Yes. The nurses say he'll stare at the same spot on the wall all afternoon.'

Dr Allen nodded calmly, noting this down. If he resented

giving up his Saturday afternoon he was hiding it well. He seemed more at home here in his consulting room in the Whitchurch Hospital in Cardiff than in the borrowed room in Chepstow. His other-worldliness fitted perfectly with the grand Edwardian building surrounded by parkland. Jenny found it intimidating. Making her way along vast corridors, passing semi-catatonic women drifting aimlessly in their nightdresses, she was struck with the fear that she could become one of them. She had wanted to turn and run, but Steve had gripped her arm and steered her to their destination, insisting she do it for Ross if not for herself.

'A patient with Alzheimer's as advanced as your father's is not a reliable witness of anything, Jenny,' Dr Allen said. 'The brain is disintegrating. The connections it makes are broken and nonsensical. I appreciate it's difficult, but you must treat his accusation as nonsense.'

'But now I know she existed. We were virtually the same age. No one ever mentioned her.'

'It's not unusual for families to draw a veil of silence over a tragic event.'

'They weren't silent about much else.'

The young psychiatrist put his notebook aside and looked up with a bright, optimistic expression. 'The good news is that we've been pursuing exactly the right course. There is an event in your past which I'm sure we can now expose, and that opens the way to recovery.'

'I can sense a "but" on the way.'

'It's like any medical treatment. There's always a likelihood of short-term pain.'

'How much?'

'I couldn't predict, exactly.'

'I can't stop work, not now.'

'A week or two, surely—'

'And what would it say on my sick note? How many times do I have to tell you? When I'm working, I'm fine.'

'It's up to you, of course, but if you're hallucinating, even mildly—'

'It was a trick of the light.'

Dr Allen sat back in his chair and frowned. 'Let me put it this way. When a patient starts to see things, it tells me that we may have crossed the threshold from anxiety neurosis into something a little more serious.'

'It was one minor incident. It was late. I was exhausted.'

'There are other signs: delusional beliefs, difficulties in social interaction—'

Jenny gave a dismissive shrug. 'I don't have any of those.'

He gave her a searching look. 'You told me you genuinely believed the man and child your partner saw outside your house were ghosts.'

'I was frightened they *might* be. There's a difference. They were probably just a father and daughter out for a walk. Perhaps he's related to the old woman who used to live in my house; people are always doing that, going back to look at a place—'

Dr Allen held up his hand. 'Calm down. Of course there will be a logical explanation, but think objectively for a moment. You're dealing with a number of cases all at once; how would the parties feel about your involvement if they knew of your state of mind?'

Jenny thought of Paul Craven and Father Starr, and of the worshippers spread-eagled in ecstasy on the floor of the Mission Church of God. Compared with them, she was relatively sane. 'I think they'd take their chances.'

'If you insist. But you do understand that I am obliged to record my advice on your notes.'

In his quiet way he was telling her that this was a point

of no return. If she came unstuck, if for any reason the Ministry of Justice ever requested a report on her mental health, the record would state that she had willingly ignored doctor's orders. Her dismissal would be a formality: *inability in the discharge of duty.*

Jenny said, 'Of course. Are we going to do the regression now?'

As Dr Allen talked her down she sank with little resistance into a state of near-unconscious torpor, neither sleeping nor waking. His voice grew steadily more distant as Jenny descended deeper into the caverns of her subconscious. She found herself in a warm, dark space and followed a pinprick of light that slowly widened into a street scene. Neat rows of pre-war semi-detached houses in a seaside town.

'Tell me where you are, Jenny.' Dr Allen's voice came to her as if from the far distance.

'In the street where we lived when I was a child, in Weston. I can see the houses, the sun shining on them. One of them is painted white with a green roof. I can smell a bonfire, leaves burning.'

'Good. And how are you feeling?'

Jenny tried to isolate the sensation she was experiencing. 'Odd.'

'In what way?'

'I'm not sure.'

'Do you know how old are you?'

'Small. I'm wearing the buckled shoes, the blue ones that Nan bought me.'

'What's happening?'

Jenny drifted for a moment. 'They sent me out. There are men in the house . . . their car's parked outside.'

'Who are these men?'

'I don't know.'

'Did you see them?'

Jenny flinched, balling up her fingers into fists.

'What? What is it?'

'The shouting again. It's my mother. I can't bear it.'

'Stay with it, Jenny, stay there. What's she shouting?'

Her chin lolled from one side of her chest to the other, her face creasing with pain.

'Tell me, Jenny. Tell me what's she saying.'

' "Don't take him! Don't take him!" There are people coming out of their doors. The woman from next door, she's pulling me to her, not letting me see.'

'See what?'

'It's my fault. It is. It's my fault.'

'What's your fault, Jenny?'

'What they're doing to Dad, what's happening to him. The policemen are taking him away.'

Steve turned off the main road and threaded through single-track lanes. Overgrown hedgerows brushed the sides of the car. The dipping sun danced off the wings of a million insects. Jenny closed her eyes and felt the warm evening air playing over her face, neither of them saying a word. He pulled up at the entrance to a forestry track and led her along a winding path through thickets of birch and hazel, emerging into a meadow that wrapped around an oxbow bend in the River Usk. They waded through the long grass and sat at the edge of the water, where fat turquoise dragonflies, more brilliant than peacocks, came to sip in the shallows.

In no hurry, he waited for her to speak first, happy to smoke a cigarette and gaze at the two swans on the opposite bank elegantly preening themselves after a lazy afternoon swim.

When the heaviness of the hospital began to lift, Jenny

found her voice and told him what had happened in Dr Allen's consulting room. She had regressed before, retrieved many snatches of buried memory, but nothing had been as vivid as today. There was sharp detail: the gaudy orange flowers on the neighbour's dress, the click of the detectives' shoes on the pavement, the raw fear in her mother's voice.

Steve said, 'And that was it, just that scene?'

'It's like that. It's as if I can only bear to take so much at once.' Jenny wiped her eyes, the tears stinging her cheeks. 'Maybe I'm making it up, putting together pieces that don't belong together.'

'What did the doctor say?'

'He seemed pleased. I'm seeing him again next week.'

Steve tossed aside the blade of grass he'd been picking at and tenderly touched her face. 'This is good, Jenny. You've started to open the door. You're going to get free of all this.'

She looked at him dubiously. 'I don't know why you're still here. Your last crazy girlfriend cost you ten years.'

He let his hand drop down to hold hers and kissed both her eyelids in turn. 'You know why.'

'You're betting a lot on me. I hope you know what you're doing.'

'What do you mean?'

'You don't believe I did it, do you?'

'You were just a witness to something upsetting, that's all. A very long time ago.' He drew her closer. 'Don't let it poison your whole life, Jenny. Try thinking about where you are now.'

He kissed her lightly, and with no demand, in a way that took her back to more innocent times. She wished she could stay there for ever.

# NINE

MONDAY MORNING GREETED HER WITH the small mountain of death reports that a weekend in high summer inevitably generates. Hot weather, even more than cold, was the undertaker's friend. In addition to the usual post-operative deaths were numerous suspected coronaries, a gory motorcycle accident and a drowning. The police had emailed photographs of the body of a teenage boy stretched out at the side of a reservoir. There were livid bruises on his chest from desperate attempts at resuscitation. Even after handling over twelve hundred cases, the sight of those who had been torn from life in an unexpected instant never failed to appal her. It was less the physical spectacle than the injustice of it; the inability of the deceased to prepare, to say goodbye to loved ones and make their peace.

She had come to appreciate that a death faced with foreknowledge and a clear conscience was a rare privilege granted only to the few.

Jenny hurried through the hospital reports, certified the cause of death in the cases in which post-mortems had already been completed and by mid-morning finally summoned the courage to call the family of the drowned boy. She spoke briefly to a hung-over-sounding man who said he was the mother's boyfriend. In the background a woman yelled obscenities at screaming younger children, their voices competing with a blaring television. The atmosphere of aggressive chaos hit her like a shock wave. She could understand why the fourteen-year-old might have swallowed a bottle of cheap vodka and gone for a swim. The mother refused to come to the phone and conversation fizzled to an inconclusive end.

Turning to the boxes sent by Paul Craven's lawyers, Jenny skimmed through the papers the police had seized from Eva's house. There were domestic bills, bank and credit-card statements, correspondence with her mortgage and pension companies and documents relating to her work on behalf of Decency. It didn't take an accountant to work out that Eva had been in financial trouble. Decency paid her a salary of three thousand pounds a month plus travel expenses, but she had refinanced her house twice in as many years and was paying eighteen hundred pounds each month in mortgage payments. Her current account was forty-five thousand in the red and between half a dozen credit cards she had racked up another thirty-five thousand pounds' worth of debt. Jenny found a letter marked 'COPY' dated the previous November, in which Eva had written to Michael Turnbull c/o Decency's London office requesting an increase in salary to reflect her importance to the campaign. There was no evidence of a reply.

Despite their volume, the papers cast little light on Eva's personal life or state of mind. Jenny flicked back to the sheaf of itemized telephone bills to check for frequently called numbers, but on close examination Eva appeared to have made only one or two calls each day from her home number, some days none at all. There were no bills for a mobile phone. She checked the statement made by DC Sarah Munroe, the exhibits officer, and noted that no mobile phone records had been seized, nor even a handset. Buried in the credit-card statements she had spotted a payment for a laptop computer Eva had purchased the previous August, but it was absent from DC Munroe's list of items seized. It was apparent that not everything she would have expected the police to have taken had been recorded, let alone copied and forwarded to Craven's lawyers.

Jenny flicked back through Eva's work papers, searching for some hint of a clue. Most of them had been generated by the Decency campaign office: strategy papers, statistical information for use in interviews (one in three men in the UK has a pornography habit, one in six an addiction), and minutes of meetings with ministers and civil servants. The few personal letters were from campaign supporters or church groups requesting Eva to come and talk to them. Only one item, caught up in the middle of briefing papers for an appearance on television news, gave an insight into the side of Eva's life that most interested Jenny. It was from her solicitors, Reed Falkirk & Co., writing to inform her that having reviewed her contracts with GlamourX Ltd, counsel had confirmed that she had a good claim for unpaid royalties for *Latex Lesbians* Parts 1 to 4 and all six films in the *Lil' Miss* series. The solicitors awaited her instructions, reminding her that they would require ten thousand pounds to be paid on account of their fees. The letter had been written in mid-March, just under two months before her death. Jenny checked her bank statements and realized there were none on the file after January.

DI Vernon Goodison was a hard man to get hold of. It took three separate calls to track him down to a CID office in Trinity Road police station, and impatient threats to a junior detective to extract his mobile number.

'Jenny Cooper, here. Severn Vale District Coroner. I understand you led the investigation into the murder of Eva Donaldson.'

'Ah, the infamous Mrs Cooper.' She could picture his patronizing smile. 'I was the interviewing officer. DI Wallace was heading up the investigation.'

'It's your signature certifying that the unused material handed to Craven's solicitors was complete.'

'I think I remember that.'

'There appear to be documents missing.'

'Then I suggest you contact the solicitors. We had no reason to hold on to anything.'

'They're missing from your lists. You can't tell me you didn't find mobile phone bills or bank statements after January. It looks as if the deceased had a computer, but there's no mention of you having seized one.'

'Have another look at the exhibits list. Have you got a copy?'

'Fire away.'

'Top of the second sheet, as I recall.'

Jenny turned the page and read, 'Item: document shredder.'

Goodison said, 'A woman with a bit of a past, you might say. Wouldn't want things falling into the wrong hands I expect. You can understand why.'

Jenny said, 'How far did you dig?'

'We don't spend money for prurience alone, Mrs Cooper. Once we'd established Craven was our man, we moved on.'

'What happened to the computer?'

'As far as I know, we never found one. You know as well as I do it'd be the first thing in the bag.'

'Did you check her email server?'

'We searched her one known address. There should be a statement in the file covering that. She was a scrupulous woman, liked to cover her tracks. I suppose she had plenty to cover.'

Jenny opened the file containing the prosecution statements. She must have missed it the first time she skimmed through. A single paragraph from DC Anya Singh recorded the fact that a search had been made of Eva's only known email account and that it had been closed down at the request of Eva herself on 12 February. There was no surviving record of her previous email correspondence on the operator's server.

'Did you find out why she closed the account?'

'No. The best guess is that she was doing a spot of housekeeping before this bill came before Parliament. You can imagine the kind of press attention she would have attracted.'

'And ditched the computer for safe measure?'

'Put it beyond reach, that's for sure.'

Jenny instinctively mistrusted the DI and had to remind herself to remain objective, to remember that the police had no interest in gleaning the whole truth, only in gathering sufficient evidence for a conviction. Once they had a confession, details such as Eva's tattoo or why she might have dumped her computer would be of no concern to them.

But she couldn't resist a final dig. 'I read your interview with Craven. Seems like you had to tease it out of him.'

Goodison laughed. 'Not at all, Mrs Cooper. He couldn't wait to put his hands up. He was good as gold.'

No money. No phone. No computer. A contractual dispute with an adult movie company and a new tattoo two weeks before she died. Eva had been in a mess and Jenny felt a sudden and profound shift in her feelings towards her. She wasn't a porn star or an evangelist, she was a lonely and frightened young woman whose short life was heading for disaster. If she didn't try to understand her, no one ever would. But why Eva more than a drowned boy or the innocent victims of a crane collapse? Jenny didn't have an answer, only a powerful feeling that if she were to turn her back on Eva now, she wouldn't be able to live with herself.

Alison bustled in with coffee from their local Brazilian cafe balanced on top of a tray of mail. Ever since the good-looking new waiter had greeted her as 'my pretty lady' she had been making daily trips.

'Good weekend, Mrs Cooper?'

'Yes,' Jenny lied. 'You?'

'Oh, all right.' There was something uncharacteristically girlish in Alison's non-committal reply.

'Not too lonely without Terry?'

'Goodness no. I think it's probably been good for both of us. Things get a bit stale after thirty years. We probably both felt like a bit of excitement, only he was the one who acted on it.'

'Do you think you'd have him back?'

'I'm not sure, Mrs Cooper. I suppose it depends what happens. People change.'

Jenny sensed she was being asked to delve deeper. Too proud to gush, Alison's way of revealing herself was in-variably to drop tantalizing hints that she was supposed to pick up on. Something of the parent and teenage child had developed in their relationship, Alison craving Jenny's approval but never daring to let down her defensive guard.

'Have you met someone?' Jenny ventured.

'Me?' Alison said, feigning surprise. 'I've had a few dates. Why not? Terry's certainly making hay.'

With a knowing look, Jenny said, 'What's his name?'

'Who?'

'The man you were meeting on Friday night?'

'Oh, him,' Alison said casually. 'That was Martin. A friend put me on to one of these dating sites. It was the last thing I'd have done if she hadn't suggested it, but he turned out to be rather charming. Very gentlemanly.'

Jenny smiled. 'Sounds promising. What does he do?'

'He's a consultant, advising companies on their security, that sort of thing.' Alison's cheeks coloured. 'He's only forty-three. He thinks I'm forty-nine.'

Jenny had never seen her look this excited. 'Just dinner, was it?'

'Mrs Cooper. What do you take me for?'

Jenny offered absolution: 'I'm happy for you, really. You deserve some fun.'

Alison gave a grateful smile, knowing it wasn't just her wayward husband Jenny was referring to, but also Harry Marshall, Jenny's predecessor as Severn Vale District Coroner. Twelve months had eased the pain of his sudden passing, but during their five years working alongside each other, Alison had come to idolize him. In an unguarded moment, Alison had confessed that Harry had once tried to seduce her and that she had shied away. She regretted it still, and probably always would.

'I'm afraid there's not much fun in your postbag this morning,' Alison said. 'You might want to read that email first.' She handed a printout across the desk.

It was from Patrick Derwent, the father of the girl who had hanged herself in the Conway Unit. He was angry, and had been moved to write after reading local newspaper reports of the proceedings at Jacobs's inquest. Why was the truth of Jacobs's wholly inappropriate behaviour towards his daughter skimmed over, he asked? It wasn't just a matter of him attempting to subvert her psychiatrist's diagnosis; he had pestered her with his simplistic religious beliefs, plied her with evangelical literature and even forced her to pray with him, promising her that being born again could open the door to her recovery. It was bad enough that all this had been hushed up until after the cursory inquest into his daughter's death. It was unforgivable that it hadn't even been exposed following Jacobs's obvious suicide. Did Deborah Bishop's unit have something else to hide? How many other needless deaths had it contributed to?

'What do you think?' Alison said. 'His wife never mentioned any of that, did she?'

'I'd better talk to the coroner who dealt with Emma Derwent's death.'

'It would have been Mr Rogers. Do you want me to call him?'

'I'll do it.'

As Jenny picked up the phone to call her colleague in Bristol Central, she found herself wondering what it might do to Ceri Jacobs to reopen the wound. Who would it serve to go back and heap more ignominy on her dead husband's name? Weren't some things better left undisturbed?

Nick Rogers was of the curt, ruthlessly businesslike school of coroners, notorious for conducting his inquiries by the letter of the law and with the minimum display of compassion for the bereaved. Jenny secretly suspected the gruff exterior disguised a delicate soul, but Rogers would have scoffed at the notion and accused her of being a bleeding heart.

The girl never complained about Jacobs, Rogers said. As far as he had been able to ascertain, she had merely mentioned the prayer incident to her parents in passing. It wasn't strictly NHS practice, but it was hardly a crime in his book. It was only after the girl had hanged herself that the parents said anything to Deborah Bishop, and it was the first she'd heard of it.

'Did Jacobs give evidence at the inquest?' Jenny asked.

'Oh yes,' Rogers said. 'Poor man was visibly distressed.

He said the prayer incident was all at her request. They got chatting about this and that and she found out he was a believer. As far as I could tell it was all perfectly innocent. There was no doubting she was very sick. She killed herself during a major psychotic episode. I found no reason to suggest that he had contributed to it in any way.'

'The father says he pressed literature on her.'

'I felt he was wrong about that. Jacobs was a Catholic, or trying to be. What Emma Derwent had got hold of was some hardcore evangelical tracts from that bloody great place with posters all over town.'

'The Mission Church of God?'

'That's the one. Jacobs said other kids in the unit had brought it in. It was nothing to do with him.'

'Did you believe him?'

'I had no reason not to.'

Not altogether convinced by Rogers's bluff certainty, Jenny sent Alison to talk to Patrick Derwent. Her mind had moved on to Eva Donaldson. She needed Jacobs laid conclusively to rest.

Michael Turnbull's assistant offered Jenny a meeting with him at five p.m., informing her that he was attending a House of Lords committee all morning and had to chair a Decency board meeting back in Bristol during the afternoon. This was intended to impress, perhaps even to intimidate her; Turnbull's staff seemed to relish their connection with a powerful man. Jenny had read that he shuttled around the country in a helicopter, relentlessly spreading the word like some latterday apostle. His campaign was certainly gathering strength: the latest newspaper polls put public support for the Decency Bill at 74 per cent. Not for nearly two hundred years, the leader writer commented, had the country's mood jolted so radically in a puritanical direction. Why it

had happened was a source of fevered debate. Some claimed
it was a fearful retreat from modernity, others that society
was finally striking a sane balance between permissiveness
and personal responsibility. Jenny was torn on the issue.
The pornography she had seen was crude and brutal, but
she had always believed that censorship, too, bred hypocrisy
and shame.

She had still reached no clear conclusion by the time she
arrived at the Mission Church of God later that afternoon.
School kids, some still dressed in their uniforms, mingled in
friendly groups. Boys and girls were good-naturedly kicking
a football together. There was an atmosphere of reassuring
innocence, a sense of sanctuary, like the embrace of a large
and loving family.

In the lobby more children were sitting at rows of trestle
tables stooped over schoolbooks. A familiar voice called out
to her. The red-haired boy jumped up from one of the far
tables and bounded over. Along with all the others he was
wearing a name badge. His said: Freddy Reardon.

'Hi. How d'you get on with the book?' His fingertips
anxiously gripped the cuffs of his school shirt, his freckled
face bright with excitement.

Jenny couldn't bear to disappoint him. 'I'm going to start
it this evening.'

'You'll be blown away,' Freddy said. 'What happened to
her, it's unbelievable. And when you've finished that one,
you've got to read *Forgiveness*. She wrote that one with
Lennox. You should hear him talk about it – they finished it
in a week. That's not like humanly possible, so it means
those words can only have been coming from one place, you
know what I'm saying?'

'I'll make sure to give it a go.' Jenny smiled, his enthusiasm was infectious. 'So tell me, what's going on here?'

'Evening service is at five-thirty. You don't get in unless you've finished your homework.'

'Wow.' She looked at the children's faces, pictures of concentration, and recalled her nightly battles with Ross, having to drag him from the computer and stand over him like an ogre. 'Everyone's behaving themselves.'

'It makes you feel good,' Freddy said earnestly. 'Everyone here looks out for each other. No one's giving you any trouble.'

'Are you all like this at school?'

Freddy grinned. 'Not really, there's no Lennox Strong at school. I keep telling him he should set one up here. I'd come. It'd be wicked, man.'

Jenny said, 'He's got your respect, huh?'

Freddy said, 'They're gonna have to invent a new word for it. See that kid over there, the one with the Afro? He's at my school. This time last year he was smoking rocks and mugging, pulled a knife on me one time. Now he's in my study group. You want proof, you're looking at it.'

'I'm impressed,' Jenny said. 'And I'll read the book, I promise.'

Freddy beamed, confident he'd closed the deal. 'It'll change your life. Guaranteed. See you around.'

Joel Nelson greeted Jenny with a warm smile and a soft handshake and brought her tea while she waited for the board meeting to finish. The ten or so staff in the slick church offices could have passed for employees in an advertising agency. Young, stylish and quietly efficient, they radiated confidence. Pretending to be absorbed in the latest edition of the church's glossy magazine, Jenny strained to make out the odd muffled exchange that escaped through the closed boardroom door. She gathered they were discussing media relations in the run-up to the parliamentary debate, but the detail eluded her. What she did hear were snatches of Michael Turnbull's rousing final address to his colleagues: 'The public is with us, the newspapers are following and the politicians are being sucked along in their wake. What we've got, ladies and gentlemen, is momentum, and if it keeps building this fast, nothing on God's earth is going to stand in our way.' He was greeted with a burst of applause which prompted the office staff to look up from their desks and smile.

Jenny counted eight board members as they filtered out, upbeat and cheerful. Middle-aged, white, suited, six of them men, they looked a conservative bunch, but their excitement was palpable. Several of their faces were vaguely familiar. They weren't smooth enough to be politicians; Jenny guessed they were businessmen and other professional leaders.

Michael Turnbull came out to meet her, still bathing in the afterglow of a successful meeting. 'Mrs Cooper. Come on in.'

Jenny followed him into the cool, spacious boardroom, where two others were waiting.

'Let me introduce you,' Michael Turnbull said, closing the door behind him. 'This is my wife, Christine, co-founder and treasurer of the Decency campaign, and this is Ed Prince, our chief legal adviser.'

Jenny shook hands and exchanged polite greetings with Lady Turnbull, an elegant, well-spoken woman who, she had gleaned from a profile in the church magazine, was forty-two and the former director of a PR agency. Even in artificial light she didn't look a day over thirty. Jenny's confidence evaporated in the glow of her perfect smile.

'Mrs Cooper.' Ed Prince enclosed her hand in a powerful fist. He was in his late fifties, powerfully built and with a battle-ready glint in his eye. He reminded her of the lawyers she was dealing with in the crane collapse: hardened litigators with a merciless instinct for an opponent's weakness.

'It was Ed's idea that he and Christine sit in, if you don't mind,' Michael said, almost by way of apology.

Prince said, 'Lady Turnbull probably knew Eva better than any of us, and quite frankly I'm here to protect the interests of this campaign.' Ignoring Michael's glance, he pressed on. 'You know, Mrs Cooper, it would be greatly appreciated if you could delay whatever you have to do for a few weeks. The man's pleaded guilty – there's surely nothing more to be said.'

At least she knew what she was dealing with: a bully, and one who thought a provincial coroner would retreat in the face of a big hitter from the City. She felt prickles of perspiration on her back, but her heart wasn't threatening to explode as it often did in the face of unexpected aggression.

Helping herself to a seat, Jenny said, 'I'm sure I won't need to explain coronial procedure to you, Mr Prince, but in case you're not entirely familiar with it, I'll remind you that being an independent judicial officer means what it says. I carry out my inquiries independent of all outside interference or influence. And for the avoidance of doubt, I have had no contact with the media over Miss Donaldson's death, and I intend to keep it that way.'

'That's a little naive, isn't it?' Prince said.

Christine Turnbull interjected. 'Mrs Cooper, you'll understand our anxiety, nearing as we are the end of a multi-million-pound campaign in which Eva was so involved. I suppose what's making us anxious is the thought that something unexpected could come up.' She paused to consider her words carefully. 'I'm sure it won't have escaped your notice that we're threatening a very powerful industry, and not one renowned for its probity.'

Jenny said, 'My concern is to get full information about the circumstances of Miss Donaldson's death. I'd be grateful for your help with a few points.'

Michael Turnbull held up his hand to restrain Prince before he objected. 'Of course. We'll assist in whatever way we can, Mrs Cooper.'

The lawyer frowned, keeping his eyes trained on her as she took a legal pad from her briefcase. She guessed it was he who would have been part of the discussion with Eva's father; the complaint to the Ministry of Justice had probably been his idea. No doubt he was furious that she hadn't been warned off.

Jenny opened her notebook to a page in which she'd jotted some questions. 'This isn't a formal evidence-gathering session,' she emphasized, 'just a chance for me to find out what was going on in Eva's life.'

Prince couldn't help himself. 'Are you seriously entertaining the possibility that it wasn't Craven who murdered her?'

Calmly Jenny said, 'A coroner must entertain whatever possibility the evidence supports.'

Prince gave a dismissive grunt.

Ignoring him, Jenny continued, 'I understand Miss Donaldson had been working for Decency for a little over a year.'

'That's right,' Michael Turnbull replied. 'Though it seemed like a lot longer.'

His wife nodded in agreement.

'What would you say was her chief motivation?'

'She didn't want other women to suffer what she had,' Christine Turnbull answered. 'She wrote at length about it in her two books. There was the simple humanitarian side, the desire to prevent cruelty and exploitation; and there was the spiritual side. She genuinely believed that pornography is an addictive drug, something that destroys moral integrity.'

Jenny said, 'I've no doubt she was committed to the cause, but she was in trouble financially. Were you aware of that?'

Michael Turnbull cut in ahead of his wife. 'I'll be straight with you. This has only come to light since she died. Decency paid her a very reasonable salary, but obviously, if she'd told us how bad things were, we might have tried to offer more help.'

'She wrote to you last November asking for a rise.'

'That's right. Her request was put to the board and it was felt that increasing salaries wasn't the best use of funds. I talked to her about it afterwards: she perfectly understood.'

Michael and Christine Turnbull exchanged a glance, as if there was something they weren't sure should be said.

'Yes – ?' Jenny prompted.

'Of course, we knew the campaign wouldn't go on for ever,' Michael said. 'I'd talked with Eva about what she was planning to do afterwards, and to be honest she was struggling to decide between some quite profound alternatives.'

'Such as?'

'She had become a very committed Christian, but she was also a natural performer,' he said with a fond smile. 'I know she and Lennox, our chief pastor here, talked a lot about her maybe entering the ministry, but she was also attracted to a career as a serious actress. I couldn't tell you if she had made up her mind, but I know what I would have wanted for her.'

'She was a very powerful preacher,' Christine Turnbull added. 'Personally, I think she'd made a decision to minister.'

'And live on what?'

'A very modest wage,' Michael Turnbull said. 'Money can't buy a vocation. Even a well-endowed church like this one has to live by the obvious principles.'

Jenny made a note that Eva was on the horns of a dilemma. Maybe it began to explain the bizarre tattoo? Perhaps 'Daddy's Girl' referred to her relationship with God? It didn't seem the obvious way to express it, but what could she know about the mind of an ex-porn actress?

'How would you describe her state of mind in the weeks before her death?' Jenny asked.

Michael Turnbull gazed at the ceiling for a moment, a trace of sadness, or was it regret, in his expression? 'Like the rest of us she was apprehensive, anxious to succeed. But having become the face of the campaign she probably felt personally responsible in a way the rest of us didn't quite appreciate.'

'You mean she was showing signs of strain?'

'No more than any of us,' Christine Turnbull said. 'I suppose it just bothers all of us that she was at home that Sunday evening, too tired to be here as she usually was. She had been to Manchester and Birmingham and made several radio appearances that weekend.'

Yes, it was regret. Jenny saw it Michael Turnbull's face.

'If there's one thing I should have insisted on,' he said, 'it was that she have full-time security. I offered on several occasions but she always refused. I suppose we all had faith that we'd be looked after. But sometimes one has to stop and remind oneself that we live in a fallen world.'

'Did she receive much negative attention?' Jenny asked.

'Quite the opposite,' Christine Turnbull said. 'We had piles of letters and emails for her every day, from well-wishers all over the world.'

'No threats? She can't have had many admirers in the pornography business.'

'There were a few,' Michael Turnbull said, 'but nothing particularly sinister as far as I'm aware.'

'What about close friends? Was she seeing anyone?'

Husband and wife exchanged a look.

Christine Turnbull shook her head. 'No boyfriend as far as I know. I don't think she had much time for a social life beyond what she had here. You'll have to ask Lennox, he was probably the closest to her of all of us.'

Ed Prince glanced impatiently at his expensive wristwatch, no doubt anxious to get on the phone to the office and hear what they'd come up with to torpedo her.

Jenny said, 'One final thing: her computer. She'd shut down her email in February and there was no sign of her laptop at her house. Do you know what happened to it?'

Ed Prince turned to her. 'All those connected with the campaign were advised to take steps to secure their personal communications. From what I saw of Eva, she was a sensible young woman who would have taken the advice to heart.'

It was Christine Turnbull who showed Jenny to the door. Over the course of their interview, Jenny had gradually warmed to her. She had expected a beautiful woman in what she suspected was a Dior suit to be aloof and judgemental. In fact, Christine gave every impression of being eager to assist and appeared profoundly saddened by Eva's death.

As they parted at the door, Christine Turnbull spoke quietly, 'I'm sorry if we seem agitated, Mrs Cooper. We're nearing the end of a long road, and what happened to Eva . . .' She shook her head, at a loss for words. 'When you see how much good has been achieved you know evil's never going to be far away. Eva was like a light in the darkness, and even though she's not here for us, she's still shining.'

'I can see that,' Jenny said, and bid Christine Turnbull a warm goodbye.

Walking back across the lobby skirting the busy bookshop, Jenny felt the last vestiges of cynicism dissolve. The people browsing the shelves were young, keen and intelligent. They were looking for meaning beyond themselves while most of their peers, her son included, would currently be alone in front of a computer or a TV screen, part of a vast global generation too over-stimulated and self-obsessed to muster any idealism or sense of greater purpose.

She stopped to study the big plasma screen above the closed door to the auditorium. Bobby DeMont and Lennox Strong were laying hands on some teenagers who had come up onto the stage. Lennox was saying, 'In the name of Jesus, we call upon you, Lord, to fill this young man with your spirit, to guide him to do your will and to give him strength to resist temptation.' The kneeling subject rose to his feet and turned to face the audience. It was Freddy.

'Can I tell them something, Lennox?' Freddy said.

'Sure.'

Gripping his cuffs in his clenched fists and rocking up onto his toes with excitement, Freddy addressed the crowd. 'When I first came to this church I was sick. I was drinking, taking drugs, most of the time I didn't know who or where I was. The doctors said I was depressed, but there was nothing they could do to help me . . . I tried to kill myself twice. I mean, *really* tried. All I wanted was for the pain to end. But then a friend told me about this place. No way did I want to come to a church. I thought that's somewhere for old people and weirdos –' Bobby DeMont threw back his head and laughed uproariously – 'but something said to me just try it, just once.' Freddy's face cracked into a grin so wide he could hardly force out the words. 'That day changed my life. When Lennox called for people who were ill or suffering to come to the front, it felt like a hand was guiding me. And when he prayed over me – you know the feeling when you jump off a high diving board? It was like that, only angels caught me in the air. From being in so much pain, I felt like I was flying, I was so *light*, so happy—'

'Here.' Lennox handed Freddy a Kleenex to wipe his streaming eyes. The young congregation cheered.

His voice cracking with emotion, Freddy continued, 'I'd never heard of the Holy Spirit. I hadn't even read the Bible. But from that moment I knew I was saved. That's the power of the spirit. It doesn't matter who you are, it doesn't matter what you've done, just open your heart the tiniest crack and I promise you, it'll come rushing in. And if I can be saved, anyone can.'

Bobby DeMont stepped up to his side and clapped a powerful arm around his narrow shoulders. 'Thank you so much for that, Freddy. You see, folks? God does not judge you on your past sins. Some of the greatest Christians of them all have been evil men, persecutors, slave traders, even murderers. That is the miracle of grace, my friends. When you ask to be born again Jesus lifts that sin from you in the twinkling of an eye.'

'How many of you out there haven't been born again?' Lennox chimed in. He scanned the hands going up in the audience. 'OK. Well, if you people want to change your lives for ever, all you have to do is join me in this prayer.' He pointed a finger to the big screens above the stage. 'Say after me: Dear Lord, I recognize that I am a sinner, and I truly repent . . .'

Jenny turned to see Ed Prince approaching. He stopped alongside her, following her gaze to the screen. The camera picked out individual young men and women earnestly mouthing their prayers of commitment: 'I believe that He is risen from the dead, and I accept Him as my personal Lord and Saviour . . .'

'Are you a believer, Mrs Cooper?' Prince said.

'After a fashion.'

'See all those young black kids, boys who'd have been out with knives, girls who'd have been pregnant? Lennox Strong has led them here like Moses through the wilderness. And the white kids looked up to Eva.'

'I've no intention of harming your good work.'

Focusing his deep-set eyes on her, Prince said, 'Do you know who our greatest enemies are? People who call themselves Christians but don't believe it should be happening like this. You know who I mean?'

Jenny shook her head.

'Oh, I think you do, Mrs Cooper. I think you know perfectly well.' He glanced briefly at the screen – born-again faces overcome with emotion – and headed for the exit.

'Ha-le-lujah!' Bobby DeMont's cry blasted out through the auditorium doors and into the lobby. Freddy Reardon and two young women were convulsing on the floor of the stage.

# TEN

CREEPING THROUGH STOP-START TRAFFIC Jenny checked her answerphone. Alison had called to say she'd spoken to both Patrick Derwent and Deborah Bishop and that Father Starr had been phoning the office badgering for Jenny to get in touch. The only other caller was Steve, saying that he'd found some information about her cousin that she might find interesting. His message sent a shot of panic through her. She dialled his number with clumsy fingers.

'Steve, it's Jenny.'

'Hi,' he said, sounding perfectly relaxed.

'What is it?'

'I dropped into the library at lunchtime and looked up the local newspapers from those dates we turned up.'

'And?' She struggled to control the steering wheel, her palms slippery with sweat.

'You sound like you're driving. Why don't I come round this evening?'

'Where are you now?'

'Just leaving the office.'

'Then meet me in town. Do you know Rico's?'

'Around the corner from your office.'

'I'll be there in ten minutes.' She rang off before he could make any excuse and dialled Alison's number, her heart pressing hard against her ribs.

Alison answered from what sounded like a busy wine bar.

'Hello, Mrs Cooper,' she said agitatedly.

'How did you get on with Derwent?'

'He's adamant Jacobs was trying to convert his daughter, but he hasn't got a lot of evidence. He found the text of a prayer in her belongings that he's convinced Jacobs gave her, and the rest is just suspicion. He says that in the three days she was off the drugs she was experiencing some sort of religious euphoria. He claims he didn't put all the pieces together until he read about Jacobs's death.'

'What sort of prayer was it?'

'One for healing.'

'Catholic?'

'I wouldn't know, but there's no mention of Our Lady.'

'What did Bishop say?'

'No change from her evidence at the inquest. There was no official complaint, and as far as she knew Jacobs never pressed religion on any of his patients. She admitted some pamphlets from the Mission Church of God were found in the reading room, but she didn't think there was a problem. As long as it's not pornographic or racist, the kids are free to read what they like.'

'Do you think she's telling the truth?'

'I couldn't say. To be honest, I don't think she's got much of a clue about what goes on on the shop floor. Her office isn't even in the unit, it's over the other side of the road.'

'I suppose I'd better have another talk with his wife.'

'What for, Mrs Cooper?' Alison said. 'We know what the poor man's problem was. Shouldn't we just leave it at that?'

Jenny considered the prospect of knocking on Ceri Jacobs's door once more and felt her determination to dig out every last grain of truth quickly fade. In the weeks before his death Alan Jacobs was clearly upset and confused; the pressure cooker was starting to blow. Even if she could place every event in sequence they might not add up to a logical picture. All she would have achieved would be yet more agony for his humiliated widow.

'Maybe you're right,' Jenny said. 'What would it achieve?'

'You've done all you can,' Alison said, sounding relieved, and anxious to end the call. She had rung off before Jenny had a chance to ask what Father Starr wanted, but he could wait. There was something far more daunting about to confront her.

Steve was waiting for her at a table in the little cobbled yard at the back of the cafe, where you could smoke a cigarette with your cold beer and tapas. Despite the warm evening they were the only ones sitting outside. Jenny was glad they were alone. She felt fragile enough without having to worry about who might be listening. If she hadn't been so on edge it would have made for a pleasant date: gentle samba music playing on the stereo and Otavio the handsome waiter treating her like a princess.

'You didn't tell me you were going to dig around in my past,' Jenny said, reaching for Steve's tobacco tin and helping herself. One of these days he would decide he could afford cigarettes that came in a packet.

'It was almost an accident.'

'Yeah, right,' Jenny said.

He unbuckled his briefcase and brought out a handful of photocopied newspaper articles.

'They're from the *Weston Mercury*, October 1972.' He looked at her hesitantly. 'Do you want to see or not?'

'Give them to me,' Jenny insisted.

The first headline read: *Girl Dies in Fall*. In three short paragraphs the article stated that five-year-old Katy Chilcott had been killed in an accidental fall down the stairs of the family home at Pretoria Road. Her parents, named James and Penny Chilcott, were said to be being comforted by relatives.

Feeling numb, Jenny quickly turned to the next article. A photograph of her father in his early thirties sat beneath the words, 'Weston Man Questioned Over Girl's Death'.

*Following the death last Thursday of five-year-old Katy Chilcott in what was initially thought to be a tragic accident, detectives yesterday arrested the dead girl's uncle, Brian Chilcott.*

*The owner of Chilcott Motors was taken from his home on Sunday afternoon and is believed to have spent the evening helping officers with their enquiries. He was later released on police bail. Detectives are said to be awaiting the results of a post-mortem examination.*

*Neighbours of the dead girl's family saw Chilcott arrive at the address at approximately 5 p.m. on Thursday afternoon. Shouting was afterwards heard coming from inside the premises. Chilcott was seen leaving with a young child believed to be his daughter shortly before an ambulance arrived.*

*A hospital spokesman said that Katy Chilcott died as a result of 'significant trauma' to the head.*

'Does it bring anything back?'

'The arrest bit does. It's what I was remembering with Dr Allen.'

'What about what happened inside the house?'

Jenny shook her head. It was a blank.

She looked at the final article. It was dated Friday, 24 November. Under the headline, *Girl's Death Ruled Accidental*, was a brief report of the coroner's finding that Katy had died as a result of falling down the stairs at the family home, striking her head on the tiled floor. The coroner, Mr C. R.

Benedict, was quoted as saying, 'Katy's death was a tragic and sadly unavoidable accident to which no blame can be attached.'

'What is it?' Steve asked.

Jenny shrugged, placing the articles back on the table.

'There's something. I can tell.'

'It's Dad, I suppose.' She tried to untangle the knot of emotions that had been disguised by her initial shock.

'What about him?'

'He could have quite a temper. I can remember him smacking me, the look on his face, more than angry, enraged.' She drew on her cigarette, assailed by fragments of long-forgotten memory: her father erupting at a spilled glass of milk and a sharp slap on the legs; his face, boiling red, yelling at her mother, the sound of her shriek as he hit her, her sobbing as he thundered down the stairs and crashed out through the front door.

'You look tired,' Steve said. 'Shall I drive you home?'

Jenny didn't answer. She was remembering the helpless, terrified feeling her father's fury stirred in her. Even as a small child she had intuited that it came from somewhere deep within him, a place neither she nor her mother could reach.

'Jenny? Why don't we get the bill? We'll pick something up and cook at your place.'

She shook her head.

'You've got to eat. You look like a ghost.'

'I'm going to see my dad.' She stood up from the table, grabbing the photocopies and stuffing them into her handbag.

'Now? Isn't it a bit late?'

'He doesn't care what time it is. He doesn't even know.'

'Jenny, I really don't think—'

'You started it.'

She marched inside, making for the exit. Steve chased after her, grabbing her arm. Otavio looked round from tapping an order into the till.

'Jenny, please.'

She turned, sharply. 'What do you expect me to do?'

'At least let me come with you.'

Brian Chilcott had been confined to the nursing home in Weston-super-Mare for nearly five years. When Alzheimer's struck in his late sixties, his second wife left even more quickly than she had arrived. 'What would I be staying *for*?' she said to Jenny. 'He's not my Brian any more, but he'll always be your father.'

It was the time of the evening when the elderly residents of the home were being given their night-time sedatives and hoisted into bed. With Steve in tow, Jenny passed along the carpeted corridor that smelled of urine, disinfectant and cold tea, catching nightmarish glimpses of decrepitude through semi-open doors.

Her father's door was shut. Jenny paused to gather strength.

Steve put a hand on her shoulder. 'You don't have to do this.'

'I do.' She reached up to touch his fingers. 'Come in with me.'

'You're sure?'

'For me. He won't know who you are.'

She pushed open the door and found her father propped up in bed, wearing bright blue pyjamas buttoned all the way up to the neck. For once the television was silent. A magazine lay open but untouched on his lap.

'Hello, Dad,' Jenny said quietly.

The old man, seventy-four years old and as strong as a carthorse, turned to look at them, but said nothing.

'Dad, you know me, don't you? It's Jenny?'

He stared at her blankly, seeming to focus on the wall behind her.

Steve sat on the arm of the stiff-backed armchair in which Brian spent most of his waking hours. 'Hello, Mr Chilcott. I'm Steve. Pleased to meet you.'

Brian appeared to respond. His eyes moved briefly to Steve's face before travelling to Jenny. She thought she detected a faint hint of recognition.

'I'm sorry it's been such a long time. I've been busy,' Jenny said, adding the lie: 'Ross sends his love.'

Brian turned his gaze back to Steve.

'That's not Ross. That's my friend, Steve. There's Ross.' She pointed to one of the few framed family photographs arranged on the shelf at the far end of the bed: Ross aged fourteen, posing with a surfboard on a Cornish beach.

There was a long moment of silence. Brian seemed to lose concentration and drift back to wherever he had come from.

'Dad—'

No answer.

Jenny was beginning to abandon hope, when her father said, 'He's the spit of me, that boy, and trouble with it.' He smiled.

It was a phrase he'd coined long ago, but at least it was something. The nurses had told her there were days, even weeks, during which he said nothing at all. But on some days he would bellow obscenities and hurl his belongings around the room without provocation. There was no pattern to his behaviour. His ex-wife was right, Jenny thought, he wasn't himself any more, so much so that she scarcely connected him with the man who, after her mother had left, had brought her up single-handedly from the age of twelve.

She reached into her handbag. 'Dad, I want to show you something.'

Steve shot her a look, losing his nerve now that he was confronted with the reality.

Ignoring him, she produced the crumpled photocopies and smoothed them out on the blankets.

'You remember last time I was here I asked you about Katy – Jim and Penny's little girl? I want to know what happened to her.'

She held the first article in front of him. 'The newspapers said she died falling down the stairs. You must remember that.'

'He's got a man's shoulders, that boy. He'll be a strong 'un. We worked on the trawlers when we were lads.'

'Please,' Jenny said. 'I need to know. Look.' She held up the article bearing his picture. 'The police took you in. They came to get you from our house, I remember. I was outside in the street and they took you away in their car.'

Brian appeared to look at the article and study it. There was nothing wrong with his eyes. He'd never had glasses, not even for reading.

'They thought you'd hurt her. You were at Jim and Penny's house before the ambulance came. There was a row, the neighbours heard it. Please, Dad. Try.'

The dim lights in his eyes went out. He yawned and tugged awkwardly at the pillow that was keeping him upright.

'Dad, wake up,' Jenny said urgently, and thrust the third article under his nose. 'They said it was an accident. She fell down the stairs and hit her head. Why didn't you ever talk about it? Why didn't anyone ever tell me about her?'

The old man batted her hand away. Sensing that she was getting through to him, Jenny persisted. 'You called me Smiler – do you remember? Do you remember the swing in the garden? You used to push me. I remember that.'

Her father grabbed a handful of blankets and brought them tight up under his chin.

'I think maybe that's enough,' Steve said.

'You can understand, can't you, Dad? I know you can. You wouldn't forget a thing like that.'

He closed his eyes, a sound somewhere between a sigh and a groan escaping from his depths.

Jenny shook him by the shoulder. 'Dad, tell me.'

Steve got up from his chair. 'Jenny—'

Suddenly her father snapped out a hand and seized Jenny's wrist with an iron grip that her made her cry out in pain.

'Stop that.' She tried to prise his fingers away. 'Steve, help me.'

'You know the deal, Smiler. You keep my secret, I'll keep yours.'

'What do you mean? Dad?'

He slackened his grip, a lost, bewildered expression taking the place of the anger that had briefly contorted his face. Sucked back into the void, he was an empty shell again. If there was a fate worse than death, Jenny thought, it had come to her father.

# ELEVEN

JENNY WOKE LATE, the alarm clock telling her it was nearly eight-thirty. Leaden, she hauled herself out of bed, vaguely recalling Steve leaving shortly after daybreak, kissing her cheek as she had drifted back into sleep. As the fog cleared she remembered they had been talking until nearly three, Steve trying to convince her that if anyone had a sinister connection with Katy's death it was almost certain to be her father. He had been impressive, piecing together the evidence like a criminal lawyer, almost persuading her that Brian was responsible for the year-long gap in her childhood memory. He wanted to hide something, Steve said, and he's terrified you into hiding it too.

'Like what?' she had asked.

Steve had answered with a look. He didn't have to spell it out.

She had always rejected the idea that her father had molested her. Her feelings towards him weren't hostile or ambiguous enough; and she could swear that nothing had happened during the years when they had lived alone together, her mother having fled with her Jaguar-driving lover. Yet if he had, the dark dreams that had haunted her for so many years would make perfect sense: the ominous crack opening in the corner of the bedroom in her family home, the unseen, malevolent presence that lurked in the darkness beyond. She almost wished it were true.

Steve had pressed her to make another appointment with Dr Allen. It was her moment finally to drag the memories from her subconscious while the door was still open, he had said. She had resisted, pretending to him that she couldn't face it while she was so busy at work, too afraid to admit the full extent of her terror. Not only was she frightened of falling into a place from which she would never escape, but she feared that the truth might reveal her as a monster from whom Steve would recoil.

She staggered to the window and drew back the curtains to reveal a perfect deep-blue sky. A pair of buzzards circled above the oak woods opposite; to the right of the cottage the patchwork of meadows and copses that sloped all the way down to the Wye was a vision of Eden. It's all there for you, Steve would have said, you just have to reach out and take it.

The phone disrupted her moment of tranquillity. She stumbled stiffly down the narrow stairs to answer it in the study.

'Oh, you're still there, Mrs Cooper,' Alison said with mock surprise. 'I only tried you at home to make sure. I thought you'd be over the bridge by now.'

'I've been catching up here where it's quiet,' Jenny said, in a voice still thick with sleep.

'If it's quiet you want, I should stay at home. Father Starr's on the warpath. He's insisting on speaking to you. I've got his number.'

'What about?'

'Do you think I didn't ask him?'

Jenny's call was answered by an elderly, austere-sounding priest. She could hear several male voices in the background and footsteps on wooden floors. Father Starr took a long time to come to the phone and spoke to her curtly. Could she please meet him at Clifton Cathedral, he asked.

'Can you tell me what this is about?'

'I'm afraid not.'

'I see. Don't you think some indication would be courteous?'

'Please grant me this one interview, Mrs Cooper. I would be most grateful.'

Each year, as summer reached its zenith, there were a handful of days during which the Wye valley radiated such transcendent beauty that it was impossible not to be inspired to a vision of a clear and uncomplicated future. Meandering through the graceful corridors of beeches that reached out and touched each other over the five miles of road between the villages of Tintern and St Arvans, Jenny felt her spirits lift. The sun spiking through the branches brought a simple, brilliant thought: she could rise above the tribulations of her past, and set her own parameters. It didn't need prayer or divine intervention; she could choose, right here and now, to take control.

She could begin with Starr. He was an obsessive who couldn't believe one of his converts capable of murder. He was manipulative, too, taunting her with mention of Alec McAvoy. It wasn't hard to understand his motive. And who but an egotist with fragile self-esteem could spend his life ministering to a captive audience of prisoners for whom the Church offered the only viable prospect of hope? A multitude of inadequacies could hide behind the priestly mask. She resolved to leave him in no doubt about what she thought – that he was wrong about Craven.

Father Starr was waiting impatiently on the steps of the brutally arresting modern cathedral. Built in the early 1970s largely of concrete, its three-pronged spire seemed to jab accusingly at the sky: a monument to the hubristic century that had created it, demanding rather than inspiring awe. Jacketless, a short-sleeved clerical shirt hugged his lean frame.

'Good morning, Mrs Cooper.' He didn't offer his hand. 'It's a little too hot to talk out here, don't you think?'

Without waiting for her answer, he turned and led the way through the cathedral's glass doors into an interior which, if it hadn't been for the abstract mosaics of stained glass, struck Jenny as having all the magic of an airport terminal. Vast concrete beams welded the building's pre-cast sections together. The altar stood beneath a hexagonal concrete dome of which even Calvin might have approved.

'You don't appreciate the modernist architecture?' Starr said, reading her thoughts.

'No,' Jenny said, determined to follow through on her resolve.

'I try,' Starr said, with a suggestion of a smile. 'And invariably fail.'

He nodded to the altar, crossed himself, and directed her to the end of one of the many rows of chairs that substituted for pews.

'I think the architect's idea was to allow for purity of thought,' he said. 'In that, at least, I feel he succeeded.'

Jenny was about to ask him what was so urgent that couldn't wait, when she realized his small talk was veiling a silent prayer. His eyes were focused inwards, his folded hands perfectly still.

After a moment's meditation he said, 'I would usually be performing my duties at the prison on a weekday, but apparently I have been the cause of complaints. I have been asked to hand over my responsibilities to another priest.'

'Complaints from whom?'

'Two prisoners is all I have been told. Their identities have not been disclosed to me, of course. That would allow me to defend myself, which would never do.'

His sudden bitter tone surprised her. It was that of a man unused to rejection.

'Have you been told the substance of the complaints?'

'The governor informs me that I have exerted "indecent ideological pressure" on certain prisoners, thereby offending their freedom of conscience.'

'Have you?'

Starr shook his head. 'Never. I offer myself to prisoners to talk, that's all. To force myself on them would be anathema. My order's way is always to lead by example. If others see you have something they wish to possess, they will make the approach. In truth, Mrs Cooper, I am bewildered. Five years in La Modela, every day in the presence of evil, and not a single word of complaint.'

'You must have some clue what prompted this.'

'I have a suspicion, but I'm afraid you'll accuse me of being paranoid.' He turned to look at her, the first time she had seen genuine humility in him. 'Believe me, I'm not prone to conspiracy theories, but these complaints mean I can no longer contact Paul Craven. I fear for him. His behaviour has become erratic, his thoughts disjointed. I had become the one person whom he could trust.'

'You think the complaints against you were manufactured?'

'I hesitate to believe that—' He checked himself and gazed at the altar.

'But you do?' Jenny said. 'Who does this benefit? I thought priests were welcomed by prisons.'

'It may be a perfectly valid grievance,' Starr said, in an effort to convince himself, 'but I suppose there may be some who would like to see me discredited. A priest suspended from his post for browbeating doesn't make the most compelling witness at an inquest, for example.'

'I wouldn't pay it much attention,' Jenny said. 'Besides, any evidence you gave would hardly be critical.'

'But the allegations can be put, and repeated in the press. I will be called a zealot and my belief in Craven dismissed as delusional.'

Jenny thought of Ed Prince's parting words at the Mission Church the previous afternoon: his sly allusion to those Christians who didn't like the way his clients conducted themselves. She'd guessed he was referring to Starr, but in the turmoil of the evening she had left her thoughts half-formed. Was Prince implying that the priest had an agenda beyond exonerating Craven? She had come intending to tell Starr she couldn't help him, but he had headed her off and was dragging her into the mire.

Be direct, that was the only way. Hit him with the hard questions now and gauge his response. A would-be Jesuit couldn't deny the power of logic. If all he had to offer was blind faith in Craven with no facts to back it up, she could let him down with a clear conscience.

'Let me ask you something, Father,' Jenny said. 'What do you make of Eva Donaldson?'

'In what sense?'

'Her life story. Her conversion. What she represented in a spiritual sense.'

He gave her a sideways glance, reading her with eyes from which there was no hiding place. 'Are you asking me if I believe God was working through her?'

'If you like.'

'And whether I approve of her church?'

'You couldn't be much further apart,' Jenny said.

'Protestants forget we have "phenomena", too. But we subject them to scrutiny. The Catholic Church treats the experience of a solitary individual with caution. Doctrine, scripture and the accumulated wisdom of two thousand years must all play their part in discerning truth.'

'You're sceptical about her.'

'What would you expect?' He smiled. 'But just as for you there is only truth and untruth, for me there is only that which is from God, and that which is not. I am touched by Miss Donaldson's story, but I am also aware that human beings can generate a level of collective emotion that apes the action of the Holy Spirit. You can experience it in a football crowd – the collective surge of passion that physically lifts the exhausted player.'

'Football crowds don't reform young criminals or eradicate pornography.'

'I don't believe anyone has ever asked them to.'

'Have you been to the Mission Church? What they're achieving with children is very moving.'

'God isn't sentimental, Mrs Cooper: consider what happened to his son. We all enjoy interludes of happiness, but it's through our suffering that we progress.'

'All I have to offer is unrelenting pain and hardship—'

'I beg your pardon.'

'Captain Bligh. You must have seen *The Bounty*?'

'I don't believe I have.'

'It's the line he uses to entice loyal men to join him when the mutineers cast him adrift.'

'And does he prevail?'

'Yes. He survives and the mutineers become marooned in a paradise that turns into a hell.'

Starr nodded in amused approval. 'I must watch it. But I can assure you, no matter what you may have heard, I've no desire to persecute a crew of mutineers. My concern is purely for Paul Craven, and of course the truth.'

'What makes you so certain he's innocent? It must be something more than what he tells you.'

Starr said, 'You're impatient with me, Mrs Cooper.'

'Do you blame me?'

'What if I were to tell you that I had had a "word"?'

'God spoke to you?' Jenny said.

'If you wish.'

'And that's why I should put my neck on the line? The Ministry of Justice are already piling the pressure on me to steer clear.'

'You've rowed against the tide before. Alec McAvoy told me himself.'

'Can you please not mention him again?'

Father Starr persisted. 'I'm appealing to your conscience, Mrs Cooper. Something is not right.'

Jenny shot up from her chair and turned to face him. 'Do you know what I think? I think you're reading all sorts of things into this that don't exist. You're dramatizing, casting yourself in the middle of some imaginary struggle between good and evil, when the simple truth is Craven killed her.'

She started off across the stone floor, the click of her heels ricocheting like bullets off the cathedral's unadorned walls.

Starr jumped up and pursued her. 'Mrs Cooper—'

She kept on walking. 'I'm sorry, but I can't be used this way.'

He came alongside and reached into his shirt pocket. 'Please. I didn't know whether to show you this.' He brought out a folded piece of paper. 'I still don't.' There was anguish in his voice. 'Really, I've prayed, but I've no idea what's right.'

Jenny came to a reluctant halt. Avoiding her gaze, Starr handed her the single sheet.

'I've heard Eva Donaldson was friendly with a boy,' Starr said. He swallowed a guilty lump in his throat. 'His name's Frederick Reardon.'

'I've met him,' Jenny said. 'What of it?'

'He's got a violent past.'

She looked at the unfolded document. It was a standard printout from the Criminal Records Bureau. Two convictions were listed beneath Freddy Reardon's name. Both were on the same date a little over two years ago: possession of an offensive weapon and assault occasioning actual bodily harm.

'Where did you get this?' Jenny said.

'That I can't say,' Starr said.

'How did you know about Freddy?'

Starr shook his head. 'I didn't. This was given to me.'

'What's going on? Who's doing this?' Jenny demanded.

'I've told you all I can,' Starr said. 'Make of it what you will.'

With a look that told her his loyalties lay to a far higher authority than hers, he said a hurried goodbye and walked quickly away.

'He's playing games with you, Mrs Cooper,' was Alison's blunt assessment.

'Why would he?'

'He's a fanatic. Plausible, but the maddest people often are.'

'How would you get hold of a criminal record? It's not an employer's copy, it's come out of a Crown Prosecution Service file.'

'Maybe he's using a private investigator. A lot of my old colleagues from CID have gone that route. I dare say they could tickle up a few contacts in the CPS if they needed to.'

'He hasn't got the money, he's a penniless priest.'

'But think what he's got behind him.' Alison handed back the criminal record with a dismissive frown.

'I can't see why the Catholic Church would go out on a limb for a convicted murderer.'

'It's not about him, is it?' Alison said. 'Priests are like politicians, they tell you what you want to hear. With his own kind, I guarantee all the talk will be of false prophets and wolves in sheep's clothing. Every night when he flogs himself, your Father Starr will be praying for the Mission Church of God to be torn to the ground.'

Jenny said, 'Before I saw this, I'd made up my mind to certify cause of death and close the file.'

Alison gave her the sort of pitying look that could only come from an ex-detective who believed she had seen it all. 'Sometimes I think not even you know what drives you.'

# TWELVE

Eva Donaldson had dialled only six different numbers in the final fortnight of her life. Ringing each in turn, Alison established that they were Decency's Bristol and London offices, Michael Turnbull and Lennox Strong's direct lines, the Mission Church of God's main switchboard and Freddy Reardon's mobile. She had called Freddy five times in eight days, but she had spoken to Lennox Strong only twice.

Protocol dictated that Jenny should have sent Alison to interview a potential witness, but there were occasions, and this was one of them, in which she couldn't entirely trust her officer to put her prejudice aside. She told herself it was an exploratory visit, that she was approaching Freddy merely for background information. It was stretching the rules to their outer limits, and as she parked beneath the tower blocks of the Langan Estate she stopped to reconsider. Who was she doing this for? Was it really for Eva? Did she actually need to be here or was she allowing herself to be bullied by Starr? She stared through the windscreen at a carrier bag drifting across a scrubby patch of grass littered with crushed tins and broken glass and hoped for an answer. None came.

It was an image of McAvoy which formed behind her eyes. She pictured his face the day she confronted him in the courtroom, at the moment he confessed his fear of what, or more precisely the one, he had called the 'author of all this sadness'. He had managed at one and the same time to be both a wicked and a good man who feared for his soul. During the months since he had gone, Jenny had scarcely dared acknowledge the fact that their coming together had been something far more than mere sex could consummate. Without exchanging a word, they had both known that she was offering him a route to redemption and he was doing the same for her. It might have happened, only in wringing out the truth he had killed a man, and then thrown himself into purgatory, leaving her to face the conclusion alone.

The lift that took her to the fifteenth floor of the Molyneux Tower was plastered with obscene graffiti and smelled so overpoweringly of ammonia that it burnt her nostrils during its painfully slow ascent. Bursting out of the doors, Jenny found herself looking down a long, noisy corridor. As she made her way along its full length to number 28, she was assailed by the sound of domestic arguments, barking dogs and the heavy thump of bass permeating the flimsy apartment walls.

The woman who eventually shuffled to the door and half-opened it looked old enough to be Freddy's grandmother. Eileen Reardon was heavily overweight with unkempt greying hair that straggled to her shoulders. A loose, kaftan-style dress did little to disguise her bulk. Around her swollen neck she wore a pewter Celtic cross.

'Mrs Reardon?'

The woman peered at her suspiciously.

'Jenny Cooper. Severn Vale District Coroner. I called earlier—'

'Freddy's not back yet.' She looked Jenny up and down. 'I suppose you want to come in.'

'If you wouldn't mind.'

Mrs Reardon moved back along the small, stuffy hallway. Jenny followed her into a dingy living room. The only natural light was the little that leaked around the edges of shabby, tie-dyed drapes tacked permanently over the windows. Two mismatched sofas smothered in cheap ethnic throws were arranged on either side of a low table. The air was stale with the smell of Indian incense and cigarette smoke. Jenny had the feeling that Mrs Reardon spent most of her waking hours in this room.

'Would you like some coffee?' Mrs Reardon asked.

Jenny eyed a collection of filthy mugs sitting next to a grubby ashtray. 'No thanks. I'm fine.'

She took a seat and noticed her host's badly swollen ankles and the wheezing sounds she made as she lowered herself onto the sofa opposite. A heart condition, Jenny thought, and wondered if Mrs Reardon was even aware that she was ill.

'You want to talk to him about this girl, do you?' Eileen Reardon asked in a manner which suggested that she didn't approve of Eva Donaldson.

'Yes. Did you know her?'

'No,' she said, as if the idea was ridiculous. 'I don't go in for any of that.'

'Church, you mean?'

'All that puritanical stuff. I ask you, who cares? She regretted her past – so what? So do lots of us.' She gave a self-conscious laugh.

'She seemed to have a lot of time for Freddy.'

'He's that sort of boy, friends with everyone.'

Jenny glanced at a rickety set of bamboo bookshelves jumbled with books on the New Age: titles on crystals, auras and chakra healing.

'I know,' Mrs Reardon said, following her gaze, 'Freddy and I aren't exactly peas in a pod, are we? I'm afraid I haven't read the Bible since I was at school, if I ever did then.' She shrugged. 'Whatever works for you, I suppose.'

'How did Freddy get involved with the Mission Church?' Jenny asked as innocently as she could. 'I've got a son almost the same age, I can't imagine how it happens.'

'I don't remember,' Eileen said dismissively, 'probably someone at school. It seems to be a bit of a craze – a weird one, but I suppose that's the point. You don't rebel by doing something your parents would like.'

'You don't quite approve.'

'It's not the only way people get better, I know that much.'

'I'll confess, I was there yesterday. I saw him speaking. He gave the impression that he as good as owed his life to the church.'

'I was helping him, too,' Mrs Reardon said defensively. 'I'd been giving him healing for three years. They can't take all the credit.'

'He said he'd been suffering from depression.'

Mrs Reardon shifted her large mass uncomfortably beneath her. 'You can give it a label if you like. I don't put much store by doctors, personally, especially psychiatrists.'

Jenny gave an understanding nod, hoping she would tell her more. It worked.

'Freddy lost his father when he was younger and didn't get on with the man I was with,' Mrs Reardon said. 'But once the quacks get their claws into you it's hard to escape. I never wanted him in hospital but you're just the parent, you don't count for anything.'

Becoming agitated, she heaved herself to her feet. 'Where is he? He said he'd be here by now.' She produced a cordless phone from amidst a heap of clutter on the table and dialled his number.

'Freddy, it's Mum. Where are you? She's here, waiting for

you.' She sighed. 'I don't care, it's up to you. Please yourself. All right, I will.' She stabbed the off button with a puffy finger.

'Is everything all right?'

'He doesn't want to talk to you in front of me.'

'I don't want to force him.'

Mrs Reardon was quiet for a moment, then suddenly flared. 'How about telling me what the hell it is you want from him?'

'He was one of the people Eva spoke to a lot before she died. I just want to know what she said.'

'I'm not stupid. He was at church the night she was killed, we went through all that with the police. He's only a boy – why can't you people leave him alone?'

'I'm sorry. I didn't mean—'

'He's got nothing to say to you. He's had enough trouble without you stirring it all up.'

Jenny wondered if it was Freddy or his mother who was the more fragile. Her face was beetroot; she laboured for every breath.

Deciding there was nothing to be gained by imposing herself, Jenny said goodbye and let herself out.

She could tell it was Freddy skulking on the bench at the far end of the stretch of grass, even though from this distance all she could see was a shadowy outline, stooped forwards staring at the ground. She hesitated, in two minds whether to disturb him. She was tempted not to upset his delicate equilibrium, but the mother in her wouldn't let her leave him looking so pathetic. She had to make contact, if only to offer some reassurance. She approached slowly, picking her way around the broken beer bottles, giving him every chance to retreat, but he wanted her to come, she could feel it.

'Hi, Freddy.'

He was silent for a moment, then said, 'I told them. I didn't touch her. I didn't even know where she lived.'

'Of course,' she said gently. 'It's hard to explain how I'm different from the police, but I am, very. My job is to find out how someone died.'

'She was stabbed by a nutter.'

'It certainly looks that way, but I have to make sure all the facts are known. I don't feel the police asked all the questions that needed to be asked. That's why I'm talking to people who knew her, people like you who knew what was going on in her life before she died.'

'Nothing was going on,' Freddy said.

'Do you want to tell me what you talked about on the phone? She called you a few times in her last week.'

'I was in her study group. We talked about that, how the new people were doing.'

'Did you ever discuss anything else? Did she talk to you about her life outside the church?'

Freddy shook his head.

Jenny could see why Eva might have taken him under her wing. Any thoughts she had entertained of a sordid connection between them dispelled. He was like a much younger child at the mercy of his moods, trusting and easily hurt.

'I get the feeling she was very precious to you,' Jenny said.

'It wasn't easy for her. People treated her like some sort of saint, but she was only human. She had feelings like everyone else.'

'What do you mean?'

'She got tired and depressed sometimes, but that's what your friends are for. Eva prayed for me when I first went to church and I prayed for her.'

'What did she get depressed about?'

'All the work she had to do, what people expected of her.'

'She talked to you about that – the demands of her work?'

'Sometimes. It wasn't that big a deal. She was tough. Tougher than most people.'

Jenny wondered why Eva would choose a vulnerable teenage boy as a confidant, and presumed it was because she felt unthreatened by him. Michael Turnbull and his immediate colleagues were educated and successful. No matter how high her media profile, Eva would always have felt their inferior. Even the most pious would have seen her as the ex-porn star.

'Freddy, do you think she was in any sort of trouble? Was anyone threatening or hassling her?'

'She never said anything.'

'She didn't get any problems from people who knew her from before?'

'She never talked about that,' Freddy snapped. 'When you're born again, that's it, you're changed for ever. There's no need to go over the past. Your sins are taken away. The Holy Spirit drives out the bad spirits, that's the whole point.'

Jenny nodded, longing to put a comforting arm around him.

'That's what her book's about.' He looked at her with wounded, accusing eyes. 'I bet you haven't even read it.'

'I've started,' Jenny lied.

She could see he didn't believe her. 'You might learn something,' he said. 'God changes people. Not just a little bit, completely. And for ever. All you have to do is let him.'

His heartfelt belief made her feel doubly deceitful. The idea that Freddy's closeness to Eva had tipped into a frenzy of murderous emotion seemed absurd; she despised Father Starr

178

for having planted the poison in her mind. He was worse than a sly detective, moving in the shadows, forming baseless theories to suit his prejudice, not even man enough to tell her where he was getting his grubby information from.

Jenny said, 'Freddy, I'm going to be straight with you. I may have to call you as a witness at my inquest. I know how much you've changed since going to church, but the fact that you've a criminal record will come out. I'm just preparing you for that.'

Freddy shrugged. 'I waved a knife at my stepdad. It was stupid, but so was he. I told the police he did far worse to Mum, but they weren't interested in that.'

'I see you got a supervision order.'

A hint of a smile lifted the corners of his mouth. 'It's like Eva said, it was all part of God's plan.'

'What happened?'

'The social worker took me to a psychiatrist and put me in hospital. They said I was psychotic. Maybe I was.' He looked at her with the same bright expression with which he'd greeted her the first time they had met. 'The doctor told my mum I could be on pills for the rest of my life. You should have seen his face after Lennox had prayed for me. He wouldn't believe it. He said it must have been my hormones or something. I haven't had pills for over a year. I don't need them any more. I've got peace of mind.'

'Which hospital was it?'

Freddy paused, a hint of suspicion in his eyes. 'What do you want to know that for?'

The rock returned to Jenny's throat, bigger than ever.

'Was it the Conway Unit?'

'Might have been.'

'And was there a nurse called Alan Jacobs there?'

Freddy was quiet for a moment. 'He was one of them.'

'Was it him who told you about the Mission Church?'

'No. He had nothing to do with it. I thought you said you weren't like the police. I've had enough of this. You people are all the same.'

He shot up from the bench and took off across the grass.

'Freddy—'

He broke into a run and didn't look back.

It had been there all along. Buried in the police files was a rough photocopy of a barely legible handwritten list entitled, 'Persons spoken to informally'. All the big names at the Mission Church of God were listed: Bobby DeMont, Michael and Christine Turnbull, Lennox Strong, Joel Nelson, and more than twenty others. Two-thirds of the way down she made out Frederick Reardon and, a little further on, Alan Jacobs.

Jenny had called DI Goodison, who made no attempt to disguise his annoyance at being troubled by her a second time. He had had a team of five detectives going through the church, he said. In the two day after Eva's death they spoke to whoever they could find who had been associated with her. They stopped when they did because Craven had come forward and confessed. There was no particular significance in the names on the list.

'But are they all people connected with the Mission Church?' Jenny had asked.

'As far as I recall,' Goodison answered, and made his excuses. He was far too busy to waste his time on a nit-picking coroner.

She had tried DI Wallace, but he was no more forthcoming. There was no evidence of any connection between Jacobs and the Mission Church, he said dismissively, and even if there was, it would do nothing to shake his belief that Jacobs had killed himself.

The two policemen probably occupied next-door offices,

but might as well have inhabited separate continents. Each had their own teams and caseloads and seemed to run their fiefdoms with no interest in their colleagues except in beating them to their clear-up targets. In the race for results, the truth was an inevitable casualty.

The prospect of meeting Mrs Jacobs again filled Jenny with a dread she could only suppress with another Xanax. The one mercy was that the widow had insisted on coming to see her at her office rather than have her daughter's routine disrupted by the appearance of another sombre stranger. She arrived a little after five, but when Alison brought her in, it was with a companion. Jenny recognized him as the priest who had sat at the back of the inquest.

'Good afternoon, Mrs Cooper,' Ceri Jacobs said stiffly. 'This is Father Dermody from St Xavier's. I asked if he'd come with me. I trust you don't have a problem with that.'

'I've no objection,' Jenny said.

'I'm very grateful to you, Mrs Cooper,' Father Dermody said, and gave a kindly smile as he shook her hand.

The widow and her priest settled into their chairs as much at ease with each other as man and wife. Jenny observed their exchange of glances and decided that Ceri Jacobs trusted him more than she trusted herself.

'I'm sorry to trouble you again, Mrs Jacobs,' Jenny said, 'but it's not so much your husband's death I need to ask you about, as what he may, or may not, have known about someone else's. I presume you've heard of Eva Donaldson.'

Ceri glanced nervously at Father Dermody, who answered for her. 'Of course we have. What about her?'

Jenny opened a file and extracted the list. She passed it across the desk, placing it between them.

'After she was killed the police informally questioned a

number of people at the Mission Church of God who had been in contact with her. You'll see your husband's name appears on it, towards the bottom of the page.'

Ceri Jacobs shook her head. 'I don't know anything about this.'

Jenny said, 'I'll try to find out which detective it was who spoke to him, but I was wondering if he said anything about this to you.'

'No.'

Father Dermody frowned. 'Where would this questioning have taken place?'

'If wasn't at your home, Mrs Jacobs, then I assume it was at your husband's workplace, or perhaps at the Mission Church itself.'

'Why would he have been there?' Mrs Jacobs said with a note of panic.

Jenny said, 'I'm conducting an inquiry into Miss Donaldson's death. Since the inquest into your husband's death there have been several separate indications that he was connected with the Mission Church in some way—'

'He bought one book, that's all,' Mrs Jacobs protested. 'He didn't go to that church, he went to St Xavier's.' She appealed to her priest. 'Father, tell her.'

'He was with us every Wednesday evening, Mrs Cooper, at our enquirers' class.'

'I made some calls this afternoon,' Jenny said. 'During the last two months he was also attending a study group at the Mission Church. He'd signed up to the mailing list using his work address, and also to their email newsletter.'

'He can't have done. He wouldn't have gone behind my back. We told each other everything.'

'Calm yourself, Ceri,' Father Dermody said gently. 'It's hardly a grave sin.'

'What day of the week was he meant to have been going there?' Mrs Jacobs demanded.

'Fridays, it seems,' Jenny said.

'He told me he was working late, the staff shortages. Why would he lie? He never lied to me.'

Father Dermody laid a hand on her arm. 'The poor man was suffering, Ceri. He didn't want to burden you. We prayed for him, we did what we could.'

Fighting angry tears, Ceri Jacobs said, 'Please tell me you're not going to open this up again. I couldn't face that.'

'I don't think that would help anyone. But so that I can rule him out, I would like to know where he was on the night Eva Donaldson died. It was Sunday, 9 May.'

'He worked an extra half-shift Sunday evenings,' Ceri Jacobs said. 'He had done for several months.'

Jenny stepped outside into reception to make the call. She caught Deborah Bishop just as she was leaving the office and persuaded her to return to her computer to check staff rosters. The answer was as she expected: Alan Jacobs hadn't worked on a Sunday evening all year, and on Fridays he had worked one hour of agreed overtime and clocked off at six.

Ceri Jacobs listened to the news wearing a look of pure contempt, not for her husband, but for Jenny for shattering her already fractured illusions beyond any hope of repair.

Father Dermody did his best to soften the blow. 'I know how much you wished for him to enter the faith, Ceri, but there are other types of Christian.'

Deaf to his soothing words, Mrs Jacobs said, 'You won't stop here though, will you, Mrs Cooper? You won't be happy until every last sordid detail is dragged out and paraded in public. Can't you let the poor man rest in peace?'

How can there ever be peace without truth? Jenny wondered, but kept the thought to herself. Now was not the time for preaching.

# THIRTEEN

THE CHILLY, GREY MONDAY MORNING could as easily have been in March as late June. Jenny gave an ironic smile as she gazed out at the bleakness of the scene that perfectly reflected her mood. All attempts to persuade the Courts Service to provide a courtroom in the handful of intervening days had failed. The only venue Alison had managed to find which could accommodate an inquest at short notice was a former working men's clubhouse on the fringes of Avonmouth, the area of heavy industry where the River Avon emptied into the Severn estuary. Nestled between the factories that lined the shore from the sprawling docks to the east to the new Severn crossing in the west, it was a single-storey cinder-block building with a sheet tin roof, surrounded by a weedy area of gravel which merged into the surrounding wasteland. Nearby the massive chimney of a bitumen plant pumped out foul, cream-coloured smoke that smelled of hot tar and burning rubber. It was an unloved place that existed only to be passed through on the way to somewhere else; a fitting location, Jenny decided, to unpick the details of Eva Donaldson's death.

She had had five days including the weekend to prepare and summon witnesses, and had fully expected the Ministry of Justice to intervene to make her think again. But apart from a solitary email from Amanda Cramer, they had remained eerily silent. Cramer's message had been tersely headed 'FYI', and contained a link to a newspaper article reporting insider gossip that the government and Decency were in advanced negotiations to secure the Decency Bill's safe passage through Parliament. It was to have its first reading in a week's time. Michael Turnbull himself was slated to open the debate in the Lords. Jenny interpreted it as a warning for the long term rather than as a threat. It was intended to remind her that as a junior member of the Establishment, she had a duty not to throw a spanner into the machinery of government. Even if she was technically within her rights to conduct an inquest, it would count as yet another black mark against her.

To make matters worse, Steve had been asked to stand in for his boss at a series of meetings with prospective clients in Edinburgh. He had been stuck in the office at the weekend, and Ross had cancelled their fortnightly Sunday lunch, claiming he was overwhelmed with coursework. Jenny had made the mistake of calling her ex-husband while she was still smarting with the pain of rejection, and had humiliated herself by bursting into tears. It was the excuse David needed to suggest she should try a new psychiatrist. He recommended a colleague at the hospital. She had felt so wretched she had taken the woman's number. Before he rang off, David said, 'I'm so glad you can talk to me like this now, Jenny. You do realize how far you've come in three years?'

Pushing open the creaking door to the former Severn Beach and District Working Men's Club, Jenny couldn't be sure if this was progress or not. Before her 'episode', the formal beginning of which she marked as the day she dried up and broke down in the middle of a family court hearing, she had been a well-respected lawyer running an entire local government department. Colleagues told her she could have applied to any of the big London law firms specializing in millionaire divorces and negotiated a six-figure salary with prospects for an equity partnership. By the time she was forty-five she could have been earning more than David and heading for a place at the top of her field.

Instead she was a local coroner making just enough to get by, and surviving on ever-increasing doses of anti-anxiety medication. Ignoring Dr Allen's warnings, she had been taking double doses for most of the past week and was still starting at shadows and imaginary phantoms. Entering the clammy, featureless room that had once been the club bar felt strangely like reaching the end of a long road. As soon as this was over, she told herself, she would take a holiday. Then she would attempt to drain the poison once and for all.

She retreated to the former committee room which would serve as her office, while Alison directed workmen arriving with hired-in chairs and trestle tables to set out the main room in a way that vaguely resembled a court. In between sips of coffee from a Thermos flask, she touched up her make-up with shaky fingers and tried to resist the temptation to swallow another Xanax.

Even with her lipstick perfect and all her lines concealed, she remained too edgy to rehearse the questions she had planned for her first witnesses. Unable to relax, she closed the tatty brown curtains, leaving a tiny gap through which she watched a steady stream of people start to arrive. Despite the sign saying CORONER'S COURT Alison had planted outside, prospective jurors, witnesses, press and lawyers all appeared equally baffled by the incongruous building. Jenny smiled to herself as she watched Ed Prince and his entourage disembark from a chauffeur-driven Mercedes van and drag their smart pull-along briefcases across the rough gravel between a jumble of parked cars. The squalid building had one virtue: it would be a great leveller.

Alison knocked shortly before ten and announced that Dr Kerr and all the police witnesses were present.

'What about Craven?'

'The prison has promised to get him here later this morning. That's the best they can do.'

'Then we'd better make a start,' Jenny said with starchy formality, but under her tightly buttoned jacket her heart was racing. The air felt suddenly muggy, a bead of perspiration trickled down the centre of her chest.

Alison stepped out in front of the now crowded courtroom. 'All rise.'

There was an obedient scraping of chairs and a subdued chorus of coughs.

Jenny entered and took her place at the head of the room at a table which had been draped with green baize. Fifty people waited obediently for her to sit before they resumed their seats. She picked out the face of Eva's father, Kenneth Donaldson, sitting alone at the end of a row, surrounded by a brood of journalists eager for a titillating story. From the brief statement he had reluctantly tendered, Jenny knew that he was sixty-six years old and the recently retired managing director of a respected and successful local company which engineered aircraft parts. Sitting stiffly in a pinstriped suit, he looked every inch a man used to being in command who wasn't going to let his suffering show in public. Three rows behind him, also unaccompanied, sat Father Starr. He fixed her with a still, penetrating gaze designed to remind her that she was answerable to only one authority, of whom he was the official representative.

No fewer than eight lawyers were spread across the two rows of tables ranged opposite Jenny's. The most senior of them, Fraser Knight QC, rose to make the formal introductions. A tall man with elegant features and an aristocratic bearing, he had earned a formidable reputation representing the Ministry of Defence in a succession of awkward inquests involving the deaths of badly equipped British soldiers in Afghanistan. An eloquent advocate whose deadliest weapons were studied charm and feigned deference, he greeted her with a courtly nod and declared that he represented the Chief Constable of Bristol and Avon police. Two further members of his team sat behind him: junior counsel and a young instructing solicitor. Representing Kenneth Donaldson was Ruth Markham, a solicitor from Collett Abrahams, one of the oldest and most prestigious firms in Bristol, though one noted for its expertise in wills and probate rather than coroners' inquests. In her late thirties, expensively dressed and with a slender figure of which she was evidently very proud, she exuded confidence. In a team of one, Ruth Markham gave the impression of being more than able to cope alone. Decency and the Mission Church of God were jointly represented by a pugnacious rising star of the criminal bar, Christopher Sullivan. Good-looking in a slightly rough-hewn way, and supported by Ed Prince and two further junior solicitors armed with laptops and imposing piles of textbooks, Jenny recognized Sullivan from a recent article in the *Law Society Gazette*. Tipped to become the youngest Queen's Counsel of his generation, Sullivan had battled his way up from tough working-class roots in Bradford to a Cambridge scholarship. But rather than turn his skill into millions at the commercial bar, he had chosen criminal law and become a notoriously fearless prosecutor. The pundits said he was certain to make a move into politics before he was forty.

It was an impressive array of legal talent and the nods and smiles they exchanged amongst themselves told Jenny that despite representing different clients they were united in wanting the same result, and quickly. Her suspicious were confirmed when, as Alison swore in the eight jurors who had been chosen by lot from a pool of fourteen, the lawyers huddled and whispered to one another, as if finalizing battle plans.

The preliminaries dealt with, Jenny turned to address the newly empanelled jurors, who sat in two rows of seats to her left positioned at ninety degrees to her and the advocates' desks. In an arrangement far more intimate than that found in a regular courtroom, the six women and two men would sit in the thick of the action, almost within touching distance of the small table and chair which would serve as a witness box; close enough to Jenny and the lawyers to spot every tic and gesture.

Hoping that only she was aware of the hint of a nervous tremor in her voice, Jenny explained to the eight puzzled faces that a coroner's jury had a completely different task from that in a criminal case. Their job was to listen to all the evidence called concerning the violent death of Eva Donaldson, a twenty-seven-year-old former adult movie actress whom they had doubtless known as the public face of Decency. At its conclusion they would be asked to use their common sense and good judgement in completing a questionnaire known as a 'form of inquisition'. The most important questions they would have to answer were when, where and precisely how she died. Finally, Jenny reminded them that there had already been a brief but well-publicized criminal investigation into Miss Donaldson's death, which had concluded with Paul Craven's confession and subsequent guilty plea to her murder. Given that fact, they might be forgiven for thinking there was nothing more to be investigated, but, she stressed, the coroner's court had a duty to look at the evidence independently from the criminal court. What had gone before must not influence them in any way.

Sullivan couldn't contain himself. 'With respect, ma'am,'

he said in a thick, combative Yorkshire accent, 'the jury must be reminded that they have no power to contradict the finding of the criminal court. Craven has been properly convicted of Miss Donaldson's murder and therefore this tribunal cannot, under any circumstances, contradict that finding.'

His aggression hit her like a fist. Battling a fresh eruption of anxiety, Jenny said, 'I don't agree, Mr Sullivan. The law is very clear on the point. In the *Homberg* case the High Court said, "The coroner's overriding duty is to enquire how the deceased died, and that duty prevails over any other inhibition." '

'As I understand the law, ma'am, the only verdict this jury is entitled to return is one of unlawful killing. And with all due respect, given Craven's conviction, it could be argued that these proceedings are of doubtful legitimacy at best.'

Jenny's apprehension was overwhelmed by a rush of anger. 'I will forgive you for not being familiar with the status and procedures of the coroner's court, Mr Sullivan, but you should know that it is neither inferior nor superior to the Crown Court. Although there are many who wish it were not so, a coroner has an entirely separate jurisdiction and must conduct her inquiry in a spirit of uncompromised independence. Is that understood?'

Rocked by the ferocity of her response, Sullivan was briefly silenced. 'We'll have to agree to differ,' he muttered, and returned slowly to his seat with a look to the jury as if to warn them that they were being sorely misled.

With adrenalin now coursing through her veins, Jenny informed the jury that despite what Mr Sullivan might believe, their duty was only to the truth, whatever they found that to be. They would spend the morning hearing from police witnesses and the pathologist who had most recently examined Eva Donaldson's body. Later in the proceedings they would hear from her friends and colleagues, and finally from Paul Craven himself.

Sullivan and Fraser Knight exchanged a glance. They were looking forward to that.

Dressed in a crisp charcoal suit with a purple silk tie, Detective Inspector Vernon Goodison strolled to the witness chair with the air of a man only too happy to help. Jenny immediately marked him down as one of the new breed of media-savvy detectives, outwardly benign and aware that every word they uttered in public and published by the press would be forever recorded on the internet. Jenny watched the jury respond warmly to his trust-me smile.

With impressive fluency, Goodison recounted how he received a call early on the morning of Monday, 10 May to say that Eva Donaldson's body had been discovered by her cleaner. Together with four scene-of-crime officers, he had arrived twenty minutes later. The paramedics had had the good sense to realize she was irretrievably dead and had left the scene virtually undisturbed. Alison handed the jury copies of various police photographs showing the body lying on the kitchen floor, and views to and from the front door through the hallway. Jenny saw several of them flinch at the pin-sharp images: Eva curled up like a baby, her silky blonde hair trailing in a huge, sticky pool of coagulated blood.

Goodison confirmed that there was no sign of forced entry to the property, nor any indication that it had been ransacked. An extensive search had been made for the murder weapon – presumed to be a knife with a blade approximately seven inches long – but none had been found.

Jenny said, 'You must have seen many murder scenes in your career, Inspector. What was your initial assessment?'

'I thought it was a domestic,' Goodison said, 'a row with

a boyfriend that had got overheated. But there again you take care only to respond to the evidence.'

'Was there evidence that anyone had been in the house with her?'

'Nothing that we could find. None of the neighbours had heard anything. There was a bottle of wine open on the counter, only one glass.'

'Where did you and your team conclude the stabbing had taken place?'

Goodison held up the photograph that was taken from just outside the front door. 'It's exactly twenty-seven feet from the threshold to where she was lying. There was no evidence of blood in the hallway, but some spots were found just inside the kitchen here. It's possible they could have sprayed out from across the room, but my best guess is it happened here, near the kitchen door. If I was forced to speculate, I'd say she was backing away from someone who'd come through the front door.'

'And there were no signs of sexual assault?'

'No.'

'Did that strike you as odd?'

Goodison said, 'When he got to the house, I don't believe Craven had the courage to go through with what he intended. She opened the door to him, he forced his way in, stabbed her and ran.'

'Not pausing to steal anything?'

'There was no evidence of that. Nothing of interest was recovered from his bedsit.'

'But there were items missing from Miss Donaldson's house you might have expected to find: a personal computer, a mobile phone.'

Goodison smiled patiently, as if to congratulate Jenny on spotting the obvious. 'We were informed by Miss Donaldson's employers that they had advised her to cease electronic communications in February of this year. We think she may have disposed of her laptop computer altogether. We do believe she possessed a mobile phone, though she hadn't retained a regular contract for more than a year.'

'Was it recovered?'

'No. But there are several possibilities. Craven may have taken it, or even an opportunist thief. Miss Donaldson may have mislaid it. We simply can't say.'

'Did you discover her phone number?'

'Yes. I'll have one of my officers provide it if you wish.' He nodded to Fraser Knight and his team. The police solicitor made a note.

Jenny said, 'You didn't recover the murder weapon either?'

'No. That was slightly more troubling. Craven said in interview that he threw it in some bushes, but he couldn't remember where. It's seven miles from Miss Donaldson's home to his address, and he claims to have covered the entire distance on foot. We did all we could within our resources.' He turned to the jury. 'Obviously once Craven had confessed and his DNA was confirmed at the scene, our efforts were better spent elsewhere.'

The power of a taped confession was such, Jenny soon realized, that only the most cynical and experienced of lawyers could resist its allure. As the film played on an old-fashioned television monitor, Jenny observed the jurors frown and shake their heads as Craven told his story about going to visit Eva to help her with her good works, and claimed that she had touched him, saying, 'Fuck me for the devil.' She studied their faces as Goodison teased out his final admission: 'And that's when I picked up a knife from the counter and stuck it in her, right there, in the chest.'

They shuddered, appalled at the casualness of his delivery. His obvious lies and vagueness over detail only confirmed the impression of guilt. He was the perfect embodiment of the inexplicable face of evil.

'Did you collect the doormat before or after this interview?' Jenny asked Goodison when the film was over.

'We already had it bagged up. It was sent for analysis after Craven said he had urinated on it.'

She cut to the chase. 'I appreciate you had a confession from a man a psychiatrist deemed sane enough to be telling the truth, but once he had said those words, did you consider any other possible explanation for Miss Donaldson's death?'

'No, ma'am,' Goodison answered. 'There was no need.'

'Did you ever doubt the reliability of his confession?'

Goodison considered his answer carefully. 'He clearly wasn't as sane as you or I, but this was a man who had killed before, and once we had his DNA on the doormat there was no question.'

Jenny gestured to Alison and handed her a copy of the list of people Goodison's team had spoken to at the Mission Church of God. Alison passed it to Goodison, who pulled a pair of designer reading glasses from his breast pocket and took his time fully digesting it.

'One of your officers recorded the names of people your team spoke to informally. I presume these conversations happened on Monday, 10 and Tuesday, 11 May before Craven presented himself at the police station.'

'I would presume so,' Goodison said.

'Do any records of these conversations exist?'

'It's unlikely unless anything of interest was said, in which case we would have taken a statement.'

'Did any suspects emerge?'

'No,' Goodison said confidently.

*You liar*, Jenny thought to herself, but let nothing show on her face. 'Who compiled this list?'

'That would have been Detective Constable Stokes,' Goodison replied. 'He was coordinating the inquiry team.'

Jenny turned to Alison. 'Ask DC Stokes to come to court this afternoon.'

Goodison glanced at Fraser Knight, who remained inscrutable, his only gesture a slight, disinterested raising of his chin. Jenny knew it would be no use her pressing the point any further with this detective. He would bluff and obfuscate all morning.

She changed the subject. 'The time code on the interview tape says you commenced at four thirty-five p.m. According to the duty sergeant's log, Craven presented himself at the police station at two minutes past midday. Did you or your officers have any informal conversations with him during the intervening four hours?'

'Only a brief one,' Goodison said. 'He wanted to talk straight away. I asked him to keep it for the interview. It took four hours for his solicitor to arrive.'

Jenny made a note to check what Craven had to say on the subject.

'One last point: Craven said he picked up the knife from the kitchen counter. Did you check the cutlery drawers to see if there was a seven-inch carving knife missing? Was there an incomplete set, perhaps?'

Goodison said, 'You know as well as I do, ma'am, without concrete proof that a knife was missing, evidence that one *may* have been missing wouldn't have been let anywhere near a criminal court.'

'Was there or wasn't there a knife missing? You must have a view.'

Out of the corner of her eye, Jenny saw Fraser Knight give the tiniest shake of his head.

Goodison said, 'No, ma'am. I don't.'

Fraser Knight offered no cross-examination of his man, calculating that while Jenny might have revealed her suspicions, the jury needed no reminding of them. Sullivan preferred the head-on approach, and set to with the energy of a boxer stepping up to the mark.

'I think what's being suggested to you, albeit in code, Inspector, is that you had a quiet word with Mr Craven before his interview to make sure he remembered his lines.'

'No,' Goodison said, with a faint smile. 'It's absolutely out of the question.'

'Maybe I'm reading a little too much into the subtext,' Sullivan said, 'but we might as well air it. In the back of some people's minds might be the thought that Craven urinated on the doormat of a former female porn star, but that he didn't actually kill her. Is it possible that he left his deposit hours, or even days before she died?'

Goodison said, 'This is a man who had spent his entire adult life in prison and had only recently been released.' He looked towards Father Starr. 'I know there are some who believe he'd experienced a genuine religious conversion, but in my view this was a psychopath capable of murder and deceit; a man beyond redemption.'

'Thank you, Inspector,' Sullivan said, as if with relief that the truth had at last been heard. 'You have been most helpful.'

Ruth Markham, the lawyer representing Kenneth Donaldson, took up the baton, greeting the detective with a polite, unchallenging smile.

'Can you confirm for us please, Inspector, that your

inquiries didn't reveal any other suspect with a motive for murdering Miss Donaldson?'

'I can.'

'And can you also confirm that her home address was in fact listed on contact-a-celebrity.com, as Craven claimed?'

'It was.'

'Thank you, Inspector. That is all.'

His cross-examination over, Goodison stepped down from the witness box without having suffered a single uncomfortable moment. Jenny began to wonder if her suspicion of him had been misplaced.

She took the uncontentious witnesses next, and dealt swiftly with two scene-of-crime officers and a senior forensic scientist, Dr Jordan, who had tested the doormat and the various scrapings and tissue samples taken from Eva's body. There was no evidence of foreign DNA under Eva's nails, Jordan confirmed, nor any traces on the swabs taken from her lips, cheeks, eyelids and the backs of her hands. If there had been a physical struggle he would have expected the attacker's saliva to have sprayed onto the victim's skin; its absence suggested their contact was extremely brief. He produced a photograph of the doormat which had successfully trapped the small number of epithelial cells present in urine. He attempted to explain the finer points of mitochondrial DNA amplification to a glazed jury, but with no evidence to contradict his findings, Jenny saved him the effort. She was satisfied that Dr Jordan had proved beyond doubt that some base male instinct had caused Paul Craven to urinate on the threshold of Eva Donaldson's home. The only question in her mind was what had happened next.

Father Starr's expression grew darker and more censorious as the morning drew on; Jenny deliberately avoided his accusing gaze as Alison read aloud the original post-mortem report filed by the Home Office pathologist, Dr Aden Thomas. Starr had expected her to confront and challenge aggressively, to test each witness to the limit and upbraid them for not having exhausted every possible explanation for Eva's death. Justice was something his spiritual brothers had frequently died for, she could imagine him saying, and here she was letting partial truth pass unchallenged. But there was a limit to how far she could question the integrity of witnesses, a barrier of convention beyond which she simply could not go, even for a priest.

As Alison recited the final sentences, the flaking double doors at the back hall creaked open. Michael and Christine Turnbull entered, followed by Lennox Strong. Heads turned and even jaded members of the press smiled in acknowledgement of the famous couple. Jenny noted Kenneth Donaldson's nod of greeting and their smiles in return.

A knot of tension formed in the pit of Jenny's stomach at the prospect of what she now had to do.

She called for Dr Andrew Kerr to come forward.

The pathologist was not yet a confident public performer. He was capable of spending entire winter evenings alone in the mortuary, but giving evidence to a room full of people was an ordeal she knew he dreaded. Jenny would have to lead him by the hand.

'Dr Kerr, recently you examined Miss Donaldson's body and carried out a review of the findings of the first postmortem carried out by the Home Office pathologist, Dr Aden Thomas.'

'That's correct.'

'Did you agree with Thomas's conclusion?'

'Yes,' Dr Kerr said cautiously. 'Broadly.'

'We've seen the photographs of the single stab wound. You do accept that was the cause of death.'

'It was. But with respect to Dr Thomas, he didn't comment

on either the angle of the wound or the force needed to inflict it.' He glanced at the restive lawyers. 'The blade penetrated to a distance of six and a half inches and pierced the aorta. Blood pressure would have collapsed in seconds. The victim would have been unconscious in moments, dead in a minute or two at the most.' He brushed his face nervously with his hand. 'But to force a blade, even that of a slender carving knife, right through the chest wall, would take considerable force.'

'Can you quantify that for us?' Jenny asked.

'An average person's full strength.' He paused to take a gulp of water, wilting under the sceptical glares of lawyers sitting less than six feet away from him. 'And the blade went in almost exactly horizontally, whereas most aggressive knife wounds are either angled upwards or downwards—'

'Because?'

'I'll show you.' He took a pen from his jacket pocket and held it in a clenched fist. 'You're either stabbing down from the top of the chest, or up from beneath the ribcage. And it's hard to kill someone with a knife. That's why you read that victims have been stabbed twenty or more times. The attacker doesn't often get the penetration to deliver a fatal blow.'

Ed Prince leaned forward and whispered urgently in Sullivan's ear. Sullivan frowned and gave a dismissive shake of his head. He wasn't impressed so far.

Jenny said, 'Are you able to say precisely how this wound was inflicted?'

'Not precisely, but I can draw certain reasonable conclusions.'

'Such as?'

'It was either a lucky blow or the killer acted very deliberately, aiming the knife horizontally so as to pierce the ribs with a single deep strike.' He rubbed a finger around the inside of his shirt collar. 'What it doesn't look like is a frenzied, emotional attack such as you might see following a rape, for example; it feels too calculated for that.'

The lawyers frowned. The police solicitor tapped Fraser Knight urgently on the shoulder and handed him a note.

Jenny said, 'Why do you think Dr Thomas failed to raise these points?'

'Each pathologist tends to draw their own frame of reference. He obviously didn't see it as his job to speculate.' He shrugged. 'Times change. I was taught differently.'

Jenny watched two women in the front row of the jury look again at their shared photograph of Eva's body. They were starting to think, to imagine different possibilities.

Bracing herself, Jenny said, 'Was there anything else about the body which you noticed that Dr Thomas hadn't remarked on?'

'It's not of any forensic value,' Dr Kerr said, eager to get to the end of his ordeal, 'but I noticed that there were two tattoos on the body. The first was a butterfly design just above the base of the spine, and the second two words tattooed just above the pubic bone on the left side of the mid-line.'

'Can you say when she had these tattoos done?'

'The one on her back had been there for some time, years perhaps. The one on her front was very fresh, perhaps only a few weeks old.'

Jenny nodded to Alison, who handed out two photographs showing the front and back of Eva's body to the jury and to the lawyers. Inset on each was a close-up of the corresponding tattoo.

'Did you take these photographs, Dr Kerr?'

'I did. Early last week.'

Sullivan rose abruptly to his feet. 'Can I ask you, ma'am, why these photographs weren't disclosed to the interested parties before this hearing?'

Jenny glanced at Kenneth Donaldson, who was in whispered conversation with one of Ed Prince's assistants.

'There's no legal requirement for a coroner to disclose in advance, Mr Sullivan.'

'There's a right to see a post-mortem report in advance,' Sullivan snapped back.

'And copies were sent to your instructing solicitors.'

'It contained no mention of these tattoos.'

Praying that Andy Kerr would hold his nerve, Jenny said, 'Perhaps Dr Kerr didn't consider them relevant. And I fail to see what difference disclosure of this detail would have made.'

'Ma'am, I wish to raise a matter of law in the absence of the jury.'

'No, Mr Sullivan. There is no reason for this evidence to be withdrawn, and there is certainly no reason for its existence to be suppressed.'

Sullivan jabbed the air with his forefinger, 'Ma'am, there are extremely important issues of public interest that need to be addressed with a full consideration of the law.'

'You misunderstand the nature of a coroner's court, Mr Sullivan. I am not an arbiter between competing cases, I decide what evidence I consider relevant. If you have a complaint you make it to the High Court.'

'Then I request an immediate adjournment.'

'Out of the question.'

Prince's second assistant hurried to the door, phone in hand. Jenny had no doubt that within the hour a London QC would be in front of a judge pleading for an injunction to prevent reporting of the existence of Eva's dubious body art.

Jenny turned to the jury. ' "Daddy's girl" is what the tattoo says.'

Kenneth Donaldson fixed her with an expression of icy contempt.

Ignoring Sullivan, who remained stubbornly on his feet, she continued, 'In a moment you'll be hearing from the artist who drew it.'

In a matter of seconds, half the twenty or so reporters in the room had dashed from their seats and hurried for the exit to phone the revelation through to their editors. In a tight race against a possible injunction they could have their story on the internet in minutes and spread out across the social networks and blogs seconds later. Even if a High Court judge could be persuaded on spurious grounds to rule that the public had no right to know, it would be already too late to put the genie back in the bottle, and the lawyers knew it.

Calmly, Jenny said, 'You can sit down now, Mr Sullivan.'

The frustrated prosecutor slammed into his chair and turned to plot his revenge with a furious Ed Prince. Jenny didn't dare look at the Turnbulls and Lennox Strong, but she did catch a glimpse of Father Starr: for a fleeting moment he was smiling.

Jenny turned to Dr Kerr. 'Is there anything else you wish to add, Dr Kerr?'

'No, ma'am,' he said apprehensively.

Fraser Knight rose to his full imposing height and fixed the young pathologist with a look of disappointment tinged with disbelief. 'How long have you been a fully qualified pathologist, Dr Kerr?'

'Thirteen months.'

'I see. And Dr Aden Thomas?'

Dr Kerr reddened with embarrassment. 'I've only met him once or twice—'

'Thirty-two years,' Fraser Knight said. He looked down at his legal pad and cast a disapproving eye over its contents. 'You have seen fit to "speculate" – your word – in a way in which he didn't.' He delivered his question while looking at the jury: 'Do you think that in his thirty-two years of practice he may have learned that it's not a wise, let alone a scientific, thing to do?'

'I've no idea.'

'No,' Knight said, with an indulgent smile. 'Nor do you know the state of mind of Miss Donaldson's killer, or the exact manner in which he held the knife, or the exact sequence of events leading to her murder.'

'No,' Dr Kerr admitted.

'From the evidence gleaned from her body, all you can say for certain is that she was killed by a single, powerful stab wound.'

'Yes, but—' Dr Kerr hesitated in mid-sentence, losing courage.

'So you would accept, therefore, that your speculation does not help us to establish any key fact. It is only speculation.'

With an apologetic glance to Jenny, Dr Kerr answered, 'Yes,' his authority all but destroyed.

Sullivan asked only one question of the witness: 'You have no factual evidence whatever, do you, for suggesting that anyone other than Paul Craven murdered Eva Donaldson?'

'No, I don't.'

Sullivan gave a theatrical sigh and threw the jury a look that said he pitied them for having their time so needlessly wasted.

It was almost one o'clock, stomachs would be aching with hunger, but Jenny called the tattoo artist, Alan Turley, to give his evidence before the lunch break. With a shaved, tattooed head, and nose and ears peppered with rings and studs, he was a man Jenny would have crossed the street to avoid. But Turley, who practised his craft under the name Doc Scratch, was quietly spoken, and gave the impression that he was a gentle soul, devoted to his work.

Alison handed him a copy of the photograph of Eva's body. He looked at it briefly and lowered his head, visibly upset. Jenny took him carefully through the evidence he had given in a statement he had made to Alison the week before, making sure that he repeated every detail. He told the jury that Eva had booked the appointment by telephone several days in advance under the assumed name Louise Pearson. When she arrived for her appointment she wrote down the words she wanted tattooed and selected the font from a style book. It took no more than fifteen minutes to apply and she paid in cash: sixty pounds.

Jenny stole a glance at Kenneth Donaldson. What she saw in his face surprised her. In the back of her mind she had invented a story of abuse for Eva's tattoo: riddled with guilt at her years prostituting herself, it was to be an ironic testament to the true cause of her pain, a mirror image of the scars that disfigured her face. Marking her body in this way was a form of therapy: sex could never be had for the sheer hell of it again; it would always be married with the truth. But Donaldson's expression didn't fit with her neat version of history. In her many years in the family courts dealing with men who had done unspeakable things to their daughters, she had learnt to recognize the benign, detached, self-deluding smile the guilty ones adopted. There was nothing self-deluding about Kenneth Donaldson's reaction; no, he was in genuine pain.

'Mr Turley,' Jenny said, 'did Miss Donaldson talk to you at all while you were drawing the design?'

'Very little. She seemed sort of distant.'

'Did you ask what it meant to her?'

'No. It didn't seem right.'

'Why was that?'

Sullivan rolled his eyes. Ed Prince drummed his fingers impatiently. Jenny ignored them and urged Turley to answer.

'It was just a feeling,' he said. 'A lot of people want tattoos when they've just lost someone – it's like a memorial. The young lady felt like that. Sad. As if she'd just come to the end of something.'

# FOURTEEN

What had she done?

It had been less than twenty minutes since Dr Kerr had revealed the existence of Eva's tattoo and it was already the major headline on newspaper websites. Jenny surfed through them in her office. All grasped the opportunity to print photographs of Eva from her porn-star days, and took care to mention the fact that her father was a retired industrialist who had been widowed for almost fifteen years. Jenny could picture Michael and Christine Turnbull and their colleagues wincing at the damage the story would already have done to their campaign: even as she was championing anti-pornography laws that would have turned the clock back forty years, Eva was marking her body with a tattoo which was ambiguous at best. Somehow it smacked of hypocrisy and mixed motives, and far more damagingly of buried secrets from a woman who claimed to have none left. Out of a simple desire to have the whole truth told, Jenny realized that she had unleashed a story that wouldn't die until there was an answer. She slammed down the lid of her laptop and grabbed her pills from her handbag.

She had barely forced the tablet down when Alison arrived to tell her that Ed Prince had nearly come to blows with reporters who had swarmed around the Mercedes van he and his team were using as their mobile office. The

Turnbulls and Lennox Strong were in there with them, besieged by a news-hungry mob who had blocked the van's exit from the car park.

Jenny said, 'Can you call the police?'

'They're on their way.'

Sensing Alison's disapproval, Jenny said, 'I had to do it—'

'Mr Donaldson wants to give evidence,' Alison retorted. 'His solicitor would like you to call him this afternoon. He's writing a statement now.'

'Good. I'll hear from him whenever he's ready.'

'Her old boyfriend Joe Cassidy's finally answered his summons, but there's no sign of Freddy Reardon yet. No one's picking up the phone at his home address.'

'He'll be nervous. He might need a bit of encouragement. Maybe you can ask the police to send someone to get him.'

'And if he doesn't want to come?'

'I'll give him a chance to cooperate before I issue a warrant. I'm sure he will.'

Alison gave a doubtful grunt.

'What is it?' Jenny said. 'I've done something you don't approve of. I can tell.'

Alison stalled at the door. 'It's not you. It's that priest, Father Starr—'

'What about him?'

'It's just an instinct – there's something not quite honest about him. Even when we were at the prison, it didn't feel as if he was being completely straight with us.'

It was a concern that had been nagging at Jenny too, but she had put it down to her insecurity on being confronted with a man who led such an austere and observant life. His triumph over normal human weaknesses served to make her more painfully aware of her own.

'What has he got to be dishonest about?' Jenny said, asking herself as much as Alison.

'You wouldn't find me at the Mission Church of God,' Alison said, 'but at least they're achieving something. On the brink of changing the law, churches all over the world, getting kids off the street and out of crime. How many would turn up to hear Father Starr on a Sunday morning?'

'You think he's jealous?'

'My husband's a Catholic, or was,' Alison said. 'They might pretend to be tolerant, but believe me, there's only one road to heaven as far as they're concerned, and it goes through Rome.'

The ranks of journalists had swelled and the air was stuffy with the smell of too many bodies crammed tightly together. The Turnbulls and Lennox Strong had yet to return to their seats. Jenny assumed they were still outside in their vehicle, being tutored by members of their legal team. The faces of the lawyers in the courtroom had hardened. All three advocates seemed to have united to form a single opposing front. Sullivan wore a permanent threatening scowl. Behind him Ed Prince brooded like a wounded bear. Attempts to secure an emergency injunction had clearly failed. Jenny had out-manoeuvred them and embarrassed their clients. Human nature alone dictated that they would be seeking revenge.

Ruth Markham half-rose from her chair. 'Ma'am, might it be appropriate for Mr Kenneth Donaldson to give evidence first?'

'Very well,' Jenny replied.

Donaldson marched to the front with the cold determination of a battle-scarred general about to testify before a committee of cowardly politicians. He completed the opening formalities with no hint of emotion.

The jury listened respectfully as Donaldson gave a brief, but moving history of his daughter's early life. She was an only child, he explained, and had been particularly close to her mother, a successful fashion model turned photographer, whose own life was cut short by cancer when Eva was only fourteen. It was a loss from which she would never fully recover. She spent most of her teens at boarding school, where initially she did well, but as she grew older increasingly found herself in mild bouts of trouble for all the usual teenage reasons – drink and boyfriends, though fortunately never any mention of drugs. Despite several near misses, she clung on and gained a place at Bristol School of Art. It was then that rebellion tipped over into outright rejection and defiance. Despite his best efforts to share in his daughter's life, Eva drew further away, refusing to visit home even in college vacations. He was hurt and confused at her behaviour, but listened to the advice of friends who told him to trust that in time she would mature and reconnect.

'I'd send her money, but she'd post the cheques back or never cash them,' Donaldson said. 'She was very determined to be independent. She kept saying she didn't want to be reliant on me. I did what any father would do: I told her I would always be there whenever she needed me.'

'And she continued to go her own way?' Jenny asked.

'Yes. She would phone occasionally but never tell me very much. For example, I didn't know she had abandoned her college course until six months after the event. It was a schoolfriend of hers who told me that she had left to become involved with films. I tried to persuade her out of it, but she was twenty years old and hell-bent on doing as she pleased. She was clearly making plenty of money, so I didn't exactly have much leverage.'

'Did you have any contact with your daughter during her career in the film business?'

'Very little. There'd be the odd birthday card. She came to visit one Christmas, but she was very remote. I hardly saw her in four years – until she had the accident, in fact.'

'What happened then?'

'We spoke more often. I wouldn't say it was a normal relationship, but things certainly started to thaw. Once she became involved with the Decency campaign we spoke quite regularly.' Eva's father hesitated, showing the first hint of emotion since entering the witness box. 'We started to meet. She would come round every few weeks. Wc had dinner once a month, perhaps. Eva talked about her work, her life at the Mission Church. I was very pleased for her. Her life had a purpose.'

Jenny said, 'Did she seem to be having any particular problems in the months before her death?'

'She wasn't earning what she was used to, but she seemed determined to manage somehow. She certainly never asked me for support.'

'And emotionally?'

'She was always tired; she had a tough schedule of commitments. That apart, I would say she was the happiest I had seen her in years.'

Jenny looked down at her notes, feeling three sets of eyes boring into her. She pretended to read for a moment, preparing to broach the subject she had so far managed to avoid.

'Mr Donaldson, we heard evidence this morning that several weeks before she was killed, your daughter had a tattoo—'

'Yes.'

'Did you know she'd had it done?'

'No.'

'Have you any idea why?'

'None. If Mr Turley's dates are correct, we met the following day – the Saturday. She was in good spirits.'

'You don't know what the words mean?'

'No.'

Sullivan interjected, 'Ma'am, before you go any further—'

'A witness here has the same protection against self-incrimination as he would in a criminal court, Mr Sullivan. I presume that's your concern.'

'Yes, ma'am,' Sullivan barked.

'Then you have nothing to worry about, have you?'

Reluctantly giving way, he dropped back into his seat.

Jenny turned to the witness. 'I am obliged to remind you that you do not have to say anything which may incriminate you, Mr Donaldson. Nevertheless, I would like to ask you if your daughter ever suggested to you or anyone else that she believed you had at some time behaved inappropriately towards her.'

'You're asking if I interfered with my daughter. Never. Never. Never.' His denial rang around the silent courtroom. 'Eva undoubtedly slept with young men while she was still at school, possibly when she was as young as fourteen. But there was never anything untoward between us.'

'I understand, Mr Donaldson,' Jenny said gently, 'but my question was whether to your knowledge she believed there *might* have been.'

'No. Definitely not. She expressly told me that her decision to appear in pornographic films was nothing to do with me or how I had behaved. If I'm forced to psychoanalyse, I would say she was deeply hurt by her mother's death and sought love elsewhere, but I'm not sure I would even go that far. She made a foolish mistake and she accepted that.'

'Mr Turley said that she seemed sad when she came to his studio. He likened her to someone who was grieving.'

Kenneth Donaldson then dipped his head as if he had been suddenly assailed by unexpected emotions. 'I've had very little time to think, but I wonder if the truth is that Eva was grieving for a lost childhood, a lost innocence even.' He struggled to find words to express his confusion of feelings. 'These marks that people make on their bodies strike me as elemental. It's possible she didn't know the reason for it herself.'

Jenny felt a pang of sympathy and wrote a note to herself: *At a loss to explain. Believe his reaction genuine. Unpolished. Thinking aloud.*

'Where were you on the night your daughter was killed, Mr Donaldson?'

'At my home in Bath. I was entertaining former colleagues, the MD of my former firm and his wife. I gave details to the police.'

Jenny could have concluded her questioning there, but her gut told her that having opened Donaldson up, he had more to offer.

'Is there anything else you would like to tell the court?'

She saw Ed Prince trying to catch Donaldson's eye, shaking his head from side to side, urging him to remain silent. Donaldson ignored him, frowning through painful memories. 'Only this: that she was a more complicated young woman than I think any of us can or will understand. We talked once or twice about forgiveness; the church had asked her to contribute to a book on the subject. I remember she was a little melancholic about a conclusion she'd reached. She said she had come to realize that giving and receiving love wasn't the profoundest experience in this life, it was giving and receiving *forgiveness*. To her, sadly, it meant that our highest expression is always bound up with sin.'

'Thank you, Mr Donaldson,' Jenny said, still struggling to make sense of his evidence. She addressed the advocates' bench. 'Cross-examination?'

All three lawyers shook their heads.

\*

Detective Constable Ray Stokes immediately struck Jenny as the safe pair of hands DI Goodison would have needed to organize the investigating team on the ground in a sensitive case. Well into his fifties, he was a solid, reassuring character who had managed to maintain a sense of humour after nearly thirty years of front-line police work.

Alison handed him the handwritten list of people spoken to at the Mission Church of God on Monday, 10 and Tuesday, 11 May.

'Yes. I wrote that,' he answered.

'Did you make any more detailed notes?'

'Individual officers might have done, but if they didn't form any part of the investigation they wouldn't have made it into our files.'

'What sort of notes might they have made?' Jenny asked.

'I had a team of half a dozen detectives. I sent three of them into the church to ask anyone who knew her if they had heard anything of interest, whether she was having a problem with anyone, that sort of thing.'

'And this is a list of people they spoke to?'

'It is. And we didn't get anything out of it as I recall. We'd already established from Mr Strong that she'd stayed at home on the Sunday evening feeling tired, but that was about all of any use we learned there.'

'Why was that useful?'

'It wasn't particularly. It just served to rule out everyone who was at the service. We had a time of death at about eight or nine p.m. The service wasn't over until nearly ten.'

Jenny said, 'One of the names on the list is Alan Jacobs. Do you know who questioned him?'

'It was me. I had a list of people in her study group. There were about four or five names. I spoke to each of them.'

'Do you recall the conversation with Mr Jacobs?'

'Yes. I caught him at work, up at the Conway Unit. He was very helpful as I recall. He said that he had met Miss Donaldson a number of times in a group at the church, and that he'd been at the service on the Sunday night.'

'Were you able to verify that?'

'I think he gave a few names, people who confirmed he was there.'

'You *think*?'

'It was early days. If Craven hadn't come forward so soon the investigation would have dug deeper. As it turned out, it wasn't necessary.'

'Would you have made a note of the names he gave you?'

'If I did,' DC Stokes said, 'I'm afraid I haven't got it now. It was just preliminary stuff, running around. You scribble something down or make a note on your phone and don't necessarily hold on to it.'

'You didn't follow up on his movements or those of anyone else at the church?'

'Not in detail, no, ma'am,' the detective said with a shrug. 'Like I said, we talked to lots of people.'

Jenny considered what a study group might mean. She assumed it was a sociable gathering and that the conversation must have drifted to the group's families and work. It was hard to imagine Alan Jacobs and Eva Donaldson not having found each other interesting. It must have occurred to Jacobs that Eva could have served as an inspiration to many of the kids in his care, particularly the drug-addled teenage girls who'd have sold themselves for their next fix. And she in turn must have been intrigued by a man who worked with young people of precisely the sort her church was setting out to reach and help.

Jenny said, 'It must have struck you that professionally at least, they had much in common. Did you ask him if he discussed his work with Eva?'

'No. We didn't get much beyond the basics I'm afraid.'

Ed Prince and his team were in whispered conversation with Fraser Knight and his solicitor. What the hell is she driving at? Prince was undoubtedly asking. Nobody seemed to have any answers. Neither did Jenny. There was only a hunch, a vague, uneasy suspicion that two deaths in one study group amounted to more than mere coincidence. She knew there were many more answers to come – her problem was finding the right questions. From his seat at the back of courtroom Starr held her in his calmly critical gaze, judging, assessing, and fiercely willing her on.

Michael Turnbull returned to the hall accompanied by his wife and Lennox Strong. The three seemed inseparable. As he came forward and prepared to testify, Jenny could tell that it wasn't facing the court that daunted him, but the fact that his words would be broadcast around the world within moments of him uttering them. There was no room for error.

The consummate professional, Turnbull sat angled towards the jury, speaking to them as if they were concerned friends. Jenny wanted them to hear Eva's story from his perspective and led him through the chain of events which had brought them together. Turnbull began by describing the occasion when Pastor Lennox Strong first introduced her to him. He had been wary at first, he admitted, but over the course of several discussions in the following weeks Eva convinced him that she had been led to the Mission Church for a reason: to combat the industry that was corrupting a generation. He offered up many prayers before presenting her to Decency's board as a potential ambassador, but they were unanimous in their decision to take her on.

'She made me rethink the whole issue,' Turnbull said. 'Before I met Eva, my focus had been on the damage done to consumers by this material, how it engendered brutal feelings towards women and led to a spiral of dishonesty and guilt. But I always struggled against well-intentioned, liberal-minded people, both men and women, who said the effect was the opposite; that tolerating pornography was a necessary part of a free and honest society. Eva's argument was simple: no one can be set free by watching men and women debase themselves. To obtain pleasure from that is to be corrupted. That is how corruption works – by preying on our greatest vulnerabilities.'

Eva's media appearances, Turnbull said, took the Decency campaign from a fringe group treated as an object of derision by the popular press to the heart of the mainstream. Here was living, breathing proof of the damage the so-called 'adult entertainment' business wrought. Without Eva Donaldson, he conceded, he would not, in only a few days' time, be faced with the realistic possibility of taking the first steps to passing a stringent anti-pornography law. Her contribution had been nothing short of miraculous.

'This was a multi-billion-pound business you and she were attacking,' Jenny said. 'You must have collected enemies.'

'There was a steady stream of abusive correspondence, certainly.'

'Were you aware of Eva receiving threats to her personal safety?'

'Quite the contrary. Eva was deluged with messages of support. Much of it from men addicted to pornography. They wanted to be set free.'

'But what about the vested interests, the companies such as the one Eva used to work for?'

'They're very sophisticated. Like the tobacco business, they hire lobbyists and seek to persuade politicians with the economic arguments. And no doubt they've prepared amendments to our bill designed to allow material which has passed certain ethical standards. If they play the politics right they could still be the big winners. Instead of a ban they would get regulation in exchange for legitimacy.'

'So you're saying they had no motive for silencing Miss Donaldson?'

'I'm sure they would have loved her to support their compromise position, but I don't think for a moment they thought she ever would.'

'Do you think they might have tried to win her over?'

'I can guess what you're driving at,' Turnbull said. 'But I can assure you Eva was as committed as it was possible to be. No amount of money would have bought her. Ask anyone – once Eva was set on a course there was no persuading her from it. She had a will of iron.'

Jenny saw Kenneth Donaldson nodding in agreement.

She moved on, touching briefly on Eva's financial problems, but Turnbull was dismissive, saying that if she had needed more money there were any number of PR companies who would have paid her many times the salary she earned from Decency. She was acting out a vocation; money wasn't her focus.

She broached the issue of the tattoo, but Turnbull denied all knowledge and refused to speculate on her state of mind. He was her employer, not her confidant, he insisted.

'Are you honestly saying you have no thoughts on what might have motivated her to have that tattoo?' Jenny asked.

'Yes.'

'No insight into her state of mind at the time?'

'As far as her work was concerned, she remained determined and focused. That's all I can tell you.'

'You didn't notice her showing signs of strain?'

'She seemed to be coping well. But you have to understand: ours was a professional, not a personal, relationship.'

Resigned to the fact that Turnbull wouldn't deviate from a well-rehearsed corporate line, Jenny moved on to the night of Eva's death. Turnbull explained that he and his wife had been in London the previous day. Christine had caught the train home to Bristol on the Sunday morning. He had meetings to attend and had followed later in the afternoon. His driver delivered him straight to the Mission Church, where they met at approximately six-thirty. There were more than four thousand in the congregation that evening and the service lasted for several hours. It was after ten when he and his wife finally got to leave.

'I understand Eva stayed at home that evening,' Jenny said.

'Yes. We'd hoped she'd say a few words about the campaign, but I got a message from the office to say she was feeling too tired after a weekend on the road.'

'Who gave you the message?'

'That would have been our administrator, Joel Nelson. I think he took Eva's call.'

'Did anyone else apart from you and Mr Nelson know that Eva was at home that evening?'

'The entire congregation. As I recall, Lennox Strong made an announcement explaining that she couldn't be with us.'

'Had she done this before?'

Turnbull had to think before answering. 'No, I don't remember her having missed an important engagement.'

'So this was a formal engagement?'

For the first time since he started giving evidence, Turnbull glanced at his lawyers, looking for a prompt. Jenny's eyes were on Sullivan before he could offer one. Turnbull was left to answer alone.

'Not formal in the sense that she was being paid for it,' he said without conviction.

'But she was expected to address the crowd?'

'She had offered to.'

'And instead she stayed at home and opened a bottle of wine.' Jenny picked up the booklet of police photographs and turned to a shot with a clear view of the bottle. 'It looks as if she had drunk about two-thirds of it by the time she died.'

Turnbull made no comment.

'Was she much of a drinker, do you know?'

'Not that I was aware of.'

Jenny studied the photograph again. There was a single, partially full glass of wine on the counter, and next to it a corkscrew and an ashtray containing several butts. On the counter opposite, a peninsula unit, was some broccoli wrapped in cellophane. There was no sign of cooking in progress. It looked as if Eva had opened the bottle and stayed at the counter drinking.

'Lord Turnbull,' Jenny said, 'are you aware of any reason, other than the one Miss Donaldson gave, as to why she might have stayed at home that night?'

'No.'

'I see,' Jenny said, leaving him in no doubt that she wasn't persuaded. Up to her eyes in debt, alone, traipsing around the country delivering the same lines for an employer who refused to give her a rise: it was impossible not to suspect that Eva was becoming more than a little resentful. Added to the fact that two weeks before she'd had her crotch tattooed, it painted a picture of a young woman who was going through a rough patch of turbulence, to say the least.

Sullivan was the only lawyer to cross-examine. 'Miss Donaldson's indebtedness has been alluded to. Am I right in saying she wrote to you in November of last year asking for a pay rise?'

'She did. I put the request to the board and they decided

it would be inappropriate, given the fact that she had been employed for less than a year.'

'How did she react to that refusal?'

'She understood the reasons and accepted them.' He turned to the jury. 'Look, I think we have to acknowledge that we are talking about a fallible human being here, not a saint. Eva came under the same pressures as the rest of us.'

'One more thing,' Sullivan said, with a dismissive glance in Jenny's direction, 'I think what Mrs Cooper may have been intending to ask, but didn't quite, is whether to your knowledge Miss Donaldson was planning to meet someone at her home the evening she was killed.'

'I don't know of any such arrangement.'

'And she's not the only one of us to have had a glass of wine alone at the end of a hard day.'

'Quite.'

Jurors smiled. They liked the idea of Eva having an Achilles heel.

Christine Turnbull was just as skilful as her husband at evading the issue of Eva's state of mind. Composed and dignified, she described a purely professional, arm's length relationship between them. In her capacity as a member of Decency's board, she met Eva mostly to discuss forthcoming engagements and to plan strategies with their media consultants. Eva had impressed everyone with her ability to operate under pressure without letting emotion intrude, which was a remarkable feat given her painful history. Their social contact had been limited to a few dinners and the odd cocktail party Decency had hosted at the Houses of Parliament. Even on these occasions their conversation had rarely become personal, let alone intimate. 'I got the impression that in public she was above all concerned to maintain her dignity,' Christine said. 'To have discussed intimacies would have been out of the question. I'm sure there were people with whom she did have such discussions, but they weren't with me. I think she saw me very much as an employer. She was comfortable with that, and so was I.'

Jenny said, 'You didn't try to establish a personal relationship?'

'No,' Christine replied. 'Much as I liked her, it didn't seem right. I'd go so far as to say that Eva preferred to have purely working relationships that didn't cross borders. She had a very strong sense of propriety. It was one of the things I admired about her.'

Jenny could quite believe their relationship was a distant one, but not for the reasons Christine Turnbull gave. Surely they would have been wary of each other: Eva intimidated by Christine's age and experience, Christine both intrigued and repelled by Eva's years in front of the camera. Christine wouldn't have been human if she hadn't wanted to know what it was like for a young woman to walk onto a crowded set and copulate with half a dozen men before lunchtime.

Wearing an open-necked ivory-coloured silk shirt beneath his black suit, Lennox Strong looked more like a TV host than a man of God. But Jenny's hopes of getting him to shine a light on the Eva Michael and Christine Turnbull claimed not to know were soon dashed. He happily described the night when Eva first came forward to give herself to Christ, how he had laid hands on her and seen the burden lifted from her shoulders, but when Jenny asked him what they had discussed in subsequent conversations he answered with a phrase that had Ed Prince written all over it: 'You'll understand I'm not able to repeat things said to me in confidence in my role as pastor.'

'Even after the subject is dead?' Jenny pressed.

'A confidence doesn't end with the confider's death,'

Strong said with a patient smile, 'not unless that was her request. Eva never made such a wish, so her confidences go with me to my grave.'

For nearly half an hour Jenny pushed and probed for the slightest detail to prise open Eva's mind. There were hints at her complexity – Strong described how writing their book on forgiveness had pushed Eva back to the brink of depression – but for the most part he described her as a woman who had embraced a simple, uncomplicated faith which she used to banish her past. She didn't discuss her time in the porn business, Strong explained, because she didn't want to dwell on it. 'Through my own experience I was able to prove to her that God gives you the freedom to move on. You don't have to drag the past around behind you like a ball and chain: that's what being born again means.'

'Can you say how having the tattoo squares with leaving the past behind?' Jenny asked.

'I don't have an answer, but I do have a theory. It's not breaching a confidence to say that Eva and I had been talking about her future. She was thinking of coming to work for the Mission Church full time after the Decency campaign had finished. It was a huge step for her. The one bit of security she'd had in life was money. Working for the church would have meant she had enough to survive, but no more. When you're making that sort of commitment you're tested in all sorts of ways you're not expecting. It's as if you're questioning every aspect of your character, peering into every dark corner. You ask yourself, am I truly worthy of this? Can God really want *me*, of all people? And that rebellious part of your spirit, it's going to show itself one last time before you can put it away. That's what was happening to Eva.'

'Did you see any evidence of this "rebellious spirit" in her?'

'Not explicitly, no.'

'Had you noticed any change in her, anything of the mood Mr Turley detected when she came to his studio?'

'Eva was just like the rest of us. Some days she was full of enthusiasm, other days the world got on top of her.'

He fell silent.

'Mr Strong?'

'You know, I don't know if this is the right place to say it, but the reality for Eva was that she was in the middle of a battle. It doesn't matter how hard you try to surround yourself with good and trustworthy people, evil's always going to come and seek you out. That's why we pray, every day, "deliver us from evil"; having faith alone is no protection, in fact it puts you on the front line. She was caught off her guard. She made one bad call and that was all it took; the enemy got her.'

There was a moment of stillness as all in the courtroom seemed to share in his grief; all except Father Starr, whose features remained as hard-set as the concrete in his cathedral.

As the pastor stepped away from the witness box and made for the exit with Michael and Christine Turnbull, Alison came and whispered to Jenny that police had gone to Freddy Reardon's address but no one had answered; did she want to issue an arrest warrant? Jenny pictured officers arriving at the flat and staving in the door to drag a frightened Freddy to court.

'We'll leave it for now,' Jenny said. 'I may not need him.'

Joe Cassidy was the final witness of the day and, save for Freddy Reardon, the last on Jenny's list. He had cut his hair for the occasion and was dressed in a movie star's suit, but beneath the slick exterior he was edgy and impatient and cast nervous glances at the lawyers, who whispered to each other behind their hands.

He stated his profession as company director and claimed to have known Eva for over five years. 'We acted together, then we lived together,' he said. 'We broke up after her car accident, when she became depressed, but we stayed friends.' He spoke directly to the jury. 'I might not have been on the same religious kick, but no one could have known her better than I did.'

Jenny was taken aback by his abrasive tone. He was hardly recognizable as the tousle-haired TV producer who had tried to flirt with her over drinks.

Jenny said, 'Shall we rewind a little and hear how you and Miss Donaldson met?'

'Can I say something first?' Cassidy asked. 'In all the time I worked with Eva, she never once failed to turn up for work, even when it was the last place she wanted to be. I've heard a lot of speculation about her today, but one thing I guarantee is that she wouldn't have let down four thousand people without one hell of a reason.'

Anticipating Sullivan's objection, Jenny said, 'Do you have any evidence for this, Mr Cassidy?'

'Yes. This is a woman I've seen climb out of a sickbed at dawn and scrape the ice off her windscreen to shoot a gang bang with a bunch of strangers.'

'I meant, do you have any evidence that she was told not to come to the Mission Church the night she was killed?'

'I don't know who told her to stay away,' Cassidy said, 'but I'm pretty sure I know why.' He aimed his last remark at the press. 'I don't think Eva believed any more.'

# FIFTEEN

CASSIDY'S STATEMENT CAUSED UPROAR. As the journalists rushed to file their second sensational story of the day,
Sullivan furiously accused him of being in the pay of the
pornography business, and of having used his sham TV
company to solicit young women for adult films. Cassidy hit
back with the claim that Eva wouldn't have approached him
to help her start a straight acting career unless she was
planning on leaving the Mission Church of God behind.

Jenny fought a losing battle to restore order. The session
ended in disarray with Cassidy swamped by reporters as he
tried to leave the building, and Sullivan demanding that his
evidence be ruled inadmissible. Shouting above the commotion, Jenny declared the day's proceedings over and sought
sanctuary in her office.

She emerged twenty minutes later to find Alison straighten-
ing the empty rows of chairs. She didn't have to say I told
you so – it was written in her every pernickety gesture,
restoring order where Jenny had unleashed chaos.

'Has everybody gone now?' Jenny asked.

'All except *him*,' Alison said, nodding towards the exit.

'Who?'

'Who do you think? The Grand Inquisitor. I asked him to
wait outside.'

'Oh . . . Did he say what he wants?'

'That'd be far too polite.' She crossed to her desk and tidied her papers. 'Are you planning on calling any more witnesses tomorrow? We'll save fifty pounds if we're out of this place by lunchtime.'

'I haven't decided. I might have to call Michael Turnbull back to answer Cassidy's allegations.'

Alison looked up with a worried frown.

'Why would you do that? There's not been one shred of evidence that's made me doubt for a second that Craven killed her. Don't take this the wrong way, Mrs Cooper, but if you keep on, it's just going to make you look worse.'

'Worse than what, exactly?'

'Than you do already. Someone has to tell you – that priest thinks you're an easy touch. He preyed on your conscience because *he's* feeling guilty for what Craven did. It's not your job to make him feel better.'

Jenny picked up her briefcase and marched to the door.

He was waiting in the car park, standing with his back to the building and looking out across the choppy estuary to the shadowy Welsh hills ghosted on the horizon. He turned slowly, unsure of himself as he addressed her.

'Am I permitted to speak to you during the proceedings, Mrs Cooper?'

'I don't see why not. I've no plans to call you as a witness.'

'Then I'll be brief.'

He moved towards her, hands clasped awkwardly behind his back. 'You're going to pursue this allegation of Cassidy's?' he asked.

'I doubt it. My job is to determine cause of death, not to pick over her relations with her employer.'

'If she was asked to stay at home that evening, it surely raises a number of questions. Other suspects may emerge—'

'I can't drag respectable people through the mud without a very good reason, you must understand that.'

'She was clearly unbalanced. Perhaps they were frightened she would say something inappropriate, or damaging?'

Jenny said, 'My apologies, Father. I made a mistake. This isn't an appropriate conversation after all.' She started to unlock the car door.

'I see you have lost faith, too.'

'I beg your pardon?'

'It was our friend Mr McAvoy who once told me that, for a lawyer, believing in a client's innocence is like a priest believing in the possibility of redemption. No matter what the outcome, it is the pursuit of that belief that brings us closer to—' He checked himself. 'That dignifies us.'

Jenny rounded on him. 'Is that your trump card, mentioning his name again? Do you really think I'm that stupid? I know what you want, Father. You want to believe your faith in Craven wasn't misplaced. Because if you're wrong about that you can be wrong about anything. Am I right?'

He looked at her defiantly. 'I am not wrong about Paul Craven.'

'Because he said some prayers and told you so?'

'No.'

'Oh, yes. I remember, God told you.'

'Is it so ridiculous? It's my job to act to the full extent of my faith, yours to act to the full extent of the law.'

'There are limits. For both of us.'

She yanked open the car door and threw her handbag onto the passenger seat.

'If it's of any interest, I had a word for you, too, Mrs Cooper.'

'Really?' She climbed in and reached for the door handle to pull it closed. Starr put out a hand and held it open. 'Please let me go,' Jenny said.

'I was told you're carrying a terrible burden and want to be set free. Am I right, Mrs Cooper?'

She heard the telephone ringing from the street outside her office. As she pushed angrily through the door and made her way along the gloomy corridor it ceased as the answerphone cut in, then seconds later it started again. She entered the empty reception area and glanced at the caller ID screen on the console on Alison's desk. 'Number withheld.' She flopped into Alison's chair, braced herself and lifted the receiver.

'Mrs Cooper? Amanda Cramer here.'

She needn't have bothered with the introduction. There was no mistaking the owner of the sinister, robotic voice. Jenny flicked on the monitor of Alison's computer.

'How can I help you?' Jenny said, checking her email.

'Have you seen the newspapers?'

'I've glanced at them.'

'You've certainly given the press a sensational story.'

'Not me, the evidence did that.' Her in-box started to load with the day's messages.

'But you called the evidence, and at a time of your choosing. All matters undoubtedly within your discretion, but a coroner does have a duty to use her discretion wisely.'

Jenny scanned the list of forty new messages. 'In what way are you suggesting I haven't, precisely?'

'It's not just the specifics, Mrs Cooper, there is a wider public interest to consider – a highly sensitive bill being introduced to Parliament.'

Jenny struggled to hold her temper. Still furious with Starr, Amanda Cramer's interference was making her feel murderous. 'The day causing embarrassment to politicians is a good reason to soft-pedal an inquest is the day justice has died, don't you agree?'

'I should have known you'd be belligerent.'

'Fearless independence is my legal duty.' She arrived at the end of the list and a message marked 'urgent' from Bristol CID. She clicked it open.

'All manner of sins can masquerade as principle,' Cramer said.

'What exactly are you asking me to do?' she said, her attention shifting to the few brief lines of text on the screen. A young man's body had been found on the Langan Estate.

There was a pause. 'The right thing.'

'Or?' Jenny stiffened with shock. The brief email ended with: '. . . thought to be that of missing teenager Frederick Reardon.'

'Let's not be childish, Mrs Cooper. It's in nobody's interests not to bring this inquest to a rapid close.'

Jenny didn't answer.

Amanda Cramer said, 'Can we expect a conclusion tomorrow?'

'I think that's very unlikely now.' Jenny put down the phone.


A small rag-tag crowd of residents had been drawn out of the surrounding tower blocks and stood at the cordon that marked off a section of the car park and the rough parkland beyond. Jenny pushed between them and announced herself to the young constable holding them back.

'Can you wait a minute? I've been told not to let anyone through.'

'I'm the coroner.'

'Yeah, but—'

'Do you know what that means?'

He looked at her uncertainly. 'Yeah—'

'Dear God.' Jenny ducked under the tape.

'Ma'am—'

'It's all right, Constable, she's with me.' Alison hurried out from between the assortment of police vehicles.

'Can you please explain to this idiot who the coroner is?'

'Sorry,' Alison said to the young policeman.

'Don't apologize, tell him!'

She strode off towards the scene of activity that centred on an area of undergrowth. It was near the bench on which she'd sat alongside Freddy only a few days before.

Alison caught up with her halfway across the grass, out of breath and perspiring.

'I only just got here, Mrs Cooper. I tried to call you.'

Jenny cut through her lie with a look.

'I was just about to.' Alison searched for an adequate explanation. 'I was trying to find a way of breaking it to you.'

'Because I'm so unused to people dying.'

'No. I just thought you might feel—'

'What? Responsible?'

'He hanged himself, Mrs Cooper. Some time last night they think.'

Jenny felt nothing. A complete absence.

'Does anyone know why?'

'There was a note in his pocket,' Alison mumbled. 'It said, "I'm no good."'

They approached a thicket of spindly birch and hazel clogged with nettles and bindweed. Two officers in white overalls emerged from a break in the undergrowth, peeling off their masks and hoods.

'Jenny Cooper, Severn Vale District Coroner,' Jenny snapped at them and pushed past with Alison at her heels.

DI Wallace was standing in his shirt sleeves talking into his phone as two officers dressed in white overalls zipped the body into a nylon bag. Directly above it a length of blue plastic washing line hung limply from a branch.

Wallace hurriedly ended his call as Jenny approached.

'Hello again, Mrs Cooper,' he said, a trace of apprehension in his voice.

'May I please see him?'

Wallace gestured to his officers to comply.

The zip came down to reveal Freddy's swollen face. A purple welt where the line had cut into his flesh circled the front of his neck and rose vertically behind his jawbone. He was dressed in the same yellow T-shirt he had been wearing the afternoon they had met at the Mission Church.

'Time of death?'

'Between one and three this morning.'

'Where's his mother?'

'In her flat. Family liaison's with her now.'

'Have you spoken to her yet?'

'No.' He was in a hurry to get on. 'Seen enough?'

Jenny nodded. 'What about the note?'

'I'll get you a copy sent over.' He gestured to the body. 'To the Vale, is it?'

'Yes.'

The two officers hoisted the stretcher and pushed out of the thicket. Jenny looked up at the dangling length of line.

'Any idea why?' Wallace asked.

Jenny pictured Freddy stooped forwards on the bench only yards from where they were standing, the way he'd gripped on to his cuffs with clenched fists as he told her, 'God changes people. Not just a little bit, completely. And for ever. All you have to do is let him.' It was the one thing he had seemed certain of, and the one thing that had reassured her.

'He was fragile,' Jenny said, 'with a history of psychiatric problems. I don't think his grip on life can have been very strong to begin with.'

'I'll tell you what, I'm happy to treat this one as suicide for now,' Wallace said. 'This looks more like your territory than mine.' He turned to Alison. 'You'll drop me a copy of the p-m report?'

'Of course.'

Wallace glanced up at the line. 'I'll have someone take that down.' Dipping his head to avoid the low branches, he pushed his way out to the light.

Alison said, 'You really mustn't blame yourself, Mrs Cooper. If he's had mental problems—'

'I don't,' Jenny said. 'When you lift stones you find worms. That's just the way it is.'

Several ragged bunches of flowers wrapped in cellophane lay on the dirty tiled floor outside the door to the Reardons' flat. Jenny pushed them gently aside with her foot and lifted the knocker. A female liaison officer who didn't look any older than her son answered. Jenny asked to see Mrs Reardon alone, leaving the girl to dither over whether to bring the flowers in or to leave them outside. Were these unsolicited offerings which had become part of the modern death ritual, a private gift or a public memorial? It was hard to say.

Eileen Reardon was sitting with the curtains drawn in the airless sitting room. It reeked of stale smoke. Sniffling into a grubby handkerchief, she looked up at Jenny with eyes that seemed to have sunk into her face. Propped up against the empty cigarette packets littering the coffee table was a photograph of a smiling Freddy in front of a roller-coaster.

'That was on a trip last year,' Eileen said. 'He went with the church.'

Jenny sat on the edge of the sofa opposite, trying to tolerate the foul-smelling air.

'I'm sorry, Mrs Reardon. I truly am.'

Eileen lowered her chin, her exhausted marbled features telling Jenny that Freddy's death was less a complete surprise than a tragic conclusion to events she had been powerless to influence.

'How had he been?'

'Quiet.'

'Last night?'

'Went to church, came home about half-past ten. I left him in here watching the television.'

Jenny tried to imagine what it must have been like for Freddy returning from an evening of euphoria to this pit of despondency.

'When did you notice he was gone?'

'He gets up before me in the mornings, you know, takes himself to school.'

'Did he mention the inquest?' Jenny asked. 'I'd asked him to give evidence today.'

'I didn't know a thing about it.'

'There would have been a letter in the post.'

She shook her head.

'The police came here today—'

'I don't talk to the police.' She glanced at the partially open door. 'Rotten, hypocritical bastards.' She looked at Jenny. 'They can't do enough for you when they're dead.'

'You've been told there was a note in his pocket?' Jenny ventured.

Eileen nodded.

'This probably isn't the right time, but if there's anything you want to tell me—'

The corners of Eileen's mouth twisted downwards as she

seemed to struggle against a feeling of overwhelming revulsion. 'He'd talk to me about Jesus. Walk with Jesus, love Jesus. Jesus is going to save you. Jesus is going to heal you. All that crap.' She spat out the words. 'I told him I didn't do bullshit any more. I'd had enough of that from his father and every other man I'd ever known. If there are answers in this world you find them yourself, you don't get taken in by some church that wants to send us back to the Dark Ages.'

'When I spoke to you before, I got the impression that you respected his belief.'

'Sometimes I'd pretend to. I know you've got to try to let them have a mind of their own, but all this religious stuff . . .' Running out of words, she shook her head.

'Did he ever talk to you about Eva Donaldson?' Jenny asked.

'She's sitting at the right hand of God, isn't she? I'd rather he'd been watching her movies, if I'm honest.'

'Did he ever talk about her death, the way she died?'

'It was the devil, you know. He did it. And it was unbelievers like me who were helping him, of course.'

'Freddy never talked about her wavering, losing her faith?'

'Was she now?' Eileen laughed, stirring the mucus in her rattling lungs. 'Oh, my God.'

'He never mentioned that?'

'I think I would have remembered. Oh, yes.' Her smile contorted into a mask of pain. 'He worshipped those people. But I was the one who got him out of hospital, it was me who nursed him and got him back to school.' She pounded her fist into her chest. 'But I was the one who was damned because I wasn't with Jesus!'

*

It was called the Eagle's Nest, a man-made balcony seven hundred feet above the western side of the Wye valley, midway between Chepstow and Tintern. Jenny pulled on the walking shoes and jeans that now lived permanently in the boot of her car and made the climb up the three hundred and sixty-five steps and narrow paths that snaked through the woods and traversed the jagged cliffs. The fading evening sun filtered through a dense canopy of ivy-choked oak and beech; ancient yews clung implausibly to the rocks, their gnarled roots strangling boulders like the slow-moving tentacles of sea monsters. In damp hollows and dark corners untouched by summer light, moss grew six inches deep in a carpet of emerald velvet.

It was a mythical place, like the forests of her childhood storybooks, where the trees came to life and spirits flitted between the shadows; a netherworld through which she ascended up ringing iron steps to the clearing on the summit. There she was met by the sight of twenty miles of patchwork countryside beyond the gorge. She stood at the railing, gazing out over a landscape slowly descending into twilight, and wondered, not for the first time in her brief career, why it was that she felt as if she had one foot in the place where the dead went when they were wrenched unwillingly from this world. The living part of her wanted to close the door on them, to bring her inquest to a rapid end and to deal with Freddy's death with one of the discreet thirty-minute hearings her colleagues managed to conduct without a trace of guilt. But try as she might, she couldn't force the door shut; hollow, frightened faces peered at her from the darkness, silently pleading.

She had hoped that the exertion of the climb and the majestic view would have cured her of her maudlin thoughts, but they merely brought her dread into sharper focus. For the first time since McAvoy, it had happened again: she could no sooner walk away with the truth half told than leave a grave half filled. Eva, Jacobs and Freddy felt close enough to touch; it was their voices she heard on the breeze, their faces she saw among the scattered clouds in the pink-tinged sky.

# SIXTEEN

IGNORING ALISON'S GRIM WARNINGS OF recriminations from above, Jenny postponed the resumption of the inquest for twenty-four hours and forced her officer to spend her evening making phone calls to grumpy lawyers and tetchy witnesses. She unplugged her telephone at the wall and spent the evening holed up in her study. She imagined Ed Prince pacing his hotel suite, venting his anger on exhausted assistants while concocting his plans for revenge. Michael Turnbull would be quietly sounding out friends in the government, seeking assurances that this wasn't some elaborate rouse to derail his precious bill. To them he would present the calm and rational face of a well-meaning reformer, but at home with Christine the talk would be of the devil's voice making itself heard in Cassidy's testimony.

As she lay in bed dosed with pills to deaden her jangling nerves and stamp out her unruly imagination, Jenny picked up Eva and Lennox's book, *Forgiveness*. It was trite stuff written in a folksy style, half a chapter by Lennox, half by Eva, but as sleep threatened, a passage caught Jenny's eye. Eva had written:

> *'Forgive us our sins, as we forgive those who sin against us,' is one of those little phrases I didn't think about much at first, but which changed my life. It's that little*

*word 'as'. God forgives us as we forgive others. It means that you can be free of your sins and living in peace with him only so long as you're doing all in your power to forgive those who've hurt you, including yourself. God's forgiveness is always there like water to your house, and just like the water company he leaves it completely up to you whether the tap's on or off. People wonder how someone who has been born again can so easily fall out of step with God; often the simple reason is they've turned off the tap and stopped forgiving.*

The book fell from Jenny's fingers and clattered to the floor as her eyelids drooped and closed. She switched out the light and slipped from consciousness with a picture of Eva at her kitchen sink turning the tap on and off.

A mortuary technician was sluicing down a body as Jenny arrived at the Vale early the next morning to talk to Andy Kerr. He was caught up in a call to the lab, which he took on the phone screwed to the autopsy room wall, leaving Jenny, dressed in green overalls, to watch the end of the procedure on the table next to the one on which Freddy's naked body lay. The corpse was that of a woman of about her age and bore no obvious signs of injury.

The technician, a small, wiry man with unnaturally bright eyes, said, 'A bit close to home, eh?'

Jenny gave a half-hearted smile and looked away. She didn't want to know how the woman had died.

'Sorry about that.' Andy came off the phone and pulled on a pair of gloves. 'Is there anything I should know about him?'

'I'm still waiting for his medical records,' Jenny said, 'but I do know there was a history of mental illness, I'm guessing manic depression.'

'We'll run blood tests for the usual drugs. Anything physical?'

'Not as far as I know.'

Andy began with a visual examination. Starting at the feet, he checked for signs of bruising, abrasions or needle marks. Finding nothing of note, he moved on to the mid-section, scanning the skinny abdomen and chest before levering the body onto its side to examine the back.

'No cuts or bruises. No sign of a struggle.' He leaned in close to inspect the welt left by the washing line. 'No bruising around the mid or lower neck –' he glanced back down at the legs – 'the blood's pooled in the lower half of the body. A classic case of self-inflicted asphyxiation I'd say.'

Jenny nodded. It was exactly as she had expected, but part of her had been hoping for evidence of violence having been used against him. She didn't want any doubt hanging over Freddy. She was sure she would establish that he had been at the Mission Church the night of Eva's murder, but his suicide raised a suspicion she couldn't ignore. His history suggested instability; his closeness to Eva hinted at motive.

She dismissed the thought. It was more likely that Freddy had killed himself out of despair. Having looked up to Eva and seen her as living proof of healing and redemption, her death must have shaken him to the core. Perhaps he had been in love with her. Scarred as she was, it would have been almost impossible for any young man who knew her not to have been.

'Are you OK?' Andy asked, reaching for the nine-inch knife he would use to make the first incision.

'Fine. Just thinking.'

'You've never got used to this, have you?'

She glanced at Freddy's plaster-white face, the sharp

bones jutting through his hollow cheeks. 'I was with him the other day.'

Andy set the knife down on the counter. 'Why don't you wait in my office?'

It would have been the sensible thing to do, but a voice in her head insisted she stay, telling her she owed it to Freddy to see it through to the end.

'I'll stay,' Jenny said, 'I'll just look the other way.'

She stepped back to the corner of the room and stared at anything but the autopsy table as Andy opened the cadaver, first with a knife, then with shears to crop through the stubborn ribs. Out of the corner of her eye she saw him excising the tongue muscle, drawing it down through the throat and carrying it to the counter for dissection. The small, horseshoe-shaped hyoid bone, which sat halfway between the bottom of the chin and the Adam's apple, always yielded the first major clue in a suspected suicide by hanging. If the victim had been strangled by a third party, it would invariably be broken; if he had hanged himself, the point of compression would be higher up the neck.

'Hyoid's intact,' Andy said. 'Looks like my theory's safe.'

She heard it rattle as it hit the kidney dish. Andy turned back to the opened body.

Next he removed the stomach, carefully cutting it open with a scalpel to reveal the contents.

'Empty. He hadn't eaten in hours,' he announced, and turned his attention to the duodenum. A short while later he confirmed his finding. 'I'd say he probably hadn't eaten all day.'

'No sign of pills or alcohol?' Jenny said.

'No. We'll wait for the blood tests, but I'd be prepared to bet he was completely sober.' Andy looked over his shoulder at her. 'Would it help to put some music on? I'm about to use the saw.'

'Maybe I will wait outside.'

She stepped out into the corridor as Andy fired up the fine surgical saw with which he would remove the top of the skull. She felt ashamed of herself for still being squeamish, but every post-mortem still felt to her like an act of sacrilege.

She had been loitering for nearly fifteen minutes when Andy came to the door.

'All done. Not a lot to report.'

She followed him back inside, tugging off her overalls and dropping them in the laundry bin. The bright-eyed assistant was already at work, humming quietly to himself as he stitched Freddy's bloody torso together again.

'All the major organs were very healthy,' Andy said, stripping off his gloves, 'though I'd say he liked a cigarette.'

'That would be his mother.'

'Then she's been doing enough for both of them. No sign of any trauma or anything to indicate a struggle,' Andy continued. 'I've taken nail scrapings and internal swabs. Don't ask for any results in less than forty-eight hours – you're more likely to walk on water.'

'That'll do.'

There was a sudden rush of water as the technician switched on the shower head connected to the autopsy table and began to sluice Freddy's body down.

Andy stepped over to the sink, soaped his hands and started to scrub.

'Maybe I shouldn't ask you until the inquest's over, but did you find out what that tattoo on Eva Donaldson's body meant?' he asked. 'It caused quite a stir yesterday. My name was in so many newspapers my mother's making a scrapbook.'

'I'm afraid she took her reasons with her.'

'You know what I think? It was the Marilyn Monroe thing, you know, the whole little girl act to make up for the fact she was corrupted so young.'

'What's little girl about tattooing your crotch?'

'She was what, twenty-seven? To that generation getting a tattoo's as natural as buying a new outfit. She wouldn't have thought twice. And with her public profile, beneath the bikini's the only place she could have put it without running the risk of it being caught on film.'

'It's as good a theory as any,' Jenny said, and turned to glance one last time at Freddy as Andy dried his hands on a paper towel.

The assistant casually moved a forearm to rinse down the right side of the ribs, and that was when Jenny noticed: a bracelet of red marks around the right wrist. She moved towards the table.

'Look at this.'

Andy tossed the towel away and joined her.

'Marks on the wrist. Why didn't you see them?'

'Turn that off,' Andy ordered the assistant. '*Now*.'

He stepped round to the left side of the body and studied the wrist. He reached for a clean scalpel and scraped it gently across the skin. He held the blade up to the light. 'There's some sort of concealer on there, like make-up.'

Not bothering with scrubs, Andy pulled on another set of gloves. Jenny watched as he scraped away what looked like a hardened layer of foundation cream, revealing a ring of abrasions around the wrist.

'See there, where it rubs against the bone,' Andy said, pointing at the rawest section of flesh, 'that was handcuffs.'

'How recently?'

'There's scabbing, evidence of healing. I'd estimate a couple of days before death.'

'There was no evidence of sexual contact?'

'Not on visual inspection,' Andy said. 'The swabs will tell us more.'

Jenny stepped away from the table and tried to fathom what it meant.

She called Alison from the car but there was no answer at the office. She tried her mobile and got through to her on a bad line with the sound of seagulls and motor launches in the background. Alison claimed she was out running errands, but the sounds of the harbourside were unmistakable. She could tell from her assistant's guilty inflection that she was meeting Martin again.

'I was hoping you could go and talk to Mrs Reardon for me. It turns out Freddy had some abrasions around his wrists that he'd tried to conceal. It looks as if he'd been handcuffed.'

'Oh, I might be a little while—'

'Anything important?'

'Where would you like me to begin, Mrs Cooper?'

Jenny winced; it was embarrassing to listen to. She gave up on the idea of avoiding confronting Eileen Reardon herself. Alison would hardly have her mind on the job even if she could be prised away.

'It's all right, I'll go,' Jenny said, and left Alison to her fun.

Eileen Reardon refused to answer her door. Jenny knocked and knocked again, but to no avail. The bunches of flowers which had been left the day before lay untouched, their petals browning in the heat. She pushed open the letterbox and peered into the darkened hallway. There was no sign of life.

'Mrs Reardon. It's Jenny Cooper. I really do need to speak to you.'

No answer.

'We've found some marks on Freddy's body. Please, it's very important.'

'You're wasting your breath.'

Jenny turned to see a white-haired old lady standing cross-armed in a doorway across the hall.

'Do you know if she's in?' Jenny asked.

'She'll be in there all right, never comes out. She's got a "phobia"; that's what her boy said, anyway. Fond of a drink as well, though God knows who'll fetch it for her now she's on her own.'

Jenny said, 'Did you know Freddy?'

The woman eyed her suspiciously. 'Are you with the police?'

'No. I'm the coroner.'

'Oh—'

'Nothing to do with the police.' She offered what she hoped was a reassuring smile. 'Maybe you could help me?'

The woman thought for a moment, then glanced along the corridor to check they hadn't been seen.

'You'd better come in.'

Jenny followed her into a spotlessly clean flat and sat at a small table in the kitchen.

'I didn't catch your name,' Jenny said, introducing herself.

'Maggie Harper.'

Jenny's eyes travelled over the shiny surfaces and polished cupboard doors. It was a world away from the flat across the hall. 'Have you lived here long?'

'Twenty-five years – about fifteen more than her. You wouldn't think she was the same person to look at her now.'

'I can believe it. She doesn't look well.'

'It's ever since that man of hers,' Maggie said. 'He did for both of them in my opinion.'

'Was that Freddy's stepdad?'

Maggie pulled a face as she nodded. 'He was a dropout. Hippy type, hair all matted. Didn't do a stroke all day as far as I could tell, except yell at those two and smoke whatever it was.'

'I heard Freddy got into a fight with him.'

'He was only protecting his mother. He'd hit her – Gary, was his name. You could hear it all from in here. I'd call the police when it got too bad but she'd never say a word against him. Some women are like that, don't ask me why.'

'But this man, Gary, he pressed charges against Freddy, did he?'

'Oh, yes. I told Freddy I'd speak for him in court, but he went and pleaded guilty. I think he did it to save his mum the ordeal of giving evidence.'

'What happened to this man?'

'Right after that he just packed up and left. Never heard of him again.' She looked down at the table, shaking her head. 'It's a wonder that boy lasted as long as he did. He was lovely when you spoke to him on his own.'

'Did you know him well?'

'He's been coming over for years. I'd give him his tea sometimes when she was out of it. But he was ever so loyal to her, wouldn't say a bad word.' She looked up. 'What is it you'd like to know?'

'I know Freddy had been involved with a church, but I've no idea about his personal life, who his friends were, what he might have got up to.'

'He never seemed to have any friends,' Maggie said. 'I was probably as close to him as anyone. I certainly never saw him bring anyone home.'

'Did he ever talk to you about the people he'd met at church?'

'Not much. We had our little routine, you see. He'd come over and watch TV in the front room and I'd bring him something to eat and sit with him. That's the way he liked it. Cosy. No fuss.'

'And lately? Did you see a change in him?'

Maggie frowned. 'It's not so much recently, it's more since before Christmas. He hadn't been coming over as often, maybe once every couple of weeks.'

'How did he seem?'

'Quiet. I thought he was worried about his mother – he said she hadn't been well – but I suppose I should have seen the signs . . .'

Jenny waited.

Maggie had a kind face, she thought, and she was glad Freddy had had at least one caring and trustworthy adult in his life. Her orderly flat must have been an oasis for him.

'There was one night; it must have been three months ago. It was a Friday, quite late. He came to the door all pale, as if he'd had a fright. I sat him down in the other room as usual and came in here to make him some supper. I thought it was something on the television at first, but it was him, he was sobbing. He'd dried his eyes by the time I came back in. I asked if he was all right. He said was fine, but I could see he wasn't. He was like this –' she curled her fingers into her palms and pressed her elbows to her sides – 'like a little lost soul.'

'He didn't say anything?'

'No. I probably should have asked, but I didn't want to scare him off. You can understand.'

'Of course.'

'I didn't see it as any of my business. I just wanted to be there for him when he needed me,' Maggie said. 'But it wasn't enough, was it?'

Jenny came away feeling that she'd learned more from Maggie Harper than she would have done from Eileen Reardon. With a little pressing she had established that the Friday night she had talked about was either the third or fourth in March. It meant that whatever had caused the dip in Freddy's mood had pre-dated Eva's death. Jenny wasn't sure if that was a good or a bad sign. Maggie had been certain of one thing, though, there had been no girlfriends. 'He was far too innocent for any of that,' she had said. 'He was still a mummy's boy, except his mum was hopeless.'

Back at the office Alison was tapping furiously at her computer. Jenny didn't mention her lunch date with Martin and nor did she; they didn't have to. They both knew where she had been and Alison was doing her best to demonstrate she was making up for lost time. She briskly handed over a batch of new death reports and rattled off a list of urgent phone messages, including several from various members of Michael Turnbull's legal team protesting at her demand that he return to the resumed inquest. Jenny retreated to her office and endeavoured to cram a day's work into what remained of the afternoon. There were new cases to log, hospital consultants to call, post-mortem reports to wade through, a host of deaths to certify and bodies to release, but Eva and Freddy refused to leave her thoughts. There was something she had yet to find out; she felt sure there was a person who would unlock them both, but she still felt far from knowing who that might be.

The fading sun had retreated behind a bank of dark cloud as Jenny turned off the valley road at Tintern and climbed a mile up the narrow lane to Melin Bach. The dull evening light coupled with an unseasonal chill gave the countryside a melancholy air that reflected her mood. It was an evening for ghosts and regrets, the lengthening shadows seemed to say.

She resented the fact that her emotions could shift as swiftly as a child's, that something as mundane as the changing weather could cause her mood to plunge. The thought of returning to her empty cottage filled her with irrational dread, but as she rounded the penultimate bend and spotted its slate roof through a gap in the trees, the sky opened again and a stretch of brilliant blue appeared over Barbadoes Hill. Just enough to repel the anxious, unwanted thoughts which had started to intrude.

There was no time to be neurotic, she told herself; all that would have to wait until Eva's inquest was over. Then she would set aside the necessary few weeks to resolve her problems. It would be good to feel properly human again. She couldn't wait.

She was surprised to see Steve's Land Rover parked in the lane outside the house. Alfie, his sheepdog, shot out from the verge in pursuit of a rabbit, which zigzagged along the road for several yards then disappeared into the hedge with Alfie hard on its tail. She pulled into the overgrown cart track and stepped out of the car to the smell of ripe grass and lavender. Steve wandered across to meet her from the back garden, beating a path through the weeds with a stick.

'You could do with someone to sort this place out,' he said with a smile.

'It's good for the wildlife. I thought you were in Edinburgh.'

'Signed up the client before lunch and caught an earlier plane.'

'That sounds like good news.'

'Could be. But if they kept me on to manage the project it'd mean spending a lot of time up there.'

'What about France?'

'Still stringing them along.' He swished distractedly at a clump of thistles.

Jenny absorbed his tired and thoughtful face; he'd changed in a year. Study and responsibility had diluted the carefree spirit, but she liked the man who was emerging. He was sensitive, searching, and he wanted her. Yet she remained frightened to give, scared of letting him down. And perhaps fearful of what he would ask from her. He wanted to know parts of her that her ex-husband wouldn't have even known existed.

Jenny said, 'Do you get the feeling that you're being dragged out of the woods at last?'

'Maybe I don't want to be. Something might work out.' He tossed the stick aside and looked at her. 'What about you? Do you ever think this place is just a staging post, somewhere to hide out for a while?'

'Ask me in a couple of months' time.'

'What happens then?'

'Maybe I'll be out of the trees and the world will look different.'

A gust of wind blew her hair across her face. Steve reached out and pushed it back, brushing his fingers against her cheek. He moved his lips, as if about to speak, but instead stepped closer and touched her hand. 'If you weren't here, the decision would be easy.'

Jenny wanted to tell him that his life was his own, that he mustn't let her hold him back, but as he kissed her the thought of losing him was too painful to bear. She held him tightly, pressing herself to his hard chest, aware of how selfish she was being but powerless to do a thing about it. He was her release, her glimpse of freedom.

They made love on the grass beneath the last rays of the dying sun. Afterwards, Steve ran naked into the stream, daring her to join him. When she pleaded that she was too cold, he came and picked her up, squealing, and tumbled backwards into the water bringing her with him. The freezing water took the breath from her; she shrieked and protested but he clung on to her until the feel of it against her skin was like a million hot needles. And when they walked back to the house scooping up their clothes, the blood coursed hot through her veins, and for a short while she felt alive and invincible.

Steve lit a fire in the grate and they lay entwined on the sofa sipping tea and waiting for the shivers to subside. Jenny leaned back against him as he stroked her hair. Alfie stretched out on the hearthrug, his eyes half-closed in bliss.

'How are you feeling?' Steve said.

'Good . . . tired.'

'Are you going back to Dr Allen?'

'When this inquest's over. Let's not talk about that now, hmm?' Jenny sensed that he was tense. 'What is it?' she asked.

His hand slid from her head and rested against her arm. 'I had a message on my phone when I got home. The man said his name was Detective Sergeant Gleed, based at Weston. He left a number.'

*Gleed.* It wasn't a name she recognized.

'Did you call him? What did he want?'

'Yes. He was polite enough—'

Jenny put down her mug and sat up, tugging away from him.

'What did he want?'

'He said he understood that I knew you, and had you ever talked about an event in your childhood? If so, he'd like to meet and discuss what you had told me.'

Jenny looked at him in disbelief.

'I said I didn't know anything about it.'

'A detective?' Jenny said, incredulously. 'Why didn't you tell me this before?'

'I was going to. That's why, well, one of the reasons I came—'

'But you thought you'd have your fun first.'

'That's not fair.'

'Jesus. God.' Jenny sunk her head in her hands. 'You bastard.'

'Jenny, it's not like that. You know it's not. I care about you. I—'

'Don't say it!'

'I do. And I want to be with you, but you've got to deal with this stuff.'

'Or what?'

'Or nothing. You just have to. You know you do. Why don't you call this man? See what he wants.'

'He can go to hell. I was a child, for Christ's sake.'

'He wants something. These people don't just go away.'

'It'll be Dad. He'll have said something to one of the nurses.'

'All the more reason to clear it up.' Steve reached to his shirt pocket. 'Look, I've got the number—'

'I don't want to know.'

He grabbed hold of her wrist. 'Jenny, you've got to face this.'

She wrenched free. 'Don't tell me what I've got to do.'

'How else are you going to sort yourself out?'

'Leave me alone.'

'Why don't you call him while I'm here?'

'Stop trying to control me.'

'I'm trying to help.'

'Shut up! Shut up!' She shot off the sofa. 'Get out! Go!'

She wanted to punch him, to lash out and hurt him and make him hit her back, to turn her anger and confusion into physical pain she could rail and pound her fists against, but Steve absorbed her outburst without a word. He left the scrap of paper bearing Gleed's number on the corner of the sofa and turned to leave.

He stopped briefly in the doorway with his back to her. 'I'll be here for you, Jenny, but—'

'Please go.'

Softly, but with a finality she knew was real, he said, 'You know what I mean.'

She sat and stared into the fire for the time it took the logs to dwindle to embers, her mind racing with angry thoughts and wild theories. She had never felt more exposed or more furious. Why? Why now? Who could the events of nearly forty years ago possibly be of interest to? It was past eleven when she snatched up the phone and punched in his number. An anonymous answer message played. Jenny said, 'Detective Sergeant Gleed, it's Jenny Cooper, Severn Vale District Coroner. I don't know what you think you're doing, but I'll expect your call tomorrow.'

She screwed up his number and tossed it into the grate.

# SEVENTEEN

DETECTIVE SERGEANT GLEED DIDN'T RETURN her call. Nor did Jenny manage to reach him through the switchboard at Weston police station as she sped over the Severn Bridge en route to her reconvened inquest. The detective's affectation of making himself unreachable infuriated her and she cursed him out loud for his petty attempt at intimidation.

Shouting out her frustrations in the privacy of her car was a release of sorts but, Gleed apart, Steve's challenge had been salt on an open wound. The pain had raged through a long, restless night and refused to be dampened by her morning dose of Xanax bolstered by a top-up of Temazepam. The drugs might have stopped her heart from racing and steadied her hand, but they did nothing to dull the inner ache. He had confronted her with the undeniable truth: there was something buried inside her she had to uncover, or she would be truly lost. McAvoy had seen it from the moment they met. Father Starr had interpreted his intuited insights into her unsettled mind as a word of the spirit; Alison had betrayed her suspicions in countless minor manifestations of disapproval. All of these Jenny had been able to disregard as quirks of character, but Steve was different. He knew her past and was forcing her back to it. Anyone else could be pushed away, but Steve had cornered her. He had locked her in a space alone with herself.

The news crews were already busy setting up as Jenny squeezed her Golf between their vans and parked on the rough grass at the side of the hall. They were a different crowd from those who had been present on the first day; she recognized the faces of several national television reporters among them. Making her way to the hall, she overheard an earnest young woman explaining to camera that the sudden apparent suicide of a witness who had failed to testify, coupled with Cassidy's allegation that Eva had lost her faith, suggested there were many questions the police inquiry had failed to answer. *Or even ask*, Jenny wanted to butt in.

'The parties are all assembled, Mrs Cooper,' Alison announced as she appeared in the office doorway, 'but counsel would like to speak to you in chambers before we begin.'

'What about?'

'They didn't say.'

'Didn't you ask them?' Jenny said as she gathered her papers, trying to ignore the sudden palpitations that the prospect of facing a row of awkward lawyers had caused to erupt.

Alison swallowed defensively. 'I didn't think it was my place.'

'I see. Has Michael Turnbull answered his summons?'

'I didn't notice him.'

'So he's failed to attend. Are his lawyers aware that amounts to contempt?'

'I wouldn't know.'

Jenny took a deep breath, struggling to hold her impatience with her officer in check.

Alison hovered uncertainly. 'Shall I tell them to come in?'

Jenny marched towards the door, her apprehension turning to anger. 'You can tell them to stand up.'

Christopher Sullivan and Ed Prince wore expressions of surprised indignation as Jenny took her seat at the head of the packed hall. She could see Father Starr and Kenneth Donaldson amidst the swollen ranks of reporters, but there was no sign of Michael Turnbull. She did, however, spot a new face alongside Prince: a female lawyer with the hard attractiveness and sharp-eyed gaze that could only belong to a seasoned litigator, and wearing an outfit that could only have been afforded by a partner in a wealthy firm. She was their new tactician, Jenny guessed; a woman sent to read and undermine her.

Sullivan was first to his feet. The new lawyer flashed him a look that reminded him to remain polite. 'Ma'am, might counsel be permitted to address you briefly in chambers?'

'I don't see counsel in chambers, Mr Sullivan,' Jenny said, still battling a racing heart. 'As a matter of principle I conduct my business in public and on behalf of the public whose interests I represent.'

He strained to be polite. 'As an exceptional deviation from the rule, it would be much appreciated.'

'This isn't like a criminal court, as you well know, Mr Sullivan. It is *my* inquest, and as counsel you have the right to cross-examine any witnesses I may call, but not to dictate procedure. Now do you have anything you wish to say before I call on Lord Turnbull to answer his witness summons?'

Sullivan glanced back at Prince and his female colleague and exchanged whispered words. Jenny noticed Fraser Knight QC and Ruth Markham, passive observers to their colleagues' discomfort, exchange a hint of a smile across the length of the advocates' bench.

Sullivan turned back to the front, still wearing his expression of mock civility. 'Ma'am, I have to inform you that it has not been possible for Lord Turnbull to appear as promptly as requested. You may not know – and the fault may be ours for failing to inform you – just how busy a parliamentary timetable he has at the present moment.'

'On the contrary, your instructing solicitors informed me yesterday afternoon. And I told them that he was required to give evidence here at ten o'clock this morning.'

'Ma'am, it simply hasn't been feasible—'

'Where is he, Mr Sullivan?'

'Ma'am, a degree of reasonableness is customary—'

'Where is he?' Jenny insisted.

Sullivan's eyes flared, but fighting every instinct he contained his anger. 'In London. On urgent business, I believe.'

'And when *is* he proposing to attend?'

'He's very busy with parliamentary business all next week, ma'am.'

At her desk, Alison sat hunched over the tape recorder, avoiding the lawyers' gaze, pretending she was part of the furniture. It suddenly occurred to Jenny that they must have intimidated her into arranging the cosy meeting in chambers in which they hoped to ensure that Turnbull's absence would be excused and never mentioned in front of the press.

'Members of the jury,' Jenny said, 'in the light of Mr Cassidy's evidence about Eva Donaldson's state of mind prior to her death, I issued Lord Turnbull with a summons; he was to attend this morning to see if he could help us any further with the issue. Failure to comply is a contempt of court, an offence punishable by fine or imprisonment.'

Sullivan interjected: 'Ma'am, my client can hardly be said to have wilfully absented himself.'

'That's just what he has done, Mr Sullivan. The law applies to a wealthy member of the House of Lords as much as it does to a street sweeper. I find him to be in contempt and I'll sentence him when he appears. Do I need to issue a warrant?'

'He'll be here this afternoon, ma'am,' Sullivan said, through gritted teeth.

Jenny saw Ed Prince and his companion trade a glance that said they'd taken a punch, but could ride it. She sensed there was something else in play, a deeper strategy, but right now she had neither the time nor the mental space to ponder what that might be. She glanced down at her copy of the witness list. Apart from Turnbull's name, there was only one other yet to be ticked.

'Is Mr Joel Nelson present?'

The man who had greeted her in the office at the Mission Church stood up. 'Yes, ma'am.'

'Please come forward, Mr Nelson. We'll hear from you now.'

As Nelson walked the short length of the hall Jenny noticed Prince and his female colleague both sending messages on their phones. Two rows behind them, Father Starr was sitting perfectly still, his steady, piercing gaze telling her that she was being judged, and by the most exacting standards.

Jenny studied Nelson carefully. Beneath the sober suit and tasteful tie he was an attractive young man with sky-blue eyes and sandy hair. He wore no wedding ring, she noticed, and had the slim frame and well-defined features of someone who took good care of himself. He exuded ambition and purpose.

'Could you please state your full name?'

'Joel Henry Nelson.'

'Your age.'

'Thirty-two.'

'And your occupation?'

'I am employed by the Mission Church of God based in Bedminster, Bristol. My official title is administrative director – which in practice means I run the office,' he added with a polite smile.

'How long have you worked for the Mission Church, Mr Nelson?'

'A little over two years.'

'And prior to that?'

'For eight years I worked for the corporate finance arm of an investment bank. Then I saw the light, as it were.' The smile again.

'I'm intrigued. How did a banker come to work for a church?'

'I answered an ad.'

His quip drew a ripple of laughter from the jury.

'Actually I'd become rather disillusioned with finance,' he continued. 'Money does indeed make the world go round, but among my colleagues I witnessed levels of greed and excess that made me uncomfortable. I'd started looking for something more rewarding when I went to a talk given by Michael Turnbull. It was an epiphany; here was a man who had made a vast fortune then committed himself to working for good. I knew I had to be part of his project.'

'Just out of curiosity, was this also a spiritual epiphany?' Jenny asked, aware that she was straying into territory that wasn't strictly within the bounds of her inquiry.

Nelson leaped on the opportunity to tell more of his story. 'At that time I would describe myself as agnostic. As a thoroughly rational person I believed it was the only intellectually honest position to take. Impressed as I was by Michael's work, I saw organized religion as more of a social good than an expression of absolute truth, a positive motivational force if you like; some people need it to behave well, others don't.' He smiled to himself as he tried to find the words to express what happened next. 'I was still working at the bank when I came down to Bristol to see the church for myself. To be honest, I was sceptical. There were maybe four or five hundred people present and after nearly an hour I'd had enough, I decided that I had made a mistake. But then Pastor Lennox Strong challenged any new arrivals to come forward and commit themselves to God. I was already on my way to the exit, but it was as if a strong hand placed itself on my shoulder and turned me around.' He paused briefly. 'For those who have never experienced anything similar this will make no sense at all, but I was drawn to the front of the church by a force I can only assume was that of the Holy Spirit. And when Pastor Strong placed his hands on me, I experienced something to which words can do no justice—'

'I'm sure we'd be very grateful if you'd try,' Jenny said.

'It's a phenomenon that's become known as the Rapture. If you can begin to imagine an overwhelming sense of warmth and unconditional love coupled with a sense of the physical body being transformed into something light and radiant, you're a fraction of the way there. We call it a gift of the spirit; an experience God gives us to prove that he's real. Some of us believe this has been sent to reinforce the promise of the rapture described in Thessalonians, when Christians are lifted from the earth to the heavens.'

'What happened to you then, Mr Nelson?' Jenny asked as the lawyers exchanged shifty glances.

'Within a fortnight I had applied for and accepted the job.' His eyes shone at the memory.

'I'd like to take you forward in time some seven or eight months to when Eva Donaldson came to work for Decency. Did you have much contact with her?'

'Yes. We were quite friendly. The board would meet in

the church offices, Eva would sometimes attend. She would always stop and talk.'

'Would you describe yourselves as close friends – did you socialize?'

'Not in that sense. It was a friendly, professional relationship, although we had different employers.'

'You never work for Decency?'

'They have their own staff.'

'So this wasn't the kind of friendship in which you discussed intimacies, matters of a personal nature?'

'Not in the sense that I think you mean.'

'You'll know that her former partner, Joseph Cassidy, claims that Eva lost her faith before her death. Do you have anything to say about that?'

'I never doubted her faith. She gave total commitment – you only have to consider her schedule, she didn't stop.'

Jenny turned back through her notebook to a section of Michael Turnbull's evidence she had flagged. 'Eva was killed on the night of Sunday, 9 May. She had been making a round of media appearances that weekend and was due to speak at the evening service: is that your recollection of events?'

'Yes,' Nelson answered cautiously.

'Michael Turnbull said in evidence that you took a call from Eva, who said she wasn't able to attend.'

'That's right.'

'What precisely did she say to you?'

'She said she was very sorry, but she was exhausted and wouldn't be able to make it to the evening service.'

'Had she ever done that before?'

'Not that I can remember.'

'Did you consider it unusual?'

'Not at all. I took her at her word, I had no reason not to.'

'How often did Eva address a congregation four thousand strong?'

'I couldn't say. Not often.'

'So this was a special occasion. Michael and Christine Turnbull were there, Lennox Strong. It sounds like something of a rally for the Decency campaign.'

'No. It was a service at which Eva had intended to say a few words.'

Jenny detected a hint of stiffness, or was it defensiveness, in Joel Nelson's answer.

'To your knowledge, Mr Nelson, had anything happened? Had there been any falling-out or misunderstanding which might have led Eva to stay away?'

'No.'

'Were you aware that as long ago as last November she had asked Decency for a pay rise and been refused?'

'No, I didn't know that.'

'Did you know she had money problems?'

'I had no knowledge of Eva's finances.'

'You weren't aware that all this committed work for Decency was driving her further into debt?'

'I was not.'

'Would it be fair to assume that Michael Turnbull would have known?'

Sullivan started to his feet. 'Ma'am, surely the witness can't be asked to speculate on something about which he can have no knowledge?'

For once he was right, and Jenny was forced to concede. But perhaps she had offered it subconsciously to provide a moment of distraction before she cut to the bone. 'You're quite right, Mr Sullivan, it's a question best saved for this afternoon. You don't have to answer, Mr Nelson.'

Sullivan sat down with the satisfaction of having scored his first point of the day. Behind him, Prince and his colleague remained impassive, their attention anchored in a lower realm Jenny had yet to fathom. They had the brittle stillness of people waiting for something they hoped was coming but might not; only their eyes moved, flitting from Sullivan to Nelson to each other, a glance at the time, no attempt to take notes or pass messages.

'Let me ask you this, Mr Nelson,' Jenny said. 'Did you get any sense from Eva that she was in any way resentful or annoyed that Sunday evening?'

'Not at all. She sounded a little tired, that's all.'

Jenny flicked forward through her notes of Lennox Strong's evidence and tried to picture the scene in the crowded church on that Sunday night: the excited crowd whipped up by the music, hearing that Eva couldn't be with them. Announcing that she was under the weather and had stayed at home didn't seem to fit with the way the Mission Church choreographed its services, each one a carefully staged 'happening' in which the rules of real life were suspended.

'Do you remember how Eva's absence was explained to the congregation?' Jenny asked.

'I think Pastor Strong said something. I can't recall his precise words.'

'Did he tell them she was at home?'

Nelson shook his head. 'Possibly . . .'

'Is it fair to say she had become something of a talismanic figure, a person people had come to see as living proof of the Mission Church's work?'

'I can't deny that.'

*But your answer says you'd like to. Why, Mr Nelson? What is it you'd rather I didn't know?*

'Were you ever aware of her receiving unwanted attention from any member of the church?'

'She never mentioned anything of that sort to me.'

Four thousand worshippers. There had to be more than a few who idolized her less than healthily, who had spent the day in anticipation of being in her presence. A lightning rod for the sexual and religious mania of countless confused and searching souls; the disappointment of her absence must have been crushing.

'She was friendly with a young man in her study group by the name of Freddy Reardon. Unfortunately he died two nights ago. It seems likely he took his own life.'

'Yes, I heard. It's a tragedy. I also heard he had a history of mental illness.'

Anticipating Sullivan's objection, Jenny turned to the jury. 'That's correct, members of the jury. Freddy Reardon was sixteen years old, but had suffered a depressive illness in his earlier teens. He was due to give evidence to this inquest on Monday, but as you may have read in the local press it appears he took his life on Sunday evening. It's not our job here to speculate why that was, so please take care not to read any undue significance into that event.' She turned back to Nelson. 'Did you know him?'

'Hardly at all, I must confess.'

'Were you aware that he was friendly with Eva?'

'Vaguely. I might have seen them chatting once or twice.'

Was she imagining it or was Prince's new companion now operating Nelson by invisible strings? Her steady gaze was fixed on him, but angled as he was slightly towards the jury, Jenny couldn't see if his eyes were meeting hers.

'He was a regular volunteer at your church.'

'I'm afraid I'm a back-office man,' Nelson said. 'I knew Freddy's name, but I doubt he knew mine.'

Jenny followed swiftly with a question she hoped would open a fissure. 'Tell me about Alan Jacobs.'

This time there was no doubt. Nelson glanced at the

anonymous lawyer, who gave the slightest twitch of her eyebrows as if to remind him of his script.

'I believe he's another member of the congregation who also unfortunately took his life in recent weeks.'

'Not only a member of the congregation, a member of the same study group as Freddy Reardon and Eva Donaldson. He also happened to be a psychiatric nurse who had come into contact with Freddy when he was an inpatient at the Conway Unit.'

'I'm afraid to say I didn't know Mr Jacobs either, but obviously I'm deeply sorry for him and his family.'

'I presume his death was the subject of some discussion at the church?'

'Not particularly,' Nelson said. 'When you've so many members these sorts of things are to be expected.'

*But how many study groups had two members who had killed themselves within days of each other?* She would like to have rubbed Nelson's nose in the circumstantial evidence until he was forced to say that Eva must have known things about them that no one else did, that she was their confidante and confessor, their channel from the darkness to the light and perhaps back again. Jenny had to be cleverer than that; she had to find the single weakness that would cause Nelson to stumble and drop his guard.

'Mr Nelson, as the administrator of a church with such a high public profile, you must have been particularly alarmed at Mr Jacobs's death, given his close association with Eva Donaldson.'

'As far as I know the police saw no connection, and nor did we.'

' "*We*", being—?'

'The church's trustees.'

Ruth Markham, solicitor for Kenneth Donaldson, stood up

from her chair and broke her morning-long silence. 'Ma'am, if I may say so, it strikes me that this inquiry is in danger of straying some distance from the narrow issue of what caused Eva Donaldson's death. Clearly while the relevance of evidence is a matter for you to determine, the influence of irrelevant evidence on the jury could affect the sustainability of a verdict.' She gave an almost apologetic smile.

It was a muted interjection, but the message issued in lawyerly code was loud and clear: *Stop this fishing trip and stick to hard facts or we'll have the High Court tear up your verdict before the ink's dry.* Jenny watched Sullivan and Markham exchange a glance. Working in concert, they were sharing the load, making the record show that it was clear to all parties present that the coroner was trespassing where the law said she shouldn't. She was caught in a catch-22: despite her duty to seek out and determine the truth, the ever-tightening case law told her she could only cast her net in certain well-defined waters. She desperately wanted to make the connection between Freddy, Jacobs and Eva, but almost any line of questioning hinting at one would suggest pre-judgement and bias. Reluctantly, she accepted that for present purposes Jacobs's and Freddy's deaths were off-limits.

Thanking Markham for her observation, Jenny addressed her final question to Nelson: did he know of anyone other than the man convicted of her murder who wanted to kill Eva Donaldson?

'No, ma'am. I firmly believe her killer is already behind bars, where he belongs.'

Jenny's mind swam with questions and half-made connections as first Sullivan, then Ruth Markham led Nelson through a series of questions and answers designed to banish any suspicion that Eva's mental state was anything less than stable, or that the untimely deaths of Alan Jacobs and Freddy Reardon were anything other than a cruel coincidence. The Mission Church of God had suffered more than its fair share of suicides among its congregation, Nelson admitted, but as the last stop for the ill and the desperate it was only to be expected. If they had made one mistake it was in failing to protect Eva from its most troubled souls.

Closing the door of her office to await Turnbull's arrival, Jenny attempted to crystallize her suspicions into a theory that might be tested. She had grown increasingly certain throughout the morning that what linked Eva to Alan Jacobs and Freddy Reardon went beyond the simple fact of their acquaintance and into much darker places. She recalled Freddy's hostile reaction when she had mentioned Jacobs's name to him. They had met at the Conway Unit, but Freddy had violently denied that Jacobs had steered him towards the church. Eva had spoken to Freddy frequently, telephoned him and shared her insecurities. Why him? Did she sense a kindred spirit? And what had caused Freddy's bleak mood the night three months ago when he arrived late for his dinner with his kindly neighbour, Maggie Harper?

Jenny's two brief forays into the Mission Church had taught her that it was a place of drama and catharsis; a crucible of emotion in which buried pains and passions were encouraged to erupt and spill out to the applause and wonder of the excited crowd: a theatre of the soul. It didn't surprise her that Eva had been drawn from pornography to the Mission Church's particular brand of religion. It was no coincidence that 'ecstasy' invariably described either sexual or religious euphoria.

She lifted the phone and dialled Andy Kerr's direct line at the Severn Vale District Hospital's mortuary. She had hoped to reach him in person, but her call was answered by his machine.

'Andy, it's Jenny Cooper. I need you to run a DNA test for me. It's just a hunch, but could you please establish if the semen found in Alan Jacobs's body came from Freddy Reardon. I need to know as quickly as possible. Thanks.'

She looked up to see Alison framed in the doorway.

'There's someone to see you, Mrs Cooper,' she said guiltily.

She stepped aside to make way for two men.

'Good morning, ma'am,' the older of the two grunted. 'Detective Sergeant Simon Gleed.' He passed her his warrant card and nodded to his younger colleague. 'Detective Constable Alan Wesley.'

The junior detective gave an embarrassed nod. Not yet thirty, he held a briefcase awkwardly in front of his body and glanced around the shabby room to avoid meeting Jenny's gaze. Gleed was closer to fifty and hadn't worn well; a beer drinker's stomach strained against his shirt, and his bald head was coated with a thin sheen of perspiration.

'You can leave us, Alison,' Jenny said.

She waited for the door to click shut before addressing her visitors.

'Do you make a habit of interrupting judicial proceedings, Mr Gleed?'

'We're answering your enquiry, ma'am,' he said with a pronounced Somerset burr that made him sound almost quaint. 'I understand you've been trying to reach me.'

Jenny sighed: an outward show of impatience to disguise the sensation of panic tightening her chest. 'Let's not play games. What do you want?'

Gleed helped himself to a seat, leaving his subordinate standing.

'A statement might be useful.'

'Concerning?'

'We've had a complaint, Mrs Cooper,' Gleed said, as he reached a handkerchief from his pocket and swept it across his forehead, 'relating to an investigation that happened rather a long time ago.'

'You're referring to the death of my cousin.'

He nodded. 'I am indeed.'

'A complaint from whom?

'Officially it's from your surviving cousin, Mr Christopher Chilcott. But I'll let you into a secret – it was a retired police officer who alerted him to the situation.'

'Situation?'

'Let's just say that police investigations sometimes weren't as thorough back then as they would be now.' He gave an apologetic smile.

'Hold on a moment,' Jenny said. 'I was a child. I have no recollection of the circumstances and until three months ago I had no idea I even had a cousin Katy. A little girl died tragically, but her parents are both dead and the only other adult with any connection is my father, who you may already know is so senile he doesn't recognize his own daughter.'

'Your father's medical condition is certainly something the Crown Prosecution Service will consider,' Gleed said, 'should it ever come to it. But it's not a matter that I can let stand in the way of an investigation – there's the public interest to consider, and the victim's.'

'What victim? Christopher Chilcott never even knew his sister.'

'I can appreciate a woman in your position not wishing to have this raked over, Mrs Cooper, but you'll understand my position too.'

'You don't find the timing of this complaint a touch coincidental?'

Gleed glanced at his colleague and shook his head.

'The fact that I'm in the middle of an inquest which might impact on a major murder investigation carried out by your colleagues in Bristol.'

'Nothing to do with me, nor the old fella who came forward. He's a Weston man, born and bred.' Folding his damp handkerchief back into his pocket, the detective said, 'We could take it now if you like, but I'm sure you'd prefer to make an appointment to come to the station. Would later this afternoon suit?'

'And if I tell you I have nothing to say?'

Gleed fixed his small, black eyes on her. 'We'd both know you weren't telling the truth, wouldn't we?' He heaved his bulk up from the chair. 'We'll say five-thirty, shall we?'

The detectives left as abruptly as they had arrived. Jenny went to the window and peered out from behind the curtain as they walked, unnoticed by the news crews, to their unmarked car parked at the edge of the road. She was in no doubt what was happening: fearing another humiliation at her hands, Bristol CID had dug deep and found a nugget. If she brought her inquest to a quiet close, perhaps the complaint would vanish and DS Gleed could return to chasing pickpockets on the promenade.

It was between her and her conscience. She pulled the curtains tight shut and wandered back to her desk in a semi-daze. What was she hoping to achieve? Her two main suspects were Jacobs and Freddy and they were both dead. Was it right to risk her reputation and livelihood merely in search of truth for truth's sake? Weren't some secrets better left undisturbed?

There was a knock at the door.

'I'm busy.'

Pretending not to have heard, Alison entered. 'Mr Sullivan would like to address you, Mrs Cooper – in open court this time.'

'What about?'

'He wouldn't say, but I think it might be about his witness.' She pressed the door shut behind her and kept her hand on the handle as if it might suddenly be opened from the other side. 'That new lawyer has been talking to him, the woman. She looks to me as if she's in charge.'

'Do we know her name?'

'According to the attendance form she's called Annabelle Stern. She's from the same firm as Mr Prince.'

'All right,' Jenny said, 'I'll hear him.'

News of the application hadn't filtered through to the journalists and reporters milling outside the hall. Aside from Kenneth Donaldson and Father Starr there was barely anyone occupying the rows of seats behind the lawyers. Jenny could tell at once that this was Annabelle Stern's play. While Prince sat back disinterestedly with arms folded, she leaned forward, watching Sullivan intently as he rose to address her.

'Ma'am, it's with great regret that I have to inform you that my client has been unavoidably delayed in the Lords – I understand he has been required to participate in a whipped vote. I'm afraid his business there may not be concluded until later this evening.'

'I thought I made myself perfectly clear, Mr Sullivan.'

'Ma'am, you did.' He hesitated momentarily as if losing courage. 'But those instructing me have suggested that as you have doubtless so much to consider, a short delay would make no material difference.'

Annabelle Stern and now Fraser Knight turned their gazes to Jenny, their hard, determined expressions and the empty seats behind her telling her all she needed to know: they would keep her secret if she didn't pry any further into theirs.

# EIGHTEEN

SHE SAT IN THE OFFICE with the curtains tightly drawn, aware of little except the sound of departing vehicles and the overpowering smell of mildew. Unable to form coherent thoughts, she watched the silverfish dart out from between the cracks of the bare, worm-eaten boards and go about their business of slowly reclaiming the flimsy building for the earth. Whatever Alison knew or had been told, she kept to herself as she tidied the chairs and emptied the lawyers' water jugs in the empty hall. Once finished, and knowing better than to intrude, she called to Jenny through the closed door.

'Shall I see you back at the office, Mrs Cooper?'

'Yes, thank you, Alison.'

'I'll leave the key on my desk.'

Jenny listened to her fading footsteps. Then all was silence.

But Jenny wasn't alone. Behind her, in the corner of the room where she dared not look, sat Eva, Freddy and Alan Jacobs, heads bowed and faces twisting in unanswered prayer. Outside, a small girl played hopscotch on the crumbling concrete slabs.

'Memories, and indeed the imaginings they provoke, are nothing more than chemical ones and noughts,' Dr Travis, her first and most uncompromising psychiatrist, had once pronounced. 'They may affect us adversely in the same way that a faulty code upsets a computer program. Our work is simply to isolate and overwrite the bad data.'

It had been a comforting thought, faced with the acute and exquisitely bewildering pain of her 'episode': isolate and destroy, what could be simpler?

But she, like Dr Travis, had been a rational person then, one who believed that problems could be solved by a series of logical steps, that reason and good intentions alone would triumph. She had never considered the possibility that doing the right thing could bring about the worst possible consequences.

Ed Prince, Annabelle Stern and the rest of them would bury her sooner than risk letting the truth, whatever that was, come to light. How deep had they had to probe? How many resources had they poured into excavating her past to come up with an obscure retired policeman with a lingering doubt over a case nearly forty years old? How could she meet such force and hope to achieve anything other than self-destruction?

She wanted to be brave, to shine as a light in the world and to hell with the consequences, but it took energy she no longer possessed, courage that she could no longer dredge up from her exhausted well. She was paralysed, trapped, and realized with a bitter smile that she had merely arrived at her inevitable destination several months later than she would otherwise have done. The last time she had been confronted with the end, all that had saved her had been Alec McAvoy's suicidal recklessness.

This time she had no saviour. She was alone and her own resources were not enough.

Resigned to defeat, she gathered her papers into her groaning briefcase and forced it shut. She snatched the key from

Alison's desk and retreated hurriedly from the hall, the ghosts trailing in her wake. Slamming the front door, she locked them in, feeling like a jailer turning the key on the condemned.

Hurrying across the uneven ground, she turned the corner of the building and saw another car parked alongside hers. Father Starr climbed out of the driver's seat and strode towards her as she made a dash for her Golf.

'Was that an admission of defeat, Mrs Cooper?' It was more an accusation than a question. 'One could be forgiven for forming the impression that your inquest won't be hearing from Michael Turnbull again.'

Jenny rummaged clumsily through her pockets in search of her keys.

'An innocent man is still in prison,' he said accusingly. 'I know you find me troublesome, but he has no voice but mine.'

He drew closer as she switched her search to her handbag.

'You're a woman of conscience, Mrs Cooper. If you stop your ears to him now, I can promise his cries will never leave you.'

Jenny's fingers at last closed on the keys. She thumped her bag on the roof of the car as she unlocked the door. Starr was only inches from her now, all inhibitions gone.

'Is this the woman I was told would tolerate no impediment to justice? If I weren't so angry, I'd pity you. Do you honestly think you'll find any comfort in lies, any peace though colluding with this travesty?'

Jenny flung open the door and turned on him. 'Has it ever occurred to you that it might be you who's wrong?'

'A comment unworthy of your intellect, Mrs Cooper. All I am asking on Craven's behalf is for his legal entitlement, for due process fearlessly administered.'

'That is exactly what he is getting.'

Starr gave her a wearied yet knowing look, one that penetrated her feeble protest and seemed to probe at the heart of her fear. Quietly he said, 'Do you assume that you are the only person being tested?'

She climbed into the car and pulled at the door. Starr grabbed the outer handle, refusing to let it shut.

'Please, Mrs Cooper, don't be intimidated.'

Jenny yanked hard, hit the locks and turned the key in the ignition.

Starr shouted at her through the closed window. 'Then at least afford me one last chance. There are people I can go to for help. Good people.'

She slammed into reverse and stamped on the throttle, forcing the priest to jump clear. He was still calling after her as she sped away.

Dull with indecision, Jenny arrived back in the office to find that Alison had already gone to lunch, leaving a tell-tale trace of perfume in the air. She tried to clear her head, to concentrate on the hundred mundane tasks with which she could fill the afternoon, but even lifting the overnight death reports from her in tray was an energy-draining effort.

Among the neat stacks of files on her officer's desk she noticed the latest edition of *Chambers and Partners Directory*. The annual listings usually lived on the shelves in Jenny's office. She picked it up to find a scrap of paper marking a page. It opened at the professional biography of Annabelle Stern, listed as a partner in the firm of Kennedy and Parr. The portrait photograph was several years out of date, but the reported cases in which she had featured were recent and dealt exclusively with the fast-evolving field of personal privacy. The names of show-business celebrities featured alongside football managers and a leading case described only as *A v. B* which, it was claimed, had set a new benchmark in curbing newspaper intrusion. The British civil courts accorded total anonymity only to royalty and the extremely rich. Whatever the identity of her clients, Annabelle Stern was trusted by the biggest players and had made her reputation protecting their dirty secrets.

As Jenny reached for Alison's keyboard to see what the internet might reveal about her newest adversary, her mobile rang. Simon Moreton's name blinked up on the caller display. Jenny was tempted to ignore him. She had nothing to say to her notional superior from the Ministry of Justice except that she wanted the inquest to end and as quickly as possible. But a nagging sense of duty forced her to answer and utter a matter-of-fact hello.

'Ah, Jenny. Glad I got you. I happen to find myself in your part of the world on a bit of business. Just got word you might have come free for a spot of late lunch. Shall we say the Hotel du Vin? One-thirty?'

It had taken her many months in post to appreciate the full absurdity of the genteel code in which Simon spoke. She was undoubtedly the business and there would be no ducking his summons.

Jenny made her way across the city centre on foot. A journey that began in sunshine descended into gloom as a cool westerly breeze picked up and blew in a slate-coloured mantle of cloud from across the Bristol Channel. The first fat drops of rain were splashing the pavement and filling the air with the scent of damp concrete when she entered the restaurant. Simon came to meet her, looking trim and energetic in a summer-weight suit and Liberty print tie. Running was his latest passion, she recalled, and his suntan and newly defined cheekbones were a testament to his hours of training. He could have claimed to be forty, rather than fifty-three, and probably did.

'Jenny. You're looking well,' he said, squeezing her hand.

'You too,' she replied stopping short of the compliment on his newly honed physique that he was evidently fishing for. Experience had taught her that flirting with Simon wouldn't end with a playful exchange.

Ever the gentleman, he summoned a waiter to take her coat and led her through to the dining room. A sliver of Temazepam before she left the office had taken the edge off her anxiety, and a glass of Pouilly Fumé while they waited for their salmon – no starter for the figure-conscious Simon – lulled her into a state approaching relaxation. It was strictly small talk until lunch was cleared: office gossip from the Ministry, the stupidity of politicians and a handful of anecdotes about lesser coroners designed to make Jenny feel good about herself, or at least less insecure. *You may be wrong-headed, but we know you're not stupid or sexually incontinent*, was the subtext.

It was Jenny who was first to grow tired of the pretence. 'I had a call from your number two the other day, several actually.'

'Yes.' He smiled. 'A bit keen, isn't she?'

'You normally make the awkward calls yourself.'

'I'm afraid she took the initiative on that one. I was otherwise engaged at the time.'

Jenny looked at him over her wine glass, letting him know she didn't believe a word.

'I know she lacks a certain finesse,' Simon said by way of apology, 'but she's not a bad girl.'

'She was trying to persuade me not to conduct an inquest.'

'That's a little strong. Advising you of the potential hazards might be a fairer way to put it.'

'And you left it to her because you didn't want to be

tainted by association. Better to keep clear completely than to try to dissuade me and fail.'

Simon studied the tablecloth with a thoughtful smile. 'Surely you can see it from my perspective, Jenny. Craven freely confessed to murder. He pleaded guilty in court. A coroner's function isn't to subvert the criminal process.'

'Particularly when a major witness, who happens to be a close friend of the government, is about to steer his bill through Parliament.'

Her petulance confirmed his instincts. 'I admire your tenacity, Jenny, you know I do, but the one element of holding judicial office you can't seem to grasp is your duty to the administration of justice as a whole.'

'The last time I checked, the coroner's duty was to be fearless and independent – as I pointed out to Miss Cramer.'

'But you and I both know the dividing line between admirable independence and perversity can be razor thin. It's the ability to execute that fine judgement that we look for in our coroners. Can I put it any more clearly than that?'

'I've hardly done anything outrageous.'

'Holding Lord Turnbull in contempt was a little over-zealous.'

'He ignored a summons – what else would you call it? I'll probably stop short of having him locked up if that's what you're worried about.'

'It would be appreciated.'

'Is that all this is about?'

'Not quite.' He tapped the ends of his fingers together nervously. 'There is something else, something rather more significant, you might say.'

'Oh?'

'I'll level with you, Jenny. Even before this case there were moves afoot to ease you aside, perhaps to a post some considered more suited to your specific skills.'

'Such as?'

'I did hear something in the family law sector suggested; an advisory role of some sort.'

'Sounds fascinating,' Jenny replied caustically.

'I managed to head them off, persuaded them your successes outweighed any "temperamental" issues –' he looked her in the eye – 'and that I could guarantee an improvement in that department.'

'That was rather presumptuous.'

'Yes.' He leaned back in his chair. 'It was probably a little rash of me. Foolish even. And now this matter of your past—'

'There's nothing to know.'

'Really?'

'My cousin died. The police were involved. No one was charged. The coroner recorded accidental death.'

'But the police are looking again, I hear.'

'That's hardly a coincidence. Have you read the names of the lawyers the Decency campaign has employed?'

'You can hardly be surprised, Jenny.' He wore an expression of pained regret. 'The thing is, it's not something we can weather that easily, or perhaps at all.'

'Meaning?'

Simon leaned forward, adopting a cosy, familiar tone. 'You'll have to believe me when I tell you this is an entirely informal visit. No one knows I'm here; it's not even in the diary. And the reason I came was to warn you –' his face twitched in a nervous smile – 'that if you should cause undue embarrassment, any influence I once had over your security of tenure will be gone.'

'Since when did causing embarrassment amount to unfitness for office?'

'There are more than enough grounds on the file, Jenny,' he said. 'We both know that.'

He was alluding to her psychiatric history, which she had neglected to mention when applying for her post. The anti-discrimination laws were moving in her favour, but not quickly enough to save her if Simon's superiors decided her time was at an end.

'And if I play to the rules?'

'You may survive. But you'll be under scrutiny, of course. Trust will take time to restore.'

It was the fact that he had behaved so impeccably which told her that for once he was deadly serious. On every other occasion they had met he had contrived to brush her hand, or to touch legs beneath the table, but today he had kept to himself. Even his eyes had remained chastely fixed on her face. There was a time, not so long ago, when she would have told him to go to hell and lectured him on the separation of powers, but somehow she had lost the stomach for the fight. Without the strange comfort of his flirting she felt very alone. Yes, that was the sensation hovering beneath the dulling haze of alcohol: a fear of being abandoned, a dread of finding herself at forty-five, washed up, unloved and unemployable.

They lapsed into silence as coffee arrived, then, sensing her need to reflect, Simon chit-chatted about a sailing trip he'd recently taken with friends. Jenny smiled, but it was only a surface gesture. And she knew that despite his bon-homie Simon could see that he had brought her to the point that they had both known she would eventually reach: would she give in and finally become one of them, or would she strike out alone into the wilderness?

As he called for the bill, Simon allowed himself a final, dangerous moment of sincerity. 'I do hope you make the right decision, Jenny. I've grown fond of you, I really have.' He reached across the table and patted the back of her hand, and when she didn't recoil, he let it settle and closed

his fingers around hers. 'There's a lot you can achieve
without going to war every time, you know. You could still
be a real asset to the service.'

They parted amicably with a handshake and pecks on the
cheek. Simon climbed into a waiting taxi and gave a friendly
wave as he departed. As an exercise in washing his hands of
a troublesome coroner, it couldn't have left a smaller stain
on his conscience.

Jenny retraced her steps across the city oblivious to the
passing showers. Simon hadn't spelled it out in terms, but
he had told her that despite all the high-blown academic
theory there were situations in which the law came a distant
second to politics, and this was one of them. The government had read the public mood and quietly agreed to
smooth the way for the Decency Bill. It was a near-perfect
manoeuvre: a private bill claiming massive support, striking
a death blow to permissiveness that previous adminis-
trations could only have dreamed of. And Eva's short and
tragic life neatly told the story: slain by a monster she helped
to create, saved by a faith that redeemed her. Nothing must
be allowed to sully her memory.

Jenny found herself asking what Alec McAvoy would have
said. From wherever he was, he answered her loud and
clear: *Would that oily wee bastard from the Ministry have
come all the way from London if he'd nothing to hide?
Who're you kidding, woman?*

A news bulletin blaring out of the open door of a builder's
van told her it was three o'clock, a thought which brought
her back to her appointment later that afternoon at Weston
police station. Turning the corner from Whiteladies Road,
she pulled out her phone and tried to reach Steve.

He answered with the impatient tone of a man who didn't

appreciate a personal call intruding at the office. 'Hi, Jenny. Look, I'm just going in to meet clients.'

'When can I talk to you?'

'I can't say – it could be a few hours.'

'Your detective came to see me. He wants me to go to Weston police station this evening to give a statement.'

'*My* detective?'

'Sorry. It's not what I meant—'

'I really can't talk now. I'll call you when I'm done.'

He rang off.

'Screw you, too,' Jenny said out loud to herself.

Alison emerged from the kitchenette in a pair of spiky heels that Jenny didn't recall her wearing earlier in the day.

'There you are, Mrs Cooper,' she said, sounding a little flustered. 'I've had a consultant surgeon from the Vale on the line who's just lost a twelve-year-old girl to peritonitis. He sounded in a dreadful state.' She handed Jenny a note bearing his name and direct line. 'And you had another call from Father Starr. He doesn't give up, does he? He's like some sort of incubus.'

'What did he say?'

'Do you think he'd tell me?' She sat in her swivel chair and turned to her computer with exaggerated primness.

The consultant's voice was weak with exhaustion. The fight to save the dead girl had lasted nearly two hours. She was from a strict Muslim family who had left it far too late to bring her to A & E for fear of her being examined by a male doctor. A ruptured appendix had caused septicaemia and multiple organ failure. Jenny did her best to reassure him that her inquest was likely to be a formality, but she could hear the fear in his voice. Successful litigation would push his insurance premiums through the ceiling and kill his private practice. No more house in the country, no more private school fees. She feared he might break down and weep: there was no one quite as pathetic in adversity as a professional man used to nothing but praise.

There was nothing brittle about Father Starr's voice as he answered the communal telephone in the Jesuit house, nor any trace of surprise that she had responded so obediently.

'It's absolutely essential that we talk, Mrs Cooper, as soon as possible. Are you free now?'

'I could be. I don't have long.'

'I'll come straight to your office.'

'That wouldn't be appropriate.'

'Because—?'

Because I don't want anyone to know, she said to herself. Because I'm confused. Because I don't know if you're mad, obsessed or the one person I should be listening to.

'I have to drive out of town. I'll be passing through Clifton.'

'No.' He lowered his voice. 'But I can be on the Downs side of the suspension bridge in fifteen minutes.'

The heavy clouds had blown over and bursts of sunlight cast the Downs in a luminous golf-course green. Jenny picked her way past lazing groups of college students catching the precious rays as she made her way from her car towards the toll house at the end of the bridge spanning the Avon gorge. She had been waiting no more than two minutes when a figure she only half recognized as Father Starr emerged from the pedestrian entrance to the suspension bridge. He was wearing a navy polo shirt and sand-coloured chinos, no dog collar. Without the authority of priestly clothes, his dark, intense eyes seemed more unsure than threatening: a window to a complex soul.

He glanced over his shoulder as he approached, then seemed to scan the expanse of grass behind her and the bushes beyond.

'I nearly didn't recognize you,' Jenny said.

'You mean I look human?'

'Almost.'

He smiled.

'Where do you want to go?' she asked.

'We'll just walk. It won't take long.'

He struck off across the grass, hands clasped behind his back as if he were heading for somewhere. Jenny followed in his wake, resenting the fact that he felt entitled to dictate events.

'What is it you want to discuss?' she asked, trying to regain control.

His answer came after a short pause, as if a final mental obstacle had first to be crossed. 'There are people who might help . . .' Another hiatus. 'As it seems you have reached the limits of your resources, I thought it appropriate that I should draw on theirs.'

'Who exactly are we talking about?'

'Friends. Sympathizers.'

'Would these be Roman Catholic friends?'

'Of course. What of it?'

'I'm a coroner in the middle of an inquest, Father. The only things of any use to me are credible witnesses and verifiable facts.'

'I appreciate that, Mrs Cooper. I can't provide you with witnesses at the present moment, but I can offer you information. *Verifiable* information.'

Jenny waited to hear it.

'As you probably know, the Decency campaign has a board of eight members, mostly respectable business people as well as a retired diplomat, I believe. For various legal and no doubt tax reasons, it has chosen to organize itself as a limited company. The Mission Church of God, however, is a registered charity, but with only three named trustees: Michael and Christine Turnbull and the lawyer, Edward Prince. But the actual governance of the church is conducted by a council of five. Michael Turnbull is one of them, Ed Prince another, then there's a former Assistant Commissioner of police, Geoffrey Solomon, a banker turned philanthropist named Douglas Reynolds and the American pastor, Bobby DeMont.'

'No women?' Jenny said.

'I get the impression they're rather conservative.'

'That's something, coming from a Jesuit.'

'Not a Jesuit quite yet,' Starr reminded her.

They had rounded a thicket of tall shrubs that shielded them from the road and the eyes of passers-by; he slowed his pace to a stroll as he glanced left and right.

Jenny wondered who it was he was frightened of; were his Jesuit brothers watching his every move?

'And why do you think the identities of these men are so important?' Jenny enquired.

'It's not so much who they are, as their *agenda*, Mrs Cooper. You won't find it written down in black and white because they prefer to pursue it from the shadows. But these men are puritans, in the truest sense of the word. They have an unswerving, absolutist commitment to their doctrine. Nothing is more important to them than realizing their vision of God's kingdom on earth.'

'Is that so different from yours?' Jenny asked.

Starr came to a halt and turned to her, his face filled with conviction. 'You have to understand what is most significant to these people. In my church we strive for purity, but we know it will only arrive through grace; we seek to allow God his room to move, to touch lives and to change them from within. The puritan mind insists on purity, demands it, imposes it. It believes a simple declaration can effect a personal and immediate relationship between man and God no matter how ignorant and sinful the man.' His eyes danced as he gesticulated with his hands. 'That is why it strives for phenomena, for evidence of the Holy Spirit entering the physical body. You must have heard them pray? They lecture and barrack and demand their immediate reward. They are impatient with this world, Mrs Cooper, and also with its creator. They have no *humility*.'

'You may be right,' Jenny said calmly, 'but how does this affect Mr Craven?'

Starr clasped his hands tightly in front of his chest. 'Mrs Cooper, you would listen to a doctor of seventeen years' standing and give weight to his opinion?'

'Of course—'

'And equally to a lawyer, or an engineer?'

She nodded, her heart growing heavier as she anticipated his point.

'My expertise is in the condition of the human soul. God called me to live amongst criminals and minister to them. I have accompanied Paul Craven on a journey lasting many years; I have witnessed his redemption as proof of God's grace. If it is false, then so am I, so is my faith and so is my church.'

'Father, your faith isn't evidence.'

'Perhaps not in the legal sense, but as God is my witness that will come. I have someone working on it as we speak, all I ask is for *you* to maintain a little faith.' Softening visibly, he said, 'If I could give you some of mine, I would.'

Jenny said, 'The inquest finishes tomorrow. If you wish to bring any further evidence to my attention you haven't much time.'

'I understand, Mrs Cooper.'

She felt a sudden and powerful urge to unburden herself, to tell him he was insane to stake his vocation on a woman in her predicament, but he was immovable, she realized, clinging to his belief like the last piece of wreckage in a storm-tossed sea.

# NINETEEN

THE POLICE STATION AT WESTON was uncomfortably hot and Detective Sergeant Gleed was badly in need of a shower. Seated next to him, Detective Constable Alan Wesley appeared oblivious to his superior's overpowering body odour, and sipped slurry-coloured coffee from a thin plastic cup. Jenny had taken one mouthful of hers and abandoned it.

Gleed turned slowly through the pages of a small black policeman's notebook. Jenny tried to remain calm, but her body defied her. Her heart rate picked up to a gallop, pins and needles spread from her fingertips and her vision clouded at the edges: all the symptoms of ensuing panic. She wished Steve were with her and she offered a silent prayer that he would forgive her. She needed no more proof; she wasn't strong enough to cope without him.

Gleed looked up from his notebook with a downturned, bulldog smile.

'Are you sure you don't want a solicitor, Mrs Cooper?'

'I thought I was writing a statement, not being interviewed.'

'No harm in having a little chat first.'

'Under caution?'

'If you'd prefer.'

'Is this an interview or isn't it?' Jenny demanded.

Gleed settled himself in his chair. Jenny felt his smell at the back of her throat. 'I see it more as an exploratory discussion at the moment, Mrs Cooper. No need for formality for formality's sake.'

'You say this all started with a retired detective?'

'That's right. He says it's always niggled at him.'

'Do I get to see his statement?'

Gleed gave a saggy smile and shook his head. 'You know that's not how we do things.'

'What about my cousin? Has he given a statement?'

'No. As you said, he never even knew he had a sister. But he finds it strange that you never said anything to him.'

'I didn't know she existed until a few months ago. And I haven't seen Chris in twelve years – his father's funeral.'

Gleed picked up his notebook. 'Still happy to proceed informally?'

Jenny was too tense to argue. All she could think about was escaping into the fresh air. 'What would you like to know?'

'Katy Chilcott, she died on Thursday, 19 October 1972, at her home at 28 Pretoria Road, Weston. She was five years old.'

'I'll take your word for it,' Jenny said, sounding more agitated than she had intended.

'You don't remember?'

'No.'

'But you were there, Mrs Cooper, in the house. The neighbour opposite saw you leaving with your dad.'

'Then you know more than I do.'

Consulting the notebook, Gleed scratched his sandpaper chin.

'She says you went there every day after school – two o'clock until half-past five. It must have been your first year.'

Jenny said, 'I have a memory blank. I've virtually no recollection of what happened between the ages of four and five. I've tried to remember, but I can't.'

'Really?' Gleed sounded interested. 'What do you mean, you've tried? In therapy?'

'Yes.'

'Do you mind my asking what you have been undergoing therapy for?'

'I'm recently divorced. There's been a lot of fallout.'

Gleed nodded. 'And then you started seeing Stephen Painter?'

'He has nothing to do with this.'

'Bit of a pot-head, isn't he? He has a recent conviction.' He glanced at DC Wesley, who gave an affirmative nod.

Jenny swallowed her anger and answered as calmly as she could. 'Can you please ask me what you want to know?'

'Your dad was quite the local character, by all accounts. Businessman. Freemason.'

'That sounds perfectly respectable.'

'The problem with small towns,' Gleed reflected, 'is folks sometimes get a little too close for their own good. And when your coppers are drinking pals with a fella they're investigating, things can slip by.'

Jenny took a deep breath, suppressing the rising urge to bolt from the room. His smell, the heat, the clumsy insinuation was more than she could bear.

'Mr Gleed, I'm not an idiot. There is no way on God's earth my father could be made to stand trial. We both know why you've asked me here and it's got nothing to do with what happened thirty-eight years ago.'

He studied her with patient, puffy eyes. 'The officer who was in charge of the investigation is very much alive and well, Mrs Cooper. If it turns out he was – how shall we put it – less than conscientious, then it's his head on the block, isn't it?'

'And the timing of this investigation is purely coincidental?'

'Perhaps our complainant read your name in the paper. Even I'd heard of you, and the only paper I ever see is covered in budgie crap.'

Wesley snorted with amusement.

'So it's this retired detective you're investigating?' Jenny said sceptically.

'His name's Ronald Pope, lives down on the south coast. He was a young DI back then, same lodge as your dad.'

Ron Pope. The name did have a distant echo. Why *Ron*? It was her mother's voice she heard saying it, casually in conversation, through the open door of the kitchen in their family home; Jenny standing somewhere around the corner in the hall, aware of serious adult talk she didn't understand.

'Ring a bell?'

Jenny shrugged. 'Not particularly,' she lied.

Gleed arched his back a little, lifting his arms a fraction, giving Jenny a glimpse of the damp pits of his shirt.

'You see, we think you must have spoken to Mr Pope at some point, or perhaps he spoke to you? The problem is there's no trace of the files, otherwise we'd have more to go on.'

Jenny shook her head. 'I don't remember.'

Gleed waited a moment, as if expecting her to change her mind, then nodded to Wesley, who reached into his inside pocket and drew out a photograph. It was an early colour picture of a man in his thirties with long brown hair, and a full moustache that dipped, bandit-style, around the sides of his mouth.

'That's Mr Pope. We dug out his old personnel file.'

The face was distantly familiar. She stared at it, searching her memory for the reason why. No image came to mind, but there was something else – a dim recollection of the sharp smell of tobacco smoke on a man's breath . . . and a deep voice, a smoker's voice.

'I can see it's stirring something,' Gleed said.

'Perhaps.' She shook her head. 'No, I don't think so.'

'Let me tell you what happened, Mrs Cooper, so far as I can. Your dad was seen hurrying from the house tugging you behind him at about a quarter to six in the evening. An ambulance arrived ten minutes later. They found your auntie Penny with your kid cousin lying on the hall floor. She'd cracked her skull and died of a haemorrhage. Your uncle James turned up in the middle of all the commotion and took a swing at his wife, had to be pinned down by a couple of our boys. According to Pope, your auntie's story was that your dad had already been to pick you up when Katy fell down the stairs. Your dad backed her up, said she was right as rain when he left with you.'

Jenny said, 'Wasn't any of this discussed at an inquest?'

'We don't know,' Gleed said. 'There's nothing at the coroner's office but a report from the doctor in A & E pronouncing her dead on arrival: head injuries consistent with a fall.'

*You killed her.* Her father's words rang through her head. *You keep my secret, I'll keep yours.*

'Are you feeling all right, Mrs Cooper? You look a bit queasy.'

'I'm fine,' Jenny said, but she had no feeling beyond her wrists, and now sensation was leaving her feet and legs too. It felt like the beginnings of what she termed her deep panics. There were no tangible thoughts attached to the building sensation of dread; it emanated from an unreachable place beyond the realm of words. She had once described the feeling to Dr Allen as like a seizure of the soul.

'Would you like me to fetch you some coffee, Mrs Cooper?' DC Wesley asked.

'No thank you,' Jenny whispered. The room was turning to a blur.

When Gleed spoke it was as if he were addressing her from the far end of an echoing passageway. 'It could have been an accident, but why not tell the whole truth?' He leaned insistently across the desk. 'You see, in my experience there's always something that gives it away, some little clue that all's not well. Do you know what it is here, Mrs Cooper?'

Jenny shook her head.

'There are two things, in point of fact. Firstly, I'm told your dad was a notorious shagger, and secondly my retired detective friend says your cousin had no knickers on. Just a skirt and blouse. He noticed when they lifted her onto the stretcher, but apparently no one ever said a word about it.'

He was lying, he had to be, but Jenny's heart was pounding so hard she could scarcely breathe. *My right arm is heavy*, she repeated to herself, *relax, relax*, fighting to draw back from the brink of a full-blown attack.

'I won't pull my punches, Mrs Cooper, I can see you're anxious for me to get to the point: did he ever muck about with you, your dad?'

'No,' Jenny whispered.

'You don't seem very sure.'

'It's not that. It can't be.'

'No knickers. Head injury. Running from the house . . . You've got to admit it's worth more than a few minutes of my time.'

'Why don't you speak to Pope?'

'Oh, we will,' Gleed said. 'We most certainly will.'

'Would you excuse me—'

Jenny got up from her chair, her legs threatening to buckle beneath her. Wesley reached out a hand to steady her. She pushed it away and made for the door, wrenching it open and plunging into the corridor. She heard Gleed call out from behind her, 'You can't hide for ever, Mrs Cooper . . .'

She made it down the four flights of stairs and out of the side door onto the pavement. She leaned back against the concrete wall for a long moment, sucking in the cool air, filling her lungs slowly to the count of ten the way she had learned with Dr Travis. Inch by inch the feeling returned to her limbs. She glanced back at the door, expecting Gleed or Wesley to come after her, but neither appeared. She focused on her car parked across the main road from the station, and made her way unsteadily towards it.

She waited for a gap in the traffic. Stepping out from the kerb, something caught the corner of her eye. She turned to see a figure in the driver's seat of a blue car parked to her left aiming a camera lens at her. He got the startled, head-on shot he was after, then tossed the camera aside and swept out of the space, passing behind her as she reached the far side. Jenny spun round to get a look at him, but he was gone.

The car had looked too smart for a reporter's; she couldn't tell the make, but it had seemed sleek and fast. She collapsed behind the wheel of her Golf and tried to get her panicked thoughts in order as she groped for a pill. Would Gleed have tipped off the press? No. There was nothing in it for him. He was just doing what he'd been asked: to rattle her. More than that: to scare her. Damn! She wrenched at the lid of the Temazepam bottle with wooden fingers and scattered tablets across her lap. She grabbed one and swallowed while she scooped the others up greedily like an addict.

She lay back in her seat, eyes closed, waiting for the drug to work, too jittery to drive. And then it came to her: if Turnbull's lawyers had somehow put Gleed up to this, what else might they have done? Alan Jacobs had killed himself before she had decided to hold the inquest, but not Freddy Reardon. He had died the night before he was due to give evidence.

How would that work? She tried to reason it through: Freddy knew something about Eva that the Mission Church or Decency didn't want known, perhaps something to do with Jacobs? Jacobs was in a mess, seeking truth and struggling with his sexuality. She recalled the witness at his inquest, Mary Richards, Jacobs's fellow enquirer. Jenny pictured her in the witness box, her earnest expression as she ignored the glowering Father Dermody to breach Jacobs's confidence. His words filtered back to her exactly as the witness had spoken them: *'I've become involved with some people I shouldn't have. I thought they were helping me but now I don't know. I don't know what's going on. I feel as if I don't know who I am any more.' I remember the look of despair on his face*, Mary Richards had said. *I tried to get him to say some more but he wouldn't.*

Who were the people helping him? Perhaps Eva was one; if he had confided in anyone it was likely to have been her. Freddy? Others at the church? *I don't know what's going on . . . I don't know who I am any more.* The words of a man who thought he was being taken in one direction only to find he was being led in another. Mary Richards had said he told her this about three weeks before he died. That would have been the first week of June; Eva had been killed almost exactly a month earlier.

She felt the Temazepam starting to work; a warm, slightly

giddy sensation like the first drink of the evening. It took the edge off her nerves but caused her to stumble as she groped for connections: the police claimed Alan Jacobs's hard drive had been wiped accidentally. Could it have held evidence relating to Eva, or was she letting herself drift into paranoia?

For a reason she couldn't fully explain, Jenny still believed that Ceri Jacobs was as ignorant of the truth as she claimed to be. The widow had never struck her as a secretive or knowing woman, but rather absorbed in her role as a mother at the expense of intimacy with her husband. And she had been far too disapproving for Jenny to imagine Jacobs sharing his confusion with her. No, his comfort would have been with strangers. But Eileen Reardon, Freddy's mother, was different. Broken down as she was, she had lived and suffered. Jenny could see that her physical addictions and attraction to strange philosophies were her insulation from a reality she would otherwise be unable to bear.

But even through the alcoholic fog, she would surely have seen something.

The flowers, now dead, remained on the floor of the landing collecting other scraps of litter to them, forming the beginnings of a mini rubbish heap.

The doorbell refused to ring so Jenny called through the letterbox into the dark hallway. 'Mrs Reardon? It's Jenny Cooper. I need to talk to you.'

No response.

'Please, Mrs Reardon. Just a few minutes, then I promise I'll leave you alone.'

Silence.

Jenny straightened up and cast a glance at the group of teenagers who had appeared at the end of the hall. Two boys with T-shirts stuffed in their jeans pockets were strutting bare-chested in front of the others, but at the same time letting her know they were there, and that it might be fun to scare her.

She leaned down to the letterbox one last time.

'Eileen, if you don't answer the door I'll have to assume you're in some kind of trouble. I'll need to call someone to open it. I don't think you'd want that.' She waited for a reply. None came. 'OK, Eileen, I'm going to have to call for help. I'd wait here but I'm not sure how safe it's going to be.'

Jenny took out her phone and dialled directories to get the number for the housing association. She'd try to get the door unlocked before she called in the police.

She was being connected to the tenants' welfare officer when she heard a click. She turned to see the door had opened an inch, but there was no sign of Eileen. She pocketed her phone and nudged the door open.

'Mrs Reardon?'

She heard movement. Eileen emerged from the sitting room dressed in a tatty purple dressing gown worn over crumpled pyjamas. Her eyes were lined with broken veins. She looked as if she had been drinking.

'You can't go in there, it's a mess,' she said, as thick in the throat as a morning-after drunk. She opened a door to Jenny's left and shuffled in.

Jenny followed her into the filthy kitchen, which smelled of burnt fat and festering rubbish. The only place to sit was at a small table stacked with unopened mail and old newspapers. Jenny pulled out a chair while Eileen lit a cigarette from the gas ring.

'What do you want?' she said, leaning back against the stove.

'To understand what was going on in Freddy's mind.'

'You tell me.' Eileen sucked in sharply.

'I can't. That's why I'm asking his mother.'

Eileen's eyes flicked towards her as she blew out a thin stream of smoke.

'He was part of you,' Jenny pressed. 'You knew what made him break down that time he ended up in the Conway Unit.'

Eileen looked away, studying a spot on the grimy tiles.

'I've got a seventeen-year-old son who refuses to live under the same roof as me. I know what it's like to feel you've failed at the one job you're not allowed to . . .' Jenny paused, a catch in her voice. *Jesus.* 'You needed help with him, but I'm wondering if he didn't always get the right kind. You're the only one who'd know. Deep down a mother knows most things. Am I right?'

Eileen took another lungful of smoke, unable to look at Jenny any more.

'I'm guessing that part of the reason he was unhappy was that there was no dad around. I mean, you had a partner, but Freddy didn't know where he fitted in. I picture him as a sensitive child who wasn't finding himself, but who had become so angry and hostile that you couldn't reach him . . .'

Jenny felt something between them change. Eileen reached up with the back of her hand and wiped her eye.

'Kids like that either lash out or break, sometimes both. Is that what happened to Freddy?'

'He was hearing voices,' Eileen said quietly. 'The doctors called it psychosis, but to him they were real. He thought they were evil spirits.'

'Were they telling him to hurt himself?'

Eileen nodded, still looking the other way.

'What did you think?'

'I don't know.' Her voice sank to a whisper. 'I just . . . I just wanted him to get well.'

'The senior nurse there, Alan Jacobs, did Freddy talk about him?'

'He liked him. He said he was the only one who'd listen and understand.'

'About the spirits?'

'Yes . . .'

'And the doctors told him that was nonsense, that the voices were just parts of his brain misfiring?'

Eileen nodded.

'Is that when Freddy got interested in religion?'

'That's when it began.'

'With Alan Jacobs? Did he talk to Freddy about the Mission Church?'

Eileen pushed a hand through her lank hair. 'He might have done, but it started with a black guy from the church who came in to talk to them about how he'd been a criminal, then got saved. I remember Freddy going on and on about him. He thought he was the best thing since sliced bread.'

'You mean Lennox Strong?'

Eileen met Jenny's eyes. 'That's the one. When he got out, Freddy took himself off to that church on the Sunday. He wanted me to come, but I couldn't . . .' Tears ran down her face but Eileen didn't sob.

'He came home saying he'd been cured and flushed all his pills down the bloody toilet. I was scared stiff for him, but damn me if he wasn't like a completely different kid. There was Jesus this and Jesus that, but no pills or booze or drugs . . . I didn't know what I'd done to deserve it. I thought we'd seen a bloody miracle.'

'How long did it last?'

'He stayed well, at least until Eva was killed. It was me who went down. I was happy for him, of course I was, but this God stuff . . . I couldn't stomach it. He wanted me to have what he'd got, but I just never . . .' She tossed her cigarette butt into the sink. 'It wasn't me. It wasn't for me.'

'What happened when Eva died?'

'The bad dreams and voices came back. I tried to make him see the doctor, but he wouldn't. He kept saying people would pray for him to make him better.'

'Anyone in particular?'

'I don't know. I didn't really want to know.'

'Was Alan Jacobs one of them? Did Freddy mention him?'

'Maybe once or twice. I . . .' Another rush of tears. Eileen pressed her eyes into the crook of her elbow. 'I should have done more, I know I should have. I was no good for him.'

Jenny said, 'Eva died at the beginning of May. But before that, was he OK? You didn't see any change in him before then?'

'Maybe he started to change a bit before,' Eileen said uncertainly. 'He'd get impatient with me, but you know –' she gestured to the mess around the sink – 'why wouldn't he, when all he got was promises?'

'Eileen, was Freddy getting ill again before May?'

She thought about it for a moment. 'I suppose he might have been.'

'When did it start? What month?'

She shook her head vaguely. 'March, April . . . But it was definitely worse when she died. We were both in here the morning the news came on the radio. The way he reacted, you'd have thought she was family.'

'Did the police talk to him at all?'

'Only to see where he'd been when she was killed. They checked all that out. He was helping out at church, in a prayer team or something.'

Jenny said, 'I want you to think carefully about last week, the days before he died. Did anything happen to Freddy?

Did he say anything? Did you notice anything out of the ordinary?'

'What do you mean?' Eileen said, alarmed.

Jenny hesitated, realizing that the wall she had mentally erected between Freddy's and Eva's deaths had come tumbling down. The return of his illness coinciding with Eva's apparent waning faith, and Alan Jacobs's involvement *with people he shouldn't have* were coincidences too far. 'I wasn't going to mention this until all the lab tests come back, but the post-mortem showed that Freddy had marks on his wrists, almost as if they'd been caused by rope or handcuffs. They were quite fresh. He'd covered them with concealer.'

'Handcuffs? Are you saying he was arrested?'

'It's one explanation.'

'He can't have been. He was still a juvenile. I would've been told, wouldn't I?'

'You'd have thought so,' Jenny said, but nothing seemed impossible any more.

Jenny was grateful for the mania that had gripped her since her meeting with Eileen Reardon. It pushed out her fear and banished her ghosts. The message from Steve on her answerphone had gone unanswered. The desk in her study was strewn with papers which she had covered with notes and diagrams exploring every possible connection between the spinning fragments of evidence.

She had yet to find the missing piece that linked Eva's death with those of Freddy and Jacobs, but she felt that at last she was drawing close to its essence. In life, as in nature, there were two types of attraction: the healthy sort born of affection and generosity, and the compulsive craving of the kind that had killed the moths whose burnt remains lay beneath her anglepoise lamp. Watching their death throes, she was reminded of the outstretched arms and convulsing bodies of the worshippers at the Mission Church. They had found a light, too, and it wasn't the sun.

# TWENTY

Jenny woke to the sound of the telephone. It wasn't six a.m. but the day was already as bright as noon. Blinking against the sharp light, she hurried downstairs and retrieved the receiver from beneath a mess of papers on her desk. She expected to hear Alison with news of some spectacular motorway collision, or perhaps a contrite Steve wanting to invite himself for breakfast and a little more, but it was a gruff, though polite Northern Irish voice which greeted her.

'Mrs Cooper? Sorry to trouble you so early. DI Sean Coughlin. I'm a friend of Father Starr's.'

'Oh—' was all Jenny could find to say.

'It's probably wise not to talk on the phone. Would it suit you to meet briefly, in say an hour's time? I'll be outside Tintern Abbey.'

'Hold on a moment—'

Her protest was futile. Coughlin had already rung off.

Her hair was still wet, there had been no time to put on make-up, and three cups of strong coffee had left her feeling jumpy. The early-morning sun was blindingly bright as she reached the bottom of her lane and dog-legged across the main road towards the abbey ruins. There was only one other vehicle in the visitors' parking area, a dark blue BMW cabriolet with the roof up, not a car that looked like it belonged to a policeman. Jenny pulled up and saw that it was empty. Maybe she had misheard? Her exhausted yet heightened state made her feel as if she were in a waking dream, not quite certain of anything. She turned off the engine and climbed out to get some air. It was cool and fresh against her skin. A halo of mist hung in graceful suspension over the river, tracing its serpentine path through the steep sides of the wooded valley. The abbey, a vast stone skeleton that once would have been as gilded and opulent as an Italian cathedral, was a dark, commanding shadow against the brilliant sky.

She heard the sound of solid, even footsteps. A male figure appeared around the corner.

'Mrs Cooper?'

'Yes.'

He was a man of uncertain age, somewhere between forty and fifty, tall and wiry with close-cropped greying hair.

'Sean Coughlin. Pleased to meet you.' He extended his hand.

Jenny shook it, noticing the inlaid silver crosses on his cufflinks.

'Inspiring, isn't it?' he said of the abbey. 'You live in a beautiful part of the world.'

'And you, Mr Coughlin?'

'London. I'm with the Met.' He seemed anxious to change the subject. 'Fancy a stroll down to the river?'

'Don't you think I should have a little more proof of who I'm talking to?'

Coughlin reached into his pocket and handed her his wallet. She opened it to find his Metropolitan Police ID, driving licence and credit cards. In the photo pouch there was a picture of the Virgin and Child.

Satisfied, she handed it back and decided to give him a hearing.

They wandered across the empty tarmac and turned right down the lane to the water's edge.

Jenny said, 'How do you know Father Starr?'

'We met through the Catholic Police Guild.'

'That sounds very clandestine.'

'Oh, we're thick as thieves on our side of the Tiber,' Coughlin said good-naturedly. 'I suppose some officers might use it for advantage, but I'm more on the pastoral side.'

'You're not a priest?'

'I did get most of the way through seminary when I was younger. Refused at the last fence.' The joke was offered in a way that invited her not to venture any further in that direction. He was still in conflict, she sensed, and doubted there was a Mrs Coughlin.

The tide was at its lowest point and the water rushed noisily over rocks on which a heron stood, statue-still and inscrutable. Coughlin filled his lungs and took in the view: the mist rising over an enchanted landscape.

'Beats the Caledonian Road, that's for sure.' He glanced back the way they had come. There was no sign of life except for a ginger tomcat that had wandered into the path and stretched out to bathe in a pool of sunlight. He turned to Jenny. 'I don't know if this is of any interest to you, Mrs Cooper, but I can call on certain resources to look into matters that require it.'

'I thought you were going to offer me a revelation.'

'I've read about the case and spoken to Father Starr about the evidence, that's all. I can see that local detectives wouldn't be inclined to reopen a matter they've already put to bed and, quite frankly, I wouldn't be inclined to in their shoes.'

'How does your Super' feel about you going freelance?'

Ignoring her note of sarcasm, Coughlin said, 'I've dealt with enough sexual psychopaths to know they don't tend to stick in a knife and run. If Craven was the killer he would have done more than relieve himself on the doorstep. As far as I can tell, he didn't even rifle through her possessions or look over the house. Ninety-nine times out of a hundred, a kill and run is either an execution or an accident.'

'What do you think it was?' Jenny said.

'I wouldn't put my money on it having been an accident.'

'All right, let's say we follow your logic. Who's got a motive to kill Eva?'

'The obvious answer would be someone from her old business, but then there are the two suicides – if that's what you think they were.'

'I think we can assume that. And I think we can assume neither Freddy Reardon nor Alan Jacobs killed Eva. For one thing they were both at church at the time, and for another I don't believe either of them was capable of it.'

'I'd agree with you. It sounds to me like there could have been something else going on, something bigger than all of them.'

'Bristol CID don't seem to think so.'

'Police forces don't spend money on disproving confessions.'

Jenny studied him for a moment, trying to decide what it was that was making her listen to him.

'Why exactly are you here, Mr Coughlin?' she asked. 'And please don't tell me God told you to come.'

'I've a lot of time for Father Starr,' Coughlin said with no hint of apology. 'You've got to admire a man who truly acts on his faith. But there is a little more to it than that. I had a colleague in Bristol check out the crime desk logs. It turned up something you ought to know. On the evening of Monday, 15 March this year, a woman by the name of Eva Donaldson phoned up with a rambling complaint about someone – we believe it was a male – harassing her. She wouldn't mention any names and the officer taking the call noted that she sounded drunk and incoherent. He checked the action log and saw that a follow-up call was made exactly a week later. The log says "caller denies all knowledge of having made the complaint".'

'Have you got a copy of this log?'

'It's been faxed to your office. I'm afraid the colleague who turned it up can't be named.'

'Is he a member of the Guild?'

'That would be a reasonable assumption.'

'Have you got anything else?'

'Not yet, but from what Father Starr has told me I'm inclined to have a look at Alan Jacobs. I understand he'd had sexual relations with a man on the evening he died.'

'Who told you that? I know, let me guess – Father Dermody?'

'I don't know Dermody personally,' he said, avoiding the question, 'but I thought you might like to know who Jacobs was with, whether he told him anything that could be useful to you.'

'Of course, but I might need a little time to think this through. No offence intended, but I suddenly feel as if I've got involved with the mafia.'

Coughlin said, 'We may behave like a family, but I can assure you that's where the similarity ends. Any favours I do Father Starr are strictly within the law.'

'A good Samaritan, hey?'

'We all need one of those every now and then.'

After a moment, Jenny said, 'Fine. I'm not sure why, but I think I'll trust you.'

'Wise decision. I'll be in touch, Mrs Cooper.'

He shook her hand once more and turned to make his own way back. Jenny watched from a distance as he climbed into the BMW, flicked the switch that folded back the soft top and took off down the valley at high speed. There was definitely no Mrs Coughlin, she decided, or anyone closer to him than his priest.

It was only a few minutes after eight when Jenny arrived in the empty office clutching a coffee and croissant. She dumped the mail on Alison's desk without checking it and went straight to the elderly fax machine. As Coughlin had promised, there was a single page copy of the crime desk log, Eva's call marked with an asterisk: *Caller at times incoherent, possibly intoxicated. Refuses to name male harassing her.* In the right-hand column was the follow-up note: *Caller denies all knowledge of complaint.* Jenny took it through to her room. She would have to fetch out all of Eva's papers to search for any clue as to what was happening in her life around 15 March.

She unloaded the document box that she had ferried to and from the inquest and reached for the bundle of papers dealing with her various engagements. There was a printout of an email dated 11 March giving details of three local radio interviews Eva was scheduled to conduct on Friday the 12th, but no hint as to what was in her schedule for Monday. Turning to the bundle of correspondence, she flicked through letters to and from her bank and mortgage company for dates in January and February. They showed that she was struggling with arrears – that much Jenny already knew – but a phrase leaped out of a letter dated 18 February that she hadn't accorded any significance to before. An executive from her mortgage company had written:

> *In the light of representations received via your solicitors concerning your anticipated income in the second half of this year, I have decided to grant your request for a five-month period of interest-only payments. Arrears to date will be rolled over into the principal sum.*

Jenny leafed back, looking for any sign of the solicitors' letters being copied to Eva but none had made it to the file. The several letters that followed were dry, administrative pro formas confirming the adjusted payment schedule, but the last in the sheaf was the letter headed Reed Falkirk & Co. that Jenny recalled seeing the previous week. Since her meeting with Coughlin its date now held more significance: 13 March. She re-read its three paragraphs carefully:

*Dear Ms Donaldson,*

*Further to your instructions we have reviewed your contracts with GlamourX Ltd and as agreed have sought counsel's advice. Simeon Hargreaves QC has confirmed that clause 3.2 of the contract dated 23 September 2005 clearly entitles you to 4.6 per cent of sales revenue generated by* Latex Lesbians *Parts 1 to 4 and all six films in the* Lil' Miss *series. As we anticipated, he advised that all films in the* Whorehouse Vixens *series are subject to the buy-out agreement between you and GlamourX dated 2 November 2005 and that no royalties are owing.*

*In the light of GlamourX's failure to respond to correspondence to date, we advise that there is little prospect of reaching a settlement, and that High Court proceedings should be commenced forthwith. We would, however, remind you that our invoice dated 26 February in the sum of £14,675 remains outstanding and that no further action can be taken in this matter until payment is received. In accordance with standard practice, we will require the sum of £10,000 to be paid on account of fees that will be incurred in the preparation and issuing of proceedings.*

*We await your instructions.*
*Yours sincerely,*
*Damien Lynd*

A glance in *Chambers and Partners Directory* confirmed that Lynd was one of four partners in the firm of Reed Falkirk & Co. His specialisms were listed as media and corporate law.

There was no subsequent correspondence from Mr Lynd or his firm. Extrapolating from what she had read, Jenny assumed that the bill for £14,675 had been incurred in fending off Eva's mortgage company with the promise of unpaid royalties and commissioning an opinion from Queen's Counsel. But why hadn't Eva pursued this before? Out of distaste, Jenny presumed, but her circumstances had become too straitened for such scruples. The March letter left her with the tantalizing prospect of money from GlamourX, but as lawyers do, Reed Falkirk had demanded payment on account that she couldn't afford.

One other thing struck her. Eva had negotiated five months' grace with the mortgage company. That would have taken her to the end of July. There was no significance in the date that Jenny could think of other than the fact that, if everything went to plan, the Decency Bill would have passed the major parliamentary hurdles by then, leaving her free to take up the acting career she had discussed with Cassidy. But the prospect of a TV show was far from money in the bank. It was likely that Eva felt that she couldn't be seen to sue GlamourX for personal gain until the Decency campaign was at an end, in which case might she have asked Turnbull for money? Perhaps, but Jenny was doubtful. And might the person 'harassing' her have been her lawyer, holding a gun to her head in his demand for fees in advance?

There was too much missing from the paper trail to get beyond speculation, but it raised a lot of questions. One was how Eva had racked up a lawyer's bill of nearly £15,000 for simple written advice from counsel and a handful of letters. Returning the documents to their box, Jenny thought about calling one of Eva's executors to give evidence about the state of her personal affairs, guessing her father was likely to be one of them. She racked her memory for the rules of executor confidentiality, a subject she hadn't touched on since law school. They refused to come, but by some mysterious process of association, another forgotten phrase floated to the surface: *a lien on the papers*. In Eva's case it meant that as long as her bill remained unpaid, her solicitors would have the legal right to retain her files and therefore all documents relating to her claim against GlamourX. They would eventually be paid out of her estate, but a grant of probate took months, sometimes as long as a year.

Jenny needed to speak to Damien Lynd.

She grabbed the phone and fetched out the March letter to find Reed Falkirk's number. Her call was answered by a machine. She was ready to leave a message when it occurred to her that Ed Prince and Annabelle Stern were likely to have made contact with Lynd already. Putting him on notice of her interest would only give him the opportunity to let them know. Far better to surprise him. She checked the time: eight-twenty. If the traffic was kind she could call past their offices in Queen Square and still make it to the inquest for ten.

She grabbed her briefcase and the box of documents and hurried out. As she clattered through the door and into the hallway she bumped into Alison.

'Mrs Cooper, I need to speak to you,' she said urgently.

'It'll have to wait. I'll see you at the inquest.' Jenny pushed past.

Alison pursued her.

'Mrs Cooper, I was approached by a reporter.'

Jenny stopped abruptly and turned. 'About what?'

'You,' Alison said hesitantly. 'Something about a police inquiry into your past.'

'What did you tell him?'

'The truth – I had no idea what he was talking about.'

'If he calls again, tell him he'll be hearing from my lawyers.' She turned to go.

'He didn't call—'

Jenny looked back, responding to the alarm in Alison's voice.

'I was sitting outside a restaurant in Bath. I was with Martin. He took a picture of us.'

'Last night?'

Alison nodded. 'But how did he know I was there? I can't have that in the papers. I've only just met this man . . .' She was almost in tears. 'God knows what he must think of me.'

'Oh, I see . . . I thought you meant you were worried about your husband—'

'Sod him. He's got no right to be angry.'

'Look, even if this person was a reporter, you're not the story.'

'Who else would he have been?' Alison said, panicked.

'That woman lawyer who turned up yesterday has made a career out of keeping her rich clients' grubby secrets out of the press. I wouldn't put anything past her.'

A look of relief spread across Alison's face which Jenny found curious, but their whole exchange had left her more than slightly confused. The love-struck Alison wasn't a person she knew or understood.

'I've got to go,' Jenny said, and hurried for the door.

The short drive into the city centre turned into an agonizing twenty-minute crawl through a solid jam. By the time she had made it to Queen Charlotte Street Jenny had lost all patience and cut across a silver Mercedes to beat it to a parking space. She met the driver's protest with a raised finger and a volley of abuse. She felt her face burn with shame as she hurried into the Georgian splendour of Queen Square; under pressure, she was no more civilized than a sewer rat.

Reed Falkirk & Co. occupied an elegant double-fronted building named Montego House. A frieze carved into the stonework depicted a ship in full sail with Caribbean palm trees in the background. Like all those in the square, it dated from the city's heyday, when local merchants and their bankers had grown rich on slaves, sugar and tobacco.

She climbed the stone steps and pressed the intercom.

A clipped female voice came over the speaker. 'Hello?'

Jenny turned to face the camera, trying to look imposing. 'Jenny Cooper, Severn Vale District Coroner. I'm here to see Mr Lynd.'

She entered a vestibule that opened into a spacious reception area set out to resemble a Regency drawing room: dark wood furniture upholstered in button-down velvet. Empress of this domain was a receptionist with perfectly painted nails and a silver brooch at the fussy collar of her blouse. Jenny approached her desk feeling irrationally timid.

'Good morning.'

The woman glanced up from a slender monitor. 'Do you have an appointment, Mrs Cooper? I don't see one.'

'No. But I won't take long. Five minutes at most.'

'I'll see if Mr Lynd's available.' She lifted the receiver and dialled a number with sharp, disapproving stabs of her immaculate fingers.

Jenny glanced up at the vast oil painting hanging above the mantelpiece. It depicted a tall wooden ship being un-loaded by piratical-looking stevedores, dogs and ragged children at their feet. A young black man in a wig and frock coat stood in the foreground; an older clerk at his side was recording figures in a ledger with a quill pen.

'He'll be down in a moment,' the receptionist said coolly.

'Thank you.' Jenny was struck by the fact that the young man in the picture had fine features but strangely unforgiving eyes.

'It's called *The Sugar Man*,' the receptionist explained, more friendly now. 'The one in the wig is William Clayton, the first owner of this building.'

'Really,' Jenny answered, surprised that a black man had been that wealthy.

'He had a white father and a slave mother. He was one of the richest men in Bristol in the 1790s.'

At that moment a man came down the ornate oak staircase. He was younger than she had expected, and more fashionable than the lawyers who appeared at her inquests; his prematurely bald head was close-shaved and he wore expensive Italian glasses.

'Mrs Cooper?'

'Yes.'

'Damien Lynd.' He turned to the receptionist. 'Is the meeting room free, Susan?'

'Mr Reed has a conference in ten minutes.'

'We won't be long.'

Lynd steered Jenny to a door leading to a conference room which, apart from a plasma TV screen, could have been the same one in which William Clayton had entertained his business associates two hundred years before. Dark polished boards creaked underfoot as they sat at opposite sides of a cherry-wood table.

'What can I do for you?' Lynd asked.

'I've seen from correspondence that you acted for Eva Donaldson. I'm sure you know that I'm currently conducting an inquest into her death.'

'One could hardly avoid it.'

'May I ask if you're acting for her estate?'

'No, we're not. I believe her executors instructed someone else.'

'Her executors being—?'

'Her father and his long-standing solicitor, as far as I am aware.'

'I see. Then I presume you're still in possession of her files, at least until her bill is paid.'

'Yes,' Lynd said cautiously. 'That would be the usual situation.'

'Then, if you don't mind, I'd like to see the originals and to have copies made.'

The lawyer studied the backs of his hands. 'I'm afraid that won't be possible, Mrs Cooper.'

His objection came as no surprise, but Jenny was curious to see how he would justify it. He must know as well as she did that her next move would be to make an order requiring their disclosure, and that failure to obey would amount to contempt.

'You no longer have them?'

'I'm afraid I find myself in the position of being unable to answer any questions on this subject.'

'I do hope you haven't been placed under any pressure, Mr Lynd?'

'I'm really not at liberty to discuss this any further. I know it sounds odd, but that is the situation.'

'Mr Lynd, either you make Eva Donaldson's files available to my inquest in their entirety, or I will use the full force of the law to compel you. Do I make myself clear?'

With the pained expression of a man walking an excruciatingly fine line, Lynd said, 'I understand your impatience, but if you were to take that approach I can tell you that it would trigger a different order of legal proceedings entirely.'

'What kind of proceedings?'

'Enforcement, I would imagine.' Lynd spoke in such a way that suggested there was a subtext she was expected to understand.

The light slowly dawned.

'Are you trying to tell me that there is some sort of court order preventing you from disclosing Miss Donaldson's papers?' Jenny asked.

Lynd gave her look indicating that even to answer that question was a risk he couldn't take. She was left in no doubt: he had been gagged in a manoeuvre that only a lawyer of Annabelle Stern's expertise could have executed.

'I can't claim to be an expert on the law of confidentiality, Mr Lynd, but I do know that there is no lawful means of putting Miss Donaldson's papers beyond the reach of a coroner.'

'Moot point, Mrs Cooper. And not one I'm willing to test,' Lynd said.

'And if I were to make the order here and now and summon police assistance to take the documents from the premises?'

'I would pick up the phone to a judge.'

'Any judge in particular?'

Lynd's forehead creased with the mental effort of charting a course through his complex ethical dilemma. Whichever way he jumped, he risked being found in contempt of court, and many lawyers had been struck off for less.

Jenny said, 'Don't say anything. Just listen. I'm assuming there's an injunction in force preventing you discussing or disclosing any documents relating to Miss Donaldson or her affairs, and I can guess who obtained it. I can also guarantee that the judge wasn't told anything like the whole story, nor did he intend to derail a perfectly legitimate inquest.'

'All logical conclusions,' Lynd said, starting to relax a little now that she had retreated from her earlier threats.

'I appreciate you can't tell me who the parties were or even confirm that this injunction exists, but if it does, I'm sure it doesn't contain a provision preventing you from naming the judge who granted it.'

'Almost persuasive, Mrs Cooper.' He glanced anxiously at his watch. 'I think our time's nearly up.'

'Just a moment.' Jenny fetched out her phone and speed-dialled Alison's mobile.

She answered from her car.

'Alison, I need police assistance at the offices of Reed Falkirk & Co., Montego House, Queen Square. Right now.'

'Police? What for?'

'To enforce an order for disclosure.'

'Now, hold on a moment—' Lynd protested.

Jenny cupped a hand over her mobile. 'Yes?'

Lynd pressed his fingers to his temples in an agony of indecision.

'Mrs Cooper?' Alison's tinny voice cut through the ominous silence between Jenny and Lynd.

'I'm sorry, I don't have time for this. Alison?'

'No!' Lynd said. 'Mr Justice Laithwaite.'

'Thank you.' Jenny spoke into her mobile. 'Blank that last instruction, Alison. But I want you to call the Royal Courts and get me an appointment before Mr Justice Laithwaite. As soon as possible.'

She rang off and turned to Lynd. 'If a single document goes missing from those files I will hold you personally responsible. Do you understand?'

'I think you've made yourself perfectly clear.'

'And by the way, I know about her dispute with GlamourX.'

Lynd's mouth fell open: she clearly wasn't meant to.

'Someone left a letter in her personal papers. I'm presuming the £15,000 she owed you was spent dealing with the injunction. Hard to catch everything, I suppose.'

Getting up from the shiny table, Jenny paused. 'One thing you might be free to talk about – Eva called the police on 15 March to complain that someone was harassing her. A male. Any idea who?'

'I have no knowledge of any complaint,' Lynd answered woodenly.

'I don't suppose you'd care to speculate as to who Eva had upset enough to want to kill her.'

'Why do you say "upset"?'

'I get the feeling she was a woman of extremes; you'd either love her or hate her, possibly both.'

'No comment,' Lynd said.

# TWENTY-ONE

THE NEWS VANS AND PEOPLE CARRIERS had filled the clubhouse car park and spilled out along the litter-strewn margins of the road. Jenny arrived fifteen minutes late and was forced to carry her heavy briefcase and unwieldy box of documents fifty yards along the busy carriageway, an articulated truck threatening to pull her over in its slipstream.

Alison was waiting fretfully on the front step in her usher's gown. 'I thought we'd lost you, Mrs Cooper. The lawyers have been threatening to leave.'

Jenny offloaded the box on to her. 'Did you make an appointment with the judge?'

'I don't think it's going to be possible. He's hearing applications this morning and checking into the Cromwell Hospital at three – gallstones.'

'Great. Well, I'll just have to catch him between the two.'

She pushed through the door.

'I don't think—'

'It can't wait,' Jenny insisted. 'Call his clerk and tell him I'll come to his hospital bed if I have to.'

She opened the door to the hall and walked straight to her desk at the front, the hubbub of speculative chatter dissolving to an expectant silence as she took her seat and removed several legal pads and her copy of *Jervis on Coroners* from her briefcase. Ignoring the indignant lawyers, she addressed the jury.

'I apologize for my lateness, but I can assure you that I'm as anxious as you are to conclude proceedings.' Jenny turned to face the hall and saw that Michael Turnbull was present. 'I see your client has finally arrived, Mr Sullivan.'

'Good morning, ma'am,' Sullivan said, with exaggerated deference. 'I am glad to say that Lord Turnbull has indeed been excused parliamentary duties this morning.'

'Then we'd better hear from him. Come forward, please.'

Turnbull made his way unobtrusively to the witness chair, smiling briefly in the direction of the jury before taking his seat. Ed Prince and Annabelle Stern sat side by side, watching their man closely. It was their moment of greatest danger and the tension was written in their faces.

'We'll deal with the issue of your contempt before we go any further,' Jenny said. 'The consequences of failing to attend were clearly stated in your summons.'

Turnbull stiffened. 'If I might offer my apologies—'

Jenny cut him short. 'I fine you the sum of one thousand pounds. You'll arrange payment with my officer before leaving court.'

Turnbull made no comment, responding with a not quite contrite nod she could imagine him having practised with Ed Prince.

Jenny turned to her handwritten notes of Cassidy's evidence, conscious that she was far from mentally prepared for the coming confrontation. *You can get through this*, she told herself. *You're the coroner, for goodness' sake.*

'Lord Turnbull, you weren't present, were you, when Miss Donaldson's former partner, Mr Cassidy, gave his evidence?'

'No.'

'You might have heard that he stated his opinion that by the time of her death Eva didn't have faith any more.'

'That certainly wasn't my impression,' Turnbull said mildly. 'In fact, I would say that her faith had never been stronger. Her efforts on behalf of Decency were relentless.'

'Campaigning for a ban on pornography doesn't require religious faith.'

'Eva was an ever-present member of the church. I never heard of her expressing doubts.'

Fighting the urge to go in hard at the outset, Jenny told herself to stay calm. Even the merest hint of bias would send Prince scurrying to the High Court; the Ministry of Justice would leap at the chance to remove her. She had to appear neutral, however hard Starr stared at her from his seat at the back of the room. She turned at the sound of Alison emerging from the office door behind her. She walked to her desk, giving Jenny a nod as if to say an arrangement had been made.

Jenny addressed herself to Turnbull with a renewed sense of purpose. 'How would you describe her state of mind the last time you saw her?'

'It would have been at a briefing session on the Friday afternoon. She seemed in very good spirits.'

'Was she ever prone to mood swings?'

'I think I have already stressed her levels of professionalism.' He spoke to the jury: 'I can only emphasize that.'

Jenny turned to the tab in her pad marked 'Turnbull', and brought up her notes of his previous evidence. 'Perhaps if we can just revisit the night of her death, briefly. I know that you and your wife were at the church when you received the message that she was too tired to speak that evening.'

'That's correct.'

'Are you aware of any additional strain that she might have been under which caused her not to come to the service?'

Turnbull appeared to think hard for a moment, then shook his head. 'No.'

'Did she talk to you about her mounting financial problems?'

'Not in any detail. I was aware there was an issue, but as I think Lennox tried to explain, she was considering her whole future. She clearly couldn't live as she once had while working for an organization such as ours.'

'Quite. But did you know, for example, that apart from mortgage arrears and other debts she had outstanding legal bills of nearly £15,000?'

There was a collective flinch from the Decency legal team. Annabelle Stern shot Ed Prince a frigid sideways look to which he didn't respond.

'No, I didn't,' Turnbull said with admirable calm.

He was good, Jenny thought. She could imagine him going as far in politics as he had in business.

Jenny continued, 'Mr Cassidy said that in his experience of living with Miss Donaldson it was very out of character for her to miss a professional engagement. Would you agree with that?'

'It was out of character, but not inconceivable. Her work for Decency affected her deeply. I would imagine she had become subject to all sorts of emotions she had simply shut down in her previous career.'

'You only imagine, or you know that to be the case?'

'I saw her looking tired and drained on occasions. People expected much of her and she gave it.'

'That's something I wanted to ask you about. She was the leader of a study group, two members of which have, it seems, committed suicide within days of each other. One was a young man of sixteen with a history of psychiatric problems, the other was a man in his thirties who worked as a senior psychiatric nurse.'

'It's very sad,' Turnbull said. He struck a homely tone. 'Look, churches like ours attract desperate and unhappy people, it's only to be expected. It's our Christian duty to do our best to help. It saddens me very deeply that these two were lost to us.'

'Did Eva ever speak to you about either of them?'

'No.'

'But she would have been on relatively intimate terms with them.'

'Prayer counselling has to be confidential. I'm sure if Eva thought either of them needed help she couldn't give she would have urged them to get it elsewhere.'

'You're not aware of any unhealthy aspect to her relationship with these two, and I mean that in the broadest sense?'

'The church has strict protocols. If there was any problem she would have gone straight to Lennox Strong.'

His delivery was flawless: distanced but compassionate, rational yet spoken with warmth. He was a hard man not to trust. Jenny's every instinct was to tear the facade down: to make him explain the coincidence of the three deaths following so swiftly after one another; to ask him why Freddy's psychosis had returned just as Eva was struggling with debts and crippling legal battles; to press him on the identity of the people with whom Jacobs had regretted becoming involved.

But outright confrontation wasn't an option. It wasn't just a small army of lawyers ranged against her, it was the entire Establishment. The one thing in her favour was that it played mostly by the rules. Hard as it was, she would have to try to stick to them. Keep composed and pretend that the questions she was about to ask were nothing but a regrettable necessity.

Jenny pulled the crime desk call log from amongst her papers and motioned to Alison, who, as she took it from her, whispered that Mr Justice Laithwaite could see her at two p.m. in the Royal Courts. Not a minute later. Jenny checked her watch. It was nearly eleven. She had only a few minutes left to deal with Turnbull if she was to catch a train that would deliver her to London in time. Bringing him back yet again would make her look chaotic.

Turnbull studied the log which Alison had handed him with an expression more of interest than alarm.

Sullivan rose in objection. 'Ma'am, will counsel be provided with copies of this document?'

'In due course, Mr Sullivan,' Jenny said. 'I'm afraid our resources aren't as great as those in the courts you are used to.'

There was a ripple of weary laughter from the journalists crowded on their uncomfortable seats. Sullivan sat down with a scowl.

Jenny said, 'Lord Turnbull, the document is an extract from the log of calls received by the crime desk on the night of 15 March this year. There is an entry recording a call from a Miss Eva Donaldson complaining that she was being harassed by an unnamed male. The official noted that she appeared intoxicated and incoherent.'

'That's certainly what's written here,' Turnbull said.

'And the follow-up entry next to it shows that when she was telephoned a week later she denied all knowledge of having made the complaint.'

'Yes.'

'Can you confirm that the telephone number written down there is her home number?'

'Yes, I recognize it.'

Jenny became aware that the room had fallen into unnatural silence.

'Do you have any idea as to who this man was?'

'I don't.'

'Had you ever seen Eva intoxicated or incoherent?'

'Never.'

Jenny glanced at the lawyers and could tell she had landed them in uncharted territory. Fraser Knight QC, counsel for the police, was conferring with his instructing solicitor, no doubt demanding that the original log be brought to him immediately. Annabelle Stern was whispering instructions to an underling, Ed Prince marginalized for the moment.

Jenny said, 'Had you ever seen her drink alcohol?'

Turnbull hesitated, but it was a calculating hiatus and the jury sensed it. Sullivan caught his eye and pulled him back from the brink of offering a dangerous hostage to fortune.

'I can't say I did.'

'It was unusual then, or a side of herself she kept hidden from you?'

'Unusual, certainly.'

'Except that she was also drinking alone, at home, on the night she was killed, or so the evidence suggests.'

Turnbull said, 'I can't see that I can make any useful comment.'

Jenny reached into the box at her side and brought out the letter from Reed Falkirk & Co.

'We do have some evidence for what may have been weighing on her mind on the March occasion, at least,' Jenny said. She handed the letter to Alison. 'Miss Donaldson's lawyers wrote to her on the 13th of that month. Could you please read it aloud, Mrs Trent?'

Jenny stared at her legal pad while Alison, reddening with embarrassment, struggled through the contents of the letter.

Waves of impotent fury emanated from Turnbull's legal team and crashed across her desk with almost physical force.

St Eva had been dethroned.

'Did you know that she was suing for royalties owed for her work in pornography?' Jenny asked.

Turnbull could no longer hide his disquiet. 'No, I didn't.'

'Do you find it surprising?'

'I can see that if she was struggling . . . I didn't know what was going on in her private life. I wish I had. I'm sure I could have done more to help.' His shoulders sank and the unassailable figure that had entered the witness box seemed now cut down to human size. He looked up as if about say more, but the words failed him. His lawyers watched him in horror: their man was starting to crack open.

Jenny said, 'Is there anything more you wish to say, Lord Turnbull?'

'Yes,' he said, after a pause. 'I know Eva was complex – how could she not have been? What she had lived through would have broken most people. But that's what drew others to her, her vulnerability, and her spirit. Only she knew the true depth of her faith, but I'd stake my reputation . . . No, I'd stake all I possess on Eva having been as righteously opposed to pornography on the day she died as she ever was. None of what I have heard today will change the way I feel about her in the slightest. All of us in the Decency campaign have nothing but the profoundest respect for her memory.'

*But she scared the hell out of you*, Jenny thought. *And she still does.*

She offered the lawyers the opportunity to cross-examine, but none volunteered. There had been a heartfelt quality to Turnbull's peroration and nothing they could offer would improve on it. With a final grateful glance in the direction of the jury, he made his way back to his seat.

'Ma'am,' Sullivan said, rising to his feet, 'might I ask if you are planning to produce any further documents without prior disclosure? I'm sure I hardly need remind you that failure to conform with usual practice risks compromising the legitimacy of these proceedings.'

'No, I've no further documents in my possession, Mr Sullivan,' Jenny said, choosing her words carefully, 'but I'm afraid I'm going to have to suspend our deliberations until tomorrow. I've an urgent meeting in London. I'm sure you and your colleagues will understand,' she said, aiming her pointed remark at Prince and Stern.

'I beg your pardon, ma'am? We were given no warning of this.'

'Nor was I,' Jenny said, gathering her papers. 'I'll do my best to conclude the evidence tomorrow, but I'd like Mr Joel Nelson, Mr Lennox Strong and Mrs Christine Turnbull present. I may need them to clarify some of the points raised this morning.'

Puffed up with indignation, Fraser Knight interjected. 'Ma'am, I must protest. The interested parties to these proceedings really are being treated in a quite unacceptable manner. We must at least be informed as to which witnesses will be called, and in what order.'

Jenny looked at him steadily. 'Mr Knight, this is an inquiry into the cause of death. My task is not to make life easy for you or for myself, it's to make sure we arrive at the truth.' She shuffled her papers noisily. 'Whatever that takes.'

Jenny left the building through the back door, issuing instructions to Alison not, under any circumstances, to tell anyone where she was going. The excitement of the moment was too great for the news crews, who broke with convention and swarmed around her as she fought her way through them. Reporters hurled a barrage of questions. 'Who was harassing her, Mrs Cooper?' 'What do you think the Decency campaign has to hide?' 'Is Michael Turnbull a suspect?' She kept her lips firmly closed. Talking to the media was one professional offence for which there was no excuse: a coroner who spoke to the press wouldn't be a coroner the following morning.

She piled into her car and headed back towards the city. In her rear-view mirror she caught a glimpse of reporters surging around Michael Turnbull and his lawyers as they scrambled into their Mercedes van. Jenny could only imagine how they planned to retaliate. She expected a blow to land before the end of the day; she had to make sure to strike first.

# TWENTY-TWO

THE TRAIN SLOWED TO A painful crawl through the dismal London suburbs and arrived in Paddington late, leaving Jenny just fifteen minutes for the cab ride across the centre of town to the Royal Courts in the Strand. And then there was the time it would take to clear the security check and find her way through the labyrinth of corridors to Mr Justice Laithwaite's chambers. She called Alison and pleaded with her to contact his clerk to beg for ten minutes' grace. She promised to try, but called back almost immediately to say that her request had been refused: the judge had a car waiting and would be leaving if she wasn't in his office at two on the dot. The taxi came to a dead halt on the Euston Road. It was the roadworks at King's Cross, the cabbie said, decorating his speech with expletives, you'd spend half an hour in a jam and find the lazy sods having a smoke and scratching themselves. If she was in a hurry, she'd do better by tube.

*Damn.* Jenny shoved a twenty-pound note through the slide window and jumped out between the three static lanes of traffic. Dodging the motorcycle couriers, she made it to the pavement and ran through the slow-moving tourists to Baker Street underground station.

\*

It was nearing three o'clock when she arrived, perspiring and out of breath, in the welcome cool of the Cromwell Hospital's reception area. Jenny approached the long, blond-wood reception desk and spoke to a receptionist.

'Could you tell me if Mr Justice Laithwaite has booked in? I need to see him immediately.'

The young woman tapped on her computer.

'Your name, please.'

'Jenny Cooper. Severn Vale District Coroner. It's a professional matter.'

Unimpressed, the girl ran her eyes over a list of patients. 'I'm afraid he's not checked in yet. You're welcome to wait in the lounge.'

Jenny stepped away from the desk and pondered the etiquette of buttonholing a sick judge on his way into hospital. She wasn't even sure what points of law she would argue; in the rush for the train there had been no time to consult textbooks.

'Are you quite sure? My surgeon assured me *ten* days. Well, could you please make enquiries? I'll need to speak to my insurers.'

Jenny noticed the small, round man in the beige linen suit for the first time. He was getting testy with a receptionist at the far end of the desk.

'Mr Justice Laithwaite?'

He snapped round with a startled expression.

'Jenny Cooper. Severn Vale District Coroner.'

'Good God.'

'I'm sorry to disturb you—'

'Really, this is hardly the time—'

'I know, Judge, but my inquest into the death of Eva Donaldson has reached a critical stage. I only learned this morning that you granted an injunction forbidding any disclosure of her private documents or affairs. I need to know what's in that material.'

'The moment to discuss this was at two o'clock.'

'I had to come from Bristol.'

'I'm no longer available, Mrs Cooper.'

'Judge, I need an order lifting the injunction for the purposes of my inquest. It's a formality—'

'It's out of the question.' He turned back to the desk and rapped on the counter. 'What's going on?'

'I'm trying to get through to your surgeon's secretary, sir.'

Jenny refused to give in. 'I can impose reporting restrictions. Judge, it's vital I know what was happening in her private life – the inquest is meaningless without that knowledge.'

'Mrs Cooper, don't you think the public interest might best be served by not raking over these coals until the Decency Bill has at least had its first reading? We both know how the media work. What you propose risks derailing the bill completely.'

'With respect, Judge, I can't see how the public interest can be served by anything less than the truth.'

He grunted dismissively.

'Judge, it's not Eva's Donaldson's murder that is at issue here. What you won't have read in the newspaper is that two of her close associates in the church have committed suicide in the last two weeks. One of them was a sixteen-year-old boy. I can't prove a connection with whatever was going on with Eva, but I can't disprove one either. All I know is that it smells bad, and this injunction makes it smell even worse.'

There was a pause as Laithwaite tried to absorb this information. She had stirred his conscience.

Taking advantage of the lull in conversation, the receptionist offered him the phone. 'Are you able to speak to her, sir? You might be able to explain it better than I can.'

'In a minute.' Laithwaite moved away from the counter, gesturing Jenny to follow him around the corner into an alcove that afforded a small degree of privacy. 'What sort of connection are we talking about?'

'Both of them were in Eva Donaldson's study group at the church Michael Turnbull helped to establish. The boy hanged himself the night before he was due to give evidence at my inquest. They were close.'

'And the other?'

'A married father of one who'd had sex with a man hours before he took his own life. It gets more complicated – he was senior mental health nurse at a unit the church tried to get involved with. A month before he died he persuaded a patient, a teenage girl, to give up her medication. She hanged herself too.'

'It all sounds rather circumstantial.'

Jenny said, 'The little evidence I have suggests Eva was falling out with the church in the weeks before she died. She was drinking; on one occasion she called the police and claimed she was being harassed. There – now you know more than I do.'

Laithwaite pressed a hand to his midriff and grimaced. He looked for a moment as if the pain in his stomach might overwhelm him.

Jenny reached out to steady him. 'I'm so sorry. Do you need to sit down?'

'No. Please—' He pushed out a hand to hold her at bay and waited for the spasm to pass. 'You've caught me in a weak moment, Mrs Cooper. But I can see why you considered it so urgent.' He took a deep breath and exhaled slowly. 'Given what you've told me, I'm prepared to accept there's a public interest in you being able to view any restricted material held by solicitors for the respective parties, but on strict condition that you only make public that which has a direct bearing on the case.'

'I'm not even sure who the respective parties are,' Jenny said.

'Ah, of course.' Laithwaite lowered his voice, as if fearing they might be overheard: 'They were Eva Donaldson and Lord Turnbull. I'll telephone my clerk and have him draft the order. I suppose you'll want it immediately.'

'If you could, Judge. Thank you.'

With a nod, he started back to the desk.

Chancing her luck, Jenny said, 'You wouldn't happen to recall what it was Turnbull wanted to suppress?'

Laithwaite stopped and looked her up and down, as if only now weighing the full consequences of his hasty decision. Jenny feared he was having second thoughts, but the doubt seemed to pass, giving way to an air of resignation.

'Sex,' he said, 'and a large measure of hypocrisy. A few years ago, while he was still in business, Turnbull liked to play the magnanimous host. Apparently on one occasion Miss Donaldson was part of the cabaret, a fact she chose to remind him of earlier this year.'

'They had a history.'

'More of a chance encounter.'

'And she was trying to blackmail him with it?'

'I'm afraid I can't recall every detail.'

'But the injunction must have covered more than that. She had other contractual disputes her solicitor wouldn't discuss with me.'

Laithwaite looked suddenly tired. Answering her was

becoming an effort. 'It covers anything that might bring Lord Turnbull, the Decency campaign or his church into disrepute.' He gave a pained smile. 'Do try not to be late next time, Mrs Cooper.'

He moved off to the desk, where the receptionist was waiting for him with an explanation for his query. Jenny watched him give a tired, indifferent shrug as if all the fight had drained out of him; and something told her that it probably had.

Jenny made her way to a sprawling internet cafe in High Street Kensington and hired a terminal at which she set up a temporary office among the students and travellers. It was too risky to use her phone with so many people in earshot, so she communicated with Alison via email, instructing her to request Mr Justice Laithwaite's clerk to fax copies of his order waiving the injunction to both sets of solicitors and to her office. She wanted old-fashioned hard copies to arrive in the lawyers' hands: email was too easily erased.

It was a long anxious wait for a response. Staring at the screen, waiting for a message to appear, she thought about what Laithwaite had said. It sounded as if Eva had been a hostess at one of Turnbull's parties, and more than just a pretty girl serving drinks. The judge had given the impression that Eva had been one of many girls Turnbull would have encountered while living the life of a high-rolling business-man. It was possible he wouldn't have remembered her, but she would have remembered him.

Nearly twenty minutes passed before Alison's reply arrived. Jenny clicked open the attachment long enough only for the time it took to press 'print', collected the hard copy from the desk and hurried out to hail a taxi.

The text was far briefer than she had anticipated.

# IN THE HIGH COURT OF JUSTICE
## QUEEN'S BENCH DIVISION

*CLAIM No. TD280110*

BETWEEN:

A

and

B

ex parte The Coroner for the Severn Vale District

---

## ORDER

---

Upon application by the Coroner for the Severn Vale District, the terms of the order in this matter dated 28 January are varied as follows:

1) *The Coroner for the Severn Vale District, namely Mrs Jenny Cooper, shall have the right to inspect all documents and materials which are subject to the terms of the said order, and to make whatever use of them as she sees fit in the conduct of her inquiry into the death of Miss Eva Donaldson.*

Signed on behalf of Mr Justice Laithwaite by his clerk, it bore the court office seal. It was the genuine article, but less than Jenny had hoped for. There was no mention of the contents of the previous order, and no schedule of the documents covered. It meant that even if the lawyers opened their files to her, she had no means of checking if they were complete.

\*

The cab was crossing Hyde Park Corner en route for Lincoln's Inn Fields when her phone rang. It was the office number. She pulled the glass screen separating her from the driver tight shut and answered.

'You got the order, Mrs Cooper?' Alison asked.

'It's pretty flimsy but I guess it'll do. Have all the parties received it?

'I just called both offices to confirm. It's there, or at least a PA's taken it off the machine . . .' Alison paused. 'You won't have seen the *Post*, of course.'

Jenny felt a rising sensation of dread. 'Why? What have they written?'

'Are you sure—?'

'Tell me.'

'There's a photo of you coming out of Weston police station. The article says you're helping police with their inquiry into the death of your cousin in 1972 . . . It's not so much what it says as the way they say it.'

'Say what?' Jenny snapped.

'It says the case has been reopened following a complaint by the dead girl's younger brother.'

'What other lies have they printed?'

'They quote someone—'

'Just read it to me.'

'*A former colleague described Mrs Cooper, 43, as a some-what driven but fragile character, who gave up a successful career in family law due to ongoing emotional problems exacerbated by an acrimonious divorce. She has one child of her own who lives with his father.*'

'That's nice. No name?'

'No.'

Jenny's first thought was of Ross reading the article, or, more likely, one of his college friends taunting him with it. And then there was David and his prissy pregnant girlfriend.

None of them knew about Katy. Should she phone them? What would she say?

'So, is any of it true, Mrs Cooper?' Alison asked warily.

Avoiding the question, Jenny said, 'Make sure you speak to my three witnesses. Offer them a ride to court in a police car if they've got a problem with it.'

She ended the call and thrust Katy out of her mind.

The firm of Kennedy and Parr occupied a smart Victorian building in Lincoln's Inn Fields, a quiet, green oasis set behind the roaring thoroughfare of High Holborn. Like all the pleasant central London squares, it had been built to keep the rich insulated from the poor and it had succeeded. It was now home to expensive law firms and upmarket finance houses. Quiet, discreet and reassuringly solid, it was a place in which time seemed to have stood still, and where the wealthy came for succour and sanctuary.

Jenny stopped by the railings of the next-door building and searched her handbag for the Temazepam tablet she knew was in there somewhere. She found it wedged in the folds of her wallet and swallowed it dry. It was a drug for serious insomniacs which these days barely touched her. Another thing she'd have to deal with when this was all over. They were stacking up.

She approached the front door and was buzzed through without demur. She stepped over the threshold into a reception that resembled the set of a fashion shoot.

The receptionist had been chosen to complement her surroundings. Jenny approached her with a disarming smile.

'Jenny Cooper.' She handed a business card over the counter. 'I need to speak to either Ed Prince or Annabelle Stern. I'm sure they're expecting me.'

'Take a seat.' The girl motioned her to a sofa.

Jenny flicked through a pristine copy of *Tatler* as the girl phoned around the building, evidently being passed from one PA to another. It was a full five minutes before she had any joy. 'If you'd like to pick up the phone, Mr Prince will speak to you.'

Jenny reached for the sleek handset sitting in the middle of the table. It felt unnaturally smooth to the touch, like alabaster.

'Mrs Cooper?' Prince barked, making sure to have the first word.

'I've trust you've seen the order made by Mr Justice Laithwaite,' Jenny said, dispensing with the niceties. 'I'd be grateful if you would comply. I'd like to take copy documents back to Bristol this afternoon.'

'There's nothing to copy. They were all destroyed months ago.'

'If that's true, I have to call you as a witness of fact, Mr Prince, and Ms Stern also. Are you in the building? If so, you could at least have the decency to conduct this discussion in person.'

'It doesn't matter where I am, there's nothing to discuss. Number one, there is no evidence for you to see; number two, the order doesn't say anything about lawyers giving evidence; and number three, I'd go to jail before I broke a client's confidence.'

'You may well have the opportunity to put those principles to the test.'

'I doubt that, Mrs Cooper. I doubt that very much.'

Prince hung up.

Jenny marched over to the reception desk. 'Please get me Ms Stern.'

'She's not available.'

Jenny said, 'I'm here to enforce a High Court order. She has a choice: speak to me now or I'll have her office door broken down by police officers.'

'Just a moment.' The girl dialled a number while Jenny drummed her fingers impatiently on the counter. 'Is she in the building?' Jenny asked.

'Excuse me,' the girl said and stood up from her chair. She opened a door behind her desk and went through.

'Hey—'

The girl shut the door after her. At the same moment, a large man in a buttoned-up blazer which barely met across his pumped-up chest stepped out of a doorway next to the elevator. His plastic lapel badge read, 'Kennedy and Parr, Security'. He walked towards her with no expression on his dull face.

'Could you please leave the building, madam.'

'I beg your pardon?'

'Now.' He gestured towards the door.

'Sir, I'm a coroner, and I'm here to enforce a court order.'

The man looked at her with dead eyes. 'Please comply with my instruction or I will have to use reasonable force to remove you.'

Jenny reached for her phone. 'I'm calling the police. I'd advise you not to make things any worse for yourself.'

He shot out a hand and grabbed her arm above the elbow.

'What the hell do you think you're doing?'

With his other hand he snatched her briefcase.

Pushing her towards the door, the security guard hissed, 'What are you, brain dead? Get out.' He tossed her case down the steps and shoved her after it.

He slammed the heavy door, leaving her standing outside nursing an arm that felt as if it had been crushed between boulders. A woman passing on the pavement stopped to gawp, then hurried on.

Still in pain, Jenny picked up her case with her good hand and started to plan her counter-attack. If the lawyers wanted to play rough, she would send in officers from Bristol to batter their way in. Meanwhile, Alison could take another team into Reed Falkirk. She pulled out her phone to start making arrangements. The numbers swam in front of her eyes.

She needed somewhere to sit and calm down. She remembered a cafe on a busy road nearby, but couldn't remember from which direction she had entered the square. Disorientated, she looked left and right, searching for a point of reference.

'Jenny.'

She turned at the sound of a familiar voice and saw Simon Moreton climbing out of a cab on the far side of the road. Holding the door open, he called out, 'Over here. For God's sake, come on.'

The feeling of unreality intensified as she dumbly did as she was told. Simon buckled into the seat next to her and instructed the driver to take them to the Royal Lancaster Hotel.

'Why are we going to a hotel?' she asked.

'It has a good bar. And it's near the station.'

'Soften me up and send me home?'

'Believe it or not I'm on your side, Jenny.'

'How did you know I was here? Don't tell me Annabelle Stern's pulling your strings, too.'

'There was a certain flurry of excitement when news of your coup with poor old Mr Justice Laithwaite hit the wires. It didn't take a genius to work out what your next move would be.'

'They threw me out. Their security guard nearly broke my arm. Did you know that was going to happen, too?'

'More or less.'

'What the hell does that mean?'

His ambiguous sideways glance said he couldn't decide whether to give her the full or the sanitized version.

'Unless you tell me, Simon, I'm going to have that place turned over, news cameras, the lot.'

'You could, Jenny, of course, and on one level I wouldn't blame you, but the fact is . . . the fact is you'll be out of a job before you embarrass Lord Turnbull in public, at least until his bill has passed.' He turned his gaze out of the window, as if trying to detach himself from his words. 'You have to learn to accept the way things work. Things get sorted out *in the end*. What you mustn't do is cause a cataclysm where it needn't happen. One thing at a time.'

'And if an innocent man strings himself up in his prison cell while he's waiting?'

'You're proving my point, Jenny. You've let yourself become partial. That's precisely what our measured approach is designed to prevent.'

'I have an order for disclosure of documents that Turnbull had suppressed. Laithwaite told me the story: Eva was a hostess at one of Turnbull's pre-salvation parties, screwing his high-rolling friends, probably him, too. She'd been asking him for more money since last November. She was on the skids, Simon, falling apart. Turnbull thought she was going to expose him.'

Moreton stared out of the window, smiling vaguely as they passed Charing Cross station and headed out into Trafalgar Square, a billowing curtain of pigeons rising into a clear sky.

Jenny said, 'Are you going to say something, or just sit there admiring the view?'

'I was wondering how far I would be prepared to go for you,' Moreton said. 'And if it backfired, how I'd explain it to my colleagues . . . or my wife. They'd all assume I'd had my head turned, lost my judgement.'

He shot her a look she couldn't read, but she could feel his charge in the brush of his shoulder against hers as the cab swung through Admiralty Arch into St James's Park. It would be so easy to say yes, Jenny thought, and to use him as her champion and protector. It could even prove to be his salvation from all the years of dissembling and compromise. She thought he might want that more than anything, even more than he wanted her.

Jenny said, 'Turnbull's lawyers haven't got enough to prove I'm unfit. It's my father the police are interested in, not me.'

'Judges are very sensitive creatures, these days, Jenny. You'd be removed for your own good, out of compassion, or at least until the storm had passed. We can't have a coroner working under such a burden of mental stress – it's not in anybody's interests.'

'What would happen if I didn't have any bodies buried in my garden?'

'One would be found. No one has nothing to hide, least of all the most outwardly blameless.'

'I'm not going to sleep with you, Simon, so you might as well tell me what you've got in mind now.'

'Jenny—'

'I don't think it would be in anybody's interests either, do you?'

He met her gaze, his eyes sparking briefly with hope, then slowly fading into resignation. 'No, I suppose not,' he said, as if it was his decision alone to make.

'Well?'

'You leave the disclosure issue alone and I'll guarantee the police will take a thorough look at all that evidence relating to Miss Donaldson and Turnbull later. In the meantime, you can lodge a statement with them setting out what you already know. But like I said – one thing at a time.'

'Do Turnbull or his lawyers get put on notice of the police investigation?'

'Absolutely not.'

'What *do* they hear?'

'That you've been "spoken to".'

Jenny thought about it. It wasn't attractive, but nor was the alternative. At least Moreton's deal still held out the prospect of justice being arrived at in the end. 'I still have three witnesses to hear from again. I can't be seen to have been completely rolled over.'

'I've showed you the line, Jenny. It's up to you how close you walk to it.' His face cracked into a smile.

'What?' Jenny said.

'You . . .' His hand brushed against hers. 'You'll never give up, will you?'

# TWENTY-THREE

IT WOULD HAVE BEEN BETTER to have slept with Simon
Moreton. Waking up on the sofa next to two empty bottles with a splitting head had been far lower than that. It
took Jenny back to the very bottom. She had betrayed her
promises to Dr Allen and to herself. It had happened the
first time when she had lunched with Simon at the Hotel du
Vin. Clinking her delicate glass against his had seemed the
most natural and civilized gesture in the world. Even afterwards she hadn't given it a thought. But that's how the devil
got you: before you even knew it had happened.

She prayed that she wouldn't get pulled over. The way
she was driving she deserved to be, hitting the rumble strip
as she squinted into the bright sun that hurt her eyes. The
metallic taste of the cheap wine still lingered in her mouth.
All she had managed for breakfast was black coffee, two
paracetamol and a Xanax. And in less than an hour she'd
have to face Decency's lawyers and pretend that yesterday
hadn't happened.

At least she hadn't got as far as telling Father Starr about
the injunction. In the end, when it was all over, she could
tell him a white lie: that she'd persuaded the police to have
a second look and that, lo and behold, they'd found a whole
history between Eva and Turnbull. Where that would lead,
she had no idea. There was every chance it would result in

yet another whitewash, but what could Starr expect? She was a coroner, not a miracle worker.

The very thought of the priest made her angry. He was the reason she was hung-over, about to be humiliated at her own inquest and so racked with guilt she could barely look at herself in the mirror. His selfish demands were tearing her apart. There had been messages from both Ross and Steve on her machine when she arrived home, but there was nothing she could have said to either of them apart from: *Leave me alone.* Coughlin had also called, saying that he had spoken to some regulars in a gay bar who claimed to have seen Jacobs come in and pick up once or twice. He was hoping to track one of these partners down. His call, too, had gone unanswered.

There was only one news van, as well as Alison's car, outside the clubhouse. Jenny parked close to the door, pointing outwards so she could make a quick getaway after the verdict. She planned to deal with the witnesses in the first half of the morning and sum up to the jury immediately afterwards. By early afternoon it would all be over.

Alison greeted her warmly and apologized for handing her a thick sheaf of urgent emails. Jenny sensed that she knew, and guessed that Simon Moreton had issued her with strict instructions to keep things running smoothly. She flicked through her messages and decided they could wait.

'And there was a call from Dr Kerr,' Alison said, as if preparing her for disappointing news. 'Apparently it wasn't Freddy Reardon's DNA in Jacobs's body. He's expecting the last batch of test results this morning but he said not to hold your breath.'

Jenny nodded. In a strange way it was a relief. The pressure to make a connection with Eva had dissolved.

Three separate deaths. Three separate causes. Trust Simon. One thing at a time.

Her headache had softened to a low persistent throb as she took her seat at the head of the courtroom. All eyes were on her, from Father Starr and Kenneth Donaldson at the back, through the ranks of journalists, to the jury at her side and the black wall of lawyers opposite. This was what it must have felt like for Eva going to work some mornings, Jenny thought to herself, except she had to perform naked.

If the lawyers felt any measure of shame at their part in the suppression of evidence, they weren't allowing it to show. Annabelle Stern was smiling. Ed Prince felt confident enough not even to have bothered turning up, sending an assistant in his place. No doubt there was far more money to be made back at the office.

'Members of the jury,' Jenny began, 'thank you for your patience. Before you consider your verdict, I have asked three key witnesses back to see if they can help us understand why Miss Donaldson made a complaint to the police.' She should have gone on to address the article that had been written about her in the *Post*, but when she tried to find the words, they escaped her. It was easier to behave like the lawyers, to brazen it out and pretend nothing had happened. She drew back her shoulders. 'Mrs Christine Turnbull, please.'

The witness was dressed in a navy summer suit with a light silk blouse. She managed both to be both alluringly beautiful and to radiate wholesomeness. It was impossible not to admire her.

Jenny reminded her that she remained under oath and asked her to cast her mind back nearly four months to the early part of March. Had she noticed anything out of the ordinary in Miss Donaldson's behaviour?

'She was happy. We had just commissioned polling which showed over seventy per cent of voters back our campaign. It was a real shot in the arm for us all.'

'You have been made aware, I am sure, of the evidence that she telephoned the police on the evening of 15 March in an apparent state of intoxication, complaining of harassment.'

'Yes,' Christine said, with a note of sadness. 'And I can think of only one explanation. The poll had been published the previous week. There was a flurry of articles predicting the end of the pornography business in Britain as we know it. If ever there was a time Eva was likely to have been deliberately intimidated, that was it.'

'Wouldn't she have told you?'

'Not necessarily. Our opponents are nothing if not cunning. They know everything about how to prey on human weakness. One can only imagine what they might have threatened her with. I'm sure they weren't short of material from her past.'

'But what about the fact Eva was incoherent, possibly drunk? How does that fit with the woman you knew?'

'We all have our breaking points,' Christine said. 'Even Eva.'

'That's certainly true,' Jenny responded drily, 'but we also know that Eva was pursuing a former employer, GlamourX, for unpaid royalties. If what you say about your opponents is true, wasn't that an act of recklessness bordering on the utterly irresponsible?'

The lawyers bristled. Annabelle Stern's stony face told her she was sailing dangerously close to the wind.

Unfazed, Christine said, 'Eva was entitled to what was rightfully hers; I have no doubt she would have put the money to good use.'

Then why had such draconian measures been taken to

keep these matters secret? Jenny wanted to know. And how could Christine Turnbull remain so composed when she was part of a machine that had put such pressure to bear on the dead woman? Then it occurred to her that beneath the mask Christine might be churning as much as she was, that all that was sustaining her through this ordeal was the imminent prospect of her campaign reaching its end.

'The night Eva was killed, you were at the Mission Church with your husband, is that correct?'

'Yes.'

'From what time?'

'Shortly after six, as far as I recall.'

'And when did you receive the message that Miss Donaldson wasn't coming?'

'A little while before the service. At about six-thirty.'

'Were you with your husband at the time?'

'We were in the boardroom at the church offices planning our meetings for the coming week.'

'Didn't it occur to either of you to try to persuade her to come?'

Christine said, 'No. I think we both felt that if she were exhausted we had better leave her to recover. She had a busy time ahead. We all did.'

'Might there have been another reason why Eva didn't come to the church that night?'

Christine said, 'If there was, I think we would all know about it by now.'

A pair of junior lawyers escorted Christine Turnbull to the door, where she was met by a driver who would whisk her away to her final frantic round of lobbying meetings. As Joel Nelson took her place in the box, Alison leaned over to Jenny to let her know she had received a text from Andy

Kerr saying his test results had come back with something that might be of interest. Could she call him?

'You call him,' Jenny said. 'If it's important, get him to court.'

Alison crept out to the side office as Jenny turned her attention to Nelson. His face radiated confidence.

'Tell me, Mr Nelson,' Jenny said, 'did you and Eva often pray together?'

'Not often, but we certainly did.'

'Can you tell us what about?'

Nelson said, 'I can put my hand on my heart and say there is nothing Eva ever told me in confidence that could have any bearing on this inquest. She was looking forwards, not back. She was seeking strength and inspiration, and on the whole that's what we prayed for.'

'What else?'

'Normal day-to-day things, the minor incidents of life.'

'Money?'

Nelson shook his head. 'No. That was never a subject that was mentioned.'

'Relationships?'

Nelson gave a patient smile. 'Ma'am, to tell you the truth, whenever I sat down with Eva she usually wanted to pray for others.'

'Others in the church?'

'For the most part.'

'Did a lot of people bring her their troubles?'

'Of course.'

'Such as?'

'You name it. But that's what we ask people to do – to offer up their problems in prayer.'

Jenny heard the door to the office open and close. Alison tiptoed across the creaky, uneven boards towards her. She leaned down and spoke to her in a whisper.

'Something about carbon fibre particles on both Freddy Reardon and Alan Jacobs's bodies. There might be some connection with Eva. He'll be here in fifteen minutes, but we can't keep him – he's dealing with a cot death.'

Jenny thanked her and turned back to Nelson. 'Did she ever mention Freddy Reardon or Alan Jacobs in these sessions?'

'You make it sound like a formal ritual – it really wasn't. And no, I don't believe she did.'

'How can you be sure? It sounds as if she mentioned so many.'

'I chose my words very precisely, ma'am,' Nelson said. 'I don't *believe* she did, but it's also possible I don't remember.'

Jenny glanced at Annabelle Stern and saw her features harden. The assistant next to her was punching a message into his phone. She sensed that she had strayed into uncomfortable territory. Mentioning Freddy and Jacobs was a breach of her deal with Moreton; grudgingly, she took a sideways step.

'Did the problems you prayed for ever include suicidal thoughts?'

'That came up occasionally and it still does. It's a far more common phenomenon than you might think.'

'Do you have protocols, a system to refer such people to professionals who can treat them?'

'The church doesn't hold itself out as being a substitute for medicine, if that's what you're implying.'

'But you are a church that believes in miracles.'

'That's the basis of Christian faith,' Nelson said. 'Jesus was God made flesh. He can, and does, heal all the time.'

Sullivan scraped back his chair. 'Ma'am, I fail to see the relevance of this line of questioning.'

'I'll put it directly. Mr Nelson, is it possible that someone

350

who was relying on Eva for support had become an unbearable burden? Threatening, even?'

Nelson shook his head. 'Absolutely not. Prayer counsellors are told to refer anyone they can't cope with upwards. In Eva's case that would have been to Pastor Lennox Strong.'

Satisfied, Sullivan sat down with a look that warned her not to trespass off-limits again.

Jenny took Nelson back to the first two weeks in March, but he claimed he knew nothing more than Christine Turnbull. She tried again, but he stuck resolutely to the party line.

'Can you remember the last time you spoke to her, the phone call on the Sunday evening?'

'Very well.'

'Where were you?'

'At my desk in the church office. The phone rang, it was Eva. I told her that Lennox had just been asking after her. He wanted to go through the running order before the service. She sounded very quiet. She said she was really sorry, but she was too exhausted to come. I asked if she was all right, and she explained that it had been a very long week and she just had to crash out.'

'*Crash out?* Are those the words she used?'

'Yes.'

Jenny picked up the file of documents she had received the previous week from Craven's solicitors and turned to the section containing the statements DI Goodison's team had taken in the two days before Craven confessed. She turned to the single sheet containing Nelson's.

'You gave a statement to the police on the evening of Monday the 10th. In it you say, "Eva called to say she was too tired to come in. I said we understood and would see her in the morning." You didn't say anything to the police about *crashing out*, or asking how she was. Why didn't you give them this detail?'

'I suppose I was still shell-shocked.'

'You didn't want to be as helpful as you could? It's an important detail, Mr Nelson – she didn't crash out, did she? She opened a bottle of wine when she should have been talking to four thousand people. When someone's spoken to you for the last time you think back and remember every word, don't you?'

Rocked, Nelson said, 'I apologize. That's all I can put it down to. The shock.'

'You're sure you haven't added this detail to make it sound less ambiguous?'

'It's what she said, I swear.'

She looked to the lawyers. 'Does anyone wish to question this witness?'

There were no takers.

Jenny wrestled with the feeling that there was more, that she had missed something, but reluctantly she was forced to release Nelson from the witness box.

Lennox Strong appeared unsettled as he sat in the chair. The self-assured smile seemed to require a conscious effort. He lacked the inner glow shared by his two colleagues. Jenny decided she must hit him hard and fast.

'Mr Strong, would you say that in the last six months of her life you were closer to Eva Donaldson than anyone else?'

'I suppose that's right,' he said quietly.

'You must have spent many hours together working on your book.'

'We did.'

'Where did you do that, as a matter of interest?'

'We'd find a spare office in the church, or the cafe maybe.'

'Just the two of you?'

'Yes,' Strong said, as if he were confident he had nothing to be ashamed of.

'What kind of things did you talk about aside from the book?'

He shrugged. 'Whatever came up. All sorts of things.'

'And she told you she was thinking of entering the ministry, becoming a pastor like you.'

'Oh, yeah. We talked about that a lot.'

Jenny felt the heat of Annabelle Stern's predatory eyes.

'And you discussed her doubts about that as well as her ambition?'

'Certainly,' Strong said, with a hint of caution now.

Jenny glanced down at her notes, stealing a moment to calm herself.

'Did she bring other people's problems to you also – people in the church?'

'She did.'

'Did she ever talk to you about Alan Jacobs?'

'I'm not at liberty to discuss confidences,' Strong said.

'I'm not asking you to breach any confidences, Mr Strong. I'm simply asking whether she mentioned him.'

Lennox Strong looked at the lawyers, then at his feet.

'I'd like an answer, please, Mr Strong.'

'Yes, she mentioned Mr Jacobs.'

'Thank you. And Freddy Reardon, too?'

'I think so.'

'Did they cause her a *lot* of problems?'

It was Sullivan's voice that shot back at her. 'Ma'am, we appear to be drifting a long way off the point again.'

'I decide what's relevant in my own court, Mr Sullivan. Sit down.'

'Ma'am—'

'No, Mr Sullivan. Sit.'

Sullivan unwillingly gave way.

'You were about to say . . .'

'They each had issues,' Strong said carefully, 'but they weren't alone in that.'

'But you must have known these two particularly well, Mr Strong. When Freddy Reardon was an inpatient at the Conway Unit two years ago, you went there to speak.'

'I've been there a few times, yes.'

'Was it Alan Jacobs who arranged it?'

'No. It was an idea that came up in the church – offering pastoral care to troubled kids. I was one of those once.'

'You were in a prison, not a psychiatric unit.'

'Often there's not a lot of difference.'

'Did either Freddy Reardon or Alan Jacobs cause Eva Donaldson problems, harass her in any way?'

'No. She never said anything about that.'

'Would she have done?'

'I'm sure she would.'

'Did she talk to you about her money problems?'

There was a pause as Lennox Strong wrestled with his conscience. 'She mentioned her worries once or twice.'

'Did you know she had a £15,000 legal bill?'

'No.'

'Or that she was trying to sue an adult film company for royalties?'

'No, ma'am. Eva never mentioned that.'

'Back in March, did she tell you she was being harassed by someone?'

He shook his head.

'So there was a whole side to her life you knew nothing about?'

'I guess so . . .'

'Does that surprise you?'

'Yes,' he said, quietly.

'Mr Strong, are you telling the whole truth? You're a man who every week asks thousands of people to trust him. I've seen you talk: you don't just tell people you've felt the presence of God, you tell them you've been snatched from the jaws of hell . . . I find it very hard to believe that a lonely and troubled woman like Eva Donaldson would have kept any secrets from you.'

Lennox Strong sat very still. Annabelle Stern's piercing gaze bored into him. Jenny waited for his answer, but none came. She let the silence stretch on. Five, then ten seconds passed as the pastor searched deep inside himself.

The moment was broken by the sound of the door opening at the back of the room. Andy Kerr stepped in, flustered from his hurried journey from the Vale. Under his arm he carried a leather document case.

Jenny said, 'Go back to your seat for a moment, please, Mr Strong. Come forward, Dr Kerr.'

The lawyers exchanged panicked whispers as Andy Kerr and Lennox Strong swapped places. It was Fraser Knight who spoke for them.

'Ma'am, we've had no notice of this witness.'

'We're at the same disadvantage, Mr Knight. No more interruptions, please.' She turned to Dr Kerr and reminded him that he too was still under oath. 'I understand you have received test results that may be of interest to us.'

'Possibly,' Dr Kerr said. He unzipped the document case and brought out several sheets of paper from a file, some of which, Jenny could see, displayed photographs. 'I was looking for a connection between two different corpses. They are those of Alan Jacobs and Freddy Reardon, who I believe were associates of Miss Donaldson.'

Anticipating Sullivan's objection, Jenny cut him off. 'I'm sure the relevance will become clear in a moment, Mr Sullivan. Be patient.'

Her rebuke drew smiles from the jury.

Dr Kerr continued: 'Mr Reardon had abrasions around his wrists typical of the kind caused by handcuffs, or at least handcuffs the wearer has resisted in some way. He had sought to disguise these injuries with some sort of concealer of the type usually used to cover blemishes on the face. I took a sample of the abraded skin and subjected it to microscopic examination.' He held up a photograph taken through the lens of the microscope. 'I found two things: minute flakes of lead-based gloss paint, cream or yellowish in colour, and numerous strands of fibreglass typical of the kind found in roof insulation.' He indicated several points on the photograph with his finger. 'What's the relevance? Well, I'd say there's a strong chance Reardon was cuffed to something – a railing or a pipe, perhaps – coated with this old gloss paint. Where there's glass fibre insulation, particles like this will be floating in the air, settling on the skin and being inhaled. Sure enough, there was evidence of similar fibres in the boy's nasal passages. You'd expect the mucus to clear them in twenty-four to forty-eight hours. I'm sure he inhaled them within a day or two of his death.'

Jenny looked over at Lennox Strong. Joel Nelson was trying to say something to him, but he wasn't listening. He was staring straight ahead, his jaw clamped tight shut as if he were battling an acute pain.

Dr Kerr continued, 'I checked Alan Jacobs's nasal passages and found the same fibres, only they were present in greater density, suggesting exposure in the hours immediately preceding death.' He held up another highly magnified photograph. 'They are a similar length and width as those in Mr Reardon's body.' He put the picture aside and lifted up two others. 'Lastly, I took samples from the mucus membranes in Miss Donaldson's nasal passages. There was no evidence of glass fibres in her nose, but from the sample

I took from high up inside the sinus,' he nodded towards the photograph in his right hand, 'there was a significant concentration. That tells me she was exposed on several occasions, but not in the days immediately preceding her death.' He turned to Jenny. 'A more detailed examination of the airways would yield further detail, but that's all I have at the moment.'

'Where would you find these kinds of fibre?' Jenny asked.

'Either in a roof space or somewhere where insulating fibre is being handled – in a building undergoing refurbishment, perhaps.'

Jenny's mind flooded with strange images: a place where Eva and Freddy and Jacobs had all been, a place where Jacobs had been hours before his death to which Freddy returned a week later, *handcuffed.*

There was a burst of activity on the lawyers' benches. Another assistant was dispatched from the hall. Annabelle Stern and Sullivan were locked in frantic consultation.

'Does anyone have any questions?' Jenny said.

Sullivan shot to his feet. 'Ma'am, we request an immediate adjournment to review this evidence and appoint an independent expert.'

'You don't need an adjournment to do that, Mr Sullivan. Thank you, Dr Kerr. Unless you have anything more to add, you're free to go.'

Annabelle Stern tugged on Sullivan's sleeve and whispered instructions in his ear.

'Could you come back please, Mr Strong,' Jenny said.

Sullivan interrupted again. 'Ma'am, I am instructed to inform you that an application is currently being heard in the High Court to have these proceedings halted. I request an adjournment pending the outcome.'

'And is this an application made on behalf of your clients, Mr Sullivan?'

'Yes, ma'am.'

'On what grounds?'

'Ma'am you may not wish the answer to that to be given in open court.'

So that's where Ed Prince had disappeared to. How naive of her to think he would have trusted anything to chance. He would be in court right now with the most expensive QC he could buy, who would be persuading a judge that she was barely a notch off certifiable and had spent a lifetime protecting her father, who, as chance would have it, was currently under investigation for suspected child abuse and perhaps even murder. Even if she had given Moreton the time of his life, she doubted if he would have been able to stand in the way of the juggernaut that was careering towards her now.

'If you get your order, Mr Sullivan,' Jenny said icily, 'then, and only then, will this inquiry be required to stop. Until that moment you will do nothing more to obstruct it.' She turned to Lennox Strong. 'I'm waiting, Mr Strong.'

Sullivan refused to give way. 'Mr Strong is not giving any more evidence.'

Jenny snapped. 'You're leaving my courtroom now, Mr Sullivan.' She gestured to Alison. 'Officer, see this man out.'

Alison looked up in surprise, then made her way across the floor.

'Ma'am, my clients are entitled to be represented,' Sullivan objected.

Ignoring him, Jenny said, 'Mr Strong, you will return to the witness box or go to prison for contempt. What is it to be?'

The young pastor rose from his seat. Joel Nelson snatched at his wrist, but Strong shook him off. 'Leave me alone, Joel.'

He strode forwards, ignoring Sullivan, who hissed a

warning to him as he passed. Annabelle Stern had a phone pressed to each ear.

He sat squarely in the witness chair and seemed to fix his stare on a point on the far distance beyond the confines of the hall.

'I asked you whether you had told the whole truth, Mr Strong. You have yet to answer.'

'No, ma'am, I haven't,' Strong said, his words coming from the part of his conscience that was winning the raging battle inside him. 'Some things happened in my church that were nothing to do with me, or with Eva.'

'Yes?'

Defying the threatening glares coming from Stern, he turned to the jury.

'Exorcisms. People like my colleague, Joel Nelson, and his friends believe that people's afflictions are caused by evil spirits that possess them. We're talking about people with mental illness – depression, anxiety, paranoia, schizophrenia; sick, unhappy people in need of God's help, but not like that. It was Eva who told me it was happening. They would meet in the prayer rooms at the back of the church, the old part of the building that we're still fixing up – that's where those fibres come from, we had rolls of the stuff waiting to go in the roof. Joel and his friends would take them there to drive out the devils, in the little room at the far end where you can't be heard. It was Freddy who first told Eva about this practice. He was going along with it. He said it was making his voices go away, but it didn't sit right with her, nor with me.'

'Did you or Eva witness these exorcisms?'

'She did. She walked in on them praying over Alan Jacobs. He was crying like a child, she said, begging them to make him clean. She didn't know what to do – he was there of his own free will, but it's not the way we would pray for people, telling them they're possessed by devils. I went to the trustees thinking that as pastor they'd respect my wishes.' He dipped his head in shame. 'I was told that Bobby DeMont exorcized homosexual people all the time and that I should be grateful we were doing God's work. The next day I was called in by Mr Prince, the lawyer. He made me sign a document promising I wouldn't discuss any church business with anyone outside the organization. If I did, I'd lose my job. Eva held out for a few weeks, but eventually he bullied her into signing too.'

'When was that?'

'March. She was furious. She said Michael and Christine were running the church like a cult. I tried to talk her down, tell her we'd sort it out, but she disappeared inside herself. She would hardly talk to me.'

Jenny said, 'What was going on the night she was killed?'

Lennox shook his head. 'I came into the office about quarter to seven looking for her. Joel was making phone calls saying he didn't know where anyone was, not Eva, Michael or Christine. We had four thousand people coming and I was the only one of the team who'd showed.'

Annabelle Stern suddenly rose and stepped forward to Sullivan's vacant seat. She was brandishing her phone. With no trace of emotion, she said: 'Ma'am, I have to inform you that as of this moment, these proceedings are stayed pending full judicial review. Any attempt on your part to call further evidence will not be lawful.'

All Jenny could do was stare at her and wonder what unearthly hour she had to get up in the mornings to look that perfect.

# TWENTY-FOUR

'YOU COULDN'T HAVE DONE ANY MORE, Mrs Cooper.'
Alison spoke quietly, hovering in the doorway to Jenny's
office in Jamaica Street.

'No,' Jenny said from under a dark shroud of failure and
humiliation.

'It's not even as if you wanted it to get this far. It was
virtually forced on you.'

'Yes . . .' she answered, wishing Alison would leave her
alone.

'I'll see you in the morning, then. You're sure you can
manage?'

'I'll be fine.'

'Thank you . . . thank you, Mrs Cooper.' With one last
anxious glance in Jenny's direction Alison closed the door
and left the building as swiftly as she could without appear-
ing indecent. If she had been disappointed by the eleventh-
hour abortion of their inquest, she had yet to show it. Jenny
worked out that she must have been on the phone to her
new boyfriend, Martin, within minutes of Annabelle Stern
bringing down the guillotine. She'd retouched her make-
up even before they had left the empty clubhouse. It was a
powerful drug, sex. Observing Alison's conscience dissolve
under its spell, she could begin to understand how people
could kill for it.

Jenny looked again at the order issued by Mrs Justice Delaney, a newly appointed judge, who, a little research revealed, had been instructed many times by Ed Prince and Annabelle Stern during her career at the Bar. They had been clever. They had not argued that Jenny had been biased or had mismanaged proceedings: rather they had persuaded the judge that her decision to hold the inquest in the first place was wrong; that she had never possessed any evidence that would begin to displace Craven's plea of guilty to murder.

There was nothing in the dry wording of the order to suggest that the judge had been informed about Jenny's personal history, and perhaps it was never mentioned in open court, but one way or another she would have been told. And later, in the privacy of her chambers, she would have lifted the phone to Simon Moreton to ask if it were true. And Moreton, the snake, would have replied that on reflection perhaps this wasn't the best moment for Mrs Cooper to be conducting such a sensitive inquest . . .

In a day or two he would call to commiserate. He'd tell her she was lucky to have survived as a coroner at all, and that if she wished to continue she would have to be altogether more sensitive to her place in the system. No more upsets, no more embarrassments. This was to serve as her final warning.

She looked at the fresh heap of papers on her desk with a sense of foreboding. More deaths, more tears, more loose ends and jagged edges. She was tired. She needed some respite before starting over again.

She had no right to expect Steve to respond, given the way she had treated him, but she had at least to try to salvage the wreckage of their relationship. And besides, there was no one else, nor likely to be. She dialled his number.

'Jenny?' He sounded concerned.

'I'm sorry. I was busy.'

'I've been worried sick. The story in the paper—'
'I know . . . It's complicated. They stopped the inquest.'
'Because of your past?'
'No . . . Not that they'd admit to. I'll have to explain.'

She paused, not sure how to make the move, or even whether she still wanted to.

Steve said, 'Have you spoken to Ross? I've tried to call him.'

'I've left messages, but he's not called back . . . I'm almost glad. I don't know what I'd say.'

It was Steve's turn to fall silent.

'Steve? Are you still there?'

'Jenny, look . . . the reason I was trying to call you, *one* of the reasons, is that the firm in France wants a decision. They'd need me in September. I thought things might work out here, but the Edinburgh contract's got snagged up with egos and politics . . . I don't want that.'

'You're going?'

'What do you want, Jenny?'

'Right at this moment? Some company would be nice.'

At five-thirty she was locking the office door and thinking of what she would wear that evening for Steve. She had a daisy-print sundress which she'd only worn once, but which he'd gone wild for, saying it made her look girlishly beautiful and innocent.

'Mrs Cooper?'

Startled out of her daydream, she looked left to see Sean Coughlin climbing out of his double-parked BMW, the engine still running and the roof down. Father Starr was in the passenger seat wearing sunglasses, a character from a gangster movie.

Coughlin walked towards her. Starr stayed in the car, letting the detective handle the business.

'I hear you've a problem,' Coughlin said.

Jenny wondered which one he meant. 'The police at Weston? I doubt that'll go much further.'

'With the inquest.'

'It's been stopped, Mr Coughlin. I did my best to explain to everyone present – Father Starr was there.'

'I understand that they got you on a technicality – not enough evidence to justify the inquiry.'

'Something like that.'

He nodded. 'That's good, because I've found you some.'

He let the statement hang in the air, waiting to see her reaction.

Jenny said, 'It's over.'

'We've taken advice from a friendly lawyer: with evidence, you could start another inquiry.'

'Now really isn't the best time. Why don't you call me on Monday?'

She started towards her car. Coughlin's footsteps followed her.

'It's only circumstantial, but it's solid. A detective constable in CID took a statement from a woman who lived across the road from Eva. She said she saw a maroon-coloured sports car taking off from outside her house, at about eight forty-five on the night she was killed. He was trying to trace the vehicle when Craven put his hands up. DI Goodison told him to forget it and put him on another case.'

Jenny stopped at the driver's door of her Golf and stuck the key in the lock. It jammed halfway. Damn. She been meaning to do something about it for weeks.

Coughlin came to her shoulder, close enough that she could hear him breathe. 'This came from a colleague of his, one of the faith. I've no doubt it's true. Mrs Cooper, do you know who happens to own a maroon-coloured sports car?'

She stopped her struggle with the key. She'd just remembered the car she had seen parked outside the Mission Church.

Coughlin said, 'What do you know, Mrs Cooper? What happened on your trip to London that made them so panicky?'

Jenny looked from Coughlin to Starr and noticed they had the same stillness about them, the same certainty behind the eyes. A pair of celibate warriors who wouldn't have much sympathy with her plans for the evening.

'I'm not sure how much good this will do any of us,' Jenny said.

'It's not about us, is it, Mrs Cooper? It's about a man who's in prison for a crime he didn't commit. Surely you can't sleep easy with that on your conscience?'

'Take my advice and get him a good lawyer.'

She tried the key again. It refused to turn.

'We're all afraid of the dark, Mrs Cooper,' Coughlin said, 'none more so than those of us who have found ourselves lost in it.' He spoke to her softly, like a priest. 'Don't you believe that we find ourselves at these crossroads for a reason? It's a privilege to be truly tested, don't you think? Imagine a life without even the opportunity for redemption.'

He reached for Jenny's car key and turned it in the lock without effort.

She touched the handle, but her fingers stiffened. An image of Freddy's fragile body lying on the mortuary slab flashed before her eyes, and she experienced a moment of overpowering grief. Coughlin sensed it and leaned in even closer.

'Let your conscience speak, Mrs Cooper.'

Jenny felt her resistance fall away. She began to talk.

'Before he was saved, Turnbull had parties for his business associates,' Jenny said, the words spilling out of her.

'Eva was at one of them as part of the entertainment. It seems she reminded him of it when she was arguing for a pay rise. He got a court order gagging her. Her lawyers can't discuss her affairs with anyone – it's a total blackout. I persuaded a judge to grant an exception for the purposes of my inquest, but the Ministry of Justice stepped in to shut me up.' She paused. 'This bit I shouldn't tell you . . .'

Coughlin stayed silent, leaving her to make up her own mind.

'I've been promised the police will investigate Turnbull eventually, but only after he's got his law passed.'

'And you gave what in return?'

'I promised not to rock the boat . . .' She glanced over at Starr. 'It seemed like the best deal at the time.'

'This order you got from the judge – could you still use it?'

She shook her head. 'My inquest is over.'

'It was stayed for want of evidence – that's different, surely?'

Jenny thought for a moment, guessing he had been on the phone to a friendly lawyer. 'I can see there might be an argument.'

'Eva's lawyers are the firm in Queen Square, right?'

'You know them?'

'The DC who took the statement about the sports car says they make most of their money from the pornography business – everyone in the trade uses them. One of the partners even owns the warehouses out in Filton where they shoot all the films. He tells me it's a regular little blue Hollywood out there.'

'If that's true, I'm surprised they didn't put up more of a fight against Turnbull,' Jenny said. 'A well-placed leak and they could have wrecked him.'

'A man with his money would have shut them up for small change.'

Jenny thought of Damien Lynd and his pretence of being ethical. No doubt he had performed the same routine while telling Eva that he couldn't sue GlamourX until she had paid his bill for contesting Turnbull's injunction. And at the same time he and his partners would have been negotiating their pay-offs with Ed Prince.

Jenny said, 'Why don't I talk to them after the weekend? I need to think this through.'

Coughlin said, 'I understand Mr Craven didn't take the news of what happened today too well. Between you and me, Father Starr's worried he might do something stupid.' Before Jenny could object, Coughlin said, 'Why we don't we pay these crooks a visit now, while the spirit's with us?'

Jenny sat on the back seat of Coughlin's convertible. Father Starr didn't say a word as they drove the short distance across the centre of town to Queen Square, his eyes unreadable behind the dark glasses. At first she thought he might have been embarrassed into silence, but then she spotted rosary beads in his fingers and realized he was praying.

Coughlin cruised past the rows of parked Mercedes and pulled up on the double-yellow outside Montego House. He told Father Starr to stay in the car and followed Jenny to the office's front entrance.

'Let me do the talking,' Jenny said.

'You're the boss.'

'Do I use your real name?'

'Certainly. This is lawful business, right?'

'Maybe.'

Coughlin smiled and pressed the buzzer.

The uppity receptionist looked baffled at the arrival of two unexpected visitors. 'Can I help you?'

'Jenny Cooper,' Jenny reminded her. 'And this is Detective Inspector Sean Coughlin of the Metropolitan Police. We're here to speak to Mr Lynd.'

'Good afternoon, ma'am,' Coughlin said.

'I'm afraid he's with clients.'

'Could you please tell him it's urgent?'

The receptionist looked from Jenny to Coughlin, then down at the phone, searching for a reason not to pick it up.

Gently touching Jenny's arm, Coughlin said, 'Why don't you tell us where we can find him? You looked as if you were about to go home. We wouldn't want to hold you up.'

Eyeing him warily, the receptionist got up from her chair and pushed it under the desk. 'I believe you'll find Mr Lynd in the meeting room at the end of the corridor on the first floor.'

'You're very kind,' Coughlin said, and waited for her to start towards the front door. Quickening her pace, she left the building without a backwards glance.

Jenny glanced up at the painting above the fancy fireplace: the half-caste man with cold eyes, rich on slave-grown sugar.

'Are we going to find him or admire the antiques?' Coughlin said. He headed for the stairs.

They arrived at a wood-panelled landing on the first floor. The Persian carpet and expensive fittings gave an impression of old-world opulence.

'You'd never think they were in the skin business,' Coughlin said.

Jenny stepped ahead of him and led the way along the passage, passing a number of ornately carved oak doors and heading for the one at the end with a brass plate that said Meeting Room.

She knocked twice and turned the handle, entering to see Damien Lynd starting up from the conference table. His meeting was with two attractive young women, scarcely more than girls, and a middle-aged man with a ponytail and a pot-belly that bulged over the top of his skinny jeans. He looked seedy enough to be their pimp.

'Sorry to interrupt, Mr Lynd, but it can't wait. This is Detective Inspector Sean Coughlin. Could we have a word?'

'My apologies,' Lynd said to his startled clients, his face colouring. 'I shan't be a moment.'

Lynd followed them into the corridor and marched several yards from the door before turning to confront them. 'What do you want?'

'I'm here to enforce Mr Justice Laithwaite's order,' Jenny said. 'It was served on you yesterday afternoon. I'd be grateful if you'd hand over Miss Donaldson's files.'

'Out of the question,' Lynd said, confident of his ground. 'Your inquest was stayed this morning. I've seen that order, too.'

'For want of evidence. More has since come to light. As of this afternoon I've started a fresh inquiry.'

Lynd said, 'Even if you're entitled to do so, Mrs Cooper, Mr Justice Laithwaite's order relates to your previous investigation. I don't think we have anything more to discuss.'

Jenny stepped in front of him. 'We can read the words together if you like, Mr Lynd. It says I'm entitled to disclosure for the purposes of my inquiry into Miss Donaldson's death. Now you can either assist me, or Mr Coughlin here will have to assist you in fetching what we've come for.'

'Even if I could lay my hands on the files, I really can't comply without clarification from the judge. This will have to wait.' He held up his hands. 'I'm sorry, Mrs Cooper, that's my final word.'

Lynd turned to the office door behind him and reached for the handle. Coughlin pushed past Jenny and clamped a hand on his shoulder.

'I don't think you understand, Mr Lynd.'

Lynd spun round, his face twisted in anger. 'You've no right to be here and you know it. Get out.'

Coughlin said, 'If you'll pardon me, you don't look like a man with the balls to tough this one out. In fact, I'd say you were as anxious as we are to get this done and yourself in the clear. You're not the boss here, and I don't suppose it was your decision to protect Turnbull, even though he'd like most of your clients out of business – am I right?' He looked Lynd in the eye. 'Think of it as your one chance to do good, Mr Lynd. Believe me, you'll feel a better man for it.'

The meeting-room door opened and the pimp looked out. 'What's going on, Damien? I've got to be somewhere.'

'Five minutes,' Lynd apologized. 'Help yourself to coffee.'

The man grumbled and slammed back inside.

'They're in the storeroom,' Lynd said. 'There's a copier you can use.'

Jenny said, 'If it's all the same, I think we'll make do with the originals.'

Lynd thought about arguing, but instead pushed his designer glasses up his nose and took off towards the stairs.

Coughlin said, 'Looks like you've got the place to yourself, Mr Lynd, or are your colleagues just keeping their heads down?'

The lawyer didn't answer.

They followed him across the reception area and through a door into a short, windowless passage that led to a secure storage room protected by a heavy steel door. Lynd typed in the access code, then heaved it open. They entered a large, low-ceilinged vault with a bare concrete floor. Archive boxes were stacked on rows of industrial shelving separated by narrow aisles.

Jenny and Coughlin followed Lynd to end of a row. He pulled a box off the shelf. 'This is hers.'

Jenny said, 'You're sure that's everything you've got?'

'Film contracts, house conveyance, terms of employment. The lot.' He set it on the floor and took off the lid, revealing ten or more files stacked on their sides. 'Do I get a receipt or something?'

'I'll fax one over.'

Lynd glanced up at Coughlin. 'Is this all you want from me?'

Coughlin said, 'Hand me one of those files.'

Lynd stalled for a moment, puzzled. Coughlin leaned down and took one from the box. Lynd stayed crouched on the floor, staring at the concrete as Coughlin opened it.

'What's this, Mr Lynd? I don't see Miss Donaldson's name.'

He showed it to Jenny. It looked like an old set of company accounts for a restaurant business. Coughlin pulled out another file and wrenched it open: a bunch of letters in a tenancy dispute. 'Did Miss Donaldson own a fish restaurant? Or have you got her mixed up with another one of your whores?'

Lynd pushed up to his feet and took a step back. 'I want a guarantee . . . I was just one of her lawyers. I want to know I'm not going to be implicated in whatever it is you're investigating.'

'You're not helping yourself, Mr Lynd.' Coughlin said. Jenny flinched, as, without warning, he threw the file in Lynd's face, the pages fluttering to the floor at his feet. 'Now get the right fucking box before I rip your balls off, you piece of shite.'

Jenny gave Coughlin a look, but his eyes were locked on Lynd, who was slowly shuffling backwards, shaking his head. 'I can't . . . I can't do it.'

Coughlin kicked the box aside, shot out a fist and drove it hard into Lynd's stomach. As the lawyer slumped forward, the detective grabbed his shirt with a powerful left hand, hit him hard across the face with his right, then reached down and grabbed his crotch.

Lynd made a pathetic croaking sound. His broken glasses dropped to the floor.

Jenny was appalled. 'What the hell are you doing?'

'Do you think I was kidding you, Mr Lynd?' Coughlin said, ignoring her. He tightened his grip. Lynd's face twisted in agony.

Jenny started at a splintering crash that echoed down the hallway and through the open door.

'You devious wee bastard!' He slammed his fist into Lynd's temple. Jenny saw the lights go out even before his neck had snapped back onto his shoulders and his legs folded beneath him. 'Turn this shit-hole over,' Coughlin shouted at her, shoving past and heading for the door.

Jenny looked down at Lynd, who was now slowly stirring and groaning. Thank God he was moving. She glanced up at the shelves, the hundreds of identical boxes. Where would she start? From out in the hall she heard sounds of a struggle, furniture being thrown, Coughlin yelling. She ran out into the short passageway. The door to the reception area was wide open. Next to an upturned sofa, a thug in a camouflage jacket was holding Coughlin from behind, while a shorter man in a business suit drove the butt of a night stick into his stomach.

Jenny had no control over the scream that came out of her. The two men dropped Coughlin to the floor and started towards her.

'Hey!'

They spun round at the sound of another male voice. Walking towards them was a priest holding a spray can at arm's length as if it might explode in his hand. The one with the night stick was raising it over his shoulder as the dirt-brown jet of pepper spray snaked out of the nozzle and hit his face. Starr switched aim to his friend and caught him while he was still off-guard.

Jenny had never heard grown men howl. Their eyes on fire, they floundered like pole-axed drunks, the thug dropping to his knees, the suit collapsing against the reception desk.

Father Starr was as surprised as she was, and crossed himself twice. Coughlin was on his feet now, but with a hand clamped across his middle. He hobbled towards Jenny.

'Did you find them?'

She shook her head.

Coughlin pulled her out of the doorway and went back down the passage to the storeroom. There was a brief, pitiful cry from Lynd and a few moments later the detective returned with a box under his arm.

He placed a hand in the small of Jenny's back and steered her around the two blinded men.

As the three of them left the building Starr said, 'I found it in the glove box. Did I do the right thing?'

Coughlin replied, 'God was with you, Father.'

# TWENTY-FIVE

COUGHLIN INSISTED IT WAS TOO risky to take the files back to Jenny's office or his poky hotel room at the Holiday Inn, so they went instead to a room in Clifton Cathedral Starr said would be empty at this time of the evening. The air inside the building was heavy with incense. Watching Father Starr and Coughlin dab their foreheads with holy water and genuflect to the altar, Jenny had a vision of crusaders in the Middle Ages, thanking God for helping them slay the heathen.

They made their way to an office on the lower floor. Jenny stationed Father Starr by the photocopier and had Coughlin make a list of the most important documents she brought out, giving each a reference. Like all law firms that charged per hour what the average person made in a week, Reed Falkirk & Co. kept immaculate files. There were eight in total, the earliest containing papers dating back several years to some of Eva's early film contracts. Jenny worked methodically through them, charting Eva's rise from secondary artiste to star. For the last year of her performing life she stepped up from 'consulting' to 'executive' producer, and even shared screen-writing credits. Her final acting fee was £43,000 for a two-picture deal. Not bad money for three weeks' work.

File number six began with Eva's contract of employment with the Decency campaign. Her salary was £36,000 for the year, in return for which she pledged her exclusive services, to undertake whatever media assignments were arranged for her, and to 'conduct herself at all times in a morally impeccable manner and in accordance with the principles of the Decency campaign'.

The problems had begun the previous autumn, when GlamourX refused to pay her royalties, asserting that her involvement with Decency contradicted the terms of their agreement. Eva wrote a stream of increasingly emotional letters to Michael Turnbull complaining that she was losing £8,000 per month and could barely afford to pay her mortgage. Lynd had done his best to argue her corner, but Kennedy and Parr had stonewalled him, claiming Eva's disputes with former employers were nothing to do with their client.

Eva had exploded the bomb the previous November. A letter signed by Ed Prince warned Lynd that his client had made 'allegations of a sexual nature relating to alleged previous contact between her and Lord Turnbull at a business reception in 2003', and that unless she retracted the accusation and signed an undertaking never to repeat it, 'serious consequences' would ensue. Another angry letter from Ed Prince dated two weeks later stated that, as she had failed to sign, High Court proceedings would be started immediately. The next item in the file was a copy of Mr Justice Laithwaite's original order, dated 3 December. The injunction prohibited Eva (who in the secret proceedings was referred to only as 'B') from disclosing any details of any past meetings or sexual contact between her and 'A' to any third parties. In particular, she was to make no mention of any past connection or relations between her and 'A' to his wife, colleagues, friends or associates.

Jenny handed the order to Coughlin. 'Look at that. It means Christine Turnbull didn't know.'

Coughlin was sceptical.

Jenny continued. 'It's an injunction to protect privacy. If the cat was out of the bag there would have been no point mentioning her in the order if she knew already. It also explains why Eva wasn't sacked – how would Turnbull have explained that to his wife?'

Starr and Coughlin exchanged a glance.

Jenny turned through the following pages of the file. There were a number of letters about unpaid fees and Eva's angry reply.

'Wow,' Jenny said, 'things were really turning ugly in February.' She was looking at a note Lynd had made of a meeting with Eva. Turnbull's lawyers had demanded that she hand over her laptop computer and mobile for 'security reasons'. Eva was objecting, saying she needed the phone for her producing work. Jenny read out the note:

*E. D. ill-tempered and truculent, claiming that Christine Turnbull is encouraging violent exorcisms that are taking place at the Mission Church targeting gays and the mentally ill. Claims to have witnessed an incident involving a disturbed teenager. I advised that such complaints were unconnected with her employment dispute with Decency and should be directed to the church trustees. E. D. pointed out that Christine Turnbull is chairman of the trustees. I repeated my former advice and stressed the need for payment of outstanding bills before Reed Falkirk would undertake further contractual work or litigation. E. D. became increasingly irrational, threatening to break the terms of the December injunction. I advised of consequences.*

Jenny said, 'That must have been Freddy Reardon. It's a miracle Eva held out as long as she did.'

Starr said, 'Surely the opposite of a miracle, Mrs Cooper?'

'What does *contractual* work mean?' Coughlin asked.

Jenny had reached the end of the file and opened the last one. It contained a handful of loose documents, some of them stamped *DRAFT*. She fanned them out across the desk.

There were forms relating to the formation of a new company to be called, 'Fallen Angel Ltd'; the directors were named as Eva Donaldson and Joseph Cassidy.

'She was starting a production company with her ex-boyfriend,' Jenny said, then pulled out a document headed *Actors' Agreement* and ran her eye down the page. 'Oh . . .'

She couldn't explain why she was so disappointed with Eva, or even why it came as a surprise.

Father Starr stepped towards her. 'What is it?'

She handed the paper to him, preferring not to read it aloud. She glanced through the other papers – technicians' contracts, actors' medical warranties, a studio-hire agreement – while Starr and Coughlin read about the production Eva was planning to mount in August: *Daddy's Girl*. Among the papers Jenny found a letter Damien Lynd had drafted to a potential investor in the movie. It contained what he called the 'elevator pitch': 'Eva plays a beautiful young woman who, following a disfiguring attack by a jealous boyfriend, turns to the only man who'll still love her – her daddy.'

Jenny showed the letter to Starr and Coughlin.

The two men read in silence, then Coughlin said, 'Do you believe she would have made this film?'

Jenny thought about it. 'No. I think she was testing God, and hoping one way or another he wouldn't let her.'

Starr didn't comment and put the letter back on the table. 'What do you think, Sean? Do you have enough to make an arrest?'

'We've got a car and a motive,' Coughlin said. 'The only person I've got to convince is my Presbyterian Super'.'

'We'll pray for him,' Starr replied.

It was past nine when Coughlin dropped her back at her car, an hour later than she'd told Steve she would be at his farm for dinner. She dialled his number repeatedly as she sped out of the city and across the Severn Bridge, the low evening sun making the water beneath her glow an unholy red. Each time it rang and rang without answer.

Evening had faded to dusk as she bumped along the rough track and turned into the yard. There was no sign of his Land Rover or the dog. She climbed out of the car and made her way through the empty lower storey of the barn. She called his name up the rickety stairs, but there was no reply. The door to his loft was bolted shut. She went out into the yard and around the edge of the vegetable garden to the area of grass, somewhere between a garden and a small meadow. She saw that he had set two places on the table he had made himself from a fallen cherry tree.

Jenny sat on one of the bentwood chairs listening to the faltering grasshoppers and watching the bats flitting in the fading light. She left him a note under the water jug. It said: *One last try? Jx*. It could have been a perfect evening. Instead, it felt like an end.

Steve didn't call back that evening, or at all. The weekend had felt as if it would never end. His silence, which for days had been so convenient, now felt like a yawning void. On Monday morning, Jenny sat in her car outside her office, hoping that in the last few minutes before nine he'd phone and say he'd forgiven her; he didn't. She would have phoned him, except she was too frightened of what he'd say, terrified that he'd tell her now was the time to face everything she had been putting off.

Alison muttered a muted good morning as Jenny came through the door carrying the box containing Eva's files. Jenny noticed she was dressed more soberly than of late and, through the fog of her own emotions, realized that her officer was close to tears.

'Are you all right?'

'Perfectly, thank you, Mrs Cooper,' came Alison's brittle reply. She fetched a single sheet from the fax machine. 'I presume this is for you. I'm just making a cup of tea. Would you like one?'

'Coffee would be good.'

The fax was a copy of a statement Coughlin had taken late the previous evening from a Mrs Diane Grant. She stated that on the evening of 9 May she had been on her way out of the house to collect her daughter from the railway station when she noticed a well-dressed woman walking briskly towards a large, maroon-coloured sports car on the opposite side of the road, some twenty yards from Eva Donaldson's house. The woman had climbed into the driver's seat and driven away fast. She had appeared relaxed enough, Mrs Grant said, but she had been carrying a tatty carrier bag, which had looked odd for someone driving such an expensive car. She confirmed that she had told this to a detective on the morning of Tuesday, 11 May, and that she hadn't been contacted by the police since.

Competing with the sound of the heating kettle, Jenny said, 'I paid a visit to Eva Donaldson's solicitors last Friday evening. I forced disclosure of her files—'

'I know where you went, Mrs Cooper.'

'You do?'

Alison didn't reply. She banged cupboard doors and noisily clinked spoons and cups, managing to channel what felt from Jenny's end of the passage like boiling rage into the act of making their drinks. There was a short silence, followed by a sob.

'Do you mind my asking how?' Jenny said.

Through sniffles, Alison said, 'I was with Martin. He was at my house . . . He had a call, said he had to go . . . I'd been a bit suspicious, I thought he mightn't have been telling the truth about being separated from his wife, so I followed him . . . I followed his car to Easton, where another man got in, then to Queen Square . . . I saw him go into the office and then you coming out with the others . . . I should have gone after you, but I didn't know what was happening . . . I promise you, Mrs Cooper, I had no idea, I really didn't. He seemed so genuine.'

'Did he ask many questions?'

'Not really . . . not that I noticed.' She broke down into a fit of sobs.

Jenny felt her anger subside. 'I'm sorry, Alison. You weren't to know. I knew those lawyers were capable of some pretty low things—'

'I've no excuse, Mrs Cooper . . . I should have—' She left the entence unfinished as tears overwhelmed her. Jenny hovered ineffectually, not sure how to comfort her, when the telephone rescued her from making a decision.

'I'll get it,' Alison sniffed.

'No. I will,' Jenny said, and hurried into her office, terrified it would be Steve.

'Bloody hell, Jenny. Did you know about this?' It was Simon Moreton. He was furious.

'About what?'

'The *arrest*. The bloody Met have arrested Christine Turnbull outside the House of bloody Lords. In front of the world's press, on her way in to watch her husband open the debate. Dear God . . .' he stammered. 'What the hell have they got on her?'

Jenny spoke quietly: 'I'm not sure you want to know.'

'Fuck, fuck, fuck. It's the Lord Chancellor on the other line. Wait there—'

Jenny rang off and switched on her PC.

She brought up the live news on the internet. A near-hysterical reporter spoke over a replay of images taken outside the main entrance to the House of Lords in Parliament Square. A smiling Michael and Christine Turnbull climbed out of a familiar black Mercedes van and made their way towards a scrum of media corralled behind a barrier. As they paused to field questions, two police cars pulled up, sirens blaring. The camera caught the look of shock on Christine Turnbull's face as Sean Coughlin and a female detective walked towards her, Coughlin saying, 'Lady Turnbull, I regret to inform you that you are under arrest . . .' The rest was lost in the explosion of hysteria among the reporters. The cameraman fought to hold on to the image of Christine being led to a police car, shaking her head as her husband stood paralysed. He made a half-hearted attempt to follow her, but was swallowed up by the crowd who had broken out from behind the barrier and were swarming the police car as it pulled away from the kerb. The cameraman caught a brief shot of Christine crouched in the back seat, her hands shielding her face.

Coughlin was in the seat in front of her. Jenny could have sworn she saw him smile.

As the footage played in a continuous loop, the studio anchors reported that police had confirmed that Christine Turnbull had been arrested in connection with the murder of Miss Eva Donaldson. There was speculation that, despite his wife's arrest, Michael Turnbull would go ahead and open the debate on the Decency Bill, but at ten-thirty it was confirmed that the reading had been postponed. At eleven a.m. Annabelle Stern stepped in front of the cameras and announced that Decency had been well prepared for acts of sabotage, but not even in their direst predictions had they imagined something so malicious or elaborate. She promised that Christine Turnbull had no involvement whatever in the death of the former actress, Eva Donaldson, and that the campaign would only be strengthened by these events.

For the next few days it seemed that Annabelle Stern might be proved right.

# TWENTY-SIX

CHRISTINE TURNBULL MADE NO COMMENT in her police interview and (according to the word on Alison's grapevine) became increasingly confident that the circumstantial case against her would be too weak to support a conviction. Apart from the eyewitness who had placed her at Eva's house, only the Turnbulls' nanny had implicated her, and it was rumoured that the young woman had already retracted large portions of her statement. Against all the odds, it seemed that Decency was witnessing a miracle.

But late on Thursday afternoon, former Assistant Commissioner Geoffrey Solomon, a member of the Mission Church of God's council, emailed an unsworn statement to the police from a rented villa in Morocco, a country with which the UK had no formal extradition treaty. His price for converting his statement into sworn testimony was a guarantee of immunity from prosecution. DI Coughlin forwarded a copy to Jenny in confidence, saying in the attached note that he was happy for God to be Solomon's judge, as was the Attorney General: Solomon would be the principal witness for the prosecution.

As Jenny read through Solomon's damning testimonial she finally heard the prison gates closing on Christine Turnbull:

... I received a telephone call from Michael Turnbull early on the afternoon of Monday, 10 May. He said he needed to meet straight away on a matter he couldn't discuss on the telephone. I caught a train to London and we met at his Kensington flat. Michael was in a dreadful state, he looked ill and distracted. After much prompting, he told me that his wife, Christine, had gone to confront Eva Donaldson at her home the previous evening and had returned later saying that she thought she had killed her. Michael called his lawyers, who immediately sent a car for her. He hadn't seen her since late the previous night.

I had been aware of some tension between Eva and the Decency campaign over money, but I had no idea what had transpired between her and Michael. He told me that in the previous November they had argued over Decency's decision not to increase her salary. Eva then confronted him with the allegation that six years previously she had been one of a number of hostesses at a party Michael had held for business associates. Eva claimed that she and the other girls had had sexual contact with Michael and a number of his guests. I didn't ask him whether or not this was true, but I gained the distinct impression that it was.

By this time Eva had become critical to the Decency campaign. Michael had no choice but to seek an injunction preventing her from repeating her allegation elsewhere. He deeply regretted having kept all this from his wife, but he feared that she was under such pressure of work it would have been an unnecessary burden to place on her.

Once Eva had been served with the injunction she abided by its terms, but in recent weeks she had started to complain about methods of prayer counselling at the Mission Church of God. Michael was aware of at least two occasions on which Eva confronted Christine Turn-

*bull at the church offices over the issue, leading to heated exchanges.*

*On the evening of Saturday 8 May, matters came to a head. Eva telephoned Christine from a hotel in Manchester and told her that unless the prayer counselling was stopped, she was going to resign from the Decency campaign and go public with a number of allegations, including the details of the sex party. She also claimed to have been threatened by Ed Prince, the Turnbulls' personal lawyer and a trustee of the church, that if she broke the terms of her injunction her life 'wouldn't be worth living'.*

*Christine Turnbull reacted exactly as Michael had feared. They spent the whole of Saturday night and Sunday arguing bitterly. Personal issues aside, Christine believed Eva was intent on destroying the Decency campaign just as it was nearing a successful conclusion, and the Mission Church of God too. Michael spent many hours pleading with her to stay away from Eva, and eventually she promised she would. He had no idea that she had driven straight from the church on the Sunday night to Eva's home. According to Michael, Christine claimed to have acted in self-defence, saying she took a knife with her only for protection in case Eva became violent, but it was clear to me he wasn't convinced, and in the light of the evidence that has since come to light, nor am I.*

*My experience of Christine Turnbull was that she was a woman of extremes. Nearly all of the time she was remarkably calm and relaxed, but on several occasions I witnessed her erupting into violent rage, even lashing out at her husband. To say that her personality altered beyond all recognition during these episodes is an understatement. I believe Michael Turnbull tolerated these* outbursts because they were rare. On this occasion I have no doubt that, faced with the prospect of Eva Donaldson derailing the Decency campaign and disgracing the church, Christine Turnbull lost all self-control and set out deliberately with the intention of killing her. I would describe her as a woman possessed.

The following two days were spent in crisis mode. I held numerous meetings with Ed Prince in which we monitored the progress of the police investigation and made contingency plans. It was decided that if evidence emerged which placed Christine at Eva's home, she would say that she had gone there out of friendly concern but that Eva hadn't answered the door. She would explain the delay in telling her story on advice given to her by her overly cautious lawyers.

When Craven came forward and confessed, it seemed our prayers had been answered. The officer in charge of the investigation, DI Vernon Goodison, had been a long-standing junior colleague of mine and had kept me fully informed of all major developments. He was convinced of Craven's guilt, but was very concerned that his confession could be undermined by psychiatric evidence; he desperately needed evidence that placed him at the scene. It was Prince who came up with the idea of Craven's urine being found on Eva's doormat, and he urged me to plant the idea in Goodison's mind. I resisted at first, but Ed Prince is a very persuasive man; after two hours of talking it over with him, he convinced me I would be doing God's work.

I met Goodison for a drink and suggested that he plant Craven's DNA at the scene. I pretended that all senior officers knew such things had to be done from time to time, and that it would almost be expected of him.

*Goodison thanked me for the advice. In so far as it's possible, I believe he was acting out of the best of motives.*

*As far as I was concerned, the only fly in the ointment was a series of complaints from one of our congregants, Alan Jacobs. In the days following Eva's death, he sent the church trustees a number of emails claiming that he and several others, including a young man called Frederick Reardon, had been psychologically damaged by prayer counselling they had received at the church. I spoke to our administrator, Joel Nelson, about these complaints and he assured me they were groundless. He told me that Jacobs was a confused and unhappy individual who had been close to Eva and was very upset by her death. As I was especially determined to protect the reputation of the church at a difficult time, I sought Ed Prince's advice on how to deal with Jacobs. Prince then interrogated Nelson at length about prayer sessions he had conducted with Jacobs. I know he also spoke to Jacobs in person. I wasn't privy to exactly what was said, but afterwards Prince told me he had 'explained the facts of life' and that Jacobs wouldn't be making any more complaints.*

*A few weeks later Joel Nelson called me late on a Saturday night to say that our night security officer had found Jacobs's body outside the main entrance to the church. I telephoned DI Tony Wallace, who is a loyal and longstanding member of our congregation and a man I have known both professionally and personally for over twenty years. We met at the church and both agreed that it was obviously a case of suicide. Initially, we resolved to report the death in the normal way. In fact, Wallace had already contacted the coroner's office when Ed Prince became aware of the situation and demanded that the body be moved elsewhere, to protect the reputation of the church.*

On this occasion I objected strongly on the grounds that the risk to the church was far greater if we were discovered, but I was overridden by Prince, who persuaded Wallace to organize the body's transfer to another location.

Again, I convinced myself that we had done nothing substantially wrong and had saved the church from potential scandal.

About this time I became aware that Ed Prince was concerned about the possibility of a coroner inquiring into Eva's death. In particular he was worried that the local coroner, Mrs Jenny Cooper, had a reputation for asking uncomfortable questions. Together with several of his colleagues he held a number of meetings with potential witnesses to an inquest, including Michael and Christine Turnbull, Joel Nelson and Pastor Lennox Strong. On one occasion he telephoned me to ask about one of the church's young congregants, Frederick Reardon. Prince's team had discovered that Reardon had a criminal record and wanted to know if there was any way of finding out if he had been arrested for or was suspected of having committed other offences. I told him that it might take some time to persuade former colleagues to access police files. Prince said that was no good – he demanded the information immediately. If it wasn't forthcoming, he threatened to 'scare Reardon into doing what he was told'.

I have no idea what contact Prince had with Reardon, but I am in no doubt he would have spoken to him. Whether there was any direct connection between this and the young man's suicide, I am unable to say, but from what I have since learned, Reardon was an extremely fragile personality who relied on the church, quite liter-

*ally, for his sanity. I sincerely regret that I didn't intervene to protect him. This, more than anything, weighs most heavily on my conscience.*

The following morning Christine Turnbull appeared at Horseferry Road Magistrates' Court in central London charged with murder. The news photographs showed her smiling and serene as she arrived with her police escort, still convinced, perhaps, that an angel would be sent to save her. But there was no miracle, only a brief five-minute hearing at the end of which she was remanded to Holloway women's prison. Jenny could only imagine how she would be faring amongst the addicts and prostitutes. She would need every ounce of her unnatural strength to survive among them.

Other arrests followed in rapid succession. Within hours of Solomon swearing his statement, Michael Turnbull was charged for his part in a conspiracy to pervert the course of justice, along with Ed Prince and DIs Goodison and Wallace. Other associated lawyers and detectives would follow. The Reverend Bobby DeMont swiftly issued a press release from the safety of his Montana ranch to say that he had no knowledge whatever of recent events at the Mission Church of God, Bristol, and that he saw them merely as one small setback in his ever-increasing struggle against the principalities and powers that were always poised to strike at God's chosen people.

Jenny hadn't expected a fanfare, but some small acknowledgement of her efforts would have been appreciated. There was none. Not a word from the Ministry of Justice, and not so much as a note of thanks from Kenneth Donaldson, Eva's father. She supposed that, like sudden converts to a cause whose faith had been suddenly and spectacularly shattered, they felt foolish, perhaps even ashamed. Their vision of the truth had been destroyed. The world wanted, it seemed, quickly to forget.

Father Lucas Starr, too, had fallen eerily quiet. Jenny called the Jesuit house several times, only to be told by the various brothers who answered that they would pass her message on to him. Mystified by his silence, she pursued Coughlin and caught him briefly on a bad line. Starr would probably be on retreat, he said, but you could never be sure with Jesuits; if a novitiate had got too involved or too comfortable, he could be spirited away to the far side of the world.

'Something tells me you know where he is, but you're not letting on,' Jenny said.

'I've been asked to respect his privacy,' Coughlin answered. 'I'm sure you can understand that.'

'He left me with a lot of unanswered questions,' Jenny said. 'We didn't exactly have a deal, but I more than delivered on my side of the bargain.'

'What kind of questions?' Coughlin asked.

'He'd been in contact with a friend of mine, a man who went missing.'

Coughlin didn't answer.

'Mr Coughlin? Are you there? Do you know what happened to Alec McAvoy?'

'I'll pass your message on, Mrs Cooper. Take good care of yourself.'


Jenny spent the afternoon tying up loose ends. She visited Ceri Jacobs with the news that she would hold a fresh inquest into her husband's suicide after Wallace's case had been dealt with by the criminal courts. She was hopeful of finding whoever he had been with in the final hours before he took his life outside the Mission Church. Neither Ceri Jacobs nor Father Dermody, who had sat with her during the meeting, had looked pleased at the prospect, but Jenny had felt unmoved. For the first time in her career as coroner she experienced a true state of professional detachment. It felt good.

She delivered a similar message to Eileen Reardon, promising that Joel Nelson and his colleagues would be forced to confess every last detail of their encounters with Freddy. She even heard herself say that if she could prevent anything similar from happening in future, some good might yet come from his death. Delivering her message of hope in Eileen's gloomy sitting room, she imagined this being a turning point for the grieving mother, a last chance to make a life beyond the permanently drawn curtains. She had seemed to rally a little. When it was time for Jenny to leave she showed her to the door. Waiting for the lift, Jenny glanced over her shoulder to see Eileen scooping the dead flowers outside her flat into a rubbish sack.

Driving home, she took a detour past the Mission Church. The barrier to the car park was padlocked. Steel shutters scarred with fresh graffiti were drawn down over the windows of the cafe. The huge white cross still stood outside the main building, but the lights that had given it the holy aura had been switched off. Now raucous seagulls perched on the cross-beam. It seemed to her like the mast of a sinking ship.

Too restless to spend the bright evening confined by the cottage's garden, Jenny had an urge to strike out into the woods and purge the city from her soul. Full of excitement she pulled on her old jeans and boots, like a child embarking on a longed-for outing. She strode up the lane, running her fingers through the cow parsley, and turned onto the forestry track which meandered its way beneath a vaulted canopy of beeches towards Barbadoes Hill.

The woods, which had frightened her a little when she had first moved out of Bristol, were now a place of wonder to her. She had learned to identify the different trees from the shapes of their leaves and the texture of their bark, she knew her way to a secret glade in which a five-hundred-year-old oak stood, slowly shrinking and dying a death that would linger over two centuries. She had discovered a beech whose lower branches had rooted to form fresh shoots where they touched the ground, and the stump of an ancient lime coppice, the hollow centre of which formed a pool of rainwater that teemed with tadpoles in early spring.

She covered the two uphill miles that took her to the lookout spot high above Tintern without breaking sweat. Through the gap in the trees she looked down on the abbey from her favourite angle, with the sun slanting through the empty windows and casting magnificent shadows across the meadow beyond. It was impossible to believe that less than twenty miles away there were high-rises and screaming sirens, and a multitude of people who would spend a lifetime entombed in concrete, disconnected from all that sustained them.

Jenny drifted down the hill in a dream, letting thoughts float in and out of her mind as lazily as dandelion feathers on the breeze. She'd call Ross when she got home. Now she was in a better state of mind she could trust herself not to rise to his spiky moods. What they needed was some time together so he could see how she had changed. In a little over a year he'd be at university or off travelling the world; there was no time to lose. She had to make him her first priority: from now on, whatever work threw at her, her precious and only son would come first.

She picked up her pace for the return journey, anxious to get home and make the call. Approaching the final leg, the path dipped steeply through a dense stand of conifers and she passed from light into shadow. A twig snapped behind her, a foot scuffed on loose ground. She glanced back to see the silhouette of a slender male some thirty yards distant.

'Is that you, Mrs Cooper?'

The voice was familiar, yet not one she could place. He sped up to a jog, his features catching the light as he drew closer. Jenny felt suddenly cold.

'It's Paul. You remember me.'

'Yes—' She continued walking. There was a long S-bend and a straight, one-hundred-yard stretch between her and the road. A quarter of a mile or thereabouts; three or four minutes' walk at the most.

'I hope you don't mind. I read in the paper you lived near Tintern. A man in the pub told me you were up this lane.'

*But you must have been following me for nearly four miles*, Jenny thought. *Were you lurking in a hedge, or hiding inside the cottage, perhaps? Why choose this moment?*

'I got bail pending my appeal,' Paul Craven said.

'So I heard. Congratulations.'

'My solicitor reckons there won't even be a hearing. I'll get a pardon, from the Queen he says.' He laughed.

Jenny glanced at his smooth, angular face, unlined by the stresses of the world outside prison walls. He had the restless, coiled energy of a feral child.

'I wanted to say thank you, Mrs Cooper.'

'I appreciate it,' Jenny said, quickening her pace as much as she dared. Some instinct told her to take the initiative, to distract him. 'I hope they've found you somewhere to stay.'

'Probation hostel. It's not bad . . . At least I'm in with some other blokes this time.'

'What about Father Starr? Has he been in touch?'

'It's a different priest who visits the hostel, Father Jason. I like him, he's a good man. Takes a while to get to know someone though, doesn't it – so that you can trust them, I mean?'

'I should make good use of him, if I were you, it's his job to help.' She'd made it to the first bend. If she kept him talking she could reach the road. But then what? She'd be lucky to see a car between the end of the track and the house. 'Have you thought about work? Is there anything you'd like to do?'

Craven looked at her strangely. 'The thing I didn't say to you, Mrs Cooper, is why I confessed to something I didn't do. You'd like to know that, wouldn't you?'

'It's up to you,' Jenny said cautiously.

'Father Starr always warned me that the devil would come when I least expected it,' Craven said. 'When I saw her picture on the television and heard what had happened to her, I could see myself doing it. I actually saw her face, the knife, the look in her eyes as the life went out of her. It was him put it all in my head, made it so I thought it was real. It was the devil . . . I can see that now. And then Father Starr found you. You know what I thought when you came to see me in prison? I thought you must be an angel. Who else would come to help a man like me?'

Heart thumping, Jenny visualized the terrain ahead. There was a drainage ditch on the left that was overgrown with nettles. She'd push him in then take off, get the five seconds' head start she needed to break clear. She glanced down at his shoes: a pair of ill-fitting leather lace-ups. Another few seconds' advantage.

'I'd been praying for an angel to come, Mrs Cooper, just like Father Starr told me to.'

'Believe me, Mr Craven, I'm no angel. I'm just a coroner doing my job.'

'You're wrong about that, Mrs Cooper. It's like Father Starr says, God works in ways you can't even begin to imagine. Maybe you can't see how he used you, but he did. You're looking at the proof.' He smiled, as if he were experiencing a sudden rush of ecstasy.

They were rounding the middle of the bend – only a few more yards to the home straight. Perhaps Father Starr had been right to trust him? He might be perfectly harmless, just a little gauche and bewildered.

She had to drive the agenda, set the boundaries. That must be what he needed, an authority figure. 'What time do you have to be back at the hostel, Mr Craven?'

'Doesn't matter, does it, if they're going to pardon me?'

'It might be as well not to upset them. What if I were to drive you home? You can be back by nine.'

'No need, Mrs Cooper. I'll be fine.'

She attempted a sterner tone. 'You know, if you break the rules they could turn you out, or even send you back to prison. You don't want that.'

'No . . . I'm never going back there. Never.'

Good. She was in control, making him feel safe again.

'Well, this is what we'll do. I'll call the hostel and arrange to get you home. I'll make sure Father Jason's looking after you and everything will be fine. Does that sound good?'

Craven nodded. 'Yes . . .'

The end of the track was in sight. A tractor drove past on the road, a car tucked in close behind it.

She groped for some words to fill the void. 'Have you made any friends yet? I expect it takes a while in a new place.'

'No,' Craven mumbled.

'Give it a couple of days,' Jenny said encouragingly.

'You don't want me here, do you?'

'I'm just concerned you don't get into trouble.'

'You think I'm shit.'

'No, Mr Craven. I wouldn't have gone to the trouble I did—'

'You think I'm a worthless piece of shit. Say it!'

He didn't give her a chance.

His fist hit the back of her neck like a hammer blow, exploding stars in front of her eyes. She splayed forwards onto the ground, her palms striking the sharp stones as she held them out to break her fall. She tried to scramble away on all-fours, but her legs refused to move. She clawed at the dirt, trying to get some purchase, but Craven kicked her hands from under her and drove another kick hard into her ribs. Drifting in and out of her body, Jenny saw only his feet as he walked around her in circles, ranting and yelling. Flecks of spittle landed on her cheek, but her hand wouldn't lift to wipe them away. He crouched at her side and grabbed her by the shoulders, rolling her over onto her back. She felt him tugging at the belt of her jeans, scratching her stomach with his sharp fingernails. He dug a knee into her chest and wrenched at the buckle. No! No! The words screamed silently inside her head. He thrust his thumbs inside her waistband, pushing it down with impatient jerks of his narrow shoulders. The rough ground grated against her thighs as his fingers dug into the flesh above her knees. He turned around to face her, one hand forcing downwards on her chest, the other fumbling with his zip.

She felt the low vibration of the engine in her bones before she heard it. Craven looked up, still tugging at his fly, then down at Jenny with a startled expression, a frightened child again. She felt his fingers tightened momentarily on her T-shirt, then he flung himself away from her, crawling crab-like across the track as he scrabbled to his feet and ran, arms flailing, up the hill. Jenny half-rolled onto her side, tasting warm blood in her mouth as the tractor rumbled to a halt and heavy boots jumped down from the cab and came running towards her.

# EPILOGUE

JENNY SAT WITH HER BACK to the ash tree by the stream, hugging her bare knees while Steve read the notes Dr Allen had copied for her at the end of their third session of the week. It was important for her to keep reminding herself of what had happened, he had said: conscious recall of buried memory wasn't always an instant process, it could take time and reinforcement for what had been recovered in regression to make its full journey to the surface.

In the first and second sessions she hadn't been able to get clear of what had happened with Craven. Each time she closed her eyes she saw his face bearing down on her, felt his cold, dry hands pawing at her legs. On the third attempt Dr Allen had waited a full hour while she wept it out of her system, before pushing her back to another time in her life when she had been helpless. The symmetry of events wasn't lost on her, but that wasn't a subject to be dwelt on in the present – perhaps in another thirty-eight years the shape of her life would make sense – for now it was enough just to know, and to work out where it left her.

When the memories finally came it had been as simple as pushing open a door: she was right there in Aunty Penny's house, aged five, dressed in her knee-length skirt and buckled shoes. She and Katy abandoned the television in the front room with its snowy black and white picture and climbed the stairs to play with their Sindy dolls. The top floor of the house always smelled of cigarette smoke and sickly rose-scented air freshener, but when Dad came to collect her it smelled of him too. It was the smell of his bedclothes first thing in the morning and his dirty shirts in the washing basket. There were noises coming from under Aunty Penny's bedroom door, frightening noises: Aunty Penny in pain, Dad grunting as if he was hurting her. Jenny pretended not to hear, but Katy stood at the top of the stairs and burst into snivelling tears. Jenny attempted to drag her into her room, where a closed door would separate them from the monstrous sounds, but Katy wouldn't move. She clung to the banister, her sobs becoming more and more hysterical, and when Jenny yanked on her arm she lashed out and scratched at her face.

She hadn't meant to push Katy down the stairs – just away – but she couldn't deny that there had been a murderous intensity to her sudden eruption of rage. Through streaming eyes she had watched her cousin fall backwards, her limbs windmilling as she turned a half-somersault in mid-air. The back of her neck struck the treads with a sharp report, and she flopped in a rag-doll tumble onto the patterned tiles of the hall floor, her skirt thrown up, exposing her white knickers.

Dad burst out of the bedroom, still buttoning his shirt, and raced to the foot of the stairs. Aunty Penny had followed moments later, holding his shoes, her normally sleek black hair in an untidy mess. Dad shouted at her to call an ambulance, but she just stood over Katy's twisted body and screamed. Peering through the banisters, Jenny saw that something was leaking from Katy's mouth and that she had wet herself. It was Dad who grabbed the phone from the hall table. He spoke into it with the same tone of voice he used talking to customers at his garage. He seemed to forget about Aunty Penny as he yanked on his shoes and came back up the stairs. Jenny was ready with a lie, she was going to protest that Katy fell trying to push *her* down the stairs, but Dad didn't ask what happened. He held her chin in his rough hand, so tightly that it hurt. Quietly, so that Penny couldn't hear, he said, 'Breathe a word of what happened to Katy, and you'll end up like her. Do you want that, Jenny?'

Jenny shook her head.

Steve came to the end and looked out across the stream at the meadow.

Impatient for his reaction, Jenny said, 'You wanted it to be my father, didn't you?'

'It was. And your aunt.'

'No. It wasn't. I could have turned away, I could have run down the stairs, I could have shouted at them to stop, but I didn't . . .'

'You were five years old.'

'Age has got nothing to do with it. What I did was *in* me. I can still feel it, how I felt then . . . the rage.'

'It wasn't your fault, Jenny.'

A cool gust of breeze caught her legs and gave her goose-bumps. She hugged them tighter, beginning to wish she hadn't shown Steve the notes after all. 'It *was* my fault. And in this life there's no redemption, only the hope you'll never do anything like it again. Some manage, some don't.'

'You can't bracket yourself with psychopaths like Craven, Jenny. It's completely different.'

'He did me a favour though, didn't he? It took staring a murderer in the face to understand what was staring back at me in the mirror every morning.'

'You're *not* a murderer.'

Jenny nodded, not because she believed him, but because

she was tired of talking about it already. She knew what she was and would just have to live with it. All that separated her from Craven and his kind was a degree of self-aware-ness, an ability to spend a lifetime striving to atone without delusions of having been cleansed by a higher power.

Steve said, 'What will you do? Will there be more therapy?'

'Dr Allen thinks I'm doing exactly the right thing. Every day I go to work I soothe the wound a little more.'

'Haven't you ever thought there might be something else, something that doesn't tie you to the past?'

'I think it's you who's longing to move on, Steve, not me.'

'Not from you, Jenny.' He held the notes up in his fist. 'And not because of this.'

He looked beautiful with the ripples from the water reflected on his face, his body taut and lean beneath his T-shirt. Delicate, that was the word. He looked delicate. She thought she might cry.

Jenny said, 'You don't want me to be the mother of your children.'

'Who said anything about children?'

'You'd make a good father.'

'I want you to come with me. Try it for a while, a few weeks. I'm not asking you to leave your job. Treat it as a holiday – you can't tell me you don't need one.'

She was tempted, painfully so. She could think of nothing she would rather do than run away, but she knew that she couldn't. It was time to stand and face the truth. Her cure, if there could ever be one, was right here, and in her office, and in the mortuary and the courtroom, one by one laying the restless dead to rest.

'You know what you should do, Steve? Go to France. Get a new life and a pretty girlfriend, and if she doesn't mind too much, look me up every now and then.'

She stretched out her legs and got to her feet, moving carefully so as not to jar her sore neck. Steve stepped over to help her up.

'You've got leaves stuck to your back.'

She let him brush them off with his hand, feeling the warmth of his skin through the thin cotton dress, but as he moved to kiss her she dipped her head and his lips grazed her forehead.

She took the notes from him, and eased away.

Steve said, 'Do you mind if I sit here for a while? I'd like to say goodbye.'

'Of course not.' She smiled. 'Watch out for the ghosts.'

And she left him standing by the stream, watching the brown trout flick this way and that, quick as lightning. But when she stepped inside and glanced out through the kitchen window he was gone.

# ACKNOWLEDGEMENTS

I am grateful once again to Maria Rejt for her guiding hand, and to my wife, Patricia, for her unfailing encouragement and support. Also, I would like to thank all those readers who have so kindly written to me from the far corners of the world over the course of the last year, many concerned about Jenny Cooper's welfare. I will do my level best to look after her, I assure you, but she doesn't always make it easy.

If you enjoyed THE REDEEMED you'll love

# THE FLIGHT

The next Jenny Cooper thriller

*It would have been easy to have sent the bodies on the beach to the D-mort and to have washed her hands of them, but the moment the suggestion had been made, she had known it would be impossible. The little girl wouldn't let her. The past and the present were still too entangled; she had still to atone.*

When Flight 189 plunges into the Severn Estuary, Coroner Jenny Cooper finds herself handling the case of a lone sailor whose boat appears to have been sunk by the stricken plane, and is drawn into the mysterious fate of a ten-year-old girl, Amy Patterson, a passenger on 189, whose largely unmarked body is washed up alongside his.

While a massive and highly secretive operation is launched to recover clues from the wreckage, Jenny begins to ask questions that the official investigation doesn't want answered. How could such a high-tech plane – virtually impregnable against human error – fail? What linked the high-powered passengers who found themselves on this ill-fated flight? And how did Amy Patterson survive the crash, only to perish hours later?

Under pressure from Amy's grieving mother, and opposed by those at the very highest levels of government, Jenny must race against time to seek the truth behind this terrible disaster, before it can happen again . . .

Out soon
The first chapter follows here . . .

# ONE

Ransome Airways Flight 189 to New York was one of seven hundred and fifty-three scheduled to depart from London Heathrow that Sunday in early January. During peak times at the world's busiest international airport, one plane would take off and another land every minute. There was little room for error, either human or mechanical – still less in the uncertain realm where the two connected.

At forty-six, Captain Dan Murray was one of the oldest pilots on the pay-roll. With a wife and three teenagers to support, he had chosen to sacrifice union representation, and the perks he had enjoyed with his former company, for the money-in-the-hand offered by Guy Ransome's buccaneering airline. His basic salary barely covered the weekly groceries bill, and stopovers were spent in the cheapest airport hotels, but each transatlantic return trip earned him a little over £2,500. As a Ransome pilot he had to meet the cost of his own aviation medicals and the eight hours of simulator time it took every six months to renew his licence, but even carrying his own overhead he was still taking home more than he could elsewhere. In a shrinking industry you had to make your money while you could.

Departure was scheduled for nine-thirty. Murray hauled himself out of bed at five, slowly came to life in the shower, and minutes later was behind the wheel of his eight-year-old Ford. The persistent headache that had been bothering him lately had thankfully failed to take hold, and for once he didn't have to spend his morning commute waiting for the painkillers to kick in.

It was an hour's drive to Heathrow and, even at this ungodly hour of the morning, the motorway was filling up with angry traffic. He pulled into the car park of the Ransome building on the outer fringes of the airport at a little after six-thirty, collected his flight case from his locker and took a shuttle bus to Terminal Four. The short journey was shared with a dozen drowsy cabin crew dressed in Ransome's trademark purple uniforms. Some would join him on the flight to New York; others were bound for Dubai, Abu Dhabi or Taipei. The younger hostesses discussed rumours of staff cuts on long-haul flights, but the older employees kept their thoughts to themselves. Experience had taught them that Ransome Airways had little patience for gossips or troublemakers.

First Officer Ed Stevens was already hard at work in the landside crew room when Murray joined him for breakfast. The twenty-eight year old had a newborn daughter and a wife who had been made redundant from a freight company as soon as her pregnancy had started to show. He needed his job even more than his captain did, and was keen to impress. After a few moments' chit-chat and greetings to other familiar faces in the room, Murray opened his company laptop, hooked into the firm's intranet and listened while Stevens talked him over the flight plan.

The precise route they would follow from London to New York was contained in the electronic flight-information pack – a series of files forwarded in an email issued in the early hours of the morning by Sky Route, one of several independent companies that provided route-planning services to the major airlines. Sky Route's sophisticated software was designed to get aircraft to their destinations as cheaply as possible, taking account of weather conditions and passenger and cargo payload. Ten per cent of flight costs were incurred in landing fees and charges for exceeding the flight times, ninety per cent in aviation fuel. A strong headwind could add thirty per cent to the cost of a flight, meaning that the airline ended up making a loss. Finding the cheapest route on a given day was one of the most critical aspects of the airline business.

Sky Route had taken account of all the satellite-generated weather data and decided on a southerly course avoiding strong winds in the North Atlantic. Flight 189 would fly due west from Heathrow, level off at thirty-one thousand feet over the Severn Estuary and make its way towards the southern tip of Ireland. Midway across the Irish Sea they would climb to their cruising altitude of thirty-nine thousand feet and follow an almost direct route across the ocean. An estimated flight time of eight hours would have them on the ground at New York JFK at midday, Eastern Standard Time. Having talked his captain through the main points, Flight Officer Stevens drew his attention to several Notices to Airmen (NOTAMS) that warned of pockets of thunder cloud over the western British Isles and Irish Sea. It was unremarkable weather for the time of year and nothing to cause either pilot anxiety.

Captain Murray had always preferred flying across the Atlantic to complex routes over a patchwork of countries. Beyond Irish air space there would be no air-traffic controllers to deal with until they skirted southern Canada. And once aloft, the Airbus virtually flew itself; in fact, if correctly programmed, it would fly and even land itself, coming to a full halt on the JFK runway without human intervention.

Satisfied with their proposed course, Murray ordered a

second cup of coffee and set about double-checking the fuel calculations – something even more important than the weather. It was standard industry practice to calculate the fuel burn-off for the projected route and take on board five per cent extra as a contingency, which in practical terms amounted to an extra thirty minutes in the air. Sometimes that wouldn't be enough – in the event of having to navigate around an unexpected and violent patch of turbulence, for example – in which case a pilot might be forced to rely on reserve fuel and the small amount factored in for taxiing on the ground. The problem was that every thousand kilos of fuel loaded required an additional five hundred kilos to transport it. Operating on the tightest of margins, Ransome Airways insisted its captains take on only the regulation minimum three per cent of total fuel load as a contingency. If a captain chose to take on more and didn't use it, he would be fined according to a sliding scale. Satisfied that there were no weather systems reported over the Atlantic likely to require a significant deviation, Murray confirmed the order for one hundred and five tonnes of kerosene and hit the send button, filing his flight plan with the company dispatcher.

It was ninety minutes before take-off. The two pilots made their way to the staff check-in, deposited their overnight bags, passed through the security channel and made their way to the aircraft.

Greg Patterson was having a bad weekend. His ten-year-old daughter, Amy, was in tears, people were staring and nothing he said would console her. To make matters worse, he could feel his wife's disapproval, even across the three thousand miles of ocean that separated them. Taking the vice president post in London had seemed to him just the sort of fillip his tired marriage had needed, but Michelle had refused to leave Connecticut. A professor in applied mathematics at Hartford University, she had been offered a visiting lectureship at King's College, London, but when departure day loomed she claimed she couldn't bring herself to desert her ailing mother. Greg knew full well there was more to it than that, but for the sake of his daughter he had agreed to go alone and suffer a monthly inter-continental commute.

Michelle had brought Amy over for Christmas but had had to fly home four days early to attend to her elderly mother, who had fallen and broken her hip during her absence. Greg had persuaded Michelle to let Amy stay on with the promise that he would fly to New York with her en route to a business trip to Washington. He had seen very little of his daughter during the previous eight months and relished the prospect of a few days alone with her. All had been well until the previous Friday morning, when, in typical autocratic fashion, Greg's CEO cancelled his Washington trip, dictating that he had more pressing business to attend to in London. He had briefly toyed with the crazy idea of flying to New York with Amy on Saturday and back to London the next day, but his plan was skewered when late on Friday evening the airline bumped them onto a Sunday flight claiming that their Saturday departure had been unwittingly overbooked. Michelle had failed to be understanding. As far as she was concerned, Greg's intention to fly their daughter home as an unaccompanied minor was tantamount to child abuse. And in a way it was. At ten years old, Amy Patterson had scarcely left her mother's side and, except for these last few days in London, had never spent a night away from her.

Amy now clung on to her father and wept at the desk in the departure hall as he completed the forms entrusting her to the airline. The Ransome hostess tried her best to soothe the little girl, promising movies, video games and an endless supply of treats until she met her mother at the other end, but Amy wouldn't be mollified. Greg attempted and failed three times to get her to put on the purple tabard that singled her out as a child travelling alone, and it was the hostess who finally insisted that he just go and leave them to it. With a lump in his throat and cursing his boss – a man lucky enough to have a doting wife who had happily followed him to London with their three children – Greg disappeared into the crush of travellers with his daughter's tearful pleas ringing in his ears.

One aspect of service on which Ransome didn't skimp was its VIP lounge. Economy class tickets barely covered costs; the entire airline's profit was made in business and first class and attracting wealthy passengers was a priority. One such was Jimmy Han – a name the young entrepreneur had adopted for the benefit of his Western business associates – who had clocked up more miles with Ransome Airways than any other customer. Once every two weeks he travelled from his company's manufacturing plant in Taipei to its offices in Frankfurt and London. This week, for good measure, he was adding a three day hop across the Atlantic to his schedule. He had spent the previous night at the Savoy, but its luxurious spa had felt a little tired compared with the one he was currently enjoying in the newly overhauled Ransome lounge.

The semi-educated boy from Shanghai had come a long way in twenty years. He had worked hard, been lucky and grown exceedingly rich. There was much he intended to give back in return for his success, but that was no reason not to enjoy his wealth. When an interviewer had once asked him if he ever tired of the high life, Han had replied that those who came from nothing appreciated luxury like no one else;

for at the back of their minds was always the thought that it might all be suddenly snatched away.

The Airbus A380 was the world's largest commercial airliner. Seventy-three yards long, twenty-four yards high and with a wingspan the length of a football pitch, it dwarfed the 747s that stood alongside it. Designed to carry five hundred and twenty-five passengers in a normal three class configuration, Ransome Airlines bunched things up a little tighter in economy to squeeze in closer to six hundred. The ethical compensation for the cramped conditions was the knowledge that your seat had the lowest carbon footprint in commercial aviation. Ransome proudly billed itself as 'the greener airline'.

Pre-flight preparations were in full swing. Outside in the freezing drizzle a pumping truck transferred fuel from underground containers into the tanks in the aircraft's wings and the ground engineers carried out their final inspections. Inside, a team of cleaners was working against the clock as the eighteen cabin crew checked that the galleys had been correctly loaded and searched the passenger lists for those with special requirements: the 'problems'. There were unusually few: three in wheelchairs and a smattering of fussy eaters. Amy Patterson was the only unaccompanied minor. The words 'Will need attention!' had been entered next to her name. The crew unanimously decided that she would be the responsibility of Kathy Flood, the newest and youngest of their number, whether Kathy liked it or not.

After twenty years flying US-made Boeings, Captain Murray had found retraining to fly the Airbus a challenge. But having overcome his initial reservations, he was now a fully committed convert. It wasn't all to his liking – he would have preferred a conventional centre stick to the arcade-style electronic joystick positioned at his right side – and a nostalgic part of him would have liked at least a few mechanical analogue instruments for use as a last resort – but he accepted that he was flying an incomparably safe machine.

Fly-by-wire technology meant that all vital systems were controlled by a highly sophisticated network of computers and electronics. Rather than the rudder, spoilers and tail elevators being moved by cables and hydraulics operated manually from the cockpit, the pilot's controls transmitted only electronic signals to the various moving parts.

Instead of conventional instruments, the Airbus captain and first officer each sat before a console containing a number of LCD screens. In total, each pilot had four screens of their own, and two that were shared between them. Directly in front of each was the identical primary flight display – the principal flying instrument – which showed the aircraft's altitude in the air in relation to an artificial horizon, and its flight mode. Each pilot also had a navigation display providing a constant visual of the aircraft's position, the weather up ahead, and constant readings of ground speed and true air speed. An onboard information terminal contained the library of electronic documents – the tech logs and manuals – that in older aircraft were contained in several thick and unwieldy paper files. In the middle of the centre console that ran between the pilots' seats, were the engine-warning and system displays, and beneath them, the four thrust levers. Either side of the levers was a multi-function display – the pilots' main interface with the aircraft's computers. Using a keyboard and tracker ball, either pilot could flip between many pages relaying the status of various onboard systems or send and receive messages to air-traffic control and the airline's home base.

The intention behind this impressive array of technology was simple: in so far as it was possible, to remove pilot error. If a pilot erred, the computers would detect and correct. And during all stages of normal flight, the Airbus's computers would make minor automatic adjustments to the roll and pitch of the aircraft. Whether the pilot wished it or not, his commands were constantly being modified or over-ridden. But by far the most controversial of the Airbus's fail-safe features was its refusal to allow the pilot any more than thirty degrees of pitch up, fifteen degrees down and sixty-seven degrees of bank. This was intended to prevent a potentially catastrophic stall by keeping the plane safely within the flight envelope – the safe limits of speed and altitude – but left some pilots feeling that in an emergency they would be unable to take full control. The aircraft's designers took a dispassionate view: in a crisis a computer flies better than a human. A computer is rational. A computer suffers no emotion. A computer has no desire to be a hero.

The chief ground engineer, Mick Dalton, arrived in the cockpit thirty minutes before take-off and briefed Captain Murray and First Officer Stevens on the few defects he had found as he entered the pilots into the e-log book on the onboard maintenance terminal. He advised them that an intermittent fault with an actuator operating one of the spoilers on the starboard wing had not recurred, but warned them to keep an eye out for it and scheduled a precautionary repair to take place on the aircraft's return. There was the usual crop of niggles from inside the passenger cabin – several faulty video screens, a malfunctioning toilet pump – and a report from the previous flight crew of an anomalous auto-pilot action. While Auto-Pilot One had been engaged it had apparently skipped a pre-programmed level-off on ascent, climbing straight through to cruising altitude. Dalton was dubious. He suspected that the first officer, a new recruit to the airline, had mis-programmed the auto-flight system. Ed Stevens promised he wouldn't make the same mistake and double checked the flight data he had already entered on the multi-function display. Despite his doubts, Dalton recorded the reported error in the deferred defect log and certified the aircraft fit for flight.

Half an hour before scheduled take-off, the three wheel-chair-bound passengers and a tearful Amy Patterson were brought along the gantry by ground staff and handed over to the cabin crew. Kathy Flood led the little girl to a seat near an exit door in the mid-section of the lower cabin where she could keep a close eye on her. She showed her where to find the kids' movies on the seatback screen and how to press the call button any time she needed something. Before joining Ransome Airways, Kathy had spent two years as an au pair to a wealthy Italian family with six spoiled children. Compared with them, Amy Patterson was a delight. Kathy helped her to send a text message to her mother saying the plane was due to leave on time, and gave her some sweets to suck during take-off. After a few minutes of Kathy's reassuring attention, Amy's mood lifted and she finally smiled.

First-class passengers embarked ahead of the crowd and were ushered upstairs into a spacious cabin. Forty luxury pods with fully reclining seats upholstered in cream leather were arranged around a kidney-shaped champagne and seafood bar. At the very front of the aircraft were six individually self-contained 'ultra suites' – glorified versions of the first-class pods separated from the cabin by sliding Perspex doors.

Jimmy Han usually made do with the relative comfort of

a regular pod, but it had been a hectic few days in which he had already travelled more than halfway across the globe. As soon as he slid the door of his suite shut and drew the blind he knew that he had made the right decision. Kicking off his shoes he eased into the seat, stroking the controls until it moulded to the small of his back. Today was a rest day, a time for reflection. He closed his eyes and recalled a long-forgotten moment from his childhood: his father had kicked a stray dog that lay sunning itself in the street outside their drab apartment building. When he had asked him why, his father had said, 'Because he looks more comfortable lying on the hard ground than I'll ever be.' Han smiled. Even now he wasn't as relaxed as that flea-bitten bag of bones, but he was worth more than seven hundred million dollars.

At nine-twenty the last of the sixteen cabin doors was secured and Captain Murray turned the simple ignition switch which commenced the automatic start-up of the four Rolls-Royce Trent engines. He watched the changing images on the engine screen as the aircraft's computers started each in turn and pressurized the hydraulic systems. Sophisticated sensors relayed a constant stream of information; the computers tweaked and adjusted fuel supply, finessing the many interconnected electrical and mechanical processes in a way no human ever could. It was as if the vast machine had a life of its own.

The ground crew disconnected the push-back tractor and radioed the cockpit to set the brakes to 'on'. The aircraft's computers calculated where its centre of gravity lay, based on the size and distribution of the payload, and decided on the correct angle at which to attack the air: too shallow and it would struggle to leave the ground, too steep and the centre of lift would slip behind the centre of gravity risking a disastrous stall. The wing flaps and stabilizer on the horizontal section of the tail adjusted themselves accordingly. On older planes the pilot would feel his way into the air, instinctively responding to the feedback on his centre stick and the pressure on his rudder pedals, but the Airbus pilot had no feedback, no tactile sense of the air pressing against the flying surfaces. He relied instead on the streams of information on his visual displays. Among the many acts of faith highly computerized aircraft demanded, those required on take-off were the most profound.

First Officer Stevens received the go-ahead from the tower and Captain Murray manoeuvred the Airbus towards the start of Runway Two. Thirty seconds passed; the tower confirmed 'cleared for take-off' and Captain Murray pushed the thrust levers fully forward to the take-off-go-around setting.

The aircraft started to accelerate; the windshield streaked with rain. First Officer Stevens called out, 'Eighty knots'. Both pilots cross-checked their air-speed instruments; both were in agreement. Had they not been, take-off would immediately have been aborted. Upwards of eighty knots the pilot was obliged to ignore any minor faults and abort only to avoid imminent disaster. An automated voice called out, 'V1', indicating that the critical speed of one hundred and twenty-two knots had been reached. Captain Murray removed his hand from the thrust lever now committed to take-off. As they reached one hundred and forty-one knots, First Officer Stevens called out, 'Rotate', and Captain Murray pulled gently on the joystick, easing the aircraft's nose up through three degrees a second until at twelve point five degrees the massive craft began to lift and climb.

At one hundred feet Captain Murray called for 'Gear-up', then 'AP one'. Like many pilots, he would have preferred to fly the aircraft manually to ten thousand feet before switching to autopilot, but Heathrow being a noise restricted airport, any deviation from the Standard Instrument Departure – such as a sudden throttle-up – risked infringing volume regulations triggering a hefty automatic fine, a portion of which, under Ransome's uniquely harsh rules, would have been docked from his salary.

The auto-pilot engaged. Only a few hundred feet from the ground the two human pilots became virtual spectators as the aircraft banked left and headed out on a westerly course, slowly ascending towards ten thousand feet. Their displays showed the constant subtle movements of the rudder, spoilers and stabilizer countering the effects of a blustery north wind. To have flown the aircraft as skilfully by hand would have been a physical impossibility.

At fifteen hundred feet Captain Murray pulled the thrust lever back to the 'climb' setting as they entered low-lying cloud and encountered minor pockets of turbulence. First Officer Stevens swapped formalities with air-traffic control and obtained permission to pass through the first altitude constraint of six thousand feet. At four thousand, the flaps retracted from take-off position and the engines responded to the reduced lift with an increase in power, accelerating to two hundred and fifty knots. The cloud was thick and dense, making for a bumpier ride than many passengers would be finding comfortable, but the weather radar showed conditions clearing over the Welsh coast. The latest reports from the mid-Atlantic were of a clear, bright day.

At ten thousand feet, both pilots called out, 'Flight level one hundred': standard procedure designed to keep them working as a tight-knit team. Now high enough above the ground to be free of noise restrictions, the engines powered up to a more efficient climb speed of three hundred and twenty-seven knots. Captain Murray switched off the passenger seatbelt signs and enabled the in-flight entertainment system. First Officer Stevens checked in with air-traffic control who handed him over to Bristol. A brief exchange of messages secured permission to continue to an initial cruising altitude of thirty-one thousand feet.

Both pilots began to relax. The hardest part of their day's work was already done.

A polite tap at the door of Jimmy Han's suite signalled the arrival of a pretty stewardess who handed him the complimentary drinks menu. It was too early in the day for champagne, so he ordered freshly squeezed orange juice, giving her a smile which promised a handsome tip if she looked after him well. Reaching for the remote he flicked to CNN, hoping for updates on the latest diplomatic spat between China and Taiwan. But the studio anchor was dwelling on another minor story and he impatiently scoured the ticker at the foot of the screen before a knot of tension stiffened his neck and reminded him that he was meant to be taking it easy. Business could wait. He switched across to the movie channels and picked out an old Clint Eastwood picture: *Dirty Harry*. It was one of his favourites. He had learned one of his most valuable lessons from American films: the good guys are ultimately more ruthless than the bad.

The altimeters ticked past thirty thousand feet prompting both pilots to call out, 'One to go', affirming that their instruments were in sync and that they were nearing level-off. First Officer Stevens checked in with Bristol and learned that aircraft up ahead had reported a belt of thunderclouds but that no deviation was necessary. At thirty-one thousand feet the auto-thrust pulled back, downgrading to a softer mode which caused the engines to quieten to an almost inaudible whisper and settle to the optimum fuel-efficient cruise speed: a steady four hundred and seventy-nine knots.

'How's the baby?' Captain Murray asked his first officer. 'Getting any sleep?'

'Doing my best – on the sofa.' Stevens unbuckled his belt and rolled his stiff shoulders.

'Like that, is it?'

'I told her, I'll change all the dirty nappies you like, but getting up in the night, forget it. I've got a plane to fly.'

'Off the leash tonight, then? I hope she doesn't expect me to keep an eye on you.'

'In New York? You really think you'd keep up?'

'You'd be surprised.'

The interphone buzzed.

'Coffee time already?' First Officer Stevens glanced up at the entry screen and saw a stewardess standing beyond the outer of the two doors which separated the cabin from the cockpit. 'She's keen. They could have sent the pretty one.'

'Who's that?' Captain Murray asked.

'You know – the little blonde one. Kathy, with the – ' He held his hands out in front of his chest.

'Oh, yeah – *her*.'

Both men laughed.

'You are definitely on your own tonight,' Captain Murray said. 'Not my responsibility.'

Stevens tapped in the entry code, which would let the stewardess through the outer door. It would first have to lock behind her before the inner door would open and allow her into the cockpit.

'Speed! Speed!' the automated warning voice called out from speakers mounted in the instrument consoles.

'What the hell is that?' Captain Murray said, 'We're at four-seventy—'

'Speed! Speed!'

'Jesus—'

'Speed! Speed!'

There was a loud clatter and a scream of alarm from between the cockpit's two doors as the aircraft's nose pitched violently upwards and the stewardess was thrown off her feet.

'I'm sorry, say again, Skyhawk . . . Skyhawk, uh, are you still on?'

At his seat in the tower at Bristol airport Guy Fearnley saw Skyhawk 380 on his radar screen but heard nothing but static through his headset.

'Skyhawk, are you there?'

The brief message from the Airbus had been too fractured to make out. He switched channels and tried again. 'Skyhawk this is Bristol eight-zero-nine . . .'

There was no reply.

The air-traffic controller watched the numbers on his screen that indicated the Airbus's altitude start to fall; slowly at first, then faster and faster. He blinked twice to make sure he wasn't imagining it.

He wasn't.